DAVID BELL IS . . .

"A natural storyteller and a first-class writer."

—*Suspense Magazine*

"A master storyteller."

—*USA Today* bestselling author Allen Eskens

"A natural storyteller and a superb writer."

—#1 *New York Times* bestselling author Nelson DeMille

"A master of suspense with well-fleshed-out characters."

—*Midwest Book Review*

PRAISE FOR *Somebody's Daughter*

"A tautly told, heart-pounding read, *Somebody's Daughter* is a page-turning whodunit where every character's a suspect and no one can be trusted."

—Mary Kubica, *New York Times* bestselling author of *The Other Mrs.*

"With razor-sharp prose and a satisfyingly twisty plot, *Somebody's Daughter* is an intense, emotional thrill ride readers won't want to miss!"

—Karen Dionne, international bestselling author of *The Marsh King's Daughter*

"Both plausible and pulsating, a psychological thriller that hits perilously close to home."

—Craig Johnson, *New York Times* bestselling author of the Walt Longmire Mysteries

"A well-paced race against time that will grip you from the first chapter all the way to its satisfying conclusion."

—Jessica Strawser, author of *Almost Missed You*

"Hooks you from the start and draws you into a tale of secrets, lies, and lives haunted by the past. A suspenseful—and poignant—thriller."

—Meg Gardiner, Edgar Award–winning author of *Unsub*

"A stunner, full of twists and turns and duplicitous motivations. Bell's solid storytelling is as sharp and scary as ever. Fans of Harlan Coben will love this one."

—J.T. Ellison, *New York Times* bestselling author of *Lie to Me*

"A compulsive, twisty, race-against-the-clock thriller . . . it's also a sensitive meditation on what connects us to each other—and what we'll do to hold on when life tears us apart. Don't miss this smart and unrelenting page-turner!"

—Lisa Unger, *New York Times* bestselling author of *Confessions on the 7:45*

ALSO BY DAVID BELL

Cemetery Girl

The Hiding Place

Never Come Back

The Forgotten Girl

Somebody I Used to Know

Since She Went Away

Bring Her Home

Layover

The Request

Kill All Your Darlings

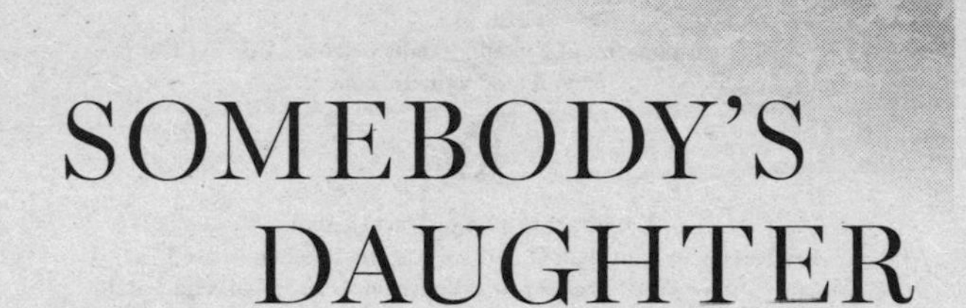

SOMEBODY'S DAUGHTER

david bell

BERKLEY
New York

BERKLEY
An imprint of Penguin Random House LLC
penguinrandomhouse.com

ISBN: 9780593337479

Berkley trade paperback edition / July 2018
Berkley mass-market edition / June 2021
Second Berkley mass-market edition / September 2021

Printed in the United States of America
1 3 5 7 9 10 8 6 4 2

Title page art by Joyce Vincent / Shutterstock Images

To Molly

part one

EVENING

chapter one

TUESDAY, 8:16 P.M.

The doorbell rang shortly after eight o'clock.

The doorbell almost never rang. Certainly not so late in the evening.

From the kitchen, Michael heard the scrape of silverware against plates, the opening and closing of the refrigerator as Angela put the leftovers away in preparation for Michael doing the dishes. It was their usual, long-agreed-upon routine for nights when she cooked.

Then the doorbell rang. At first the sound was so small, so distant and surprising, that Michael decided he'd imagined it. An auditory hallucination. Maybe two glasses clanked against each other in the kitchen, and he just thought it was the doorbell.

But then the bell rang again. Two times in a row. An

insistent ringing, a sound that said someone outside meant business about getting their attention.

Angela appeared in the kitchen doorway. Her hair was pulled back off her face, and she held her hands away from her body as though they were wet or dirty.

"Who is that?" she asked.

"I'm not expecting anyone."

"Can you get it? My hands are dirty."

"I've got it," Michael said. He looked at his watch. Eight sixteen. "Probably a kid selling something."

"A determined kid, apparently," Angela said as the bell chimed again. She smiled. "They must know who they're dealing with."

"What's that supposed to mean?" Michael held back a laugh as he said it. He knew exactly what Angela meant.

"They know you're an easy mark," she said. "You always buy from them. Candy bars, magazines. They love you."

"Should you go answer, then?" he asked. "You can be the bad cop, and I'll watch baseball."

"I don't mind what you do," she said, smiling wider. "I like that these kids know how to push your buttons."

"Admit it. You don't mind eating the chocolate I buy."

"Touché."

Michael started for the door.

"Hey," Angela said, stopping him. "Did you call your sister yet?"

"Not yet."

"Don't forget, okay? This is a big deal. Lynn's coming up on five years cancer free."

"I know, I know. You sent flowers, right?"

"Yes. But you still need to call. It will mean a lot to her."

"I will. I promise."

Michael felt light as he walked to the front of the house. He looked forward to watching some of a baseball game or maybe reading a book. He felt encouraged as he reflected on the continued good news about Lynn's health. Next week, he and Angela were going away, a trip to St. Simons Island, just the two of them. Summer was good. Languid. Less work. If they relaxed more, if they got the time away, maybe they'd finally have luck in their ongoing struggle to have a child.

If not, he wasn't sure how things would play out. He and Angela were both feeling the strain, the weight it was adding to their marriage. He hated that sex had become a chore, a duty to be performed with the specific goal of producing a baby. Michael so wanted to get back to normal.

Michael entered the foyer and opened the front door. The sun was dropping, the horizon orange and hazy with the heat that brushed across his face. Someone was grilling, the rich odor of sizzling meat reaching his nostrils.

It took him a moment to comprehend the reality of the figure on his porch. She paced from one side to the other, a cigarette in her mouth, arms crossed.

He couldn't find the words. He didn't know the words. So he just said, "What the hell?"

She stopped pacing, removed the cigarette. She looked

scared, haunted. Her eyes wide and flaring. “I need you, Michael. I need your help.”

“I don’t understand. Why are you even here?”

She took a step toward him, gesturing with the hand that held the burning cigarette. Michael caught a whiff of the smoke, leaned back as the cigarette came closer to his body.

She dropped it on the porch. The ash sparked as it hit the ground.

“I just need your help, Michael.”

“You need to back up, Erica. You need to—you need to leave.”

“Michael. My daughter. Someone kidnapped my daughter this morning.”

chapter two

"What is it, Michael?" Angela called from the kitchen. "Chocolate? Magazines?"

"I've got it," Michael said, his voice hollow and barely audible.

Michael moved onto the porch, pulling the door shut behind him. Erica stepped back, allowing Michael room. She started digging in the pocket of her jeans, which were dark and fitted, and brought out more cigarettes. While she shook one loose from the pack and flicked her thumb against the lighter, Michael took her in, observing the changes ten years had etched on his ex-wife. Some lines had formed around her eyes, some skin hung looser beneath her chin, but her shoulder-length hair showed no gray, and the cut looked more stylish and professional than the messy ponytail she had preferred in college. Michael noticed the gray Apple Watch on her wrist, the smartphone tucked in her pocket.

She looked like a grown-up. An adult. And the difference was striking.

She took a long drag on the cigarette and blew the smoke away from Michael. "You never liked this habit. I'd given it up until about twelve hours ago."

"What do you mean, your daughter?" Michael asked. "You have a daughter? How old is she?"

Erica's hand shook as she held the cigarette between her index and middle fingers. "Felicity. That's her name. Felicity."

"Your favorite show," Michael said, remembering. Erica coming to his dorm room after class, sprawling across his bed, her shoes kicked off, catching reruns of *Felicity*. She loved to analyze and debate the character's choices of men, wailed in distress when an episode played in which Keri Russell's hair was cut short.

Michael remembered it all. The late nights with friends in college. The drinking and the partying. Their histrionic fighting and the ensuing make-up sex.

The day of their wedding. And also the day a year later when he left.

All of it so long ago. When he looked back on that time, he thought they had both acted like children.

"None of this makes sense, Erica. I haven't seen you in ten years. I'm married."

"I know."

"You know? You can't just show up at my door like this."

"There's a man." She started pacing again, lifting the cigarette to her mouth, the tip glowing the same color as the sky while she dragged. "He's a music teacher at her school. He's odd. I think he liked her. Felicity. In an unhealthy way—you know? This man knows something."

Her words became more and more clipped, her gestures more frantic as she spoke. Ash fell off the cigarette and hit the concrete porch. Even when things had been at their best between them—many days in college, the early months of their marriage—Erica tended toward exaggeration. She always managed to turn even the smallest misunderstanding—either with him or with someone else—into an operatic blowup.

Michael reached out, placed a hand on her arm. "Stop, Erica. Just stop and slow down."

She did. She looked at his hand where it held her arm near the crook of the elbow, his skin touching her skin for the first time in a decade.

Michael let go. But he said, "If someone you know is in trouble, you need to call the police. They can figure it out. I have to work tomorrow."

Erica paused for a moment. She dropped the cigarette, ground it under her sneaker, a new running shoe, and scuffed her foot, leaving a smear of dark ash across the concrete. Erica had run cross-country in high school, jogged three to five miles a day in college, even on mornings after late nights of partying. She'd always been energetic, almost frantic when she did anything—walking, studying, talking, having sex. She looked at Michael as if he didn't understand something fundamental. "The police *are* looking. They've been looking all day. Do you know what happens if they don't find someone right away? Do you know what happens to the missing person? The child?"

"Erica—"

"I've been talking to the police constantly, answering questions about me and my finances and my personal life and everyone I've ever known. Including you."

"Me?"

"Everyone. Everything about my life. They look into everything when a child disappears. I've had to answer the most embarrassing questions. The most personal questions."

Michael took a step back. He reached behind him, his hand fumbling for the doorknob. *Baseball,* he thought. *A good book.* Michael craved those things. And needed to get back to them.

To his real life. Not somebody else's.

He saw a wasp's nest in the corner of the porch, where a support post met the roof. He was supposed to knock the nest down the weekend before, but he hadn't, even though a wasp had managed to get inside and zip around the kitchen, throwing itself against the window above the sink until Angela swatted it with a magazine. The nest was bigger now. More wasps stirred, floated above their dwelling. The odor of the cooking meat grew stronger as the wind shifted. The sky was transitioning from the day's blue to the evening's purple.

"You should go talk to them," he said. "The police. Go back to them. Listen to them. Tell them whatever they want to know. You were never one to keep secrets, so tell them anything that might help. I'm just a guy you don't know anymore. I can't help you."

Erica stared him down. While she did, her eyes filled with tears. She bowed her head, an exaggerated gesture like she was praying. The movement took him right back to their college days, to times she was upset and times they fought. In both the past and the present, the gesture reached something in Michael, summoning empathy and concern for the person before him. Erica could look so vulnerable at times; she seemed always to feel more deeply than anyone else. It hurt to look at her when she was in pain or distress.

And then she glanced up again, the tear-filled eyes meeting his. Her chin quivered.

"You have to help me, Michael. You have no real choice."

Her tone of voice had shifted. Gone was the manic edge, the revved-up energy. Erica sounded shaken, scared.

She spoke again, her voice just above a whisper.

"She's yours, Michael. Felicity is your daughter, and I need your help getting her back."

chapter three

"That's not possible—"

The door opened behind Michael. His hand still rested on the knob as it came open, so he let go. It was Angela. She took in the scene with her lips parted, struggling to find something to say just as Michael had moments earlier.

Finally, Angela said, "Is something wrong, Michael?"

Erica stood with her hands on her hips, her chin thrust forward in a defiant posture. But she still had tears in her eyes.

Michael looked between the two of them, feeling a strange surge of embarrassment. He and Angela had once run into his high school girlfriend, Kayla McKee, whom he dated all during senior year. Michael had felt awkward then, fumbled through introductions in the middle of the grocery store, but Angela laughed about it on the way home, pointing out that Kayla had three kids in tow and another on the way. "She's a breeder," she said. "You could have had a whole litter with her by now."

That was before their trouble having a child had grown more desperate. But Angela always talked freely of her former boyfriends and lovers, mentioned them as casually as she mentioned a piece of clothing or a pair of shoes from her past.

But she didn't laugh on the porch, not when she saw Erica.

"Angela," Michael said, "this is . . . Erica. My . . . I don't think you've ever met."

"Hi," Angela said, nodding at Erica, her voice clipped. "It's nice to meet you. We thought it was kids selling something."

"I'm sorry, but I need to talk to him," Erica said. "It's important."

"Michael, is everything okay?" Angela asked, hands on hips in an unconscious imitation of Erica's posture.

"Can you just go back inside for a minute?" Michael asked. "I'm going to figure this out, and then I'll be right in. I promise."

"It's getting *late*," Angela said. She took one more long look, running her eyes the length of Erica's body. Then turned to go back through the still-open door.

Michael knew what Angela meant. She was ovulating. They needed to try. That night. And likely again the next morning. They had a plan.

"I know you don't like me," Erica said to Angela. "You've made that very clear."

Angela kept going, closing the door as she went inside.

Erica's words stood out. They sounded like they referred to something more than the moment on the porch or the predictable distrust between two women who had dated—and then married—the same man. Michael started to ask about her words but stopped himself. He had more important things to figure out.

He remembered what she'd said just before Angela came outside.

She's yours, Michael. Felicity is your daughter.

"Erica," he said, "I don't know what you're talking about or why you're saying it, but we don't have any children together. You know that. I'm not sure why you're showing up here, trying to throw my life into chaos."

Erica maintained her defiant posture. "We were having sex up until the end, Michael. Up until you left me. We weren't always careful. You'd reach for me in the middle of the night. I don't think either one of us was fully aware of what we were doing."

"She's ten years old?"

"Nine."

"And you never told me about her? Come on, Erica. That's crazy."

"Don't do that, Michael. We're not married, but you still can't just act like I'm overreacting or hysterical. You've always done that, and it's never been fair."

Erica started fumbling in her pockets again. Michael thought she was reaching for another cigarette, but instead she brought out her shiny iPhone. She scrolled through, her finger swiping quickly, and then she turned the screen so Michael could see it.

A photo of a child. She was blond, like almost all the women in his family. Her cheeks were rosy, and in the photo, she stood in front of what looked like a barn, the red wooden boards cracked and peeling. A beautiful kid, yes.

But his?

"Don't you see it, Michael?" Erica asked. "The resemblance."

"She's blond. Lots of people in the world are blond. They're not all my kids. None of them are my kids."

"Look closer. Zoom in."

"Erica, I can't even . . . I mean, we've been trying for two years, and the doctor says I may not be able to father a child. So how could this girl—"

"Look."

Michael did as he was told. He remembered Erica's determination, her iron will once something entered her mind. He used his thumb and forefinger to zoom in on the girl's face, the picture clear even as the light faded from the day. The action didn't reveal any more to his eyes. He still saw a cute blond girl on an outing to the country, her cheeks flushed from a long run or the cold wind.

"I don't get it, Erica. A photo doesn't prove anything."

"Robyn," Erica said. "Doesn't she look a lot like Robyn?"

chapter four

Michael stared at the image a moment longer, and then tried to hand the phone back to Erica. But she didn't take it, and the two of them stood frozen like that, him holding the phone and her keeping her hands by her sides. A string of firecrackers popped up the street, followed by the laughter of children.

"Erica, I think you need to leave," he said.

"I know you very well, almost as well as anyone else on the planet. I know who you are, Michael. It's urgent when a little girl is missing like this. You would never turn your back on a child in danger. Your child. Your daughter."

"She's not—"

But how did he really know? Yes, they'd had sex near

the end of their marriage. And, yes, the timing worked out with the age of the child. Felicity. But Erica was supposed to have been on the pill. And he and Angela had struggled so much with conceiving. . . .

But she did look like Robyn.

"You're invoking Robyn to manipulate me," Michael said.

And he had to give Erica credit—she had always been honest and forthright.

"Yes, I am," Erica said.

Michael was the eldest of three children. His two younger sisters were Lynn, the middle child, and Robyn. When Michael was twelve and his sisters were nine and six, they lived in a house on the north side of Cottonsville, Kentucky, Michael's hometown and where he still lived with Angela. The house was average, certainly not as large as the one his parents eventually moved to, the one they purchased as his father's home health care company continued to grow and expand.

The first house on the north side of town sat on the edge of a subdivision that backed up to a seemingly endless cornfield. A swing set, one that had been in place before his parents even bought the house, provided hours of entertainment for the kids. But especially for Robyn, the most daring of the siblings.

It happened in summer; Michael remembered that. July 19. They were currently about a month away from the twenty-third anniversary. He still dreamed about it from time to time. He still woke up with his heart pounding, his clothes soaked with sweat at least four or five times a year. . . .

The sun had been bright that day, the sky blue and clear. Michael couldn't even say why the three of them were playing in the yard together at that point. Michael had been twelve, past the age when he could summon any patience or interest in the activities of his two younger sisters. His mom might have been on the phone or showering or tending to something in the house, which explained why the three of them were out in the yard together. Dad would have been at work. Back then and all the way to the day of his death, his dad always seemed to be at work.

Michael had grown bored with the girls, with the silly songs Lynn sang and Robyn's effervescent and constant chattering. He'd turned his back on them and started through the cornfield behind the house. He liked to walk up and down the rows, running his hands along the rough green leaves, listening to the way they rustled as he passed. He knew the sweet smell of the stalks, the rich odor of the earth. He could never get lost. The rows were so neat and orderly, the paths so straight and clear, he'd always been able to find his way back. He possessed an excellent sense of direction, and he never found himself turned around.

He couldn't say how far he'd gone that day. Not very. He knew he was supposed to be in the yard, watching his sisters so they didn't wander away or fight with each other. Even at that young age, he understood the unique place he occupied in their lives. They looked up to him.

They worshipped him. They always listened to Michael, even more than they listened to or stood in awe of their own parents. Even Robyn, the baby, the one Lynn always called the favorite. *Robyn, Daddy's little girl . . .*

Michael couldn't say why he'd turned around when he had that day.

He hadn't worried about his sisters being alone. They were getting to be old enough that he'd felt he didn't need to "watch" them all the time. He'd decided that summer that they both acted more like babies when he was around, and when they were left alone, they functioned in a more mature manner.

But still, his mom had often asked him to keep an eye on them when she was busy with something else. He knew his mom worried the most about Robyn. Even at age six, she was a daredevil. She climbed on everything—tall trees and playground jungle gyms. She rode her bike as fast as she could, jumped into the deep end of the pool whether an adult was nearby to watch her or not. She made Michael as nervous as his mother. Michael hated heights, hated the sensation of going fast or out of control. But Robyn never flinched from anything, and their dad loved it.

He encouraged Robyn every time she took a risk. He cheered her on at her gymnastics practices when she flipped so high she fell, laughed a little even when he yelled at her for climbing too high in a tree.

It bothered Michael that his father acted that way. He thought his father's behavior only encouraged more risky acts. And if Michael hated it, Lynn despised it. She always complained to Michael—and occasionally to their mom—about their father's signs of favoritism toward Robyn. How he let her get away with anything, how he never punished her. Michael accepted that it was the way things went with the youngest child. He had friends at school with younger siblings, and they all shared the same complaint: *The baby gets away with everything.*

But Lynn had never let it roll off her back. She never shrugged off Robyn's or their dad's behavior, never simply rolled her eyes and accepted the way things were. She fought against it. She balked at sharing things with Robyn, refused to let her anywhere nearby when her friends from school came over, even as those very friends told Lynn how adorable and funny her little sister was. Michael chalked it up to sisterly rivalry, the difficulty of having a younger sibling of the same gender who seemed to draw a lot of attention.

Michael took his time walking back through the corn. He had baseball practice that night. He looked forward to being on the diamond, to seeing his friends and throwing the ball around despite the growing heat. He loved the feel of standing on the dirt, the cracking of the bat, the shouts of his teammates.

He heard someone screaming in the yard as he drew close.

He recognized the sounds. His sisters were fighting, arguing with each other over some perceived injustice committed by one of them, their voices always shrill and pointed. Someone had taken a longer turn on a swing.

Someone had called the other one a name. Someone had taken something that belonged to the other. . . .

When Michael emerged from the corn, though, everything grew silent.

A hot breeze blew, but the swings were still.

Robyn lay on the ground, beneath the swing set, her head turned at a funny angle.

He knew one of her favorite things to do was to walk across the top of the swing set, arms out to her side like she was on the balance beam. Except this beam stood eight feet off the ground.

She never fell, never even wavered as she walked, even though the very act made Michael's stomach clench, made his own head spin like he was sick. The height terrified him.

She laughed as she walked, taunting her siblings. But Robyn never fell.

Until that day.

Lynn stood to the side, her mouth open, her face full of terror.

And then their mom was running from the house, her hands raised in fear and panic.

chapter five

"You can't compare those two things," Michael said. "You can't."

"Felicity is just a few years older than Robyn was. And she looks so much like the pictures I've seen of her." Erica took a step closer. Despite the smoking, Michael caught a whiff of something flowery, a shampoo or deodorant that smelled like lavender. But closer in, she looked even more wrung out and tired than he'd first realized. Her eyes were red, the whites filled with crisscrossing capillaries like a tiny map. "When we were married—hell, even when we were in college—you always told me you wanted to have children. And you always said you wanted to have a daughter, a little girl who . . . well, who might help the family move on in some way." Her tired eyes looked pleading, still filmed by tears. "I remember the dreams you'd have, how you'd still see that day, that moment, in your worst nightmares. I know all about how this affected you—your family. Your parents couldn't even talk about her. I know it all, Michael."

"Stop it, Erica."

"You even said once you'd want to name your daughter Robyn. Now, I know I didn't do that, but I thought about it. I really did. If we'd still been together . . ."

"You didn't ever tell me. You say this child is mine, but you didn't tell me."

"I was angry, Michael. I was hurt when you left me. Very hurt. The only thing I could do to get back at you was to keep the child away." Erica heaved a long, shuddering sigh. "It's getting late, and time is wasting. The police, they keep telling me the first forty-eight hours are the most important. Michael, she's gone. Felicity is. If we don't act now, if we don't hurry . . . The police won't say what they mean by that forty-eight-hour thing, but I know. They mean she's going to be dead. Killed. Murdered. Maybe . . . Well, you can imagine all the other things that can happen to a girl. My daughter. *Our* daughter."

Erica's breathing grew frantic, spastic. Her shoulders and chest shook convulsively, so that Michael wanted to reach out and grab her just to stop the painful-looking movements.

"I don't know what I can do that the police can't do. And shouldn't you be there? At your house?"

"I'll go back. Soon. I needed a break. I needed help. You went to therapy when Robyn died, didn't you? You told me. And so did Lynn."

"Why are you bringing that up?"

"People need help. From others. We can't just wallow. And sitting in that house was like being in a pressure cooker. And that's the one place Felicity isn't."

Erica brought out the cigarettes again. Her hands shook so much, she dropped the pack.

Michael bent down and picked them up. Their fingers brushed when he handed them to her. She managed to get one into her mouth, and Michael took the lighter and held it while Erica inhaled. The first long puff seemed to calm her. She regained some control of her body and her movements.

Up the street, a lawn mower roared to life, cutting through the quiet suburban evening. Someone was trying to get a few last blades of grass cut before the light was gone.

"I told you there's a man," Erica said. "He teaches at Felicity's school. I don't know what it is about him, but he always acted really interested in Felicity. He talked to me about her, sent notes home about how smart she was. He used the word 'amazing' once. It just never seemed right to me, the way he acted. It didn't seem healthy."

"Did you tell the police about him?"

"I did." She took another long drag and again blew the smoke away from Michael. "They questioned him this morning, not long after Felicity was gone. *Taken.* I thought we'd know something right then, that he would tell them where she was and why she was gone. But the cops let him go. It was so fast, Michael. So fast. They just let him go. I don't think they even searched his house. What if she's there? What if she's been held there all day and we just need to go there?"

"And you want me to . . . what?"

"Talk to him. With a man like you there, he might respond. I'd feel safer going. Just go do this and then come back. That's it, Michael. For me. I'll never ask you for anything ever again."

"Don't you have someone else who can go with you?" Michael asked. "A friend . . . or a guy in your life?"

"I'm a single mom, Michael. A single working mom. I don't have a huge circle of friends. I don't have guys knocking down my door, wanting to date me."

"Where do you even live, Erica?"

"I'm in Trudeau. On the west side."

Michael still held Erica's phone. He tapped it with his index finger, bringing the photo of the girl back onto the screen.

Yes, she looked like Robyn.

Yes, she could very well be his daughter.

And Michael knew Erica was right that time was critical for a missing child. Everyone knew that.

He handed the phone back to her without meeting her eye.

"Michael," she said in a pleading tone.

"Go to the end of the driveway," he said. "Wait there. I'll be right out."

chapter six

Quiet pervaded the first floor of the house.

Michael peeked into the dining room and then the kitchen, seeing no sign of Angela. He saw the dirty dishes he needed to wash. He smelled the remnants of their dinner: grilled onions and peppers, chicken for fajitas. A half-full glass of wine, his, sat by the refrigerator, the cabernet strangely reminding Michael of blood.

He headed upstairs, his feet brushing the carpet as he moved past the unused bedrooms—one of which, they hoped, could someday become a nursery—and walked toward the entrance of the master.

Angela looked up when Michael came to the doorway. She sat on the bed with her phone in her hand, scrolling through either news or social media. A lamp cast a soft glow on her face, but the set of her jaw was hard.

"Is she gone?" she asked.

"Can I talk to you for a second?"

"So she's not gone, is she?" Angela asked.

Angela's forehead creased with frustration. Her light brown hair was still pulled back, but a strand had worked its way loose and hung alongside her face. She tucked it away, her lips pressed into a tight line. Michael knew she had a lot to say, a lot of questions to ask, but he recognized the restraint she displayed. She excelled at patience, remaining calm in just about any storm, and possessed an inexhaustible ability to wait to hear what other people said before she responded. It made her a good salesperson at work and a good partner at home.

But in that moment, her patience felt spiderlike, a sticky spun web Michael saw no way to avoid tangling himself in.

"I'm going to go with her," Michael said, "up to Trudeau. Where she lives now."

He waited. Angela stood up, placed her hands on her hips, her face impassive. "Okay," she said finally. "Why?"

On his way through the house and up the stairs, Michael had spent time rehearsing exactly how he would tell Angela what Erica had told him about her daughter and the possibility he was the child's father. He had found no good way, and as he stood in the bedroom, facing his wife, the words were slow to come.

He started with the part he knew would elicit Angela's empathy. As a mother. As a person.

"Apparently, Erica has a daughter," he said. "And the daughter has been missing since this morning."

Angela lifted her hand to her mouth. "Oh, no. That's awful."

"Right. I can't imagine. And when someone, a kid, disappears like this, the first forty-eight hours or so are the most crucial. If they want to get the kid back . . . alive."

The hand fell away from Angela's mouth, and her eyes narrowed as she processed the news she'd just been told. "Is she married? Why is she here if her daughter is missing? Shouldn't she be out looking, or else waiting for the kid to come home?"

Michael answered the first question because it was easy to answer. "I don't know if she's married. I don't know anything about that."

Angela waited, her patience back.

Michael considered telling her something else, leaving out the most damning and painful part of what Erica had told him on the porch.

But he couldn't lie to her. He just couldn't.

So he told her.

chapter seven

Michael gathered his keys, his wallet, and stuffed them into his pockets while Angela hovered behind him.

"She can't be right, Michael. She can't just show up here and say you're the father of her child and then you just believe her. It's not logical."

"We were having sex up until the day we separated."

"I know," Angela said. "But you used protection, right? You're smarter than that."

"The pill. She was on the pill. It's not perfect."

"If she was even taking them," Angela said. "Hell, the way we're struggling with having a baby, maybe it's a long shot. The doctor said your—"

"Okay. I know the doctor says I have a low sperm count. But it's not *just* me with issues, remember?"

But the first part of her statement brought Michael up short. He didn't know for sure whether Erica had taken the pills. He'd never checked. He'd taken it on faith that Erica swallowed one every morning. What husband would want to have to check on that?

"Where does she want you to go?" Angela asked. "Do you even know what she's getting you into?"

Michael made a calming gesture with his hands, holding them out before him, the palms toward Angela. As he did it, he knew it was a bad idea. No one liked to be told to calm down when they were angry. Angela certainly didn't.

"Michael—"

"I'm sorry. Just . . . There's a guy she wants to talk to, someone who might know where the girl is. She wants me to go along. I guess she might feel safer with a man by her side."

"And you're the man? Not some other friend or a cop?"

"She might be lying or I don't know what, but she thinks the kid is mine. That's why she wants me to go."

"Do you hear this, Michael? Do you hear this?"

"Erica had issues, just like we all do, but she wasn't a liar. She was always forthright."

"Except she didn't tell you about this child. Or she's lying."

"We'll sort that out, I guess."

Before Michael could move past her and through the door of their bedroom, Angela reached out and placed her hand on his arm, stopping him from moving forward. She tightened her grip, an affectionate squeeze, a reminder that the two of them were connected in ways that didn't need to be spoken out loud. Years together. Mostly good, but even the bad. Together. Connected. "You should call the police right now. Go over to the phone and call them. Tell them Erica is here and she's upset about her daughter. She wants you to confront a witness or a suspect or whatever, and they need to come and talk her down. That's their job, not yours. It's understandable that she'd be upset if her kid is missing. I get that. The cops will understand."

"I can't do that."

"This is your life now. You and me. Our house, our future." Angela's brown eyes widened, beautiful dark pools. "We have plans for next week. We have plans for *tonight*, remember? The time of month, what we're trying to do. That's for our future together."

Michael reached down, took her hand off his arm, but held it between both of his. He loved the feel of his skin against hers, even in the most casual way. After a decade together, he found her touch could still send jolts of electricity coursing up his arms. Even with the strain of both of them working, trying to have a child, he still felt it. It was also true that over the past year, they'd snapped at each other more, neglected the little things that had once made them feel so intimate. He tried to remember that all working couples went through these things, that life sometimes felt like an out-of-control merry-go-round, and they were both desperately hanging on

"It's an hour or so up to Trudeau and then an hour back," Michael said. "A little chat with this guy. Or maybe I can talk her down from the ledge before we go very far. But if something happened to your child, if we couldn't find her, wouldn't you want anyone and everyone on earth to help you get through it? Wouldn't you want the whole world to stop if you were living in that hell and hearing that clock tick?"

Angela looked down at their joined hands. "I wouldn't go to someone I hadn't seen in a decade. I wouldn't call up any of my ex-boyfriends."

"I'm not her ex-boyfriend. I'm her ex-husband."

Angela broke free of his grip. She stepped back, her gestures and movements short and sharp. After a moment of looking at the floor, she tilted her head up, her eyes locking with Michael's again, her breath coming through her nostrils. "How do you know I won't call the police the minute you walk out the door? I can tell them your name and her name and where you're heading. How do you know I won't do that?"

"I'm asking you not to," he said.

"You're trusting everyone tonight, aren't you?"

"What if she is my daughter?" Michael asked.

Angela winced, then looked away. "Yeah, I don't know about that. I'm not sure I can think about you having a child with someone else when we can't."

"But if she is . . . She showed me a picture downstairs. She looked like . . ."

"Like who?"

"Like my family," Michael said.

Angela's eyes narrowed. She'd discovered something.

Like a terrier, she held it in her mind's teeth and worked it over. "How old is this kid? The missing one?"

"Nine."

"Nine? Oh, Michael. Do you think she looks like Robyn? Is that it?"

Michael's anger broke, his words exiting his mouth like a whip crack. "Don't make me out to be a sap. I'm worried, and I'm helping. This isn't buying magazines. This is a kid's life."

"Michael, you're not a sap. You're nobody's fool. But this issue, Robyn, I know the weight you still carry from it. I know you have the dreams. I know your mom isn't close to being over it. . . ." She paused, gathered her thoughts. "I'm sure Erica knows all about what happened to Robyn. You must have told her when you met. She must have seen how your family acts about it."

"I'm going."

He tugged the bedroom door open and stepped through, heading down the hallway toward the stairs. He wondered how any parent bore the burden of losing a child. He'd seen the toll it took on his parents over the years, his father's inability to even say Robyn's name until the day he died. The pictures of Robyn that went into a closet, the fragility and protectiveness that his parents displayed. Michael wouldn't have wished it on his worst enemy.

Angela followed him down the stairs to the front door. Before he went through it, she said, "Be careful. You don't know where she's taking you or who you're going to see."

"I will."

"No, really. Be careful. Remember when you two split up. You told me about her calls, the threats."

"Not threats. She was hurt."

"I saw the e-mails, Michael. If she lied to you about birth control and then kept this child from you, if she sent you those messages when you left her, then are you sure you know everything she's capable of?"

Michael paused for a moment, taking in the house. The cleanliness and the comfort. Problems and all, this was the life he loved. The life he held close.

He flashed to the picture on Erica's phone. The blond girl, the one who looked so much like Robyn.

"An hour there and an hour back," he said as he went out the door.

chapter eight

Michael stepped onto the porch, noting the two ground-up cigarette butts, the scattering of ashes. He briefly considered sweeping them away with his foot before Angela could see them, but he knew he'd just be wasting time. Angela was upset enough, and with good reason, so why worry about something small like the mess Erica made on the porch?

She paced at the end of the driveway. She wasn't smoking, but she held the phone to her ear, and as Michael approached, she gestured wildly with her free hand. It shook as though stricken with palsy.

She ended the call and looked up as Michael approached.

"The cops," she said, her voice shaking. "Nothing. They still don't know anything." She checked the time on the phone screen. "Almost twelve hours, Michael. It feels like twelve years. We have to get moving so I can get home sooner."

At the end of the driveway sat a white Camry parked at an odd angle to the curb, as though the driver had been in a hurry.

"I'm driving," Michael said. "You're too upset, and it's going to be dark soon."

"Fine, fine. I don't care. I'm happy to let someone else do something for a change. Let someone else worry."

Michael went around to the driver's side of his Honda SUV. He unlocked the door but saw Erica walking back to her car. "What are you doing?"

"I need something."

"I thought we were in such a hurry."

Michael stood by the open door as Erica walked to the Camry. She fumbled around inside, the dome light showing her movements, and then came out with a jacket that looked too heavy for the hot June weather. She walked back up the driveway and then climbed into the passenger seat of his car. Michael backed out of the driveway, watching his home recede behind him.

"Are you sure you don't want me to just take you to the police?" Michael asked. "Maybe if you talked to them again, they would be more responsive. Or they could give you more information."

"This guy's name is Wayne Tolliver. I have his address right here on my phone. Go north on Route 128. That's the way. He lives in Trudeau, not far from where we used to. Almost to the east side."

"What do you need the jacket for? It's eighty degrees."

"I just need it." She held the jacket on her lap, tucking it close to her body like a security blanket.

Michael did as he was told, heading for the state road that led to Davenport County. It felt awkward in the confined space of the car. Michael sensed her fear and anxiety, like being in close proximity to a jittery wild animal. She looked and smelled like she'd recently showered, but she wore no makeup, and Michael could see the worry and pain etched on her face like the work of erosion. He had next to no sense of what her life had been like over the past decade. A number of times over the past year he had checked her Facebook page, but she allowed little information to be made public, and Michael never felt right sending a friend request. Not because he didn't think he could be friends with his ex-wife, but because he didn't feel right opening that door to the past. He'd broken things off so cleanly and clearly with Erica that he felt he couldn't be the one to initiate.

And he'd never seen a photo of a child on her social media pages. Never.

"How did this happen?" Michael asked. "I mean, where was the kid taken from?"

"Felicity. Not 'the kid.' Can I smoke in here?"

Michael started to say no but relented. "Crack the window, please."

Erica did as she was asked, opening the window before lighting up. "You're more uptight than you used to be. I used to smoke in your car without you saying anything. Of course, your dad paid for that car. You live in a minimansion now. You and I lived in that little apartment. How many bedrooms does it have?"

"Five. And four bathrooms. You didn't answer my question."

"You must be working for your dad, right?" she asked, a trace of surprise and disdain in her voice. "You said you never wanted to do that. You wanted to get out of Cottonsville and not work in his company."

"Things change. They needed me when he died."

"So you just started working there when he died?" she asked.

Michael hesitated, watching the oncoming vehicles pass. "No. I started shortly after I got married again."

"Why?"

Michael lifted his right hand as he spoke. "I wanted to help my family. They matter to me. I was young when I said I never wanted to work there or live there."

"I'm sorry, by the way. About your dad. How long ago did he die?"

"Fourteen months. And how did you know about it?"

"Facebook. Where else? Is your mom okay? She must have taken it hard."

"Yeah, she did. They'd been together since college. I think she's a little directionless. So much of her life was tending to him. Now there's no one for her to take care of."

"And it was hard on you too," Erica said. Not a question but a statement. "I know you really loved him. And admired him."

"I'm okay," he said. "Life goes on. It was just sudden, that's all."

"And your family certainly already knows about losing someone. It must have brought things back up from the past."

"Okay, just, let's just not talk about Robyn and all that. Okay?"

"Sure." They rode in silence for a minute. "But you always carried that burden with you. If you ask me, they let you carry too much of the weight. Just because you were kind of watching her—"

"Erica. Can we drop it? Please?"

"Okay, okay."

Michael ignored her. He gripped the wheel tighter, staring at the road. He didn't want to think about that day or to think of his father dying. He pushed it away. It was all too much to think about, too much to remember.

It was too big.

"Boy, your dad didn't like me, did he?" she said. "Imagine if he knew we were riding around together now. He thought I was such a loudmouth. Which I am."

"You didn't answer my question from before."

"I know. I've answered it twenty times today. It makes me tired and hurt every time I have to say it. God, I've never felt so drained." She rubbed her eyes with her free hand. She rubbed so hard, it looked painful. Michael wasn't sure he'd ever seen someone look so weary and tired, as though she carried an unseen thousand-pound burden. "It's why I'm sick of talking to the police. But I guess you deserve to know, since I've brought you into this."

She sighed as she told him about agreeing to adopt a

dog for Felicity just over a year ago. Erica said she really hadn't wanted to take on the responsibility of a dog, but she'd thought it might be good for Felicity. During the summer, the two of them had fallen into the habit of taking the dog to the park in the morning, before the heat of the day set in, and leading it on a long walk. Even that early in the morning, they both ended up sweaty, but Erica still had enough time to return home and shower and get ready for work.

"This morning we went a little later than normal. I had a late meeting at work last night, so I didn't need to get in as early. I went to the park, got the stupid dog out of the car." As Erica moved to the events of that very morning, her voice took on the frantic, nervous tone again. Michael felt bad making her relive it, but his desire to know was even greater. "Felicity and I had a fight last night. She wants to get her ears pierced. I say she's too young. We went around and around about it. When we woke up this morning, she was still pissed at me. She inherited my stubbornness. So she refused to get out of the car and walk with me and the dog." Erica took one last drag and threw the cigarette out the window, and as she powered it back up, the air made a whooshing noise. "I was over it, Michael. I'm a single mom. I fight all these battles alone. So I told her if she wanted to sit in the hot car and wait for me, she could be my guest. No skin off my nose, right?"

Erica grew quiet. Michael turned onto the state road toward Davenport County. With the window up, the car seemed particularly silent with only the sound of the tires rolling over the pavement and the gentle hum of the motor and air-conditioning. Michael waited, although he might have guessed what came next.

"When I get back to the car, she's gone. Just gone. No sign of a problem. No blood or scream or anything." Her breath caught in her throat. Her voice lowered. "Gone."

"Could she have . . . I mean, kids run away."

"A nine-year-old? Where would she go? The park's in the middle of town. She had no money with her. Nothing." Erica drummed her fingers against the passenger-side door. Thrum-thrum-thrum.

"Sorry," Michael said. "Were there witnesses? Did anyone see anything or anyone unusual?"

Erica was turned away, her face pointed out the window, watching the cornfields and cattle pastures roll by.

"It was kind of early. About nine. The park still wasn't very crowded." She paused. Michael thought she wasn't going to say anything else, but then she added, "I have a problem, Michael. And it looks bad for me. Since she stayed in the car, and I walked the dog alone, people saw *me* in the park. But no one saw Felicity in the park this morning. It's like she hadn't been there at all. And they're wondering if I made the whole story up, if maybe I've done something to her."

chapter nine

9:01 P.M.

Angela went upstairs after Michael left, entered their bedroom, and grabbed a sweatshirt. She'd had a plan for the night. She wanted them to share a drink and head to bed early, and then they could take advantage of the time of month to try to finally conceive a child.

She shook her head, felt her cheeks flush. *Nothing kills the mood like your husband's ex-wife showing up. . . .*

She turned down the air-conditioning and then came back to the kitchen, taking in the dirty dishes Michael was supposed to do and finding the half-empty wineglass by the refrigerator. *Oh, I'm drinking that,* she thought, downing what remained in two big gulps and enjoying the heavy taste. She leaned back against the counter, angry at herself for wishing that when she came downstairs, she'd find Michael, his mind changed, the trip with Erica aborted.

But she knew it was wishful thinking. Michael wasn't the type to change his mind. And she had to hand it to Erica. She knew the right buttons to push, the right scab to dig into. A missing girl who might be Michael's daughter. A girl who looked like Michael's dead sister, Robyn.

Well played, Angela thought. *Well played.*

She poured another glass of cabernet, deciding not to wait for Michael's return to have another drink, and almost emptied the bottle. No way. She'd earned this one and took it with her as she left the kitchen, carrying the wineglass down the hallway to her home office, clicking on the first-floor lights as she moved. She needed to sort through reports, catch up on what felt like a thousand e-mails. With a vacation just ahead, she needed to work double time in order to be ready to go, to finally unplug and unwind with Michael and nothing else in their way.

Was it selfish to feel like the night's events had put the vacation and their peace in doubt? After all, a child appeared to be in some kind of jeopardy, a child who might be her husband's.

She tried not to dwell on that, tried not to contemplate what it would feel like if Michael had a child with another woman and couldn't have one with her. It was just too much. And too soon, since she knew nothing for certain. She also tried not to think about the night ahead, the "date" she and Michael had since she was ovulating and that was now in jeopardy. She sipped her wine and took a few deep breaths.

Calm, she reminded herself. *Calm. I'll still be ovulating tomorrow. And next month too . . .*

But she ignored work for the moment. She almost never pushed her job aside, especially during the precious evening time when Michael watched baseball or read or did his own work, but she needed to check on something, to assure herself of what was really going on.

She took out her phone and opened her Twitter app. She entered "missing child" and "Trudeau KY."

It took a moment for the information to appear. At first, Angela saw nothing, and her mind raced even faster. But then she saw it. An Amber Alert had been issued in Davenport County.

Nine-year-old girl missing from a local park. Mother distraught. Thoughts and prayers. Any information, call. No witnesses.

Police believe the child is in danger.

Angela let out a sigh, and her heart dropped like a stone. She scrolled through the feed a little more and came across a video, something posted by a news station in Trudeau. Angela pressed PLAY.

She saw a blond-haired girl, a beautiful kid, one who looked like an angel. She stood in front of a piano and sang as someone unseen picked out the notes. It took a moment for Angela to recognize the song. At first, she couldn't place the lyrics, but then the melody and the words clicked in her brain. It was that song from *The*

Muppet Movie, the one she had seen as a kid. The song about rainbows and dreamers sung by Kermit the Frog.

Angela's eyes burned with tears. The melancholy nature of the song and the sweet innocence of the singing child brought the emotion surging to the surface. She wiped at her tears as the video ended, the image freezing on the girl's face, her eyes wide, almost haunted.

Or was Angela projecting her own fears onto the child?

Or was she more emotional due to ovulating? Was her desire for a child of her own infusing everything?

She thought, *I need more wine.*

She started back down the hall, understanding that work might get passed over that night, that she might need a different kind of distraction while she waited for Michael to come home. They could deal with their problems then, discuss and understand and make plans. They'd survive whatever it was, even if the child, the missing little girl, was Michael's daughter.

She almost laughed. The girl they—especially he—always wanted, delivered to them in the craziest way possible. She again tried to ignore the little knot of jealousy in her gut, the one that arose at the thought that her husband had fathered a child with another woman. She pushed the bad feeling away.

We can handle it, she thought. I *can handle it. I can.*

What was that old curse? *May you live in interesting times.*

She reached the kitchen, pulled down a new glass since she'd left the old one on her desk, opened a new bottle, and started to pour. When the doorbell rang, her hand jumped, and she spilled the red liquid on the counter.

"Damn it."

She left the wineglass and the spill on the counter, set the bottle down. The house had turned into Grand Central Station, the front bell ringing like a pinball machine.

Could Michael have forgotten his keys? Could it be Erica? But then . . . without Michael?

Or was it simply a chance to buy overpriced candy bars to support a Little League team?

She hurried back to her desk and grabbed her phone. She opened the keypad, walking to the door with her fingers poised, prepared to dial 911 if she had to. She slipped the living room curtains aside and peered out at the almost fully dark street, the tall light poles shimmering to life.

A man she didn't know stood down at the end of the driveway, leaning close to a white Camry in an apparent attempt to see inside. Angela cut her eyes to the porch, caught a glimpse of a woman in a business suit, hands on hips. Something glinted on the woman's belt, something shiny and gold, caught by the porch light.

And when she turned her body, looking directly at Angela, the gun on her other hip, a menacing black weapon, revealed itself.

Angela stepped back, her heart thumping all over again.

Cops.

chapter ten

"Mrs. Frazier? Are you Angela Frazier?"

The woman with the badge on her belt stood with her hands on her hips, her jacket open over a simple white shirt. Angela looked over the woman's shoulder and saw the man who had been standing by the white car now walking up the sloping driveway, his movements slow and labored behind a large gut.

"I am," Angela said. "Is something wrong? Has something happened to my husband?"

"I'm Erin Griffin, a detective with the Davenport County sheriff's office." She pointed to the man who was just getting close to the front porch, the sweat beading on his forehead, his face red. "This is my colleague Jim Twitchell. We're assisting the lead detectives on a case in which your husband's name came up."

The man, who had a large moon face and a buzz cut, nodded to Angela but didn't say anything. He pulled a handkerchief out of his pocket and mopped his brow. He looked to be about fifty and wore a dark suit with a red tie, the knot loose at his neck.

The woman appeared to be in her early thirties, which made her the same age as Angela. Whether because her partner was overheated or because she was just that kind of person, Griffin appeared to be in charge. Her hair was cut short like a man's, and her blue eyes looked snowflake cool. Only the light spray of freckles across her nose softened her appearance.

"Why are you asking about your husband?" Griffin asked. "Is he not at home?"

"No, he's not. Are you here because of the kidnapping?"

"Mind if we come in?" Griffin pointed past Angela and into the air-conditioned house, and she seemed to be moving inside without waiting for permission. Angela stepped aside, and Twitchell came in too, nodding at Angela as he passed and letting out a relieved sigh as the refreshing air hit him.

"We can talk in the dining room." Angela led them through the large foyer and across the living room. She took the seat at the head of the table, the one where Michael usually sat, and the two detectives sat on either side of her. She felt like she was in a cross fire. "I'm sorry if the table is a little dirty. We haven't cleaned up our dinner mess."

"No worries," Griffin said, smiling, but her eyes still didn't show much warmth. They seemed to be scanning Angela, extracting information from her just by looking.

"Spacious," Twitchell said, his voice envious.

Angela had grown up in a cramped three-bedroom ranch-style house, sharing a room with her younger sister, then lived in dorms and tiny college apartments. She still wasn't completely used to all the space they had, still felt slightly embarrassed by the size of it all. "We're hoping our family expands to fill it."

"Can I ask you how you know about the disappearance in Davenport County?" Griffin asked. "Did you hear about it on the news?"

Angela looked back and forth between the two of them. Their patient faces gave away nothing. No hope, no fear. No encouragement or disdain. "She came to our house. Erica. She's still going by Frazier, isn't she? Erica Frazier." Angela tried not to sigh or roll her eyes. "She came here and told Michael, and the two of them left together."

Twitchell's eyebrows rose ever so slightly. He reached up and wiped his forehead with his left index finger. "Where did they go?"

"To see some guy. Erica told Michael this guy might know something, and she wanted to talk to him with Michael along."

The detectives shared a glance, their eyes cutting toward each other for one beat and then returning to focus on Angela again.

Twitchell said, "I'm presuming that when Ms. Frazier was here—Erica Frazier, that is—she told your husband Felicity is his child?"

"She did."

"Is that true?" Griffin asked.

Angela lifted her hands and let them drop back against the top of the table. "I have no idea. I'd never heard anything like it before today."

"Erica Frazier has told a few of her friends and acquaintances that Felicity is Michael's child," Griffin said. "And given the timing of when they were married, it is possible for that to be true."

Angela leaned back in her chair. "Are you investigating my husband or trying to find a missing child?"

Something crossed Griffin's eyes, a flash of anger that came and went faster than a lightning strike. A muscle twitched in her jaw. "Is tonight the first time you met Ms. Frazier?"

Angela remained leaning back in the chair. She almost laughed but didn't because she understood what the cops were doing. They were trying to see if she would tell them the truth about meeting Erica before. They knew the answer to the question. They wanted to see how she would answer.

For the second time that evening she thought, *Well played.*

"We met one other time," Angela said. "I'm guessing you have a report on that."

Twitchell pulled out a smartphone and started tapping it, his lips pressed together with concentration as his meaty fingers did their work. "This was just over a year ago," he said, his eyes squinting as he read. "The time you went to Erica Frazier's place of work and got into a screaming match with her in front of her coworkers."

chapter eleven

Angela reached up, found the strand of hair that had popped loose again. She started to twirl it but stopped herself and tucked it behind her ear. She didn't want to look like a twelve-year-old, playing with her hair in front of authority figures.

"I think 'screaming' is an exaggeration," she said.

Twitchell looked at Angela over the top of his phone. "Well, you spoke loudly enough that the police had to be called. That sounds like yelling at least."

"We can see from the report that no charges were filed, but do you mind telling us what caused this to happen?" Griffin asked.

"So now *I'm* being investigated?" Angela asked.

Griffin leaned closer. "We're investigating a missing child. A child who could right now be in grave danger.

It's a critical time, so we need to understand all the moving parts and how everyone is connected to everyone else in order to help us find her." She glanced at the clock on the wall behind Angela. "We've taken attention away from that search to come here, but we do need to get back to helping our colleagues and the volunteers. So . . . why did you and Erica Frazier have words that day at her place of employment? What happened that made you go that far just to speak to her?"

Angela felt appropriately chastened. And, regardless of what she thought of Erica or Michael's decision to go with her that night, she hated the thought of a child in jeopardy. Any child, anywhere.

"I didn't go that far just to speak to her," Angela said. "I was already there, for my job." She looked back and forth between them again, trying to gauge whether one of the faces was friendlier than the other, whether it made more sense to focus on just one of them. "I'm a sales rep for a pharmaceutical company. So I cover this whole area. I go to Trudeau and Davenport County every couple of weeks."

"Did you know Ms. Frazier was living there?" Twitchell asked.

Angela started to ask them to stop referring to Erica by the name "Frazier," but she held her tongue. Better to stick to the question she'd been asked. "Yes, I knew. I'd seen her page on Facebook before, so I knew she lived in Trudeau, and I knew she worked at the State Employees Credit Union up there. But I didn't plan on seeing her." She shifted her eyes to focus exclusively on Griffin, thinking she could register by speaking woman to woman. "I admit I was always curious about Erica. My husband married her after all. It's natural to wonder about your partner's exes. Sometimes seeing them in person deflates all the notions we build up in our minds about what that person is really like. You know, 'Oh, she's not really that pretty.' Or 'Oh, she looks heavier in person than in the pictures.' Right?"

Griffin nodded. But Angela couldn't tell if it was solidarity or an attempt to keep Angela talking.

"I had a break that day because a client canceled. And I looked at Facebook, just to be looking. And then I looked at Erica's page. Like I said, I do it every once in a while. And what do you think I saw?"

The detectives remained silent. They recognized the rhetorical nature of the question.

"I saw a picture of her and Michael. A wedding picture. She had a few other pictures of her life up, but I noticed this one." Angela held her hands out above the table, palms up, pleading to the investigators or the universe to understand how crazy the idea was. "Why was that there? My husband, years after they divorced? And she'd captioned the picture. It said something about lost love and bittersweet memories. It really bothered me. It felt like some sort of violation, to be honest."

"Was there a reason why she put it up?" Griffin asked. "Was it a special date?"

"I have no idea."

"So you went to the credit union to tell her . . . what?" Twitchell asked.

"I went there, and I parked outside, and I realized how stupid I was being. Why say anything? Why let someone from the past affect my life? After all, I was married to Michael. He walked away from her, so I didn't need to say anything." The memory brought the sting of embarrassment to Angela's face. She wasn't the kind of person to lose her cool. She wasn't the jealous type. But last year after several false alarms, she and Michael were starting to understand the struggle it would be to conceive a child. She'd felt raw that day, agitated, and as she was ready to start her car and drive off, Erica came outside, apparently on her way to lunch. "She looked so at ease, so carefree. She could post something that upset me and then just go on. I know it's silly to feel that something like that is a disruption of my life. I should have just ignored it."

"So you said something," Griffin said.

"I acted foolish. I told her to quit posting photos of Michael." Angela shrugged, lifting her hands and letting them fall to the tabletop again. "She didn't even recognize me. I had to tell her who I was. We went back and forth a little bit, and then she said the thing that really got me."

"What was that?" Twitchell asked, his eyes shining ever so slightly in anticipation of a juicy detail.

"I'll say it, but I realize now it sounds very high school."

"That's okay," Griffin said.

"She said I was just upset because nothing could erase what she and Michael shared together, that they were connected in ways I couldn't understand." Angela scratched her head, looked down at the table and then back up at the cops. "So things just escalated from there. I got out of the car. We got close to each other, yelling at each other. One of her coworkers called the police, and they came and calmed things down. No one pressed charges, and I just got back into my car and went about my day. Believe me, my own embarrassment was worse than getting charged with anything."

Twitchell nodded, his head moving as though he heard music. "What did your husband think when you told him all of this?" he asked, his head still moving.

"You all think of everything, don't you?" she said.

The two cops blinked at her.

"He doesn't know. I never told him about it."

chapter twelve

Griffin reached into her jacket pocket and brought out a small moleskin notebook. She produced a retractable pen from the same pocket and clicked it open by turning it upside down and pressing it against the top of the table. She turned to a blank page and wrote something down, something Angela couldn't read even though she tried. The sound of the pen scratching against the paper sounded loud in the quiet house. Twitchell seemed preoccupied with his phone, scrolling through using his index finger. For all Angela knew, he was looking at a baseball score, seeing how the Reds were doing against the Nationals that night.

When Griffin finished writing, she studied her words for a moment and then looked up at Angela. "This is just a routine question," she said. "We have to ask everyone. Where were you this morning?"

"We're going out of town soon, and I have a lot of work to catch up on. Reports and things. I was doing that when you showed up here tonight." Angela gestured over her shoulder with her thumb in the direction of her office, but then realized how pointless the motion was. They didn't know what her office looked like. They didn't know where it was in the house. She lowered her hand. "I had a couple of clients I needed to see, to make calls on, but I contacted them and rescheduled. I decided to just work from home today, so that's what I did."

"You were here all day?" Twitchell asked.

"Yes."

"You were here alone? You didn't see any clients or meet anyone?" he asked.

"No."

"And your husband wasn't here either?"

"He was at work. His father died a little over a year ago, and Michael has stepped in to lead the company. He works long hours and usually doesn't come home during the day."

"This is the home health care company?"

"Yes. Frazier Home Health. My father-in-law founded it. The company meant a lot to Michael's father. And his mom. I think Michael wants to keep it going. For them as much as for himself."

Griffin used her thumb to click the top of her pen. Click-click-click. "Did you have calls today? You know, conference calls? Work calls?"

"No."

"So you didn't know Felicity existed and your husband didn't know she existed, but you've been to Erica's Facebook page. You didn't see pictures of Felicity there?"

"A lot of people keep some of their information private on Facebook, unless you're friends with them. And I'm not friends with Erica on Facebook. She has a handful of photos that anyone can see, but none of them showed a child. If I had a child, I might keep their photos private on social media. Believe me, I'd have remembered if I'd seen a picture of her kid on her page."

"Just like you remembered that wedding picture," Twitchell said.

"Exactly." Angela thought Twitchell might have been trying to get a rise out of her, but the comment was accurate. She'd have noticed and remembered a kid. She'd been noticing everything about children lately. She teared up a little when she saw babies and moms in the grocery store. She felt a lump in her throat when she saw families in TV commercials. She found herself driving slowly past Babies "R" Us stores. Yes, she noticed kids.

"And there's been no other contact between you or your husband and Ms. Frazier since the two of them split up?" Griffin asked.

"He heard from her early on, when they first divorced. In fact, Erica sent him some pretty hateful e-mail messages back then, ones that just made me feel really uncomfortable."

"So this was when you were already married?" Twitchell asked.

"No, we were dating. We met just a few months after Michael and Erica split up. Some of her messages mentioned me, so she knew we were dating somehow."

"And they made you uncomfortable?" Twitchell asked. "In what way?"

"It's been a long time . . . but she said things like she wanted Michael back. And how much he meant to her. Look, I'm not insecure, but it's weird to hear that from your new boyfriend's ex-wife. And . . . Erica was pretty and fit, and I just didn't like it. Who would?"

"What did he do about the messages?" Twitchell asked. "Did he tell her to stop or what?"

"He decided to take the high road and tread lightly. He didn't want to cause Erica any more pain than he already had. Michael's like that. He tries to give people the benefit of the doubt as much as possible. He felt guilty over leaving her after such a short amount of time, so he felt like he could handle some awkward e-mails. And he said Erica had a tendency to act overly dramatic, to carry on a long time over something. He just wanted to let it blow over, and it did. He stopped hearing from her, and life went on."

"Do you know anyone else who knows Erica Frazier?" Griffin asked. "She and your husband must have had friends back then. Are you or he in touch with them?"

"I don't think Michael's in touch with most of those people," she said. "His family knew her, obviously. His parents and his sister."

"Does he talk about his ex-wife?" Griffin asked. "Ever?"

Angela thought she heard an undercurrent of emotion

in the detective's question. "Not very much. Almost never."

"Has your husband ever mentioned a man named Jake Little?" Griffin asked.

"Who's that?"

"Has he mentioned him?" Griffin asked.

"No. Is he a friend of Erica's?"

"He's an ex-boyfriend of hers. They've dated a couple of different times over the years. He was a sort of father figure to Felicity. Have you heard from your husband since he left with Erica Frazier?" Griffin asked.

"No. I'm leaving him alone. He wanted to go, so I let him. He said he'd be back as soon as he could. I'm not thrilled about it. Who would be? But I'm also not going to beg him to stay if he wants to do something like this."

"Would you mind calling him?" Griffin asked.

Angela found herself shaking her head, telling the cops no before she even said anything. "I don't want to call him. I . . . Look, I don't want to come off like some needy wife. He wants to do this, so he can do it. It's fine. Really. Whatever comes our way we can handle."

The cops again exchanged that glance, their eyes locking as though they could communicate without words. Which they probably could.

"What?" Angela asked.

"We'd really like for you to make that call," Twitchell said. "We haven't been able to get ahold of Erica Frazier for the past hour or so. She's not answering her cell phone, and she's not at her house, where we'd like her to be. Given some other factors we've learned about, we'd like to know where she is."

"What other factors?" Angela asked, her concern rising. Maybe she wouldn't get to play the cool, detached wife. Maybe there was more at stake.

Griffin nodded, and then seemed to have reached a decision. She spoke with the pen still held in her hand. "About a month ago, Erica Frazier was investigated by child protective services for endangering her child. And now the child is missing, with no actual witnesses to the events she described. She came here and has taken your husband somewhere. We'd like to know where she is. See?"

Angela did. All too well. Before Griffin was even finished talking, she was picking up her phone.

chapter thirteen

When the call went to voice mail, Angela stood up. She walked away from the table where the cops sat, turning her back to them. She pushed the red button to end the call without saying anything, cutting Michael's friendly but efficient greeting off in the middle. She walked out to the front of the house, toward the foyer, where through the drawn curtains she could see dark night, and dialed again.

She said one word under her breath. A command and a wish.

"Answer."

While she listened to the chirping ring, she looked at the wall. A picture of her and Michael at *their* wedding hung there, the two of them looking younger, smiles wide as he held her in his arms, an almost Hollywoodesque ray of sun beaming over his left shoulder. Yes, she thought, it had been so easy then. All they'd had to do was be in love, eyes cast to the endless future. Jobs, kids, a new house. New possibilities and adventures.

Something else crept into her mind, a slithering snake of jealousy. He and Erica must have felt that way once, in that picture she'd shared on Facebook.

"Answer," she said again, teeth clenched tighter.

But he didn't. So she left a message, doing everything in her power to keep her voice calm and collected. She didn't want to plead, didn't want to sound out of control.

"Michael, I need you to call me back. The police are here, and they're looking for Erica. And now they're looking for you. Can you call me back when you get the chance? I think you might be getting in over your head."

She hung up. She reminded herself of how much they had together, how much they had shared. One night couldn't erase it all. A child from the past couldn't either.

But even as she thought that, a stab of jealousy hit her in the chest. Why could he have a child with someone else and not with her? Was something wrong with her?

"No answer?"

Angela jumped at the voice. Twitchell stood behind her with Griffin at his side. She held the phone tight, her knuckles straining, the skin slick with sweat where it touched the black case.

"No. I left a message."

"You can try again in a few minutes," Griffin said. "If he doesn't call back."

"He doesn't like to answer when he's driving," Angela

said. “It goes right to the speaker in the car, but he still doesn’t like to do it.”

Both of the cops nodded, understanding. “Do you mind if we have a look around the house?” Twitchell asked. “Just a quick glance. While we’re waiting for your husband to call back.”

Angela didn’t think she could say no. Why would she? “Sure.”

Griffin started up the stairs, her flat shoes making no sound against the carpet.

Twitchell pointed behind Angela. “What’s down this hallway?”

“I have an office there. Michael does too. And a guest room. My mother stays there when she comes from out of town.” Again, she realized how much space they had, how fortunate they’d been thanks to Michael’s family. She and Michael both worked hard, but her father-in-law had built a company that made them all comfortable.

Beyond comfortable.

“Mind if I look?” he asked.

“Go ahead.” Angela stepped out of his way.

Angela didn’t know whether she was supposed to follow, but since no one told her not to, she did. She figured it was her house, her office. If the cop wanted to look around, she could tail him.

Twitchell looked the room over, taking it in like he was a prospective buyer. He pointed to the open laptop. “This is yours? For work?”

“Work and personal. Mostly work.”

He glanced at but didn’t touch the papers on her desk.

His eyes trailed around the room. He pointed to the closed closet door, behind which Angela stored a hodgepodge of more papers, catalogs, samples, and cases. "Do you mind?"

Again, Angela stepped out of the way. "Sure."

Twitchell pulled the door open. It stuck for just a moment, and Angela wondered what he expected to find in there. A bound and gagged child? A dead one? He looked around inside and then shut the door. "Is your husband's office in the next room?"

"Yes." Angela led him there.

"Does his computer have a password? Can you log on for me?"

"It does. And I can." Angela knew most of Michael's passwords, even though she almost never needed them. He knew hers as well.

But she paused for a moment.

"What are you looking for?" she asked. "I mean . . . he's not here."

"Nothing in particular," Twitchell said. "If you're not comfortable with this, if you think there's something we shouldn't see . . ."

"I don't think that." She leaned over the laptop and typed in the password. Then she stepped aside for the cop. "I want you to find this missing child too. Okay? It's horrible to think about."

"Okay. I'll just be a minute."

"Why didn't you look at my computer this closely?"

"You're here," Twitchell said. "If I wanted to know something about you, I'd ask."

"It sounds like you think I'm honest."

"I try to give people the benefit of the doubt."

"That might be a risk for a cop," she said.

"Might be." He turned away and started tapping on Michael's computer.

Angela felt like a fish out of water, so she walked to the foyer and met Griffin coming down.

"That's it," the cop said. "Thanks for letting me look."

"You're welcome."

"Is there a basement?"

"No."

"Attic?"

"Yes. But we don't keep anything there. You go in through a pull-down ladder in the garage."

"We can check that on the way out," Griffin said. "Has your husband called back?"

Angela looked at her phone, as though a call might have come through that she hadn't heard. "No. I'll try again."

She hit the CALL button and listened to the ring. Just as it went to voice mail, Twitchell spoke from the other room.

"Griffin, you out there? I think you're going to want to see this."

chapter fourteen

9:32 P.M.

Michael's phone rang again, and again he ignored it. He saw Angela's name coming up on the car's display, and it took a fair amount of discipline and control not to answer.

But he had no desire to hold a conversation with his wife while Erica sat in the car next to him. He felt it was enough to keep an eye on Erica, who had smoked what seemed like half a pack of cigarettes on their ride toward Trudeau, lighting a new one as soon as the previous one was finished. And Michael noticed the way she kept her jacket clutched tight to her body. It had started to slide off her lap once, and she made a frantic lunge, grabbing it and then pulling it back against her. Michael decided to call Angela when they reached their destination. And he promised to stick to the plan. One stop. An hour there and an hour back. And then he'd let Erica go on and do whatever she wanted to do.

"We're close, right?" he asked.

"Half a mile," she said, looking at her phone, scrolling through with the hand that held the cigarette. "Turn left here."

They entered a middle-class neighborhood, a postwar subdivision that, even in the disappearing light, looked good. Mostly ranches, the lawns well maintained, the homes lighted and bright. They passed a group of kids running across a yard, their squeals coming through Erica's open window, their bodies indistinct blurs in the fading light. Michael stole a glance at her and thought he saw a look cross her face as though she'd felt a twinge of pain.

They'd lived in Trudeau together the year they were married. Michael had worked for a startup, gaining experience before the expected move to his dad's company. He'd been to a party in that neighborhood once, a holiday thing thrown by some business acquaintance. He and Erica had gone together, she in a red dress, he in a jacket and tie. To the outside world, they must have appeared to be the perfect young couple. Happy and in love, just starting their lives together.

"Left again," she said, her voice lower. She pointed outside. "That party we went to was down that street. I don't even remember the guy's name."

"I don't either."

"Erased by time, I guess."

"What does Felicity like to do?" Michael asked. "You know, for fun. What is she interested in?"

"She loves the dog," Erica said. "She's into music and singing. That's how she got to know this teacher so well. He runs a children's choir in the summer, through the school. He heard her sing once, at an audition, and he really recruited her to join. She loves it."

"Good," Michael said.

"When she started getting into the singing, I thought of Lynn. Maybe she got that ability from her."

"I know she didn't get it from—" But Michael stopped himself before he said, *I know she didn't get it from me.* He refused to give the impression he thought he was Felicity's father. And he was trying not to be cold, given how much pain Erica must have been in.

"How is she?" Erica asked. "Lynn?"

"She's good. She had a rough time when the band broke up. And then she had cervical cancer right after that."

"She did?"

"Yeah, it was scary as hell. And then my dad dropped dead last year. But she's coming up on five years cancer free."

"Good. I'm glad to hear that." After a moment, she said, "It's weird to know people so well and then have them fall out of your life completely. Your parents weren't that crazy about me, but Lynn was always nice. Maybe we shared some kind of rebellious kinship."

"Clearly."

"And she lives in Cottonsville too?" Erica asked. "Not LA or even Nashville?"

"Her home is in Cottonsville."

"But both of you are there. That's unexpected."

Michael didn't bite. "She's happy there."

"Okay," she said. "I don't want to talk about the past either. Right now, I'm more interested in finding Felicity than anything else. We can worry about the rest later. The house is on the right. That one."

Michael eased the car to a stop in front of a modest ranch-style house. The porch light revealed two flower boxes anchored to the wrought-iron railing, and an American flag hung limply next to the door. From behind the large front window, soft light glowed, and Michael thought he saw the flickering images of a TV screen. It looked like someone was home.

"Does this guy live alone?" he asked. "And what's his name again?"

"Wayne Tolliver. And he lives alone."

"And you don't want to just ask the cops to come by and talk to him again?"

Erica threw her latest cigarette out the window and into the man's yard. She pushed the door open, pulling the coat along with her. "Let's go."

Michael went out on his side, hustling to keep up with Erica as she moved across the lawn. Above, the stars were appearing, tiny pinpricks of light, and a low moon rose behind the jagged rooflines of the houses. The temperature remained warm, the air muggy and full of swirling insects.

Michael wanted to return the call to Angela, but Erica hurried across the lawn and bounded up the steps. She rang the doorbell several times in a row, just as she had at his house, and then used the flat of her hand to pound. She took the jacket and slipped her arms into the sleeves, pulling it tight to her body.

"Hold on," Michael said.

But he watched the door come open, revealing the figure of a slender middle-aged man blinking in the face of an intrusion on his peaceful night at home. Before Michael could reach her or stop her, Erica reached out with her right hand and shoved the man back, sending him tumbling into his house and out of Michael's line of sight.

And Erica went through the door after him, her other hand, the one that hadn't done the shoving, sliding toward the pocket of her coat.

chapter fifteen

When Michael came through the door, Wayne Tolliver was on his back scrambling away from Erica like a frightened crab. She followed after him, trying to step over his pumping legs. Michael shut the front door, making sure they didn't give the neighbors any kind of show. And then he reached for Erica, trying to pull her back from Tolliver and keep her calm.

"Easy, easy. I thought we wanted to talk to him."

Tolliver managed to push himself over to the couch, and he leaned back against it, his butt still resting on the floor. Even sitting down, Tolliver looked thin and tall. He wore a button-down shirt, black pants, and house slippers, one of which had fallen off in the struggle, revealing a pale, knobby foot. His thinning brown hair fell over his forehead, and once Erica seemed to be calming down, he reached up and brushed it back off his face. Michael guessed he was in his mid-forties.

"I'm sick of talking, Michael," Erica said. "I'm sick of answering questions. I've been doing that all day. That's all you wanted to do in the car, just interrogate me and question me. I want answers now. I don't want to give them."

"You're not going to get them this way," Michael said, imagining the police bursting in at any minute and arresting him and his ex-wife for breaking and entering and assault. Michael walked over to the helpless-looking Tolliver and held out his hand.

Tolliver's eyes, wide with suspicion and fear, were two ovals of mistrust. But Michael kept his hand out, and finally the man relented and accepted the help. Michael pulled him to his feet and then eased him onto the couch. A bottle of Glenlivet sat on the end table, a half-full tumbler by its side.

"Why don't you have some of that scotch?" Michael said, pointing.

Tolliver's breathing started to return to normal. He smoothed the sweater down across his chest and stomach, trying to look dignified and composed after his slide across the floor. "I think I will. Thank you."

His voice sounded refined and thin.

Erica came close as Michael stood between her and Tolliver. She too breathed heavily, but from anger, not exertion. She remained silent as Tolliver sipped his drink, his lips pursing as the liquid went down.

"Okay," Michael said, trying to control the situation. "Now everyone is calm. No one's going to jump anybody, are they?" He looked at Erica, who didn't say anything in response. "Right?" he asked, prompting her.

"He needs to answer some things," she said.

Either the scotch or Michael's body serving as a human buffer emboldened Tolliver, because he said, his voice as sharp as a scalpel, "I already answered all the questions. With the police, this morning. Do you think that was pleasant for me? An educator dragged in there when a little girl disappears?"

"Did you tell them how obsessed you are with Felicity? How you tried so hard to get her into the choir? Did you tell them all of that?"

Tolliver rolled his eyes. He reached out and poured more scotch into his glass, his movements slow and mannered, even though his hand still shook. After he had taken another drink, he asked, "Who is this? Another male friend?"

"This is Felicity's father," Erica said.

Hearing the words spoken that way, to another person and not to himself, made them seem somehow more real, more powerful, and Michael couldn't deny that some part of him liked the sound of them. While he held himself back from completely accepting the reality of those words, he knew he was slowly warming to them.

Tolliver's eyebrows rose. He looked smugly surprised. "Well," he said, "Felicity's father. At long last we meet." He studied Michael, one eyebrow cocked. "I know your sister. Lynn."

"You do?" Michael asked.

"Not well. I'm a musician too. I admire her skill as a songwriter. I heard she had a health problem."

"She's fine. What did you tell the police?" Michael asked.

"Would either of you like a drink?" Tolliver asked.

"No," Michael said. "Just tell us what she wants to know, and then we can leave."

Tolliver sighed theatrically. He placed the glass on the table. "I told them the truth. I was teaching a class at the community center this morning. It's summer break, and that's what I do. I also told them they were welcome to come and search the house, but they didn't take me up on it. This is the condensed version of the story, of course." He looked at Michael. "I think Felicity is a great kid. I do. I think a lot of my students are great kids. But I thought Felicity merited special attention." He cut his eyes at Erica. "And not for the reasons some people think."

"Because of her talent?" Michael asked.

"That," he said, "and she needed other things."

Erica shifted next to Michael, moving in the direction of Tolliver but not going all the way. Michael sensed something easing in her posture, a resignation.

"After child protective services had been called on Erica," he said, "I thought it might be good for the kid to have *someone* paying attention to her."

chapter sixteen

Michael turned to Erica, who was standing so close he could once again smell the sweat and desperation coming off her body.

"When was that, Erica?" Tolliver asked. "Last month?"

Erica was shaking her head, and Michael noticed that her left hand had slipped back inside the coat pocket, the one her hand was in when she first went through the door into Tolliver's house. She looked less defiant and more sad, some of the steel going out of her jaw. Her features drooped ever so slightly, an almost imperceptible sagging. Michael remembered that look and pose from college. It had often come after the intensity, after the drama, when she appeared to be running out of steam, slumping back into herself as though overwhelmed by everything.

"What is he talking about, Erica?" Michael asked.

She took a step back, focusing her attention on Michael as if Tolliver weren't even in the room. The vulnerable look in her eyes took Michael back to the times in college when they'd fought or when Erica had felt sad. To the days near the end of their marriage when tears had fallen constantly. Erica seemed to feel everything more deeply than other people, to bend far but never break under the weight of emotion. Michael hated to see it, hated to see someone he once cared about looking that way after everything else she'd been through.

But he wanted to know what had happened. He needed to know before he went another step down that road.

"It's not easy being a single mom, Michael," she said. "It takes a toll. Day after day of being alone with Felicity."

"Of course." He kept the next thought to himself: *That was your choice. You could have had my help if she really is my child.*

"I admit there were times I wasn't the best parent, juggling a career with raising a daughter and trying to have some kind of life for myself. I made mistakes when Felicity was young. Maybe I partied too much from time to time. Maybe I left her alone a little longer than I should have on a few occasions."

Michael listened, withholding judgment. Behind him he heard the neck of the scotch bottle clink against the glass as Tolliver poured himself another round. Michael had to admit having a drink sounded good.

Erica said, "It's true someone called child protective

services on me a month ago. I'd gone out and left Felicity home alone. She was wrapped up in doing homework, and I hated to interrupt her. I was just going to the store to get something to bring back for dinner. Just a twenty-minute round trip. No big deal. And I kind of wanted a little break, a little time alone to clear my head." She reached up, scratched her forehead. It also looked like she was shading her eyes, preventing Michael from seeing them as she spoke. "But I ran into someone. A friend of mine."

"I heard it was a guy," Tolliver said. "An ex-boyfriend."

Erica lowered her hand, gave Tolliver a frosty look. The vulnerability disappeared. "Yes, an ex-boyfriend of mine." She looked back at Michael. "His name is Jake Little, and we dated when Felicity was young. It's the only serious relationship I've had since we split up. To be honest, he's the closest thing to a father Felicity has ever had."

Michael tried to picture the guy, wondered if he'd been acting as father to his own biological child. He felt what he knew in the moment was an unreasonable jealousy. Had another man served as Felicity's father? How much had he really missed out on?

"Jake moved back to town two or three years ago. When he and I first split up, he moved out of state, and we fell out of touch. But when he moved back to town, it was easy to pick things up. I'd been alone a long time, and Felicity knew him. And she needed a dad." She looked at Michael. "Don't you agree?"

"What happened that led to this CPS call?" Michael asked.

"Jake and I split up again about eight months after he moved back to town. It just didn't work then. Or ever. And I didn't want to get in too deep with him and let Felicity get attached to him all over again."

"So you cut it off cold with him?" Michael asked. "This second time?"

"Not cold. We talked from time to time. He knew about Felicity's life. In a pinch, he helped out with watching her a few times. He took her to the zoo once, but our romance was over. I wasn't going to play that game with him."

"So you went to the store, and what happened?" Michael asked.

"I ran into Jake in the parking lot. We talked, sitting in my car. And, yes, I opened a bottle of the beer I'd bought. We both had one while we talked. I lost track of time. I hadn't had that kind of good talk with an adult in a long while. And Jake . . . he wanted even more contact with Felicity. He pushed for some kind of full visitation rights. He pointed out that he'd been like a father to her. You know, I don't take it lightly if a man wants to come into our lives. It can jerk a kid around if she never knows who her mom is bringing home. I wouldn't do that to her."

"What else did this Jake guy want?" Michael asked. "To date you again?"

"Possibly," she said. "It's complicated, Michael. Like I said, I had to be careful. Let's just say Jake got pushy. He made me feel uncomfortable because he wouldn't stop trying to have some kind of contact with Felicity, something regular and weekly. It scared me. It's been Felicity and me for a long time. I don't want that balance upset. I don't need a man to step in, so I had to cut him off and out of our lives. It was the best thing."

"Did he hurt you?" Michael asked.

"No, it's fine."

"Back to that night," Tolliver said.

Erica glared at him before she said, "When I realized how much time had passed, ninety minutes or so, I rushed home. Felicity was fine. She was doing homework with the dog next to her, just like when I left her." She sighed. "But one of the neighbors had seen me leave and figured out Felicity was home alone. They called the cops. I still don't even know who."

"So what's the problem?" Michael asked.

"The problem is she's not telling the truth," Tolliver said, standing up from the couch. "You were gone over two hours, and you stumbled into the house. You drove that way, and you left your daughter alone."

"How do you know?" Michael asked, turning away from Erica.

"Because everyone in town knew," he said, approaching them. "I work at the school. We hear about what happens when the social workers get called out to a home."

"Did they press charges?" Michael asked, still facing Tolliver.

"He's lying," Erica said, causing Michael to turn around. "That's some bullshit rumor that went around the school. The cops asked me a lot of questions. They asked Felicity a lot of questions. But in the end, they decided no abuse or neglect had taken place. They closed the file. The embarrassment was enough punishment. I wouldn't make the same mistake again. And I didn't drive drunk or stumble in. I was talking to Jake. A serious talk over one beer. That's it."

Michael's mind churned through Erica's story, not sure what to believe. But one thing did stand out.

"But you left her alone today," he said. "You told me you left her in the car in the park while you walked the dog. I know it's not the same as leaving her at home alone, but why would you ever even let the kid out of your sight again?"

"And that's not even all of it," Tolliver said from behind, his breath brushing against Michael's neck in a way that made him shiver. "Tell him what's been going on the last few days."

Before Michael could ask, before the words could even form, Erica brought her hand out of her coat pocket and swung it in a low arc toward Tolliver's leg. Michael's mind tripped over the possibilities. A knife? A small club?

But then came the sound and the flash, something that crackled like lightning, followed by Tolliver's wail of pain and collapse to the floor. He was writhing like a wounded animal, his body thrashing.

Erica held a stun gun.

chapter seventeen

9:40 P.M.

Angela followed Griffin into Michael's office. The desk was neat and clean, not cluttered with papers as hers currently was. On the wall behind Twitchell hung Michael's two diplomas—a bachelor's degree in management from the University of Kentucky and an MBA from the University of Louisville. Alongside those were framed photos of Angela's and Michael's families, including a snapshot of the three Frazier children from many years ago with Michael standing behind his two blond-haired sisters.

"What's the matter?" Angela asked.

Twitchell pointed at the computer for Griffin's benefit. "This is Michael Frazier's," he said. He looked at Angela. "What does he use this for?"

"Mostly for work." Angela wondered what on earth

could be on there that would merit comment by the police. Even if Michael occasionally looked at porn, so what? Didn't all men?

"No one else uses it?" Twitchell asked. "You don't?"

"Almost never. I have my own."

Twitchell spoke to Griffin. "The desktop has almost all work stuff. Reports, spreadsheets, files. None of it seems relevant to us."

"But?" Griffin said, prompting him.

He looked at Angela, his brown eyes magnified by the glasses. "I looked at his social media sites. I guess he's only on Facebook, right? No Twitter account? No Instagram or Tumblr?"

"That's it. Michael doesn't really like that stuff. He always says he's going to deactivate his account and walk away. He thinks it's a time suck."

"Well, it is," Twitchell said. "I agree." He looked back at the screen. "I checked his search history. Most of it's pretty mundane. Baseball scores. He must like baseball. It looks like he's a Reds fan—sorry. They're not very good these days. Then there's weather. Stocks. More work stuff."

"Is something wrong?" Angela asked. "You didn't call us in here just to give us a rundown on Michael's browsing habits."

Twitchell leaned back in the chair and folded his arms across his chest. The springs squeaked as he adjusted his weight, tilting his head as though considering Angela in some kind of new light. "Are you sure your husband hasn't had any contact with Erica Frazier recently? You just told us you thought he hadn't. You told us he didn't know about the child, whether she's his or not."

"I've told you what I know," Angela said. She felt the return of the twisting steel worm of doubtful jealousy, a wriggling within her chest.

Twitchell uncrossed his arms and pointed at the screen. "The only thing that stood out in your husband's browser history is the number of times he's visited Erica Frazier's Facebook page. It looks like it's a somewhat frequent occurrence."

Angela's feet propelled her forward, around the side of the desk until she stood next to Twitchell. He showed her the history, and she saw the evidence.

"In fact," Twitchell said, "when you just type 'Facebook' into the search bar, it completes the URL for Erica's page." Twitchell did that very thing, and Angela saw the rest of the URL fill in after the backslash with Erica's name. "That means he must go there a lot."

"Are they friends? What have they said to each other?" Angela asked.

"Well, he's logged out. But you said you knew the password."

"Sure." Angela leaned down and entered Michael's log-in information. When she hit the RETURN button, she saw the message pop up telling her the log-in had failed. She tried again, her hands shaking ever so slightly. And again the log-in failed. "I thought I knew it."

"Do you think he changed the password?" Griffin asked.

"He might have. He must have."

"So we can't tell if he exchanged any messages with her through Facebook. And he's logged out of his e-mail account. Do you know the password for that?"

"I . . . Let me try." She leaned close to Twitchell to type it in. As she did, she smelled body odor and something like fried food, the product of the man spending his entire day running around in the heat while trying to find a missing child.

When she entered the password she thought worked for Michael's e-mail account, it also failed. After everything that had happened that day, she still felt surprised.

She straightened up, feeling the eyes of both detectives trained on her.

"Would he keep the passwords written down somewhere?" Griffin asked.

"Not that I know of."

"Does he have any other devices?" Twitchell asked. "An iPad? Another computer?"

"No." She then added, "Not that I know of. Just a phone, and that's with him."

"You just tried to call him out there in the foyer, right?" Griffin asked. "No answer, I guess."

"No. Just voice mail."

"Maybe you'd better try him again," Twitchell said. "We'd really like to know where they are."

But Angela refused to move. Her eyes scanned across the screen, taking in all the folders on Michael's computer desktop. She saw a number of things that held no interest for her, the work items listed by Twitchell. A pair of folders devoted to his fantasy baseball and football teams.

Angela couldn't have said what she was looking for. Anything that helped her make sense of the evening. Or her husband's behavior.

Her eye stopped on a folder labeled "Photos."

She almost turned away. What could she possibly see there?

But she remembered Erica sharing that wedding photo. If Michael had been visiting her Facebook page, he must have seen it, along with the handful of other photos Erica allowed to be seen by everyone. Right?

She slid the mouse around until she landed on the correct folder. And clicked.

Twitchell looked on next to her, his face patient, his large gut giving him the aura of a placid Buddha. Angela opened the file of photos, watched them pop up into a grid on the screen. She didn't know what she was looking for.

Angela knew she'd gone to Davenport County and gotten into it with Erica just over a year ago, which meant the wedding photo that set everything off had been posted around the same time. She scrolled through the photos to the previous year and looked through them.

She saw a photo of herself, a casual shot Michael had taken one morning as Angela made coffee. Her hair was messy and she wore a bathrobe, but her smile was bright and genuine. She loved the way she looked in that photo. Loved the way Michael had captured her. The photo felt intimate, a sneak peek at their lives only the two of them ever saw. Seeing the photo that way made her want to shut the computer and turn away, to quit looking for things that probably weren't there.

"Mrs. Frazier?" Griffin said. "Maybe we should call your husband again instead of—"

"Damn it," Angela said.

It was there. The wedding photo Erica posted, in Michael's file of personal photos. He'd captured it from Facebook and kept it.

Why, Michael? Why?

chapter eighteen

9:41 P.M.

"My God, Erica."

Michael kneeled down on the floor next to Tolliver, whose body was rigid, his face etched with pain.

"Oh, my," Tolliver said, over and over. "Oh, my. Oh, my."

"Just breathe," Michael said. "Breathe."

Tolliver started huffing, his cheeks puffing out as he took in and let out air like a locomotive engine.

"That hurt," he said.

"You should be okay," Michael said. "It does hurt, but it shouldn't have caused you any permanent damage." Michael leaned over and looked at the spot on Tolliver's pant leg where Erica had placed the gun and zapped him. "I don't see anything there."

"Oh, my," he said again.

Michael looked back over his shoulder at Erica, who stood behind him, her face a mixture of confusion and sadness. She still held the stun gun in her right hand, and Michael regarded it the way he would an angry, snarling dog. "Could you put that away?" he said. "Back in your pocket."

She looked down at her hand. It appeared she didn't recognize herself, as though the hand and the stun gun belonged to someone else, something detached from her own body and mind. She finally moved and slid it back into her pocket. "I'm sorry, Michael," she said. "I don't know what to do. He's not answering our questions. He's not helping us. And time is wasting."

"I don't know where she is," Tolliver said, his voice regaining strength. "I don't."

"Why don't you go get him some water, Erica? And maybe a pillow to put under his head. Or a cold washcloth."

"I didn't know what else to do," she said.

"Just go get those things. Please?"

Erica moved slowly, her feet shuffling over the carpet. The use of the stun gun seemed to have taken something out of her. Maybe it had served as the last powerful act of a long day, a moment when she was able to summon a final reserve of energy and lash out at someone. Anyone.

Or maybe the violence of her action had disturbed her so much—as it disturbed Michael—that she couldn't process it. Michael had seen the way she looked at her hand and the stun gun, the sense of dislocation and detachment.

None of it felt real. None of it.

When Erica was gone, Michael placed his hand behind Tolliver's head and helped him to a sitting position. Color started to return to the man's face, and Michael felt relieved he hadn't suffered a heart attack or stroke when the stun gun jolted his body.

"Better?" Michael asked.

"Yes. I think so."

From the kitchen, Michael heard the sound of a cabinet opening, followed by water running out of the tap. He took that chance to lean in close to Tolliver and speak in a low voice. "What were you going to say before she did that to you? You started to say something about the past few days."

Tolliver reached down and gently rubbed his thigh where the gun had made contact with his body. "I don't know. This isn't worth it."

"Just tell me. A child is missing. A nine-year-old child. That's why I'm here, to help find this girl. That's it. It's urgent. She's been gone all day, and that's not good. If you might know something, please share it with me. Erica won't do anything else—I promise. I won't let her."

Tolliver considered Michael, giving him a sideways glance. The tap shut off in the kitchen, but Erica didn't reappear. "Felicity has missed her last three rehearsals," he said. "It's summer, I know, but she's never missed so much before. I called the house after the second missed one, and Erica said Felicity wasn't feeling well. But then she was out with Erica this morning, walking the dog in the park." He leaned in closer. "Where no one saw the girl."

"Are you saying—?"

"Michael?" Erica called from the other room.

"I told the police this," Tolliver said.

"Michael! Come see this."

Michael stood up, leaving Tolliver sitting on the floor.

But the music teacher reached up and grabbed Michael's arm. "I'm worried about Felicity. About the environment she's in."

Michael pulled free and went to find Erica.

chapter nineteen

9:45 P.M.

The room grew silent, awkwardly so.

Even the detectives, cops who had probably seen a little bit of everything in their careers and who were there because a child had disappeared, seemed not to know what to say or do in the face of Angela's discomfort.

"I don't think I understand any of this," Angela said.

She thought back over the past year, over the months in which, yes, things in their marriage hadn't always been roses and sunshine. But never once had she thought they would split up or look elsewhere. They'd planned their vacation to Georgia for that very reason, to get away, to achieve a sense of renewal. Both of them looked forward to it. Or so she thought.

She shook her head, aware that the police officers were still there considering her.

No, she said to herself. No doubt. Michael looked forward to the trip too. They'd talked about it, made plans together—quiet dinners, walks on the beach. Time alone for an evening drink.

Time after that to try to conceive a child.

No. Michael was all in. She knew him too well, knew how honest he was. When she first met him, almost ten years ago, she had admired how forthright he was about his marriage to Erica. He had said they'd met when they were young, married quickly after college. A mistake, Michael had told her, a starter marriage. An attempt to feel like grown-ups when they really weren't. He'd never ducked the blame with her, never tried to shift things by demonizing Erica. He'd said they weren't compatible after all, that they were so temperamentally different, a long-term relationship wouldn't end up working. Too much drama, not enough stability and reliability. Erica zigzagged through the world, contemplating career changes, wanting to move constantly, never settling on one thing for very long, whereas Michael wanted life to go in a straight line. He developed goals and pursued them. He hated distractions and detours.

She told the police that over the years Michael seemed to want to pretend the marriage to Erica had never happened. Angela understood why he acted that way. The world saw him as competent, levelheaded, intelligent. The marriage to Erica failed to jibe with the way others—his family, his work associates, their friends—saw him. Angela didn't care about the marriage most of the time, hadn't thought about it much since her ill-fated trip to Erica's workplace.

But Michael was clearly still thinking of it to some extent.

Was that why he wanted to help Erica now?

Angela sighed. Whatever struggles they worked through, they'd always been honest with each other.

But she looked at the computer screen, the photo of Michael and Erica. Had they really been as honest as she'd thought?

And hadn't she kept her own secrets? Not telling him about her run-in with Erica?

Relief came for all of them when Twitchell's phone rang. He stood up, his stomach bumping against the edge of the desk. He eased himself around Angela and went out in the hallway, the phone pressed to his ear.

Angela sat in the vacated chair, letting it take her weight while she leaned back as far as it would go.

Griffin remained standing, and she offered Angela a sympathetic smile, one that looked much more real and authentic than the one she'd delivered on the porch. "Is everything okay in your marriage?" she asked. "Any changes in your husband's behavior lately?"

"Besides different passwords and a photo of him and his ex-wife, no." She picked at a loose thread on her jeans. "That's just it—Michael never changes. He really doesn't. He's rock steady. We started dating just a few months after he left Erica, just about a month after the divorce was final. Michael never really played the field, never cheated. On me or her. He's a serial monogamist. He works hard for his dad's company. *His* company now. He never colors outside the lines."

"Maybe that got boring. For him."

Angela shook her head. "No. He's fun too. He and I laugh all the time. This past winter, he surprised me with a weekend in St. Thomas. He arranged it all. Champagne in the room, flowers." Angela smiled at the memory. "We had a good time, I promise." She pointed at the computer screen. "This just isn't like him."

"And you're happy with everything?" Griffin asked.

"I am. We both work too much. We sometimes go in opposite directions." She felt comfortable opening up to the female detective. "We're trying to have a child. We've been trying for a while. It's kind of been a struggle."

Griffin nodded, her lips pursed in sympathy. But then the detective's eyes roamed over Angela's head and studied the photos hanging on the wall behind her. Angela spun around in the chair, trying to see what could have caught Griffin's attention.

The detective came closer, her index finger raised as she looked at the photos. "That's . . . Is it?"

"What?" Angela asked.

"Lynn Frazier. In the picture there with your husband. I heard from Erica they were related."

"Yes, she's Michael's sister. Do you know her?"

"Not personally," Griffin said. "I'm sorry. I know her band. Lantern Black. Before today, I knew Lynn Frazier from Lantern Black was from Cottonsville, but I didn't make the connection until Erica told me. Michael's sister is a rock star. I thought they were going to be the next Arcade Fire or My Morning Jacket, but then they broke up out of the blue. What does she do now? If you don't mind me asking."

"I don't mind," Angela said. "The band officially broke up a few years ago. She has a house here in town. She still does session work. Nashville, even LA. She writes songs for other artists. She's been talking about starting a new band or making a solo record, but I'm not sure where she is in that process."

"I guess she doesn't have to worry about money."

"Definitely not. She made enough to live on the rest of her life before she was twenty-five. I'm not sure how her dad felt about it."

"How so?"

"He was a buttoned-up businessman, so he didn't really get the rock and roll lifestyle. Michael went into the family business, and Lynn followed her own path. She had a little of the black-sheep thing going on."

"How does she get along with your husband?" Griffin asked.

"Well. I think they were close as kids, especially in high school. Michael has told me about the times they spent talking late at night, the way they tried to help each other navigate life with their parents. We don't see her as much as we should now, but they talk pretty regularly. Text or phone call. Their dad died suddenly last year, so that brought them closer. Unfortunately, when you grieve with someone, you feel a tighter bond with them."

"How do you get along with her?"

"We get along well. She had a health crisis about five years ago. Cervical cancer. The whole family rallied around her, and she was very appreciative of what we all did for her. We're family, so of course we'd do it. But, again, that's one of those things that makes people closer. I got to know her well when she was recovering from surgery. It's funny. . . ."

"What is?"

"Well, when she was recovering, the two of us got closer in a way we hadn't before. We just talked more, let down our guard a little bit. She was sick and vulnerable, so maybe that helped. Lynn told me that she didn't really feel comfortable with me when I first started dating Michael. I guess she and Erica got along pretty well. They were both the outspoken ones in the family, and Lynn saw me as a little uptight. I guess I could come off that way. I think about my career a lot."

"That's not a bad thing," Griffin said.

"No. And she certainly thought about her career too. But I sell pharmaceuticals, and she's an artist."

"I see."

"Anyway, I appreciated that honesty. We got over a hump then, she and I." Angela nodded. "I like her. She's really smart. And loyal to her family."

"She must be. Loyal, that is," Griffin said. "She could live anywhere, but she's here in Cottonsville." The detective smiled. "Sorry. I'm being gossipy." Griffin continued to study the wall of photos. She raised her index finger. "So, this childhood photo shows three kids, but none of the others do. Why is that?"

Angela looked at the photo again. It showed the three kids at their small house on Cravens Lake. Michael stood in front, his hair wet, his smile big and cheesy. His two sisters stood on either side of him, both of them in bathing suits and dripping water. Their skin was glowing from the sun, their eyes dancing with happiness and light. Michael always spoke of those times at the lake almost reverently, as if the house and the water possessed a magic that had evaporated from the world after Robyn's death.

Angela knew the photo had been taken just a couple of weeks before Robyn died. She sometimes wondered if the photo should be put away instead of serving as a constant reminder of the tragedy that crushed them all. But Angela deferred to Michael. He lived with the photo there. He lived with the memories, the good and the bad.

The family rarely went to the lake anymore, and Angela almost wished she could have participated in the happy times they all shared there, even though it was long before she met Michael. It felt like a part of his life she would never fully grasp. It belonged to the immediate family, especially Michael and Lynn.

"Michael and Lynn had another sister. Robyn. She died in an accident on a swing set when they were kids. She fell off the very top."

"Oh." Griffin lifted her hand to her chest, the corners of her mouth turning down. "I'd never heard that."

"Lynn didn't talk about it in interviews or anything."

"It must be awful for all of them."

"It is. Michael's mom never really talks about it either. Michael has never said too much, but I know he feels guilty. He was watching Robyn that day. He's the oldest." Angela scratched the side of her face. "Both Michael and Lynn went to therapy for it after the accident. Lynn saw it happen, you know. But they were both shaken. Michael still occasionally has nightmares about it. He won't really admit what they're about, but I know. He feels guilty." She paused. "He says her name in his sleep sometimes."

Griffin made a low grunting sound in her throat, another expression of sympathy and concern. Angela saw something else cross the detective's face, a look that suggested a deeper emotion she didn't give voice to. Angela almost asked her about it but held her tongue.

"I sometimes wonder if they both became such high achievers to try to ease their parents' pain," Angela said. "That the two of them were doing the work of three and making up for Robyn's loss."

"That's quite a burden to carry."

"The house they grew up in, the one where Robyn died, came up for sale about four months ago," Angela said. "His family moved away from there not long after the accident, and who knows how many times it's been sold since then? I swear Michael seriously talked about buying it just so he could have it torn down. He couldn't stand thinking about that house and what happened there. It's five miles away from here, so it's kind of a permanent reminder, even after all these years. You know, you asked why Lynn lives here. I think both of them also feel a certain sense of responsibility for their parents. Now it's just their mom. But they were both so deeply affected by the loss of their child that Michael and Lynn want to—I don't know—just be there for their mom. Be around her."

Griffin nodded, the sympathy on her face clear and vivid.

"I'm not sure, Detective," Angela said, "but I think Lynn might have bought that childhood home. She talked about buying it. And she has the money."

"But you don't know if she did?"

"No, I don't. She might have and kept it from the rest of us. I'm sure she'd think her mother would worry about her if she bought it. You know, that sense that she hasn't moved on."

"Has she?" Griffin asked.

"Could anybody? The house sold, but I don't know who bought it." Angela rubbed her chin. "If Lynn bought it, she'd have torn it down too. She wouldn't want her mother to know that house existed anymore."

"I guess it is the kind of place that would be loaded with memories. Good and awful."

"I've always hoped the family would go back to the lake more, maybe create some new memories. Really only Lynn goes now. If we have a child, I'd like to bring her there. Or him."

"Maybe that will get the family back there. A child."

"Can I ask you something?" Angela said. "I hate to be harsh. Do you think this kid, Felicity, is still alive? I mean . . . when she's been gone so long, and they say the longer a child is gone . . ."

"Until I see otherwise . . . it's all about bringing the kid home safe. That's all I can think about."

"I saw a video online, the one where she's singing." Angela felt the tears pushing against her eyes again. Why did she feel so much emotion for a child she didn't know? Did *everyone* feel that way over a missing child? "It's heartbreaking."

"I agree. Completely."

Twitchell came back into the room. He nodded at Angela, but then turned to Griffin. "That was the boss. If we're finished here, we need to get moving."

"I think we are," Griffin said.

"You know," Angela said, "Erica told Michael that her daughter, Felicity, looked like Robyn. That's how she tried to convince him that she is his daughter."

"And you think that's why he went?" Griffin asked. "Guilt?"

"And a sense of duty," Angela said. "If there's a chance that kid really is his, if there's a chance he can help, Michael would have a hard time saying no. He'd have a hard time saying no even if the kid wasn't his. He cares about children. He really does. That's why it's been so tough that we haven't had one yet. And, maybe because of Robyn, when a child is in harm's way, it really gets to him."

"You should keep calling him," Griffin said. "And if you hear from him, or if anything else happens, let us know. Okay?"

"Do you think Michael's in danger?" Angela asked.

The two detectives exchanged a look again. Then Griffin said, "We're really not sure what we're dealing with yet. That means anything's possible."

chapter twenty

9:47 P.M.

Michael followed the sound of Erica's voice. He went down a short hallway, past a bathroom with pale blue tile, to a bedroom on the right. Erica stood at a refinished antique dresser, both hands full of clothing.

"What's wrong?" he asked.

"Will you look at this?" she asked, holding the clothes out toward Michael.

It took him a moment to understand what she was showing him. Clothes? Who cared? But then he saw that the clothes were for a young girl. A yellow dress. A hoodie. Socks and shorts.

Michael's mouth went dry. The feeling came over him that usually preceded throwing up. "Are they . . . Do they look like Felicity's things?"

"No. That's not the point. Why does he have them here, Michael? Why does a grown man have kid things in his house? Whether they're Felicity's or not, it's weird."

"Why were you back here? We want to get moving."

"I'm looking around. Trying to find evidence. Anything."

"Maybe he has a kid, a daughter or some other relative who stays with him."

"Not that I've ever heard of, Michael. Admit this is bizarre."

He knew accidents could happen. To anyone. Michael knew they couldn't be avoided. But the thought of someone intentionally harming a child, of purposefully bringing the pain his family felt over Robyn to someone, took Michael from cold fear to white-hot anger.

His hand darted out and worked its way into the pocket of Erica's coat.

"Michael?"

He brought out the stun gun, felt the unfamiliar hard grip in his hand. He retraced his steps to the front of the house, where he expected to find Tolliver waiting. Instead he saw the man's back disappearing through the front door.

"No," Michael said.

Michael crossed the living room in just a few strides. He caught up to Tolliver on the front porch, taking hold of the man from behind by grabbing a handful of his shirt. Michael forced Tolliver to the ground, landing on top of him. Tolliver made a whooshing sound as the air went out of his body.

"Just stop," Michael said. "Stop right there."

Tolliver huffed and puffed again, and Michael's own breathing grew heavy from the quick run he'd made through the house as well as the adrenaline. He looked at the stun gun in his hand, wondering if he really would have had the guts to use it. He was glad he hadn't found out.

"Why are there a little girl's clothes in the dresser back there?" Michael asked. "Who do they belong to? Huh? Who? Felicity? Is that why you ran away?"

"No, no," Tolliver said. "Are you crazy?"

Erica came out of the house and crossed the lawn to the two men. She stood with her hands on her hips, looking down at them, to where Michael kept Tolliver in place by resting his knee against the teacher's body.

"They belong to my niece," he said. "She comes and stays with me sometimes. My sister comes with her. They left some stuff here."

Michael looked back at Erica, seeking confirmation.

"He's never mentioned a niece," she said.

"Her picture is on my refrigerator, for God's sake."

Michael eased off, relieving the pressure he'd been applying to Tolliver's body. But he didn't back up so far that the man could stand. And Michael still held the stun gun, keeping it visible as a silent threat against Tolliver.

"What do you know?" Michael asked. "Tell us something. Anything."

Erica came up next to them. She started to reach for the stun gun, but Michael pulled it away. He didn't want to see it used again. Not yet.

But something seemed off about the man. Why had he run? When they were in the other room, he could have dialed 911 and had the police come. Instead he'd bolted.

"We're waiting," Michael said.

Tolliver's eyes were wide in the dark night, the whites visible. He looked pathetic and disheveled, and Michael wanted nothing more than to be finished with him.

"You shouldn't be bothering me," he said. "I'm not telling you anything else without a lawyer. Or the cops. You can't be doing this to me."

"Are you sure you want it that way?" Michael asked.

"Yes. You're both crazy."

"Fine," Michael said. "Let's go to the cops. We'll bring those clothes. Maybe they'll want to come and search here this time."

"No. Wait. You're really going to make me go?"

Michael stood up, the stun gun still in his hand. "Car's right there," he said. "I'm going to deliver you in person instead of waiting for them. Or risking you running away again. You can ride up front with me."

chapter twenty-one

9:55 P.M.

Twitchell drove while Griffin sat in the passenger seat, observing her partner. He always kept two hands on the wheel, like a student driver, and his glasses, oversize and out-of-date, perched crookedly on his face.

"What do you make of all that?" she asked.

They'd worked together for just over a year, and she respected him. He affected an air of cluelessness at times, a goofy-dad type who acted as though he couldn't tell the difference between Beyoncé and Barry Manilow. But Griffin knew it was all an act, a way of lulling suspects into a false sense of security and convincing witnesses and victims that he meant no harm and could be trusted. It worked every time. She liked to pick his brain, to ask open-ended questions about their work and sit back while he offered his opinions.

"We're not the leads," he said. "I'm just a water boy on this one."

"Come on. What do you think?"

"I think when Michael Frazier comes home, he's going to get an earful about his social media accounts."

"And his changed passwords?"

"Yup."

"What would Peg say if you did that?" Griffin asked, teasing her partner.

"I wouldn't do it. I like to breathe too much." He sighed and shook his head. "This is every man's worst nightmare."

"What is?"

"A former girlfriend or wife showing up and saying, 'Happy Father's Day.' That's bad. Really bad. A kid your wife didn't know about. Yikes."

They left the neighborhood where the Fraziers lived. The night was dark, the oncoming headlights glowing in their faces. Twitchell tuned the radio to the Reds game, the comforting voices of the announcers, the soft cheers of the crowd providing a sense of ease and warmth, even as they investigated a horrible crime.

"Still," Twitchell said, removing his left hand for just a moment to scratch his scalp, "there's something not right there."

Griffin could tell he was warming up, putting his thoughts together and getting ready to share them.

"Michael Frazier has had some interest in and maybe even some contact with his ex-wife that his current wife doesn't know about. Hell, maybe he knew about the kid already. Maybe he's been talking to her all along."

"That could really set Angela off, couldn't it?" Griffin said. "Finding out he was still talking to his ex-wife? She already went up there and confronted her once before."

"So you think she did more than that?" Twitchell said. "Maybe she really crossed a line and harmed this child?"

"We checked her out," Griffin said. "No record. No violent history."

"Besides getting in the face of her husband's ex-wife. And then not telling her husband about it. Not good, right?"

"Yeah, right."

"And just because somebody doesn't have a record doesn't mean they wouldn't commit a crime. There has to be a first time for everything."

Griffin looked out the window, took in the lights of the passing houses. She pictured the missing girl, Felicity Frazier. So pretty, so innocent. Something stirred inside her, a protective instinct. She wanted to wrap Felicity in a protective hug and shield her from whatever pain or fear was being inflicted on her. She felt like a mama bear, could imagine fangs and claws springing from her body. She knew she'd have no problem slashing and lashing at someone who would hurt a child.

She worried she'd never get the chance to do the same thing with a child of her own.

"I can tell you're feeling all . . . melancholy or whatever," Twitchell said.

She smiled despite her mood. He knew her too well. "Melancholy?"

"You're only thirty-one. You can get married again . . . and still have time for kids. Just because you married a jerk the first time doesn't mean you're doomed to a life alone."

"Thanks, Doctor Phil." But she appreciated his concern. It had been a rough time in her personal life. A divorce from her husband, John, a free-floating examination of where she was in her life, both personally and professionally. *A third-of-a-life crisis? Is that what it is?* "I guess plenty of people have a case of heartbreak. I'm not the only one."

But it did make her empathize with Erica Frazier more than she wanted to. How could she not? Michael Frazier had left her, possibly when she was pregnant. He might not have known about the pregnancy, but Michael appeared to be living pretty well with his second wife, glorious minimansion, and successful family business. Was she wrong to feel a measure of solidarity with the woman left behind?

But what about Angela Frazier? Wasn't she getting blindsided too?

Or had she taken matters into her own hands?

She recalled what Angela said about her husband: He'd mostly stopped talking about the marriage to Erica, sometimes not even admitting it happened. Was that who she would be for John? The person from his past he pretended didn't exist?

"And don't forget," he said, "Angela Frazier went up there and got into it with the ex-wife and never told her husband. So he's not the only one keeping a secret."

"That's different."

"It is?"

"Sure. I can tell the kind of woman Angela Frazier is. She's strong and independent. She doesn't want to come off like a needy little wife. But she's still going to get her back up if she thinks someone is encroaching on her territory. Especially an ex-wife."

"So you'd do the same thing?" Twitchell asked, obviously baiting her.

"I'm a cop. I'd shoot her."

Twitchell laughed and rolled his eyes. But then he quickly grew serious as the conversation turned back to the case. "Reddick says they still don't have anything. No sign of the kid. The volunteers knocked off when it got dark, but no one found anything useful. They're going to get back to it again tomorrow, as soon as the sun rises."

"Shit," Griffin said. Her frustration manifested itself as a dull ache behind her left eyeball. "A kid. Just gone. And the sand is running out of the hourglass. You know, I can understand just about everything else these creeps do. The drugs, the murders over even minor beefs, the stealing. But can they just leave the kids out of it? Really?"

"I hear you," he said. "I remember when my girls

were that age. It makes me sick to look at that kid's picture and think about where she might be. Or what might be being done to her."

"Have we given up on the possibility she ran away?" Griffin asked. "She'd been fighting with her mom."

"It's possible of course," he said. "But no one saw her anywhere. Not even in the park. It seems more likely Erica Frazier did something to her before they were at the park than that the kid ran away. Nine-year-olds run off, but it's on the rare side. They might pack their teddy bear in a suitcase and walk up the street for an hour. Real runaways are usually teens." They stopped at a light, and he adjusted his bulk in the driver's seat. He reached down and picked up his phone. "A witness did come in and report that she saw Erica Frazier having lunch with an older woman about six months ago. They appeared to be having a heated argument."

"Really?"

"Maybe they were just disagreeing over who was picking up the check."

"No idea who the woman was, of course."

"Nope. That would be too easy. And no real description except to say the woman was older and well-dressed. But the witness saw Erica on the news and remembered." The light changed as Twitchell handed his phone to Griffin. The driver of the car behind them grew quickly impatient and honked twice. Twitchell shook his head. "This is the only time I miss driving a marked car." He pointed to the phone screen and accelerated forward. "We're going to talk to someone else. A woman who lived next door to the happy couple when they were married."

"The Fraziers?"

"The Fraziers, part one. Reddick wants us to keep looking into Erica and to follow this marriage thread a little longer."

"Erica hasn't resurfaced?"

"Negative."

"So her kid's missing, but she decides to pick up her ex-husband and strike out on her own," Griffin said.

"It's weird," he said, agreeing. "There's a car sitting on her house in case she—or the kid or anybody else—comes back."

"The phones? What about a ransom call?"

"No landline. And no calls of any kind yet. Anywhere. It's getting late, but we can still go see this woman, the former neighbor. Apparently she's eager to talk to us."

chapter twenty-two

Twitchell and Griffin drove more than an hour, back into Davenport County, and headed for the east side of Trudeau, where Michael and Erica had lived when they were first married. Back then, one decade earlier, it had been a transitional area, a place where immigrants had settled at the beginning of the twentieth century, working in the tobacco-processing factories and warehouses before moving to the suburbs along with the jobs and the better schools.

"The Fraziers, part one—," Twitchell said again, but his partner cut him off.

"Are we always going to refer to them this way?" she asked.

"I'm trying to be clear," he said, his face serious. "Anyway, Michael and Erica must have been real pioneers, moving into this area before it had really made the turn to a respectable neighborhood. It's a far cry from that minimansion he's living in. Now this area is nothing but bars and shops for hipsters. Back then, you took your life in your hands coming here."

"I know. I was in college then," Griffin said, smiling as she needled her partner.

"Thanks for reminding me." He found the address, a redbrick apartment building with four units, each of them fronted by a wrought-iron balcony. Lights glowed from three of the units, and young people walked up and down the sidewalks, in pairs and in groups, heading for the crop of brewpubs and farm-to-table restaurants that had sprung up over the past five years. "Look at this. I think you're the only member of your generation who doesn't have a beard or a tattoo."

"I'm afraid of needles," Griffin said. "And I can't grow a beard. Yet."

"By the way, what was all that about Michael Frazier's sister?" he asked. "Something about a band?"

"You didn't know? She was a member of Lantern Black, a band that did pretty well. She played guitar, wrote some of the songs. That's how you make the big money, writing the songs. One of the songs was in a movie, I think. She was young, maybe twenty, when they started. They broke up a few years back, and I guess she hasn't been doing much in the record industry since then."

"Lantern what?"

"Lantern Black. They're considered indie rock. Like Arcade Fire? Or the Decemberists?"

"Those are really bands? I've always been a Guns N' Roses kind of guy myself."

"How enlightened."

They climbed the steps to the front of the building, and Twitchell searched for the right doorbell. He pushed one with the name *Helen Winningham* written in neat handwriting next to it. It took a moment before they were buzzed in. On the second-floor landing Helen greeted them. She was an elderly woman—Griffin guessed close to eighty—in a lavender housecoat and slippers. Her apartment smelled like oregano, and the TV in the corner played a vintage game show—*Joker's Wild*?—with the sound off, the host a neatly coiffed and perfectly tanned relic from another era.

"Can I offer either of you something?" she asked.

"We're fine," Twitchell said. "Mind if we sit?"

"Please."

"Sorry it's so late," he said. "We've been doing a lot of running around. And we're trying to learn anything we can about the case while it's fresh in people's minds."

"I don't mind the hour," Helen said. "I go to bed when I want and wake up when I want. I sleep less than ever."

Helen's voice was scratchy and high, her frame so slender, a strong wind could have blown her over. But she appeared to be steady on her feet, and she sank into a recliner on the far side of the room with none of the halting, uncertain motions of an elderly person plagued by aches and pains.

Griffin looked around. She saw no family photos, no

evidence of a husband, children, or grandchildren. Helen appeared to be a lifelong single person, an old maid as her grandfather would have put it. Griffin tried to convince herself that living out her days alone in a tiny apartment while young people loved, drank, and carried on outside wasn't such a bad way to go. Maybe Helen had a John in her past, a guy she spent a brief amount of time with and then had to let him go. . . .

Stop it, she told herself. Twitchell was right. She was still young, still had lots of time.

"Why did you call us, Mrs. Winningham?" Twitchell asked.

"Miss Winningham. But just call me Helen. I called you because I saw Erica Frazier on the news." She reached up and patted her short gray hair. Nothing appeared to be out of place. "And I remember her very well from when she lived here. Right next door to me." She pointed at the wall. "I spent a lot of time with her, sort of like a surrogate mother. Well," she said with a smile, "maybe a surrogate grandmother."

"Was she married at the time?" Griffin asked.

"Of course. To Michael. I knew him too, but not as well."

"So, what did you want to tell us?" Twitchell asked. "You know, I imagine, that Erica's daughter is missing, and we're all very concerned about that."

Griffin saw a well-worn Bible on top of the coffee table, a place marked with a red tassel. Next to it sat a coffee mug, half-full and steaming.

"I know," Helen said, raising her hand to her chest, her face appropriately horrified. "That's why I called. She used to confide in me. About her marital problems."

"What kinds of problems?" Griffin asked.

"Well, Michael worked a lot. I remember that. I guess he worked for a new company, something to do with computers. I got the impression the family had some money, even though Angela and Michael were living down here with me. I think he needed to show he was his own man, you know, establish himself somewhere else before going to the family business. Lord knows the neighborhood didn't look like this back then. They must have been proving some point moving in here. It wasn't long before I could hear them fighting. Through the wall. My bedroom is next to what was their bedroom."

"They argued?" Twitchell asked.

"Oh, yes."

"More than argued? Was it ever violent?"

Helen looked shocked by the suggestion. "Oh, no. I don't think so. Michael seemed like a gentleman."

"So they fought, and you said Erica confided in you," Twitchell said. "What did she tell you?"

"First we just made casual chitchat. Then I saw her one day out at the Dumpster, and I could tell she'd been crying. So I asked her what was wrong. I'm not the kind to let a woman cry alone, not if I can help it." She looked satisfied with herself. "She felt the relationship was coming apart, even though they'd only been married a short time. And she wanted to hold on to it, to keep everything together. She could be a little theatrical, I guess, but young women sometimes are. Life sands those rough edges off over time."

"So what did she do to try to keep everything together?" Griffin asked. She'd been there herself, doing everything in her power to keep a relationship afloat and watching it all go away no matter what she attempted. "Did she tell you?"

Helen looked a little coy, her lips pressed into a tight line. "It's the oldest trick in the book, I guess. She got pregnant, figuring that would keep the man around."

Griffin looked over at Twitchell, who looked back, his eyebrows raised and easy to see without the silly glasses. She turned back to Helen. "You knew about the pregnancy?"

"I did. It was right before they split up. I remember that well. And I very clearly remember the day I drove her to the hospital."

"When she had the baby?" Griffin asked. "Felicity?"

"Not the baby. The miscarriage. Right before they split up, she had a miscarriage."

chapter twenty-three

"Are you sure about that?" Griffin asked.

Despite her age, Helen Winningham showed no signs of suffering from any loss of cognitive ability. Her words came smoothly; her thoughts never stumbled. She seemed to recall a lot of details about Erica Frazier, and Griffin's bullshit detector, the one that rang frequently while she was questioning other witnesses and suspects, remained silent in Helen's presence.

But she really wanted to be certain about this one.

"Of course I'm sure," Helen said. "I took her to the doctor. She called me and said she needed help. I went over to her apartment. I saw the blood. She was having a miscarriage." Helen paused for a moment. "She told me she suspected she was pregnant but hadn't been certain until she miscarried."

"And what happened at the hospital?" Griffin asked.

"They took her back and examined her. They confirmed the miscarriage and sent her home. It's not a big health crisis to have one, you know. Plenty of women do. My sister had three. I suppose it takes a mental toll."

Griffin remained silent for a moment. She tried to formulate a response to Helen's casual dismissal of the experience of having a miscarriage. "Yeah, it does," she said. She felt Twitchell's eyes on her, examining her. She ignored his look. "Did you call her husband and let him know what was going on?"

"She said he was out of town on an important trip and not to bother him," Helen said. "She said she'd tell him once he was home. I made sure she was tucked in over there, and I left her alone. I assume she either called and told him or else told him when he came home."

"What happened when she told him?" Twitchell asked. "Do you know?"

Helen was shaking her head. She had one leg crossed over the other, exposing a pale, blue-veined ankle, the skin almost translucent. "I don't. About two months after that, I stopped seeing Michael around the place much. I thought maybe he'd gone on a business trip again, but he was never there. Never. And I didn't hear from Erica at all. I knocked on the door a few times, but she didn't answer, even though I suspected she was inside. I think he was gone. Then a few weeks after that, I came home one day, and Erica was carrying some boxes out to the car. She said she was moving out. She and Michael were separated."

"How did she seem?" Griffin asked, her voice lower than she'd intended. "Was she pretty upset?"

"I could tell she was unhappy, but she was putting on a brave face. She was playing it close to the vest. To be honest, she seemed to want to just get out of here, like she couldn't wait to leave all of this behind."

"And that was the last time you saw her?" Twitchell asked.

"It was. I never heard from either one of them. She didn't leave an address. Never sent me so much as a Christmas card."

Griffin looked to Twitchell, who was nodding his head. She imagined tiny gears and wheels turning inside his skull, the friction generating heat as he decided what to say next. "Is that all of it, Helen?" he asked. "We didn't know about the miscarriage, so I'm glad you told us. But is that everything?"

"Isn't that enough?" Helen asked.

"Why did you think we needed to hear this, Helen?" Griffin asked.

"I just thought the timing was curious, that's all. She has this miscarriage shortly before they split up. And today I turn on the TV and see her, and she's saying she has this child who is missing, and it was mentioned on one of the news channels that the father of the child is believed to be her ex-husband. They didn't say his name, but I know who she was married to back then. I can do the math on that. If the kid's that old, then Michael is the father, right?"

"It's certainly possible," Griffin said.

Helen uncrossed her legs and leaned forward. She looked at the two detectives with a laserlike stare, as though she wanted to blast them out of their seats with the force of her vision. "If they split up a couple of months after the miscarriage, that means she would have had to get pregnant within that time. Before Michael left her. Right?"

"I guess so," Twitchell said.

"And isn't that a tight window to do that in?"

"It is," Griffin said. "But not impossible. Some women struggle to get pregnant immediately after a miscarriage. Some don't. Some research shows it's safest to get pregnant again within six months. They could have tried again right away, if they wanted to have children bad enough." Griffin's words felt heavy coming out of her mouth. "Like you said, some people think having a child will save the marriage. It's something they try. Or talk about trying, anyway." She felt Twitchell's eyes on her once again, taking her in, evaluating her as she spoke. She looked over, and he looked away.

"But what about the other thing?" Helen asked.

"What other thing?" Twitchell asked. "I don't follow."

A sour look of disappointment crossed Helen's face. "You don't even know, do you? I bet nobody around here knows anymore. I'm the only one left who does."

Despite the heat of the night and the still, close air in Helen's apartment, Griffin felt a chill in her arms. She almost shivered. "What do you know, Helen?"

"About that missing baby," she said, pointing in a vague direction. "That baby that disappeared just a few blocks away from here."

"I don't know of any missing baby, Miss Winningham," Twitchell said. "Are you saying there's another missing child?"

Helen was shaking her head again, her lips pursed. "No. Not now. This one disappeared about ten years ago, right after Erica moved out of the neighborhood. And they never found her as far as I know. And she'd be about the same age as the missing girl you're looking for, the one Erica says is her child."

chapter twenty-four

11:15 P.M.

Michael drove, with Tolliver in the passenger seat. It had taken close to an hour to get Tolliver into the car. He had insisted on changing his clothes and using the bathroom, stalling for time as long as he could until Michael forced him out of the house again. Erica rode in the back, the stun gun in her hand in case their passenger tried to escape. When Tolliver looked over and saw the weapon in Erica's hand, he rolled his eyes. "Do you think I'm going to jump out of a moving car? I'm not James Bond."

"Just being careful," Erica said.

Michael activated the child-safety locks.

"You know," Tolliver said, "when we get to the station, you're both going to be in trouble. For barging into my home and using a weapon. For knocking me down and staining my clothes."

"If you didn't do anything wrong, then they'll let you go," Michael said. "But you ran. That makes you look bad."

"You're like the cops. You can twist anything. I have an alibi."

Michael remembered that the police station was just fifteen minutes away, and as they drove, Michael felt a tightness in his chest, an adrenaline-fueled pressure. He looked back over the events of the past couple of hours, the way one ring of his doorbell had changed his evening into something he couldn't have imagined in his wildest dreams. Or nightmares.

They came to a light, a crossroads. A left turn would send him back toward home, to Angela and the house and the upcoming vacation. Just being gone for such a short time, just being with Erica for a few hours, made home seem even farther away than it was. It would have been so easy to have stayed there, to have shut the door on Erica's face. It would still be easy to head that way and leave Erica and Tolliver to their own messes.

But how could he?

If even the smallest chance existed that Felicity was his child, he couldn't.

The photo Erica had shown him came back, the little blond girl in front of the barn. She looked so much like Robyn it stabbed his heart, taking him back to the days before her death, before that black cloud settled in above his parents. And then to think of the outrage of someone harming that child, taking her from a park, snatching her away from her mother and everything she'd ever known, holding her God knew where.

Something hot twisted in Michael's gut, a searing and frustrated rage against the perpetrator. The feeling consumed him, swelled up inside his stomach like a balloon. He pounded the flat of his hand against the steering wheel, making Tolliver jump.

"What?" Erica asked.

His hand stung. "Nothing. Nothing. Just . . . frustrated. Pissed."

"I know," Erica said. "I get angry sometimes because that keeps me from crying."

As the light changed, Michael's phone rang. He saw Angela's name on the car's display. He needed to talk to her. He knew she'd called multiple times.

"You can take it, Michael," Erica said. "Just tell her she's on speaker."

Michael thought for a moment, then guided the car to the side of the road, stopping in front of a church.

"What?" Tolliver asked.

"I'm going to take this," he said. "I'll be right back."

Erica said to Tolliver, "He's afraid to talk to his wife where I can hear. He wants to pretend I don't exist. I'm pretty sure his wife also wishes I didn't exist."

"I thought we were in a hurry," Tolliver said. "Have you reconsidered taking me along?"

"No," Michael said. "But I need to take this. I left home in a rush, and I don't want anyone worrying about me."

"I'll say it again. His wife. That's who he means."

Michael ignored her and stepped outside, into the night's heat. When he closed the door, he placed the phone to his ear and answered.

"Michael?"

He heard the relief in Angela's voice, and that brought a new wave of guilt. He'd left her behind, run off like a thief in the night.

"It's me, yes," he said. He stepped up onto the curb. Through the car's windows, he saw Tolliver and Erica illuminated in the glow from the dashboard display. "I'm sorry I didn't answer sooner, but we were in the middle of some stuff."

"I'm not even going to ask you what you've been doing," she said, her voice still buoyant. "I don't need to know. I just want to know that you're okay. I just wanted to hear from you."

Her voice soothed Michael. He remembered when they first started dating, and he'd call Angela on the phone. She'd always seemed so happy to hear from him, and that enthusiasm for the sound of his voice—and the lift it always brought to him—never diminished. Her voice sounded like home. That night and all nights.

"I'm okay. Really. We went and talked to the guy Erica wanted to talk to. And now we're going to the police."

"The police?" she asked. "Michael . . . what happened to a quick trip there and a quick trip back?"

Michael offered no answer. He didn't have a good one.

"The police just left here," she said, lowering her voice

as she grew more guarded. "They're looking for Erica. Hell, now they're looking for you."

A light breeze kicked up, causing the leaves above his head to make a soft soughing. He checked the car. He still saw Erica and Tolliver in their places, but Erica cut her eyes in his direction. He saw the plea there. *Hurry up.*

"I'll tell her to call them," Michael said. "Why are they looking for her? Is there news? Did the police find Felicity?"

"Nothing like that, but she should be at home. And, Michael, we have things to talk about. You and I. They got onto your computer. *I* looked at your computer. At least the parts of it we could see."

"You just let strangers get on there?"

"They're cops, Michael. They're looking for a missing child. And Erica is telling them you're the father. They kind of need to know about you, don't they?"

"So you saw . . . I mean, what did you look at?"

"I saw the wedding picture."

Michael didn't know what else to say. He made a sound deep in his throat, something that sounded like "Ugh."

"Is that why you changed your e-mail and Facebook passwords?" Angela asked. "Because you were checking out Erica?"

"I wasn't checking her out. That sounds . . . bad. I was curious. About her life. And, yes, I changed the passwords so you wouldn't just get on there and see without context that I'd been doing that."

"Without context? That sounds like you're talking

about something on the news. And do I need context to know why you have a picture of you and your ex on your wedding day on your computer now? If you wanted to look at a wedding picture, you could have walked to the foyer and looked at ours."

"Angela, you can understand being curious about an ex."

"Curious, yes. You seem obsessed."

"Don't say that. . . ."

"Do you know they've investigated Erica? For endangering her child, the one who is now missing? Just a month ago."

"There's an explanation for that."

"Michael, listen to yourself. Are you just going to believe whatever she tells you? That the kid is yours? That she didn't hurt the girl or put her in danger?"

"I'm going to go, okay? I don't want to argue about this now. I just need to take care of this. We've wasted enough time, and we need to go."

"She's using you, Michael. The cops think that too. They think you might be in danger with her. Are you, Michael? Are you safe?"

He saw Tolliver in his own living room, and Erica reaching out with the stun gun, sending the man to the floor in pain. A child left alone while her mother spent time with a man in a store parking lot.

And he saw the face again, the one that looked so much like Robyn.

"I'm okay," he said. "I still plan on coming home tonight. Soon."

"Michael . . ."

Michael kicked at a pebble on the ground. "Look, I . . . We're still going to go away together. Next week."

"Are we?" she asked.

"Yes. We are."

"Well, I hope so."

"We will. Look. . . ." He wanted to say more. He tried to think of something he could say that would make everything feel better and normal again, to remind them both of what they shared.

But before he could say anything else, Angela said good-bye, so Michael returned to the car.

chapter twenty-five

Michael climbed back into the car, which was still running. The cool of the air-conditioning felt good against his face. Until he returned to the climate-controlled car, he hadn't realized how hot it was and how much he'd sweated just standing outside talking on the phone.

Michael said nothing to Erica and Tolliver but paused for a moment, staring at the glowing dashboard display. Erica had the back window down, the tip of a cigarette visible in the darkness. The baseball game had ended, and the announcer ran through a list of scores and highlights from games around the country. As a kid, Michael had loved listening to the game reports from far away. He'd liked to imagine the other lives progressing in other places, and he'd felt linked in some way to what was happening in another city.

Just like he still felt linked to home, even as he continued to drive away from there.

"Look," Tolliver said next to him, "just let me go. You don't need me. I didn't take Felicity. I swear."

"Shut up," Michael said, the words coming out more harshly than he'd intended.

The schoolteacher grew silent for a moment, his head moving back as though he'd been slapped. Then he said, "You know I'm not the one causing all the problems here. Erica has been—"

"Are you trying to say the mother of a missing child is causing problems for everybody else?" Michael asked.

Tolliver could tell Michael didn't expect an answer, because, for a change, he remained silent.

"Thank you, Michael," Erica said, her voice close to his ear, even though she sat in the backseat.

"You need to check in with the police too," he said, his voice still sharp. "Do you know the cops were just at my house, hassling Angela? They're looking for you, so it's a good thing we're heading there. How do you know they don't have some important piece of news to share with you?"

"Did they say they did?" she asked.

"No. I guess not. Still . . ."

"I've been checking my phone. And while you were out there talking to your wife, I texted the lead detective on the case, Detective Phillips, and told him I was fine."

"Yeah," Tolliver said, "shouldn't you be home, waiting for Felicity to come back? I mean, what if she did and you weren't there?"

Erica grew silent and thoughtful for a moment. The soft whoosh of the air-conditioning filled the car's cabin, and the baseball announcer's voice gave way to someone selling mattresses at an amazingly low price. His voice was shrill, earsplittingly so.

"The police are doing their job" she said, her voice low. "And I've been at the house or the police station all day. Don't you think I've thought of all of this? They're at the house, the cops. They're watching everything, even my e-mail." Her words came out short and sharp, like little jabs at Tolliver and anyone else who might question her. "I made a decision late this afternoon. I wasn't just going to sit by if I could possibly go out and help my daughter. I wasn't going to sit on my hands."

In the faint light, Michael met Erica's eyes in the rear-view mirror. They locked, and Erica seemed to be addressing her next words directly to him as she tossed her cigarette out the window.

"I've sat by before and let things happen that I didn't want to happen," she said. "I've let things go before without fighting as much as I could. I'm not going to do that when it comes to my daughter."

Michael put the car into drive and prepared to pull into traffic. But before he did, the run of inane commercials slipped into a newsbreak, the announcer's voice deep and serious.

"Officials in Davenport County have suspended the search for nine-year-old Felicity Frazier, missing since this morning from the Tom Haynes Municipal Park. Searchers were forced to stop looking for the missing girl due to darkness, but officials expect to resume at first light tomorrow. In national news . . ."

Erica took a long, shuddering breath in the backseat. "She hates the dark," Erica said. "She's so afraid of the dark. She still sleeps with the light on. She'd hate it if I told anyone that, but she does."

"Let's go talk to the police," Michael said. "Maybe they can bring some sanity to everything."

He accelerated, and they resumed their journey.

chapter twenty-six

11:25 P.M.

Griffin stood outside the car on the sidewalk in front of Helen Winningham's house. Twitchell was inside the vehicle, talking to headquarters. They'd already done a quick Google search, using their phones, and without much trouble located the most basic information about the missing child Helen had referred to. Griffin held her phone in her hand, the information still on the screen, and she stared at it, flipping through, hoping to learn something else.

The late-night revelers continued to pass her by. Even on a weeknight, the neighborhood swelled with young people intent on drinking and partying. She looked up from the screen, watching them pass and listening to their chatty voices. Their carefree smiles and easygoing strides tugged at something in her chest. Every once in a while, when she felt angry or confused or lonely, she wished she could be leading that life as well. To live in an uncomplicated bubble of friends and good times, to work normal hours and not suffer the emotional hangover of bringing the awful things she saw on the job home with her.

She knew it was a fantasy. She knew she would never trade her life and career for those of the people passing on the street. And she knew that every person walking by, even the ones smiling the broadest and partying the hardest, carried something with them. A sick parent, a broken relationship. An existential fear about their own future. But on a night like the one she was experiencing outside Helen Winningham's apartment building, the temptation to be someone else grew so strong, she could taste it.

Two guys passed, young and bearded. They wore skinny jeans and checked shirts, the sleeves perfectly rolled to the elbows. Both sets of eyes trailed to her, gave her a careful up and down as they walked past. One of them smiled, showing a row of gleaming white teeth, and said, "Hello" in the friendliest voice possible.

Griffin nodded, feeling the little thrill she always felt when a man paid her that kind of attention. She couldn't help the response. Could anybody? Wasn't it innate to feel a pleasant surge when someone flirted?

Not yet, she told herself. She wasn't ready for all of that yet.

But soon. At the very least, she thought, she could

stand some physical proximity to a man. And not just sitting next to her middle-aged, sweaty partner in a government-issue sedan.

She lowered her eyes and examined her phone as the men walked off.

The facts about the missing infant were sparse. A three-month-old child, Stacey Ann Flowers, had disappeared from her mother's apartment one evening two months after Erica and Michael Frazier split up and about four months after Erica suffered her miscarriage. Stacey's mother had left the child in her crib, sleeping, while she took the opportunity to shower. When she had come out, the baby was gone. Apparently, the mother, Tiffany Flowers, had forgotten to lock the apartment door. A search followed, but there were no good leads, no witnesses to the crime. Tiffany Flowers told police she couldn't imagine who had taken the child, but she did recall seeing a woman following them a few times as she pushed the baby in a stroller through the neighborhood. Tiffany had also admitted that the woman could have just been someone going about her business, not intending any harm. There was no way to know. She had provided a description of the woman, but it sounded pretty generic.

In the ten years since Stacey disappeared, there had been no leads. No hint of her.

Griffin lowered the phone. The sidewalk was clear, the street quieter. She felt the same nagging, twisting sickness as when she contemplated Felicity Frazier's being gone, but somehow it might even be worse.

An infant.

Either someone had murdered the child shortly after taking her, or the child had grown up never really knowing who she was, never knowing her mother or the life she was supposed to live.

The passenger-side window rolled down behind her. She opened the door and slipped inside. "What's the story?"

Twitchell sighed. "Still a tragedy. Not close to 'All's well that ends well.'"

"No news at home? Any sign of Erica's boyfriend?"

"Jake Little," Twitchell said. "He called in to work, told them about Felicity disappearing, said he was distraught, and no one has been able to find him. They're still looking."

"So he's a person of interest. He has to be."

"Sure. Anyone connected in any way."

"And is there anything else?" she asked.

"No real leads. Lots of silly tips, as you might expect. Still, no one has come forward who saw Felicity in the park with her mom. They do expect to have more volunteers tomorrow when they start up again."

"And it won't be long before they tail off, before everyone loses interest and goes back to their regular lives."

"People know what we know," he said. "After a certain amount of time . . ."

He left the thought unfinished. It didn't need to be said. They both knew what he meant.

"What did Reddick say about this Stacey Flowers thing?" Griffin asked.

"She listened and asked a few questions. I planted the seed."

"Yeah, but think about what we've got. A mom who isn't keeping in good touch with us, who has decided to run off with her ex-husband instead of sticking close to home while her daughter is missing."

"Erica Frazier did text Phillips," Twitchell said. "A short message just to say she was all right. But she didn't say where she was."

"Great. She miscarried right before this missing child was supposed to have been born, and has already had child protective services on her butt. And, lo and behold, a baby disappeared right near where she lived at the time of the miscarriage. A baby who would be the same age and gender as the child she claims is missing."

"A child no one saw at the spot she allegedly disappeared from," Twitchell said.

"Yup."

"And who wasn't at her summer music lessons for the last few days before she disappeared."

"Yeah." The weight of the facts pressed down on Griffin. If she'd been standing up or trying to carry them, her body would have sagged. "What do you want to do?"

Twitchell scratched his head. "There's no law that says Erica Frazier has to sit at home and wait for us. She checked in so we can find her if something breaks."

"But her kid is missing," Griffin said. "And she's out. What if Felicity came home and her mom wasn't there?"

"She's looking. Maybe." Twitchell shrugged. "I don't know what I'd do if my kid were missing. I wouldn't want to sit at home and wait like a chump. Wouldn't you go out?"

"We're cops. It's different."

"Maybe. I can understand her restlessness, her desire to act instead of just waiting for someone else to solve the problem." He drummed his fingers against the steering wheel. "When you have a kid, shit, you'd do anything."

Griffin found the sound of his tapping irritating. "Really? You too? You're going to throw that 'You don't have kids, so you don't understand' crap at me?"

"I don't mean it like that," he said, his face flushing. "I just meant . . . I understand." He paused. "And I know some of that stuff Helen was saying about miscarriages hit close to home. I do."

"I'm fine. Don't worry about it."

"You sure?" he asked.

"I'm sure."

"Okay," he said. "I hear you. But back to Erica Frazier. I kind of get that she's not at home, even if it does make her look a little . . . unusual."

"Suspicious."

"Sure. That too." He reached over, adjusted the air-conditioning vent, directing it at his large head. "I have an idea."

"What?"

"It's getting late," he said. "And we've already had a long day. And we may have more long days to come ahead of us. I think we should head in, touch base with everyone at headquarters, Reddick and Phillips, and then try to get a little sleep, even a few hours, before the craziness starts all over again tomorrow. They're going to need us to be at our best. What do you think?"

Her partner's words made sense, and she agreed to go along with them, even though she didn't like the idea. She didn't like it at all.

chapter twenty-seven

11:20 P.M.

As they drove across Trudeau, Michael's mind filled with thoughts of Angela. Their phone conversation lingered, and he could imagine her at home—reading a book, organizing the kitchen, listening to music while doing paperwork. He glanced at the clock on the dashboard. Eleven twenty. Getting late. By this point, she might be in bed, propped up on pillows and reading something for her book club, the glow from the bedside lamp illuminating her light-colored hair.

Michael caught another glimpse of Erica in the rearview. She didn't see him look, but he saw the haunted sadness in her eyes.

The loss of a child. He knew what it felt like to lose someone you were supposed to be responsible for. When

Robyn died, no one said anything directly to him. His parents never placed blame on him. No one in school or the town directly pointed fingers. Everyone who had known Robyn knew how adventurous she was, how much she liked to climb and jump and push every boundary.

But Michael *felt* it. Even if it was all in his head, he felt it. Everyone knew he was the oldest child. Everyone knew he could have been watching his sister more closely that day.

He told Angela about Robyn's death on one of their first dates. They dove into one of those "getting to know each other well" conversations, the kind that felt essential to any relationship that might make it off the ground. They sat in a coffee shop on a bright afternoon, the rich aroma of roasted beans and toasted bagels filling the air.

He had told her everything he remembered about that day with a catch in his throat, his eyes meeting hers and seeing the empathy there. She listened so intently, actively, as though hearing his words required as much energy on her part as saying them did on his.

When he was finished, she'd said, "It seems like you blame yourself."

"I do. I should have been there. I could have stopped Lynn from having to see that too."

Angela had shaken her head. "You can't. You really can't. It was an accident. And you were a kid too. If she climbed all the time, if she was a daredevil, could you really have stopped her?"

He'd heard some variation on those words a thousand times over the years, but he never believed them as much as when Angela said them. Even when his parents said them, he wasn't sure they registered. He remembered the pride and love in his father's eyes when he looked at Robyn, the way he doted on her, the way he called her his "Robbie-girl."

At that point, talking to Angela shortly after he met her, he understood they were moving toward something more serious, possibly something permanent.

"Michael?"

Erica's voice came from the backseat, cutting through his thoughts.

"What?"

"That's where it happened," she said. "Tom Haynes Municipal Park. There on the right."

"The kidnapping?" Michael asked. "Right there?"

Michael slowed. The park entrance was just off the street, and he wanted to take a look, to get a glimpse at the very place where Felicity disappeared.

"Michael, don't—"

"Don't what?"

But then he understood.

He saw a cluster of bright lights. Three news vans sat in a line near the entrance, the reporters and crews packing their equipment and rolling up cables. They'd no doubt done their live updates for the late broadcast and were ready to go home.

Michael stopped the car about fifty feet away from them.

"Get going," Erica asked. "They'll see us."

"Maybe they can tell us something. The latest news."

"You're just going to walk up and ask them for news on the case?" Tolliver asked.

Michael shook his head. "I'm not." He turned around so he could see Erica. "She is."

Erica's mouth fell open. She started shaking her head back and forth like the pendulum on a metronome. "No, Michael. I've done that all day. And if I walk out there, they're going to be all over me. And you."

"Are you sure?" he asked.

"They're hungry for a story right now," she said.

"She's right," Tolliver said. "It's better if you go."

But one of the reporters was coming closer, moving toward the car. She squinted in the dark, her heavy makeup visible in the parking lot lights.

"Mrs. Frazier?" she asked. "Is that you?"

"Oh, shit," Tolliver said.

"Go, Michael," Erica said.

"No," he said. "She saw you. Let's hear what they have to say."

chapter twenty-eight

"Keep me out of this," Tolliver said. As the reporter approached, he slunk down into his seat.

"It's just a reporter."

"I'd rather talk to the police," he said.

"Damn it, Michael," Erica said. "Now she saw me."

Erica pushed open the back door of the SUV and walked around the front, her body passing through the headlights as she approached the reporter. She looked small in their glare, almost like a child, and to some extent he always thought of her that way. Not childish but childlike. Emotional, impulsive. Carefree and high-spirited. Those qualities had attracted him to her from the first moment they met, during their junior year of college. And, at times, they'd caused him no end of frustration. School deadlines had been missed, bills had gone unpaid. But, at the same time, he'd valued the way she pulled him out of himself, made sure he didn't take himself too seriously.

He had to admit she didn't seem completely the same after ten years. Yes, the impulsiveness, the rashness, were still there and visible in her behavior that night. But Michael also detected a steeliness, a strength below the surface of everything Erica did that made her seem far more mature than the woman he knew a decade earlier.

Maybe it was motherhood. Maybe it was ten years of raising a kid alone.

Maybe it was just growing up, the scrapes and scars everyone carried as life smacked them around.

The reporter offered Erica a sympathetic smile and a hug. They talked, the reporter nodding repeatedly as two more came closer, sensing they didn't want to miss the story.

"So, is Felicity really such a great kid?" Michael asked. "Is she . . . smart and creative and all that?"

Tolliver nodded. "She is. She really is. She's also one of those kids who seem to trail a little sadness along behind them. Some kids are like that. I always chalked it up to being raised by a single mom. I know a lot of kids who are growing up in single-parent homes, and I'm not saying they're all sad. I just got the feeling it was a struggle for Erica. A lonely struggle sometimes. That must have bled over to Felicity."

"She could have told me. She could have asked for help." The words came out impulsively, through clenched teeth. Michael paused, gathered himself.

What would have happened to his life if he'd known

Erica was pregnant back then? Would he have left the marriage? He couldn't imagine it, which meant the entire last decade would have played out in significantly different ways. A marriage to Erica, a child. Maybe more children.

And no Angela . . .

He felt sick just thinking about it, a sour, acidic taste rising in the back of his mouth.

Could someone miss what he'd never had?

Nine years. Could a parent make up nine lost years?

He might never get a chance if the girl wasn't found, and the thought of that caused an aching chill to start working its way through his body from his stomach up into his chest. He might never see her, might never know who she was.

He stopped himself. He couldn't think that way. He didn't even know whether Felicity was his daughter. He reminded himself not to grieve for someone he'd never known.

But he could tell he wouldn't be able to stop that. In a way, he already felt like she was his. Some deep-seated paternal drive made him want to reach out and fold the girl in his arms, to protect her and see that she was safe from any harm.

But he understood the odds, the urgency.

More than that, he wanted Felicity to be his. He wanted a child and hadn't been able to have one, and the world seemed to be offering him that chance. A bizarre, unexpected chance, but an opportunity to be a father nevertheless. He felt that wish with an intensity that surprised him, a palpable ache at the center of his torso, something that went beyond any conscious understanding and dipped into the primal.

He wanted Felicity to be his daughter. He wanted to fill that gap in his life.

As to how he'd fit Felicity into his life with Angela . . . he'd have to figure that out later. . . .

"What is she doing now?" Tolliver asked.

Erica faced three reporters and a handful of crew. As she spoke, she gestured with her hands. They didn't appear to be filming her, as the conversation seemed casual and informal. But then Erica started walking back toward Michael's car, and the reporters and their camera operators came with them.

"What is this?" Michael asked, even though he could see what was happening. Erica was bringing the reporters to him. "I don't want to do this."

"Why not?" Tolliver asked. "Oh, I see. If you go on TV, all of a sudden everyone will know you're the baby daddy. How else are you going to introduce yourself? As Erica's chauffeur?"

When Erica came alongside the vehicle, she gestured to Michael to power down the window. He did.

"I think you should talk to them," she said.

"Why?" Michael asked. He noticed the reporters standing a respectful distance away—close enough to hear but far enough back that they didn't appear to be listening.

"They think it's a good idea too. I've talked on camera a few times today, but if you went on and said something, it might bring more attention to the case."

Michael spoke in a whisper. "Erica, I don't think I have a role here."

"Your role is doing anything you can to get Felicity back. That's why you came along with me."

"No, I can't. It's not right."

"Do you want the word to get out that Felicity is in danger?" Erica asked. "Do you care about finding her? I thought you did."

"I do. But not this way."

"I'll sit over here in the dark quietly," Tolliver said, pressing his body against the passenger-side door and hunching down in the darkness. "If they don't film me, I'll behave."

"Erica," Michael said, "this makes me uncomfortable."

"You know what makes me uncomfortable?" she asked. "Not knowing where my child is. And she's your child too." She stepped back and waved the reporters forward. "He's ready."

"Erica . . ."

The reporters and cameras moved closer. The lights went on, blinding Michael for a moment in the darkness. He blinked and rubbed at his eyes. While they adjusted to the glare, he heard a reporter say they were eager to get the footage of him for the next broadcast or maybe a special live update. "This will really help draw new attention to Felicity's plight."

Michael's heart rate increased. He wanted to drive away, to ask for a moment to gather his thoughts before proceeding, but they didn't allow for that.

"Can you just tell us why you're here and what you want for Felicity?"

The reporter was still hard to see with the bright lights shining in his face. He managed to get a vague sense of blond hair and manicured nails holding the microphone.

Michael said, "I'm here helping Erica because I'm concerned about Felicity. I want to know that she's going to be safely returned home, where she belongs."

"And what would you say to whoever perpetrated this crime?"

The question stumped Michael. What would he say to that person? How could he even imagine who that person would be?

"Just let her go," he said. "Let her return home. She's a little girl. She's probably scared out of her wits being away from her mom like this. Let her go and let her come back."

"And how are you related to Felicity?" a different reporter asked.

"I'm not," Michael said. "I mean . . . This isn't really relevant, is it?"

"You're Felicity's father, right? Her biological father?"

"I'm not sure."

"Her mother thinks you are," the first reporter said. "Could you just say you're concerned about your daughter?"

"I am concerned about her, about Felicity."

"Because she's your daughter?"

"I'd be concerned no matter what. She's a missing

child. We should all be concerned." Michael felt good about that answer. It was the right thing to say, the right sentiment to express, and he hoped it marked the end of the interview. But had he said enough? Had he made enough of an impact?

If the person responsible for the crime was watching, would he be moved in any way by what Michael had said? Did Michael need to say even more?

"Okay," he said, "yes, I'm concerned because . . . she might be my daughter. I don't know yet."

But another question came: "If you're Felicity's father, why weren't you around this morning? Did you not know she was missing?"

"I didn't—"

"Do the police consider you a suspect? Have you been cleared?"

Michael could no longer get his answers out in enough time. The questions rolled on.

"What is your relationship to Erica Frazier? Are you married to her?"

"Do you pay child support?"

"Do you think Erica knows where Felicity is?"

"Do you think Felicity's dead?"

Michael waved his hand in front of the cameras, trying to indicate that the interview was over. When they kept asking him questions, Michael pressed the button to close the window, turning the reporters' questions into a distant, muffled noise.

The door opened and closed behind Michael as Erica slipped back into the vehicle.

"Okay," she said, "do you want to get us out of here?"

"Erica," Michael said, "that was terrible. I can't believe you led me into that."

Faces flashed across his mind. Angela. His mother and sister. People he worked with. They all might see him, all might wonder what he was doing.

"You did what you needed to do," Erica said. "The right thing. And I did what I needed to do. What is your discomfort weighed against a child's life? Your child's life?"

"I don't know—"

"You don't know what?" Erica asked. "Whether she's your child?"

"No, I don't."

He saw Erica shaking her head in the rearview mirror. "Does that matter, Michael? Would you not care about her well-being if you found out she wasn't your child?"

"You put me way out on the ledge there," he said. "You dragged me into something I don't fully understand because I don't have all the facts."

"Fine, Michael," she said, her voice resigned. "But I told you not to stop at the park."

"She did," Tolliver said. "I heard her."

"Take us to the cops, and then you can go home," Erica said. "That's it. I'll release you from it all."

He wanted to say more, to tell her how much he wanted Felicity to be his, but Erica stared out the window, not making eye contact with him. And he understood that having a parting of the ways might be best for everyone.

He backed up and pulled out, leaving the lights and reporters behind them.

chapter twenty-nine

11:25 P.M.

Angela went into their bedroom and sat on the bed, her back supported by several pillows. She sent a text.

Are you still awake?

It took several minutes for a response to come. The slow reply surprised Angela, since she knew her sister-in-law was a night owl, a vestige of her many nights spent in clubs and bars playing music. Musicians operated on their own timetable, and it was a late one.

I am. Barely.

Are you up for a call?

Again a long pause. Then the response: *Sure.*

She didn't often call Lynn, not just to chat, but Angela needed to talk to someone in Michael's family. She'd almost called his mom, but then realized she'd just freak her out. And open herself up to a lot of questions she couldn't answer.

But Lynn . . . she'd be better.

Her sister-in-law answered on the third ring. Her voice sounded tired. And a little scratchy as though she suffered from a cold.

"Are you sure this isn't too late?" Angela asked.

"No, it's cool. I was working on a song, a new one. Just kind of trying it out."

"Sorry to interrupt. You sound like you have a cold or something."

"Allergies, I guess. But I'm up."

"So you were working today?" Angela asked. "Writing and recording?"

"Yeah. Long day. I'm not at home. What's up?"

Lynn sounded somewhat guarded as well, which Angela chalked up to the late hour. And it wasn't unusual for Lynn to sound that way. As a single, unattached person, Lynn was free to come and go as she pleased, and she didn't always let her family know where she was or what she was doing. It wasn't unusual for them to learn that Lynn had left town, flying to Los Angeles or Austin or somewhere else for a session or a meeting related to her music career. It was a far cry from Angela's settled life with Michael.

And while Angela would never classify their relationship as intimate, Angela always liked talking to her sister-in-law. She respected her for being a straight shooter, more of an open book than anyone else in the family. And she admired the hell out of the career she had, even if Lantern Black had broken up after only a few albums. Her sister-in-law had made it in a difficult field, made her mark on the world in a way few people did. Every once in a while, Angela envied her the travel and the attention, the adoration of people who didn't even know her. She'd been to lunch with her more than once when fans came by seeking autographs and selfies. Angela liked those moments of basking in Lynn's reflected glory.

"I got your flowers before I left," Lynn said. "Thanks. It was really sweet."

"Of course. It's a big anniversary."

"Yeah. I've been thinking about it a lot," Lynn said. "I'm still here. I'm lucky."

"And, you know, if you want to go out to dinner and celebrate or anything like that, let us know. I'm sure you might have plans with your friends, but we're around this week."

"Thanks. Maybe we can."

"And did Michael call you?" Angela asked. "He's been so busy."

"Oh, I know," Lynn said. "He's Mr. Frazier Home Health now, following in Dad's footsteps." Lynn sniffled. "Right, well, the reason I'm calling . . ." Angela hesitated. How exactly did one explain this mess to another person? Was it better to be delicate or to dive right in?

Angela tried a little delicacy.

"So you haven't heard from Michael?" she asked. Angela knew Lynn and her husband had a fairly typical brother-sister relationship. They weren't overly close, didn't confide in each other or spend a great deal of time together outside of family functions. But Michael often expressed his admiration for Lynn, his sense that she was the golden child who had achieved in her twenties what most people couldn't achieve in several lifetimes. But a buzzing current of sibling intimacy flowed between them. They shared inside jokes and memories, managed to laugh at and worry about their widowed mother, and never crossed a line into true criticism of each other. How much of that had grown out of the mutual loss of their sister, Angela couldn't say. She knew they had both been there the day Robyn died, that they'd both seen their sister's lifeless body on the ground and heard their mother's cries.

Lynn had *seen* the accident, seen Robyn fall to her death. Angela felt an aching regret between her shoulder blades every time she thought of the awful memory her sister-in-law lived with. Angela assumed, without ever asking, that Lynn's music was one way of working through what she'd witnessed and lost that summer day, an outlet to channel everything she'd seen and felt.

"You know how Michael is," Lynn said. "He doesn't always just call me out of the blue. Only Mom does that. Why? Is something wrong?"

Angela took a deep breath. Time to dive in. She told Lynn about Erica showing up at the door, as well as her claim about Felicity. While she talked, relating the story as concisely and clearly as she could, she recognized how absurd it all sounded to her own ears. And if someone had called her with the same facts, she'd doubt them and wonder whether the person telling the tale had lost her mind.

When she was finished, the line filled with silence. She checked to see if the call had been dropped and saw it hadn't.

"Are you there?" she asked.

"Yeah," Lynn said, her voice low. "I'm processing it all. So Michael went with her?"

"He did."

"And you let him?" Lynn asked. "Oh, I'm sorry. I shouldn't have said that. I just . . ."

"It's fine." But Angela kicked herself a little for letting him walk out the door. Why hadn't she grabbed him? Tackled him? Offered an ultimatum? But were marriages supposed to work that way? "I know I'm putting you in an odd position here. I never wanted to include my in-laws in anything going on between Michael and me. And I know you and Erica were friends back then." She paused and decided to fish for information. "Maybe you still are."

Silence again. Angela wanted to know how to take it. Did that mean they were still close? Or was Lynn just listening? Waiting to decide what to say next?

"Lynn, did Michael ever say anything to you about this? Do you know if he was still in touch with Erica?"

"I don't think you have anything to worry about," she said. "Michael is dedicated to you. You know how he is—Mr. Straight and Narrow. He's not going off the rails. He never has. He didn't choose to be a rock star like me."

"I know." Angela decided to go all the way, to tell the rest of it, even at the risk of upsetting Lynn. "Erica showed Michael a picture of the girl. Her missing daughter. She told him she looked like Robyn. That's part of the reason he went along. I know it."

"He went along because he sees himself as a good guy. That's all."

"Lynn, I'm sorry to bring it up. I know you don't like to discuss it."

"I don't. No. You're not going to bring this up with my mom, are you? You're not going to mention my sister to her? My mom is fragile enough right now about my dad. . . ."

"I wouldn't. I know not to. That's why I called you. . . ."

"Michael's not doing anything wrong. He never does. And I'm *not* friends with Erica anymore. Not for years, not since they split up." Music swelled in the background, and then the volume dropped. Was Lynn alone? "Look, if I were there, in town, I'd come over. We could have a glass of wine and wait this out, but I'm not. Do you think you need me to come back? I can cancel—"

"No, Lynn, I wasn't calling for . . . Look, it's late."

"Not too late for family. I hate to think of you sitting there alone while Michael is doing whatever he's doing."

"No, Lynn, really. Thanks. I don't want to interfere with your life. I just . . . I wanted your insights. About Michael. And Erica. All of it. And I didn't want to bother your mom with it."

"Are you okay?" Lynn asked.

Angela took a moment, really assessed herself. She refused to crumple, to let circumstances get the best of her. She was in the house. Their house. That mattered.

"I am," she said. "I'm good. Really. He'll be back soon."

"Are you sure?" Lynn asked.

"No, it's okay. It's late, and you're tired. And I'm going to get off the phone in case Michael calls." She nodded her head, even though no one could see. "Thanks, Lynn. If I need anything else, I'll call."

"Please do. I'm here."

"That's good to know."

Angela hung up. Her sister-in-law's words made her feel marginally better.

chapter thirty

11:30 P.M.

They continued on, taking the bypass on the south side of Trudeau, a loop that skirted some of the city's newer suburbs, allowing drivers to avoid a number of stoplights and intersections. During the small city's brief rush hour, drivers going from one side of town to the other could avoid the congestion. According to Erica, they could cut off the bypass in a few minutes and head into downtown and the police station, a shortcut Michael hadn't known about when he lived there.

Traffic was light. They passed the usual conglomeration of fast-food restaurants and car dealerships, warehouses that manufactured windows for houses, and a large plant that assembled air-conditioning units. Long stretches of the bypass remained undeveloped. Cornfields and farmland stretched away, their vast acres dark in the night. Cattle and horses grazed out there as well, a part of some farmer's or rancher's holdings.

The tires hummed against the road. The streetlights, evenly spaced, provided regular illumination.

Michael regretted every word he'd said in front of the cameras. He knew he'd looked unprepared, unconvincing. What would viewers see when they turned on their televisions? A nervous man blinking in the bright lights, stammering over his answers. And unable to respond to the simplest questions.

Are you Felicity's father? Are you a suspect?

Was he?

And worst of all, what would Angela think if she saw it? She rarely watched the local news, rarely watched TV at all. He hoped that continued. . . .

"This isn't going to look good if I go to the police," Tolliver said.

"Why?" Michael asked, but he answered more out of obligation than actual curiosity.

"Think about it. I'm a middle-aged single guy. A music teacher, no less. And there's a child missing. People jump to conclusions."

"But you already talked to them," Erica said.

"They didn't really talk to me. Not too long once I provided an alibi. They were hurried, I could tell. Overwhelmed a little. Those state budget cuts don't just hurt education. They hurt the cops as well. They're understaffed. They told me not to leave town, that they'd likely be coming back sometime tonight to talk to me more."

"We're saving them the trip."

"I've been in trouble before," he said. "I got a DUI once. And there's a misdemeanor assault charge from another incident with a friend of mine. Former friend."

"So?" Michael asked.

"I don't want more trouble," he said. "I've been thinking about this more and more since we saw those reporters. I don't want to be involved in this."

Michael looked in the rearview, catching Erica's eye. "How do you think I feel? I just got forced onto television, forced to kind of admit a child was mine when I have no idea if she is or not."

"No one forced you," Erica said, her voice carrying a sliver of resentment.

"It felt that way to me." Michael looked ahead, watching the road. "Let me ask you something. Is she really missing? No one saw her in the park. She hasn't been to her lessons. Erica, did something else happen?"

Tolliver made a low noise in his throat, a reaction to Michael's pointed question.

Erica remained silent for a long time, the tires and the passing lights the only accompaniment.

Finally, she said, "What a terrible thing to suggest, Michael. Is this what Angela told you when you talked to her on the phone? Is this her theory?"

"You aren't going to answer the question?"

"No, I'm not."

They came to a long, slow curve in the road. Michael eased off the gas but kept his eyes on Erica, waiting for—hoping for—an answer that never came.

She stared out the window, her face defiant. He remembered that look, her refusal to engage or even discuss when they encountered problems. She tended to shut down.

And shut out. And Michael felt the frost in that moment.

"Erica?" he said.

Then Tolliver was reaching over, his hands taking the car's steering wheel and turning it to the right, toward the side of the road.

"No!" Michael shouted.

But the vehicle slipped from his control. It bounded across the shoulder and the berm, the tires making a grinding sound as they left the smooth pavement. In the headlights, Michael saw a flash of cornfield, the stalks taller than the roof, and then a wire fence just before the car smashed through it.

Erica yelped in the back. The bouncing impact threw Michael off-balance. His head jerked forward, making contact with the steering wheel. His foot scrambled to hit the brake. It missed, once and then twice before he found it, before he managed to stop the car. But they'd gone fifty feet into the corn, the stalks to the left and right brushing against every window like taunting monsters.

Tolliver pushed his door open and jumped out. Michael reached for him, came up with nothing but air. Then Michael struggled with his seat belt, tried to unlatch it so he could move, but he felt groggy, dazed.

He saw the open door, the space Tolliver had vacated.

He said Erica's name, but she did not respond. He tried to remember whether she was wearing a seat belt. He didn't think she was. She seemed to be sitting close to the driver's seat, leaning way forward to watch Tolliver.

Michael felt tired. He let himself close his eyes.

Just for a second, he told himself. *Close your eyes. . . .*

part two

NIGHT

chapter thirty-one

11:45 P.M.

Twitchell parked behind the station. When they'd entered downtown Trudeau, Griffin noted how quiet the city seemed. It was nearing midnight, and the streets were nearly empty, the stoplights flashing yellow or red at most intersections. *Tuesday night in the small city,* she thought. Maybe everyone was out on the east side, drinking and partying with Helen Winningham.

When they got out of the car, however, she saw the station was buzzing. More vehicles in back, more noise and conversation when they walked inside, where the building smelled like burned coffee and fast food. They headed for the boss's office, found her staring at her computer screen. She addressed them without looking up.

"Have a seat."

Louise Reddick had turned fifty just three months

earlier. Griffin remembered because the night-shift detectives had covered her office with black crepe and Styrofoam headstones, and Louise came in, saw the decorations, and smiled about as broadly as she ever had. Which was to say . . . not very much.

But she did smile.

She tapped the keyboard a few more times and then swiveled in her chair so she could face the detectives. Her salt-and-pepper hair was pulled back into a tight ponytail, and the lines at the corners of her eyes and mouth added character and gravitas rather than making her appear old. Griffin feared her and admired her. Her own parents had been wonderful, and she felt especially close to her mother, but she sometimes secretly wished Louise Reddick had been her mother. Or at least a very cool aunt.

"Anything new?" Twitchell asked.

"Since I last talked to you? No. Phillips and Woolf are back here, but I doubt I'll be able to get them to sleep tonight." She rubbed her eyes, looking a little more frazzled than Griffin had ever seen her. "I don't know if I'll sleep much either."

"The volunteers didn't find anything useful?" Griffin asked.

The boss shook her head. "A lot of junk and false alarms. They're all so eager now to find something. They all think they're going to get on TV if they crack the case, so they pick up every discarded sock, every McDonald's wrapper."

"We do tell them anything might help," Twitchell said.

"I know, I know. And I'm so grateful to see so many people turn out. When a kid disappears like this, everybody gets shaken up. It hits everyone in the gut."

"Did they find anything on Erica Frazier's computer?" Twitchell asked. "Or anything else from her house?"

"They're going through the computer and cell phone records. We had to send everything to Louisville." She lifted her hands in a helpless gesture. "We're still kind of a stepsister out here. They have their own big-city problems."

"But a kid is missing."

"I know, Erin," Reddick said. She pointed at her own head. "Don't you see my new gray hairs? The ones that just came in today? We should hear something tomorrow. I've got a call in. I'm ready to get Congresswoman Bartel to reach out on our behalf if I have to. She and I disagree on everything, but she's also up for reelection this fall, so she's eager to do anyone and everyone a favor. I didn't go sit at her stupid fund-raising dinner to not use her when I need to."

They fell silent. From down the hallway, the sound of ringing phones and muted conversation reached them. Voices straining to make a difference, but also carrying out the routine business of the station. Domestic disturbances, car accidents, drunk and disorderlies. It all went on whether Felicity Frazier was missing or not.

Griffin held the armrest of her chair tight, her knuckles aching and turning white under the pressure.

"Have we ruled out the possibility the kid ran away?" Twitchell asked.

"Not entirely," Reddick said. "We've been looking for her everywhere. Her mother says she had no money, no wallet. No way to get around, not even a bike. Unless someone picked her up or helped her, I'm not sure how far she'd get."

"Are you sure there's nothing to this missing baby we turned up on the east side?" she asked.

Reddick rubbed her chin. She stole a quick glance at Twitchell before looking back at Griffin and saying, "You think Erica Frazier kidnapped this baby ten years ago and raised her as Felicity? You think *our* missing kid was really kidnapped ten years ago? And then kidnapped again?"

Griffin heard the skepticism in her commander's voice. It made her reluctant to go on, but she did. "It seems worth exploring. If Erica was upset enough about the miscarriage and the breakup, maybe she acted rashly."

"So how does that lead to Felicity disappearing now?" Reddick asked, her voice level.

Griffin felt stuck for an answer. She both loved and hated being surrounded by people who were equally as smart and analytical as she was. "I don't know. I just . . . The miscarriage and the divorce. It could send someone . . ."

Her voice trailed off. She saw the sympathetic looks from her partner and her boss. She knew what they were thinking: *You're taking this too personally. You're thinking with your heart instead of your head.*

She was. They were right. But she couldn't help talking about it.

"We're not ruling anything out yet, but we're stretched thin," Reddick said. "I want the two of you to get in early tomorrow and assist Phillips and Woolf again. We still have to talk to Erica Frazier more, if she ever turns up. And we're still trying to find Jake Little. The volunteers will be back out as well. It's going to be a long one. Dawn to dusk, so go home and get a little sleep."

"What about you, boss?" Twitchell asked.

"I'll sleep at some point."

They both knew she was lying. And Griffin wondered why she should get to sleep if her boss, the woman she admired the most, was choosing not to. Shouldn't she be doing more?

"What if we . . . ?" Griffin started to ask, and then stopped herself.

"What?" Reddick asked.

"I don't know," she said. "That kid is out there. I just want to do something."

"We all do. We all are. Tomorrow's a big day."

"Boss?"

Detective Phillips filled the doorway, his tie undone, his jacket off.

Reddick looked up, her eyes expectant.

Phillips said, "Better flip on the TV. Breaking news. Check this out."

chapter thirty-two

11:53 P.M.

Angela continued to resist having wine.

She decided to take other steps to calm herself down before trying to go to sleep. She checked every lock in the house, even the ones on the windows that hadn't been opened for weeks because of the early-summer heat. She activated the alarm system they rarely used. She'd insisted on having it installed as a measure of safety for when Michael traveled and left her home alone, but despite having asked for it, she almost never used it. But that night, she turned it on.

She took her time washing her face and brushing her hair, and then she settled into their comfortable bed, propping herself on a stack of pillows. She needed to read the latest selection for her book club. They were meeting in two nights, and she'd barely had time to open the title they'd chosen, a thriller about a teenage girl disappearing and the alcoholic, haunted female detective who tried to find her. Angela read a few pages, reached a part in which the narrator described in detail how the missing girl vanished from her bedroom while her parents slept down the hall, and decided to close the book.

It wasn't an escape. Not even close.

She turned off the bedside lamp and pulled the covers to her chin. It was pleasantly cool in the house, thanks to the air-conditioning. She wished she were tired, wished she could fall asleep like a child, her mind untroubled by anything resembling a nightmare. Angela could tell that wasn't going to happen. She stared at the ceiling, the faint glow from a streetlight falling across her body.

What was Michael doing right then?

She never worried about him cheating, even though they had witnessed the marriages of several friends fall apart over infidelity. She wondered if she was a fool to trust her husband as much as she did. Given what she'd seen and learned on his computer earlier, maybe she was.

But Michael? Reliable-as-the-sunrise Michael?

She'd noted his reluctance to talk about Erica or the divorce over the past few years, and while she found his desire to avoid talking about the past very different from her own approach to life, she took it as a good sign. Didn't it mean he valued the present and the future more than the past? But would he have been so eager to have another child if he'd known about the one he'd had with Erica?

She pounded the mattress with her fist. She couldn't say. She couldn't say, and she didn't know. And until

Michael came home and the two of them engaged in one of those long "Let's get it all out in the open" conversations, the ones that seemed to keep a healthy marriage alive, she wouldn't.

She just hoped he did come home and the conversation followed.

She reached up and flipped the light back on. She fumbled on the bedside table, her hand passing over the novel, a tube of ChapStick, and a balled-up tissue before finding the remote control. She clicked the power button.

Michael liked having a TV in the bedroom so he could watch sports or news as he drifted off to sleep. Angela hated it. According to her, the bedroom should be for only two things: sleep, which they didn't get enough of, and sex, which had recently turned into more of a duty as they tried to conceive a child.

When she flipped the TV on that night, she had a specific purpose. If she couldn't sleep and was going to turn the TV on, she might as well see if there was any news out of Trudeau. They sometimes replayed the late broadcast, and she wanted to know the most recent information about the missing child, Felicity.

Michael's child? My . . . stepchild?

Angela had never planned to raise a stepchild.

Does anybody plan it? Doesn't life just hand people circumstances they have to adapt to?

She flipped through the channels until she found the news, except it wasn't a replay. A banner on the bottom announced *Breaking News*, and a photo of Felicity looked out at the world from the upper-right corner of the screen.

A reporter stood in a park, her blond hair perfectly sculpted, her manicured nails holding the microphone and a piece of paper. She told the anchor back in the studio—and everyone watching as well—what Angela feared to hear: There had been no significant leads in Felicity's case. The child remained missing, and the search for her, conducted by police and volunteers, had been called off for the night.

But there was one important development in the case, the reporter said.

Angela gripped the blanket tighter, wanted to pull it up over her head and cover her eyes. Her heart sank as she tried her hardest not to contemplate the possible scenarios—kidnapping, murder, even a horrible accident.

No, she told herself. The kid had to be alive. If they hadn't found her yet, that meant they still would. And soon. Damn the statistics. They were just numbers.

She worried about what it would do to Michael if Felicity never came back. Whether she was his or not, he cared. She knew he cared deeply. Could he handle the heartache of another dead child?

As if on cue, Michael's face appeared on the screen.

He blinked in the bright lights. His skin looked washed out, pale, the stubble on his face darker than in real life.

"She might be my daughter."

And then the reporter was back, telling the viewers that while they had no idea what the current relationship was between Michael Frazier and Erica Frazier, or whether he had anything to do with Felicity's life, it was clear he was distraught over the missing girl and wanted to do everything possible to get her back.

Angela flipped the covers aside and bolted upright.

"What?" she said, her voice rising louder than she intended. But she couldn't stop herself. Had Michael really just gone on television, a broadcast everyone they knew would see, and claimed Felicity might be his child?

Her face flushed from both anger and embarrassment.

"Oh, Michael," she said as the story on the screen shifted to something more mundane. "Did you really just do that?"

Her phone pinged. She checked the screen. A friend from her book club: Just saw Michael on TV. WTF?

And then another: Everything okay, Ang?

She ached for the missing child. And she ached for Michael. She could see the pain in his eyes, the intensity of his desire to make everything right.

And there she sat in bed, unable to help.

Or was she?

She placed her feet on the floor, deciding as she did to ignore the texts from friends.

Just as she did, the phone rang. She wanted to look away, switch off the ringer. But she couldn't. She saw Michael's name on the screen.

"Thank God."

But when she answered, she didn't hear her husband's voice. She heard only the muffled sound of the wind and something rustling like leaves.

"Michael? Michael, are you there?"

Finally a voice, faint and distant, said one word.

"Robyn . . ."

chapter thirty-three

WEDNESDAY, 12:03 A.M.

When the segment about Felicity Frazier's disappearance ended, and the news went to a commercial break, Reddick turned the TV off and tossed the remote back onto her desk. She turned and faced the three detectives, including Phillips, who had stayed to watch along with them.

"Well, that was interesting," he said.

Phillips appeared to be the same age as Twitchell, and he was aging much worse. He smoked constantly and wheezed when he coughed. Griffin always thought his photograph should appear alongside the definition of heart disease in the dictionary. He rarely wasted time on polite conversation, at least with Griffin. He'd been divorced twice and was now on his third marriage, this time to a woman half his age. Griffin had met her a time or two, and always thought she looked shell-shocked and stunned. Phillips seemed to possess little regard for women, beyond liking to marry them, and he frequently questioned Reddick's decisions behind her back. Griffin looked forward to the day he retired.

"At least we know she hasn't left town," Griffin said.

"How did she get him to go in front of the cameras and say that?" Twitchell asked. "Say that this is his daughter who is missing?"

Reddick held up her hand and gave voice to Griffin's thoughts. "How do you know anyone made anyone do anything? He's a grown man. Did she force him to go along at gunpoint? He's there of his own free will."

"He looked a little spooked," Phillips said. "Ambushed."

Reddick was shaking her head. "For all we know, he *knows* he's the kid's father. It's possible he's been in touch with her for weeks or years. Maybe he accepted the fact long ago."

"Even if he isn't sure," Griffin said, "he's playing the believing game. He might hope she is his kid."

"Well, everybody's going to think it now." Twitchell looked at Griffin. "I bet his wife was thrilled to see that on the news. She didn't know he checked out her Facebook page. Now she sees this." His eyebrows rose comically to show the level of discomfort he thought the Frazier household would be experiencing. "His nightmare keeps getting worse."

"It's not our problem to worry about their marital issues," Reddick said. "Our problem is finding a missing kid." She tapped her wrist to indicate an imaginary watch, and then her words came out with an axlike sharpness. "And we're under the gun. I'm *not* interested in finding a child's body. That's not the plan."

The three detectives nodded their solemn agreement. They looked like nervous, obedient kids at a church service.

Reddick went on, pointing at Phillips. "Are you working through your list of known sex offenders in the area? Are you hitting any more tonight?"

"We have a couple of stops to make." He rubbed his chin, his palm scraping against gray stubble. "There's one interesting one. This guy, Todd Friedman. He's registered, and his ex-wife, kind of a drama queen if you ask me, says he liked to hang around in the park where Felicity was supposed to be this morning." Griffin didn't like the snarky emphasis he placed on "ex-wife." "We're going to talk to him as soon as we get out of here. After that, there are the babysitters and friends Erica Frazier told us about, people from the school like janitors and support staff. We didn't get to all of them yet."

"Is there something wrong with her?" Griffin asked.

"Wrong with who?" Phillips asked.

"This guy's ex-wife. Friedman. You called her a drama queen. Do you know this woman?"

Phillips looked around the room, first at Twitchell and then at Reddick. His eyes settled back on Griffin. "I called her what I thought. She's acting that way, if you ask me."

"Just go talk to him," Reddick said. "Didn't Erica

Frazier mention having some contact with Michael Frazier's family? His mother maybe?"

Phillips nodded. "She mentioned it in passing."

"Really?" Twitchell asked. "I don't know if Michael's wife knows that."

"We don't know if Michael knows it," Griffin said.

"Didn't Woolf talk to the mother today on the phone?" Reddick asked.

Phillips took a moment to answer. He was still giving Griffin the stare down. She ignored him. "He did. She said she hadn't spoken to Erica in a while, but she's concerned about the missing kid. Naturally."

"Interesting. Any other relatives?"

"Michael Frazier has a sister," Griffin said. "A musician. She's kind of well-known."

"And what about this sister?" Reddick asked.

Phillips said, "She might have known about the kid too, so we need to talk to her. But she's out of town right now. Working. We reached out to her earlier today."

"Might have to get her to come back," Reddick said. "Is there a dad in the picture?"

"Deceased," Griffin said.

Reddick pointed at Twitchell and Griffin. "You two go back down to Cottonsville and talk to them tomorrow, the mother and the sister too. Any red flags with them?"

"Nothing major," Twitchell said. "Michael Frazier might have been connecting with Erica on social media. He was keeping it from his wife."

"Could be major," Reddick said. "Anything else?"

"The Fraziers lost a daughter years ago," Griffin said. "An accident on a swing. The family is kind of haunted by it. And now this."

"Go see if they have anything to say. We'll have a boatload of volunteers showing up here in the morning, and history has shown that might be the day with the highest number. After the second day, they start to tail off."

"What about . . . ?" Griffin looked around the room. They were all watching her. They all looked tired. "What about this thing with Stacey Flowers? The missing infant. Are we going to look into that?"

Phillips made a snorting noise through his nose.

Griffin turned to look at him, but he refused to meet her eye.

Reddick looked at Phillips, an unspoken signal for him to answer the question. "I don't see anything urgent there. Some missing kid from a decade ago? Basing it on what some lonely, deranged old lady says?" He stared at Griffin again. "She probably just wants someone to talk to. No dice."

"But it was so close to where they lived," Griffin said, realizing as she spoke that the idea was dead.

Reddick held up her hand. "I think that's right, putting the Flowers thing a little farther down on the list for now. Our manpower is limited, so we need to be choosy. Okay?"

"Got it," Phillips said, and it sounded as though he spoke for all of them.

They started to go, but Reddick said, "Erin, will you stick around for a second?"

Griffin looked at her two colleagues. Twitchell nodded, and Phillips refused to make eye contact. She stayed behind while they filed out, and then she closed the door, leaving her alone with the commander.

"Have a seat," Reddick said.

So she sat, like a little kid in the principal's office. A principal she liked and respected as well as feared, but the principal nevertheless.

"Tough one, isn't it? Missing kid."

"It is," Griffin said.

"How are you holding up?"

"I'm great." She knew she sounded defensive. She took a deep breath, tried to maintain an even keel. "I'm tired like anyone else, but I'm holding up."

"I'm not asking about you as a cop. I'm asking about you as a person. This might be hitting a little close to home, right?"

Griffin hated having her personal life leak over into the job. She hated to think her boss might have noticed, but she knew the feelings were there, just below the surface. Maybe not even very far below, like a wisdom tooth about to break through the gums.

"I'm fine. I'm pushing the Flowers thing because I think there might be something there. Hell, we don't have anything else. We have a kid who went poof."

Reddick nodded. Behind her on a shelf sat a picture of her family—her husband, Rich, and their kids. Three brown-haired girls with perfect smiles and bright eyes. Career, husband, children. Reddick had it all. "It's tough for all of us when a child is in danger. But you've been through the divorce and the miscarriage. Very similar to what we're learning about Erica Frazier. Some wounds stay raw for a while, so I wanted to check in."

Griffin spoke in a harsh whisper. "I don't want anyone to think that. If some of these guys get wind of it . . . well, you know what they'll think. *She's a woman and she can't handle the tough stuff.* Hell, you know that as well as anybody. You've been there. I'm sure Phillips has thought that since I came on the job."

"Nobody has said anything like that to me. And I'm not trying to start anything."

"I'm fine. I'm doing my job like everybody else." She pointed at the photos on the shelf. "By the same logic, couldn't someone say you can't work the case because you have kids of your own? Same with Twitchell."

"Okay, I hear you."

"And shouldn't we identify with Erica Frazier?" Griffin asked. "Isn't she the victim here? Her kid is missing."

"But you're also thinking she might have kidnapped a baby."

Griffin said what everyone thought. "There are no easy answers here. At least not yet."

Reddick offered an encouraging smile, a gesture that accentuated the lines around her mouth and eyes. "I think that's something we can all agree on."

chapter thirty-four

12:12 A.M.

"Michael?" Angela asked into the phone. Again came the rustling sound. Like something being shaken, or the sound of soft applause. "Michael? Say something. Where are you?"

She was up off the bed, standing in the middle of their bedroom, her bare feet pressed against the soft carpet. Through the sheer curtains, she saw the quiet, empty street, the darkened houses, the moon almost fully risen.

Where the hell is he?

"Michael, you're scaring me. Just tell me you're okay."

Breathing sounds came through the line. He was still there.

"I'm in the cornfield," he said, his voice dreamy. "I'm behind the house."

"What house? What cornfield?"

Then the details came back. The family's first house in Cottonsville, the yard that backed up to the farmland.

The swing set.

"Michael?"

"I'm looking for Robyn. Mom's coming, and Robbie's in the corn. I'm supposed to be watching her. *Robbie-girl . . .*"

Angela took a step back, let her body weight go, and sat on the bed. But she refused to cry. That helped no one and solved nothing. She simply shut the fear and any potential tears off and tried to plan the next step. Hang up and call back? Call the police? Get in the car and go after him?

Then the phone jostled, as though it was moving. Something scraped against the mouthpiece, metal on plastic.

"Hello?"

A woman's voice. A little reedy. Unfamiliar. A voice she'd heard only twice—once that day in the credit union parking lot and then again on her front porch just a few hours earlier.

"Angela?"

"Who is this? Erica?"

"Michael's fine. I'm here with him."

"Put him on. What's wrong with him? He sounds like he's drunk."

"We had a little fender bender. Michael's head hit the steering wheel, and I think it dazed him. I got jostled pretty good too, but I was in the backseat."

Something muffled the phone, a hand over the speaker.

Angela heard Erica speaking in a soothing voice, like she was talking to a dog or a small child.

"Erica? Put Michael on."

She came back on the line. "It's okay. I've got him."

"Got him? What do you mean?"

"I'm bringing him back to the car. He's okay. He's coming out of it." Then Erica appeared to be speaking to Michael again, her voice still soft and cooing. "Sit down in there. You'll be okay."

Angela lifted her hand to her head. She felt perspiration, despite the cool rush of the air-conditioning. She dug her toes into the carpet and tried to stay calm. "Erica?" she said, her voice sharp but controlled.

"He's okay, Angela. Like I said, we went off the road into a cornfield, and when we smacked the small fence, he got bounced around. He hit his face and got dazed a little. So he got out of the car and wandered off. He must have called you. Maybe he just pushed the button by mistake, and you were the last call he made."

"Put him on."

"He looks better now. I don't even think the car has a scratch on it."

"Where are you?" Angela asked. "I'm coming to get him."

"We're in Trudeau. On the bypass. But you don't have to come. We were on our way to the police."

"I thought you already did that."

"We got delayed. Michael went on TV. . . ."

"Tell me where you are so I can come pick my husband up."

The phone was muffled again, a hand probably placed over the speaker. Angela heard a voice again. No, two voices.

Michael?

He came on the line. "Hey, babe. It's me." He sounded ragged and tired, as if he'd been woken from a deep sleep. "I'm okay. Really."

"Were you in an accident? Michael, are you hurt?"

"I'm not. Don't worry. That steering wheel knocked me for a loop, but I'm okay."

"You were talking about Robyn. You probably have a concussion."

"I'm okay."

"Where are you?" she asked. "Either let me come get you, or I'm calling the police."

"Don't." Michael said something Angela couldn't hear and then came back on the line. "The hospital is up the way here. We'll go by, and they'll check me out. Then we have to see the police. And then I'm coming home. It wasn't really an accident. We just went off the road."

"Where are you?" Angela asked.

"On the bypass . . ."

Erica came back on the line. "Angela. The hospital is just down the road. I'll take him there if he needs to go. It's okay."

"Erica?"

And then she was gone.

chapter thirty-five

12:25 A.M.

On her way home, Griffin drove by Tom Haynes Municipal Park. It wasn't far out of her way, and she felt restless, edgy, possessed of the kind of nervous energy usually brought on when she drank two cups of coffee in the morning just to chase the cobwebs out of her brain.

She'd been to the park that morning. In the wake of Felicity's disappearance and the issuing of the Amber Alert, about fifteen cops had descended on the spot before fanning out in all directions, searching in bathrooms, storage shelters, and distant wooded areas for some sign of the missing child. Griffin remembered the experience, the mixture of dread and excitement that coursed through her body. She couldn't imagine a more horrific event—a child disappearing—but she had also felt needed and relevant for the first time in a while. Looking for and—*she hoped*—eventually finding Felicity Frazier mattered more than any petty burglary case or any assault complaint filed by meth heads living in a trailer park. Bringing home a child . . . that was important. She'd already started imagining the look on the face of the little blond-haired girl when she was rescued from wherever she'd been taken, the benevolent hand of a cop leading her away to a patrol car and safety.

When Griffin drove by the park, she saw the news vans were pulling away, the gawkers and spectators off doing something else. The area looked quiet, deserted. Lonely. Every hour that passed nagged at Griffin's mind, weighing it down. Every hour Felicity wasn't found dripped with frightening possibilities.

She made the ten-minute drive home and parked behind her building. She barely knew her neighbors. A young couple lived downstairs, a single guy—maybe gay?—across the hall. They all exchanged pleasantries when they passed on the stairs or in the foyer, and they'd all seen her badge and gun, which caused most people, the ones who weren't criminals, anyway, to treat her with respect and a certain distance, as though she might be carrying a fatal disease.

When she opened the door, her two cats, Coco and Rory, were waiting. They voiced immediate displeasure with how long she'd been gone and the lack of food available to them, especially Coco, the calico, the one more likely to whine and cry. They were both pudgy and in no danger of starving, but Griffin felt bad, hated to think she'd been neglectful.

"I know, I know," she said as they wound around her legs, circling her calves and rubbing up against them. "Long day at work. Haven't you been watching the news?"

She went out to the kitchen, stepping carefully so she didn't trip over them, and opened two cans of food, the pungent odor of the factory-produced chicken-and-fish blend reaching her nostrils. As soon as the bowls were filled, the cats shut up, turning their attention to eating as if they hadn't seen a meal in months, their tongues making faint lapping sounds as they dug in.

"You're welcome," she said.

She opened the refrigerator and took out a beer, twisting off the cap in a way her mother would have found unladylike. She looked around. She'd been there just under a year, since shortly after she moved out of the house she once shared with John. Not much on the walls, the furniture functional. She'd never been much of a decorator, hoping cleanliness and minimalism counted as some kind of style.

Well, she thought to herself, raising the beer bottle in a mock toast, *here's to you, Helen Winningham. You're my new role model, my mentor. Solving crimes from the comfort of your housecoat.*

She took a long drink and headed to the dining room table, where her laptop sat. She ignored her e-mails and social media notifications—she struggled to summon any interest in which of her high school and college friends were getting married and having babies—and searched for more details about the disappearance of Stacey Flowers. One site shared an absurd age-progression photo, a picture of Stacey if she'd grown up to look like a blond Frodo Baggins, nothing at all like the beautiful Felicity Frazier or any other kid on the planet.

Griffin turned her attention to Tiffany Flowers, the mother. Using a people-finder site, she found several recent addresses for her, all of them in and around Trudeau. She saw no evidence of her ever marrying, no evidence of more children. She followed a link to potential social media pages for Tiffany Flowers, finding several women with the same name. She compared the profile pictures with a photo from one of the old news stories online and thought she'd discovered the right one.

If so, the years hadn't been kind. Tiffany was a year younger than Griffin, but the profile picture showed a woman who looked closer to forty. She leaned in and studied the face like an elderly person with failing eyesight. It sure appeared to be Tiffany Flowers. She clicked to see more information and saw a telling photograph, a lighted candle against a dark background, an announcement about National Missing and Murdered Children's Day.

Griffin felt something tugging on her heart, a lead weight pulling it down to her shoes.

"Ugh," she said.

Rory, the gray, jumped onto the table and sat there impassively, licking her paw and then brushing it across her face. She then licked her lips, looking like a satisfied monarch. She would need only to let out a ringing belch to complete the picture of regal satisfaction with her meal.

Griffin clicked back and found the most recent address for Tiffany Flowers. She took another long swallow of her beer and set the rest aside. She stood up and ran her hand down Rory's body, enjoyed the pleasure the cat displayed by arching her back and purring.

"I know you want me to stay, but I'm going somewhere for a little while." She wondered if Helen had ever owned a cat, ever talked to herself or inanimate objects in her apartment. Had Erica Frazier heard the mutterings of a lonely old woman through the walls? "I won't be long. You've been fed, and I'm just going to look. Just a few minutes away."

She grabbed her keys out of the dish by the door and went back outside.

chapter thirty-six

12:36 A.M.

Angela composed herself, taking a few deep breaths while the phone rang. Gail. Michael's mother. She needed to present the bravest face possible so as not to worry her no-doubt-already-worried mother-in-law. She looked down at the phone and pressed the button to receive the call.

"Hi, Gail."

"Hi, Angela. I'm sorry I'm calling so late. I bet I woke you."

Gail Frazier sounded fairly composed. Angela detected a certain breathlessness in her voice, a slight rush to her words that indicated her mother-in-law was worried and in need of reassurance. Gail Frazier rarely sounded that way. It was only when something concerning one of her children happened that she ever sounded on the verge of losing her composure. Angela had seen this for the first time shortly after she married Michael and he was hospitalized with severe food poisoning. Gail had come into the hospital room where Michael was hooked up to an IV line, and her face crumpled into tears as she caressed Michael's pale face. Only a few hours later had Angela fully understood—*Gail has already lost one child.*

"It's not too late," Angela said, standing up from the bed and pointlessly pacing the room. "I was up."

"Okay, okay," Gail said. Her voice was husky from a cigarette habit she'd given up about six years earlier when she turned fifty-five. She still sipped scotch in the evenings, played cards and golf with a group of ladies she'd known for years, and volunteered at so many charities, Angela couldn't keep track of them all. "Am I correct in assuming Michael isn't home?"

"He's not. Did you see this breaking news?"

"I did. Why didn't he call us and tell us about this, Angela? Why is he announcing this on TV? Everyone is going to see it."

"I know, I know."

When Angela first met Gail, two months after she and Michael began to date, she'd had no idea what her future mother-in-law thought of her. Gail had come across as unfailingly polite, saying and doing all the right things to welcome Angela into her home. But Angela had also detected a reserve in Gail, a caution, a sense she held something back, in contrast to Michael's father, James, who seemed open to her right from the start.

After spending more time with Gail—including an

ill-fated attempt to golf with her at the country club—Angela had asked Michael how his mother felt about her.

"Did she like Erica so much that she isn't warming up to me?"

"No, no, no," Michael had said. And he'd meant it. He'd explained that his mother didn't like Erica very much at all. Too flighty. Too unpredictable. Too willing to argue politics or religion at the dinner table. "No," Michael said. "She's protecting me. She doesn't want to see me hurt or in difficulty again. So it's about my *divorce* from Erica, not about Erica herself. Hell, on some level, Mom was probably glad to see Erica go, but she doesn't want to see me get divorced again."

Over time, Michael had proven to be right. The wall had come down. Gail had invited Angela shopping, spent time discussing books with her. Shortly before Christmas the previous year, Angela had lost her composure and broken down, crying over her inability to conceive a child. Gail had held her in a long embrace and kissed the top of her head.

"It will happen, honey," she'd said. "In good time, it will happen."

Angela had felt somewhat foolish. Shouldn't she have been comforting the woman who had recently lost her husband?

Angela squeezed the phone and wished once again for wine. She gave Gail a quick summary of what had happened that evening with Erica showing up at the door and convincing Michael to go away with her in search of the missing child.

Gail listened quietly without offering comment. When

Angela was finished, her mother-in-law said simply, "Why, that's crazy."

"Yes, it is."

"Angela, what is he thinking?"

Again, Angela felt stuck for an answer, except to point out that Michael carried a certain amount of guilt over Robyn's death and a heightened sense of duty toward a child who might be his. But she kept those thoughts to herself.

"Is he coming home now?" Gail asked. "He's been on the news in front of God and everybody, and it's getting on toward one o'clock."

Angela tried to think of a way to avoid answering the question, but nothing came to mind. She cursed herself for not being a better liar. "I don't think he is quite yet." She told Gail about the "fender bender" and Michael's desire to go on and talk to the police with Erica. She left out any mention of her husband wandering in a daze through a cornfield, searching for his dead sister.

Robbie-girl.

"Oh, my God," Gail said, her voice full of alarm.

Angela remembered her mother-in-law's fears when Michael was hospitalized with food poisoning and worried she'd said too much by mentioning the accident at all.

"He's okay, Gail. I talked to him. He's really worried about this child. I guess we all are in some way."

"Oh, yes. Of course." Angela heard a catch in her mother-in-law's voice, a protective motherly instinct that extended to all children. "I'm sick about all of this, but I worry. . . ."

"You mean you worry about Michael?" Angela asked, trying to finish the thought.

"Of course. But Erica . . . she's a piece of work. I guess I'm just worried she might be using the child to manipulate Michael, to get him to do something he wouldn't ordinarily do."

"That's what I thought." Angela enjoyed the surge of affirmation, the recognition someone else thought along the same lines she did. "I'm not crazy to think that."

"No, you're not."

Gail's voice carried something more ominous, something deeper.

"What is it?" Angela asked. "Do you know something else?"

"Maybe I should just come over now," Gail said. "I'm not going to sleep, not with Michael out there saying and doing these things."

"No, you don't have to do that. I can come over—" She stopped herself. No, she didn't want to leave. What if Michael came home? What if the police came back with more news? "We can talk tomorrow. It's late, and Michael will be back. . . ."

She *hoped* he would. She hoped.

"I'm coming over," Gail said. "My sleep has been hell since James died. And maybe we need to discuss some things in person."

"Okay, if you want."

But Angela felt relieved when she put the phone down, relieved to have the company. Did she want to sit alone all night, waiting to hear more from Michael?

What if something horrible happened? Did she want to get the news alone?

She went to the dresser, pulled out a long-sleeved T-shirt and a pair of socks. Before she changed, she looked out the window at the quiet street. In the glow of the streetlamp at the edge of their yard, a man in dark clothes walked by, shoulders hunched.

Something about the sight of the man unsettled her. No one ever walked up and down their street late at night, and she shivered a little.

But he walked the other way, in the opposite direction of their house.

She pulled the curtains shut and changed her shirt.

chapter thirty-seven

1:15 A.M.

Griffin slowly rolled by the house where Tiffany Flowers lived. Was supposed to live, she corrected herself, knowing full well that the information online might be out-of-date.

She meant what she'd said to Rory before she left the house—she simply intended to look.

But she also knew, somewhere in the back of her mind, that she was lying to herself. It reminded her of having ice cream in the freezer. Sure, she could tell herself all day she wasn't going to have a spoonful, but her mind knew better. She knew she'd be giving in at some point, succumbing to temptation.

She really wanted to knock on Tiffany Flowers's door, and she fully expected to.

And whoever lived in the house made it easy for her.

Even though it was past one o'clock, a television played inside the front room, the flickering multicolored glow from the screen lighting up the curtains. It looked like an invitation.

Griffin pulled the car over in front of the house and climbed out. As she walked across the lawn, she took a glance up and down the street. The houses were uniform, small and boxy, a working-class neighborhood. Mostly clean and orderly, not the kind of neighborhood they received a lot of calls from. The streetlight revealed light-colored siding on Tiffany Flowers's house, some neatly trimmed bushes and colorful perennials planted in the yard. A train sounded its horn in the distance, lonely and bereft. Griffin had been told not to bother with the lead about the kidnapping, so she wanted to cross it off her own mental checklist, give herself a reason to sleep better that night, if she was able to sleep at all.

She stepped onto the porch. Through the closed door, she heard the muffled sound of the television. Voices screamed and a monster roared, as though whoever sat inside was watching a horror movie. It took Griffin back to her junior high days, late nights in summer camped out on the couch and surfing cable channels for something illicit to watch while her mother slept upstairs. She'd loved the secrecy and intimacy of finding a horror movie late at night, something that made her look over her shoulder every few minutes even though the doors were locked and the neighborhood safe.

Griffin knocked loud enough to be heard over the

television. It took a moment for the sound to shut off, and then the curtains were slipped aside and a face appeared at the window. It helped Griffin to be a woman at a moment like that. A woman would be much more likely to open the door to her than a man. The face studied her for a long moment. Griffin waved in a nonthreatening way and showed her badge. When she did that, the woman's eyes opened wide, with some mixture of nervousness and surprise. The curtain fell shut, and soon the locks on the door were being undone.

The woman who revealed herself wore a baggy T-shirt and jeans, but Griffin sensed there was a taut wiriness beneath the loose clothes, the tough leanness of a person who could run fast and fight hard. Her feet were bare. Her hair looked overprocessed and slightly frizzy. Without the barrier of the window, she looked younger, closer in age to Griffin. A suspicious intensity came off her like heat.

"Is something wrong?" the woman asked, her voice slightly confrontational.

"I'm Erin Griffin. I'm a detective with the Davenport County sheriff's office. I'm trying to find Tiffany Flowers. Does she live here?"

"I'm Tiffany."

"Do you mind if I come in?"

"Can I ask what this is about? Is it because I called about the neighbor's dog? That was three weeks ago, and I think they moved."

"It's not that."

"Why are you here so late?"

"Your daughter, Stacey, disappeared a number of years ago. I wanted to talk to you about that."

Before Griffin pushed all the words out of her mouth, Tiffany's hand was at her chest, clutching the material of the T-shirt as though she were having a heart attack. Her face grew pale, and her mouth fell open like a loose screen door.

"Oh," she said.

Griffin felt like she was tiptoeing through a minefield. She'd ventured too far to go back, but the way ahead looked fraught.

"You found her," Tiffany said, her voice full of hope and dread.

"No, no. Not that. But I'd like to talk to you."

Tiffany stepped back, still clutching her shirt, and let Griffin into the house.

chapter thirty-eight

The two women settled on opposite ends of the couch. The TV still played with the sound muted. On the screen, an alien spaceship flew over an American city, firing lasers and missiles into the buildings. Huge explosions followed, and people ran through the streets, screaming as flaming debris rained down on top of them.

Tiffany folded her hands in her lap, but they refused to remain still. She tangled her fingers together, working them around and around like loose wires. Griffin wondered where all that energy was going to go.

"Just to be clear," Griffin said, "you're the mother of Stacey Flowers, who disappeared from the east side of Trudeau ten years ago, when she was an infant."

"Yes, I am." She repeated her words. "I am."

How much had the loss of her child consumed the woman's identity since then? Was there room for anything else in her life besides being *that* woman?

Did such a loss define a person forever? Would Erica Frazier's life forever be defined by the loss of Felicity? Griffin didn't want to find out.

"And the case has never been solved?" Griffin asked.

Tiffany tilted her head to the side. "You're the cop. Don't you know it's never been solved?"

"I didn't work on the original case. And I didn't have time to look up the old files."

"There's been nothing." Tiffany's voice sounded bitter, almost hissing. "After about six months, the lead detective stopped returning my calls. He didn't know anything."

"Who was that?"

"Detective Steven Phillips. Do you know him?"

Griffin kept her face neutral. *Phillips*? "I know him."

"I don't think he cared much about what went on with me. After a while, I became a nuisance to him. An embarrassment because he couldn't solve the case."

Griffin leaned forward. "Did anything unusual happen the day of the disappearance?"

"No. Except my baby was gone. Taken. I went to bed for two years after that. Depression. I was just lost." She turned her head, looking over toward the curtained window but clearly not seeing what was there. "My ex-boyfriend, Stacey's father, he left me pretty soon after. I thought about killing myself every day. Every hour. But I hung on. Somehow. I went back to school. I'm a nurse now, a CNA. It's just me and Mom living here. I never had any other kids. I had a hard enough time carrying Stacey to term."

Griffin wasn't sure what to say. Any gesture or words of sympathy seemed inadequate But she offered anyway. "I'm sorry, Tiffany. I am."

"Yeah. Me too."

"So, on the day Stacey disappeared, did anything unusual happen? Did you see anyone? Anyone who shouldn't have been there?"

"I still don't know why you're here in the middle of the night. What gives?"

"For now, let's just say I'm pursuing leads in another case. It could be related to Stacey's disappearance and it might not. So . . . my question."

Tiffany used her index finger to rub the skin above her lip. "Yes. I told them this back then. About five times. I know they suspected me too. They always suspect the parent."

"Unfortunately, it's not uncommon for a parent to harm her own child."

"I didn't."

"I didn't say you did," Griffin said. "So . . . that day?"

"There was a woman. I saw her twice, maybe three times on the street. I didn't know her, but since I saw her multiple times, I remembered her."

"Why did you remember her? Did she do or say something?"

"She stared at me. Two different times. Once in the grocery store, and then once at the post office. She just stared. I thought maybe I knew her, but I didn't. She looked . . . I don't know. Educated. Young and pretty. I even smiled at her, you know, a friendly smile. But when I did that, she got a look on her face like she was pissed off at me."

"And that was it?" Griffin asked. "She just . . . stared at you? And kind of looked mad?"

Tiffany worked her fingers over and over again. The TV switched to a commercial. A man selling cars, his face red as he yelled at the camera about his latest deal.

"She spoke to me one day. The last day I saw her. This was about . . . two days before Stacey disappeared."

"What did she say?"

"I was pushing the stroller, taking a walk through the neighborhood." She gestured toward her own body. "I've always been into exercising and working out. I run every day to burn energy and stay sane."

"I understand."

"The woman approached me. She stood in front of me, so I had to stop pushing the stroller. She stared inside at Stacey. She didn't say anything. She just stared at my baby. I felt awkward, and I didn't know what to say. I thought she might have been some nut, even though she didn't look like one. Not really."

"Did she say anything?" Griffin asked.

"She finally said she wished she had a baby just like mine. A little girl." Tiffany shrugged, her hands in the air, the fingernails on both hands chewed to the skin. "It was the way she said it too. Her voice was full of something. Regret? Anger? Almost . . . like a hungry lust for a baby. Does that make sense?"

"And then what did she do?"

"She walked off. The hairs on the back of my neck stood up, though. It was the first time I really felt that whole mama grizzly thing, the feeling that I couldn't stand it if somebody messed with my baby. Fight-or-flight, I guess. But she didn't say anything else, and I never saw her after that. Two days later . . ." She waved her hands in the air again, like a magician performing a trick. "Poof. Stacey was gone."

Griffin reached into her pocket and brought out her phone. "Do you think you'd recognize that woman if you saw her picture? It's been ten years, I know."

"I'd recognize her."

Griffin called up the image and handed the phone over to Tiffany. "Tell me if you've ever seen this woman before. And where."

Tiffany's eyes widened when she saw the phone.

"Oh, my God . . ."

chapter thirty-nine

1:20 A.M.

Angela dressed and went downstairs, her mind racing. She plugged her phone in and made sure it was fully charged. She went into the kitchen and grabbed a bottle of water, even though the wine looked much more tempting. Standing at the kitchen island, she ate a granola bar, not even tasting or enjoying it, then wiped off its sticky residue on a dirty kitchen towel.

Michael's okay, she told herself. *He's okay.*

Whatever he was doing, whatever Gail had to tell her, it was all going to be okay.

But on the way down the stairs, after changing her clothes and breezing through the house, she'd made a decision. After she talked to Gail, after she heard what she had to say, Angela was going to leave. She was going to get in her car and drive up to Trudeau, to the bypass south of town. If she didn't see them, she'd call again. She'd find them, one way or another. And then she'd get Michael home. Whatever was going on would be worked out, even if it meant incorporating a stepchild into their lives.

Her mouth was dry. She opened the water bottle and took a long swallow.

Listen to yourself. A child is missing, likely in grave danger, and you're worried about how it will affect your marriage. Your life.

The inner voice spoke true. Angela knew she had it easy if tracking down her husband on a weeknight was her biggest problem.

She heard the gentle knock at the front door. She deactivated the alarm and walked out to the foyer, her tennis shoes squeaking against the hardwood, and let her mother-in-law in. Gail greeted her with a hug and a soft peck on the cheek. Gail's every movement, every gesture, felt perfectly placed and timed. Never any awkward fumbling, never any uncertainty. Angela felt calmer just having the woman in the house.

They walked into the dining room, Gail's arm on Angela's elbow.

"I thought about this the whole way over," Gail said. "I think you should call the police. I don't care about how things look to anybody else or what Michael thinks. He's already spilled everything on the TV. What else could happen?"

Gail looked put together. She wore skinny jeans and a

lightweight black sweater. Her makeup was perfect. Did the woman ever look bad, even in her sixties?

"Yeah. I'm going to end up calling them at some point, if I don't hear from him again. I'm going up there, Gail. After I talk to you, I'm going up there and find him."

"Oh." Gail seemed taken aback by her announcement. "Is there any real reason for that? Is that safe?"

"I want to. That's it. I'm not going to sit idly by while this plays out. And if this child might be part of our lives, then I need to see that she's safe. And that Michael's safe."

"Okay." Gail stood there for a moment, the look on her face distant. Angela saw emotion welling in her eyes.

"Are you all right, Gail?"

"Silly. I can't stand to think of this child out there, somewhere. In danger. I know how bad the situation is for her. And I get more and more weepy over these things the older I get. You know, ever since James died, I cry over everything. Commercials and the news. If I see a little kid riding a bike or walking a dog, I tear up." She sniffled, used the tip of her finger to dab at the corner of her eye. "I used to be tougher."

"It's understandable. You've been through a lot." Angela decided to go farther out on a limb, to say something more direct and revealing than she'd ordinarily say to her mother-in-law. "You've lost a child, too. Some of that must be coming up."

Gail nodded. Silent. She reached out and squeezed Angela's shoulder. "I tried looking at some old photos, things from happier times. I thought they might change my energy about James. You know, at least I could think of happy times."

She stopped, but Angela felt like there was more. "I see," she finally said.

Gail looked away, but she kept her hand on Angela's shoulder. "Most of the happy times, the happy pictures, they have Robyn in them. Out at the lake, the kids playing. Our old house in town. I can't look at or think of any of it these days."

"I'm sorry, Gail. You once told me to be patient, that a baby would come to us in time. Grieving takes time too."

"Oh, I know," she said. "Believe me."

And Angela understood she meant more than James. She meant the weight of the years since Robyn died.

"You said you had something to tell me," Angela said. "Isn't that why you came over?"

"Yes, yes, it is." Gail released Angela's shoulder and shook her head. "There's a lot to say about Erica. A lot."

Angela leaned against the table, tapping her fingers against the top. "I'd never ask you this under normal circumstances, but can you tell me what Erica is like?"

Gail looked to be taking the question quite seriously. She pulled a chair out and sat down, folding her hands on top of the table, her perfectly manicured nails and simple classic jewelry showing in the light.

"She was never very grounded," Gail said. "A nice enough girl, and pretty, but the kind you worried about. Not worry like I thought she was a criminal or anything. I just always worried she would never buckle down, get serious about life. It's hard to picture her as a mother. I think Michael had the same concerns, eventually. They should never have gotten married, but you can't tell a kid that. I wish I'd stepped in more, but Michael didn't want to hear it. You know how strong-willed he is, how determined. He learned."

"I know."

"It's hard to watch your child go through that," Gail said. "The hurt. The embarrassment. Michael's not used to failing, you know. He's not someone who makes mistakes everyone can see. But he stumbled there . . . and now it might all be coming back. I worried about this."

"What did you worry about?" Angela asked. "That Erica would be pregnant?"

"Not exactly." Gail pointed to a chair. "Why don't you sit down so I can tell you?"

Before Angela could, she heard something from the front of the house. A knock? Very light. Almost a gentle tap on the door.

"Was that someone knocking?" she asked, turning around.

"I didn't hear anything."

And then the knock again. A little louder.

Angela felt like she was in one of those dreams in which a succession of bizarre events happens over and over again. In this case, the knocks at the door. Erica. The police. Gail.

And then . . . who?

Her skin felt sticky, her knees weak.

She unplugged her phone and took it with her to the front of the house.

chapter forty

1:40 A.M.

What is it, Tiffany?" Griffin asked. "Do you recognize the person in the photo?"

"That's her," Tiffany said.

"What do you mean?" Griffin asked, her voice level. She wanted to let Tiffany Flowers reach her own conclusions, not influence them in any way with her own behavior. And she hoped like hell Tiffany hadn't been influenced by anything she'd seen on the news that day. "Do you know this woman from somewhere?"

Tiffany stared at the photo on the screen again, her eyebrows furrowed. Griffin watched as the light went on.

"This is her . . . ," Tiffany said. "This . . ."

"Where do you recognize this woman from?"

Her face started to crumple. It began with tears filling her eyes, and then her mouth turning down above a puckered chin. Her cheeks flushed bright red. "This is the woman who spoke to me that day. Right before Stacey disappeared."

"Are you sure?" Griffin asked. "You haven't seen her anywhere else."

"Her hair is shorter than it was then. She looks older. She wore sunglasses that day, but she flipped them up when she spoke to me, pushed them on top of her head, so I could see her eyes." She pointed at the phone. "That's her."

"This is the woman who spoke to you on the street before your daughter disappeared?"

Tiffany wiped at her eyes. Repeatedly. Griffin looked around for tissues but didn't see any. Tiffany dropped the phone onto the couch and stood up. She walked out of the room but quickly came back with a box of tissues and started wiping her face. She resumed her place on the end of the couch.

Griffin picked up the phone, took a quick glance at Erica Frazier's picture, and then put it away. "Are you sure about this?" she asked.

"I am. How could I forget that face, even after all this time?"

"Have you seen the news today?" Griffin asked.

Tiffany shook her head. Back and forth. Back and forth. "I don't watch the news. Too sad. Too depressing."

"You don't know this woman from anywhere else?" Griffin asked.

"No. I swear."

After the words came out, Tiffany Flowers bent double, her slender body folding in half, her chest touching her knees as she leaned forward on the couch. A long, continuous sob emerged, one that made Griffin fear the woman would hyperventilate.

Not certain of what to do, Griffin reached out, placing her hand on Tiffany's thigh. She doubted the woman could feel it. They sat like that for a moment until that first long, silent sob passed. The tears came out in full force as though springing from a deep well. Ten years' worth, Griffin figured. The wound might have scabbed at some point, but it hadn't really healed.

"I'm going to get you some water."

She stood up from the couch, taking her bearings and trying to find the kitchen. Before she moved that way, a woman filled the doorway. She looked to be about sixty, her hair dyed an unnatural color of red, a floral robe belted tight across her waist. Griffin saw the resemblance in the set of the eyes, the shape of the mouth, the lean, sinewy body. The mama bear glare directed at Griffin over the sound of her daughter's sobs.

"What is this?" she asked.

Griffin introduced herself, showed her badge. She explained what had happened and why she was there so late at night. The woman listened, still keeping her distance from her daughter as though she'd started to demonstrate the symptoms of a highly infectious disease instead of the deadly pain of grief.

"You're kidding me," she said. No one seemed to know what to say.

"I was going to get Tiffany some water."

The woman jerked her thumb over her shoulder toward the kitchen sink. As Griffin left the room, Tiffany's mother moved toward her daughter, bending down and placing her arm around her.

"It's okay, honey," she said. "Shhh. It's okay. Don't let this get you down."

Griffin went out to the clean, cramped kitchen. She started opening cabinets, feeling like an intruder, and found a blue plastic tumbler with the University of Kentucky logo on it. She filled it from the tap. When she went back into the living room, the two women were in the same position, mother comforting daughter and daughter unable to speak coherently.

Griffin bent down and held the cup in front of Tiffany's face. She didn't react.

But her mother did.

She made a quick, swiping gesture with her arm, backhanding the cup out of Griffin's hands and sending it to the floor. The water splashed across the side of Griffin's body and across the carpet.

"What are you doing this for?" she asked.

Griffin's instincts took over. She stood up, took a step back. Her hands went out in front of her, prepared for either defense or offense. "Ma'am," she said, "calm down. Easy."

"I will not calm down." But her voice had lost some of its heat. She looked Griffin over, her eyes wide and angry. She shook her head, her face full of several varieties of regret. "Why did you come here? Look what you've done. Look at her, will you?"

Tiffany remained bent over, her face obscured, but the soft sobbing sounds let Griffin know she was still crying.

"I'm here to investigate the disappearance of a missing child," she said. "I know it's upsetting, but I have to ask these questions. There's a child in grave danger right now. That's my job."

"Where've you been the last ten years? Not here, that's for damn sure. Not here while she cried herself to sleep at night. Not here while she regretted taking a shower and not locking the door. Fifteen minutes that shattered the next decade. You weren't here for any of that."

Griffin's posture relaxed. She lowered her hands. "I'm sorry. But there's a child missing, a child who might be Tiffany's, and I had to know." Griffin quickly explained about Felicity, about the possibility Erica had been the one to take Stacey all those years ago. "We don't know for sure, but it's all over the news now. This gives us something concrete to go on."

"Then go. You can get out. And don't come back."

Griffin stared down at the two of them. "Tiffany, is there anything else you want to tell me about this? Anything I should know?"

The woman made no response. She remained in the folded position, her mother tending her, so Griffin made her move for the door.

"Do you think this is real?" the mother asked. "This might be Stacey?"

Griffin realized she didn't even know the woman's name. It wasn't the best time to ask.

"You have to consider all of this tenuous for now,"

Griffin said. "But we're going to look into it. I'll call you when I know more."

"And that woman in the news? The one with the missing girl?"

"What about her?"

The woman's eyes smoldered with anger. "Nail her. Nail the bitch for what she did to us."

chapter forty-one

1:47 A.M.

As Angela walked to the door, her mind raced with possibilities.

Michael? Erica? Lynn? The police?

She stepped over to the window and lifted her hand, parting the curtains as she had when the cops arrived hours earlier. Her eyes drifted over the driveway, making note of the space next to her car, which was now occupied by Gail's Lexus instead of Michael's SUV. She silently cursed him, wishing her legs were long enough to kick his butt from where she stood. She took deep Zen-like breaths, reminding herself it was far better to be married to a man who cared about others, who would drop everything to help a person in distress, than to be married to someone who simply didn't give a shit. She had friends in marriages like that.

Then she turned her head to the door and saw the man. He stood in the porch light, his hands thrust into the pockets of his light jacket. Flying insects swirled around in the muggy air, and the man reached up and brushed one away. Then he saw Angela's face staring at him.

Angela jumped back, a little gasp escaping her lips.

She recognized his shape and clothes. He was the man she had seen walking by earlier when she got off the phone with Gail.

Was he another cop? He didn't look like one. Unlike the pair of detectives who'd shown up earlier in their business attire, this man wore jeans, tennis shoes, and a light blue polo shirt in addition to the jacket.

Maybe he just had the wrong house. Maybe he was lost.

But how likely was that? How many lost wanderers showed up at their door in the suburbs?

And why had he walked by earlier?

The man knocked again. Harder. She thought she heard him saying something, his voice muffled by the closed and locked door.

Locked? She hoped it was locked.

Angela checked, saw the dead bolt turned in the correct, locked position, and took a breath of relief. She swallowed hard, choking down saliva that felt like a golf ball.

Angela heard Gail coming toward her, her light footsteps echoing in the quiet house.

"Who's there?" she asked.

"I don't know." Angela reached for her phone, sliding it out of her jeans pocket. "But I'm calling the police. It's some guy, and there's too much weird shit going on."

The man knocked again, and Gail moved past Angela and parted the curtains. When she did, she made a low grunting noise.

"What? Is he leaving?"

"No, no, he's not," Gail said. "Can you put the phone down?"

"What? Why?"

"I think we need to talk to him," Gail said.

"You know him?" Angela asked. "Who is he? Is he a cop?"

"Not that. Not exactly." Gail let the curtain drop and moved toward the door. "But he is someone who can help explain what I came to tell you tonight. I'm going to let him in."

"Are you sure?" Angela felt her chest thump, felt an air bubble in her throat.

"I'm not sure of anything," Gail said. "But I'm going to let him in."

Gail moved to the door and unbolted the lock. She stepped back, swinging the door open and revealing the man without the screen of the window and the curtains.

The man wasn't tall or physically imposing. His thick brown hair was parted to the side, and his nose and chin both looked long and thin. His brown eyes shone in the porch light like two tiny marbles.

"Who is this, Gail?" Angela asked.

The man held up his hands in a gesture that said he didn't mean any harm. "I just want to talk, Mrs. Frazier." He cut his eyes toward Gail. "I didn't know you had company. And company I actually know."

"Angela," Gail said, "this is Mr. Jake Little."

Jake Little. The name registered in Angela's brain.

The cops. They'd asked about him earlier.

"You know Erica somehow," Angela said.

"You could say that, yes." He made an attempt at a smile. It looked unnatural and forced, but he'd tried. His voice was higher pitched than she'd expected and a bit nasal. "Erica and I dated for several years around the time Felicity was born and then again a couple of years ago. I know her very well, and I've spent a lot of time with Felicity." He shifted his weight from one foot to the other. "I know all about your husband, about his and Erica's marriage. She came here tonight, didn't she? Looking for him?" He tilted his head, waiting for an answer, but there was a nervous energy in his eyes as they darted back and forth between the two women. When Angela didn't offer one right away, he asked, his voice a little higher, "Are they still here? I'm assuming maybe they're not. You know, Erica has always talked about moving away, about taking Felicity and starting over somewhere. Is it possible . . . ?"

Angela took a step back again. But she wasn't sure where she was going. "They're not here. I know that."

"Anybody else here?" He craned his neck, as if he could see through the walls and floors to the rest of the house. "Anyone? Other family or whatever?"

Angela didn't want to answer him. "How do you know him, Gail? I don't understand."

Before Gail spoke, Jake said, "Look, I want to find Erica. She won't return my calls. But I thought she might have come here. I spent the whole day driving around Trudeau, going to the parks, the malls, the playgrounds, anywhere I thought I might see Felicity. Finally, I gave up and came here to find Erica. I didn't know what else to do."

He lifted his hands in a gesture of futility, something that made him seem slightly sympathetic. Here was another person peripherally connected to events of the day, and he was every bit as confused and exasperated as the rest of them. His eyes continued to dart, bouncing back and forth like a Super Ball.

"Gail, I don't understand," Angela said. "Can you tell me how you know each other?"

The man started to say something but then stopped. He seemed to be contemplating what his next move would be, and he brought his hands together, rubbing them as though the night were cold instead of hot and humid.

"Are you going to tell her, Gail?" he asked finally, his familiar tone with Angela's mother-in-law striking.

Gail? He called her Gail?

When Gail didn't reply, Angela said, "Gail knows Erica, of course."

The man nodded, the gesture bringing some of his brown hair down over his forehead. "She does. But she also knows me. Why don't we go inside and talk more?"

Angela felt like she was in a whirlpool, the waters swirling around her. She was reluctant to move or speak, but she said, "I don't understand any of this yet."

"Your mother-in-law has been talking to Erica for years," the man said, nodding again. "She knows everything that's going on."

chapter forty-two

1:55 A.M.

"Do you want to go to the hospital?"

Michael rode in the passenger seat of his own car, while Erica drove. It had taken a while for Michael's head to clear and for them to back the car out of the corn, but they were on the bypass, the car running fine other than a low grinding noise Michael couldn't place and that didn't seem to be affecting their forward progress. No warning lights glowed on the dashboard, and Erica gently increased the speed to fifty-five. Her window was down, another cigarette going.

"I'll get rid of it," she said, tossing it away. "It's gross. And you're woozy."

He lifted his hand to his forehead. He made a tentative attempt to touch the spot where his face had made contact with the steering wheel.

"Ow," Michael said, finding the spot. He felt a small knot, one that would perhaps keep growing as the night went on. He touched it again. Not as bad but still sore. Tender. "It didn't break the skin, I guess."

"Flip that light on." Michael did, and Erica took a quick glance over. "It's a little bigger than when we were outside, but not bad. It could have been worse, having that maniac grab the wheel like that."

"Yeah." Michael chose his words carefully. "I can't say I really blame him."

"What?"

"We kind of kidnapped him, didn't we? You zapped him with a stun gun. How was he supposed to react?"

"But he clearly didn't want to talk to the police, did he? If he had nothing to hide, why did he do that?" Erica kept her eyes on the road, her body hunched close to the steering wheel. She shook her head. "What about those clothes in the dresser? The little girl's clothes?"

"You're right. I can't explain his behavior."

"The cops should have pushed him harder this morning," she said, speaking with an authority and certainty that cut off the need for further conversation. "Why don't you call them and let them know he ran off that way?"

"Okay. Sure. I don't think I need the hospital, by the way. But I wouldn't mind some ice. And maybe ibuprofen or something. Next time we pass a gas station or store, let's stop."

"Fine. I know where one is. It's not far."

Michael adjusted his body, digging around in his pocket, looking for something. "Did you see my phone?"

"Your phone?"

"I used it, right? After the accident, wasn't I on the phone? I called Angela. Shit, I barely remember what we talked about. She must think I'm a lunatic."

"I told her you were okay."

"You did? I bet she was thrilled."

"Not really."

"So where's my phone, then?"

"I think I gave it back to you. Check your pockets."

Michael felt around again. Then he ran his hands over the upholstery and down in the space between the seat and the door, feeling loose grit and dirt against his fingertips. He checked around his feet, but when he bent over that way, his head hurt. He could only do it so long, but he didn't see the phone.

"Shit. Did I drop it out there?" he asked. "I want to call Angela and tell her I'm okay. Where's your phone?"

Erica sighed in exasperation. "She knows you're fine. Besides . . ."

She left the thought unfinished.

"Besides what?"

"It's nothing," Erica said. "I shouldn't say it."

"Say it."

"I was just wondering. . . . Do you think Angela would ever hurt someone? Do you know where she was this morning?"

"Don't say things like that," Michael said, his voice

sharp and firm. "You're talking crazy. She was at work this morning, so don't say that again. Ever. The phone?"

Erica tilted her body, raising one butt cheek. "It's in my pocket." She kept one hand on the wheel and reached back, sliding the phone out. She handed it over to Michael. "The passcode is zero-six-zero-six."

Michael entered it and called up the phone keypad. He started to dial but then stopped. "Wait a minute. June sixth. Was your mom's birthday in June or July?"

"June sixth."

"How is she?"

Erica remained silent for a long moment while the dark, dull scenery rolled by. "She died a couple of years ago. She had cancer."

"I'm sorry. I didn't know."

"How would you?"

Michael wasn't sure what else to say, so he finished dialing the number. As it started to ring, he said, "I always liked her. Your mom."

"She liked you. She always wanted to have a son."

The phone rang and rang until it went to voice mail. "Shit," he said. He hung up and tried again, getting the same result. "Now she's not answering."

"Maybe she's asleep."

"She wouldn't have her phone off. Not when I'm out. Not tonight."

"Try again."

He tried one more time with the same result. Voice mail. He left a message that time, letting Angela know he was feeling better and would check in again soon. He ended the call, feeling worse about his wife. He wasn't sure why, but he worried that something had happened to her. She was alone in the house without him. He hoped she'd activated the alarm she'd insisted they buy. For the first time, he felt glad to have it.

"Where are we going?" Michael asked.

He looked up. They weren't near any stores. They were in a residential neighborhood. Midsize homes and winding streets. A subdivision.

"Erica, where are we?"

"My house was closer than any store. I thought we'd just stop there and get what you need."

"But the police . . ."

"They're near my house. No worries."

chapter forty-three

1:59 A.M.

Angela hesitated in the foyer, the door still open and Jake Little on the threshold, his hands still together in front of his body, his eyes focused solely on her as he waited for her decision. She took him in and saw in the light from above that, while his body wasn't very large, it was muscular beneath the jacket, the shoulders and biceps those of someone who exercised and lifted weights. His eyes were serious, focused, tracking Angela as though she might make a sudden move.

"Why don't we go talk in the dining room?" Angela said, and led them that way. She thought back to the appearance of the cops at the door—it felt like hours earlier—and the way her head had ping-ponged back and forth between the two of them as they peppered her with questions. She'd stood on the porch before that, her eyes cutting between Michael and Erica as she tried to understand why her husband's ex-wife had picked that night to show up on their doorstep.

And there she was again, caught in between. Was she going to spend the foreseeable future that way? Trapped between opposing forces she didn't really understand?

Not if I can help it.

"Okay, let's get this all out," Angela said when she reached the dining room table. But she looked back and saw Jake Little in the foyer, looking up the stairs toward the second level of the house. "What are you doing?"

His head was tilted, his ear cocked toward the stairs and the bedrooms above. "Are you sure . . . ?"

His voice trailed off, and then he darted up the stairs, taking them two at a time, his shoes clomping against the carpet.

Angela broke into motion. She swept past Gail, who stood there with her hand lifted to her head, and followed the man up to the second floor of the house.

She saw his back going down the hallway, sticking his head into each of the bedrooms, his movements quick and efficient.

"What are you doing?" she asked. "If you don't stop this, I'm calling the police."

Angela reached for her phone, calling up the keypad.

The man—Jake Little—stopped at the entrance to the master. He stuck his head in and then turned around. "Stop. Just stop," he said.

"Get out of here."

He held his hand out. "Put it away," he said, his voice

losing its higher pitch and nasal tone and becoming commanding. "Just put it away. That's not necessary."

"If you're not a cop—"

Jake spoke firmly. "Put it away. I had to check. I have to check everywhere, and your family is involved in this. How do I know Felicity isn't here?"

"Because I told you so. And I'm not a damn kidnapper."

"But your husband, his family . . ."

"What about them?" she asked.

"Your mother-in-law is here. What about your sister-in-law? Lynn? The rock star. Did she come by?"

"She's out of town. No one else is here." Angela summoned as much command as she could and rolled it into her voice. "I need you downstairs. Now. This is my house."

Jake considered her, a look of surprise and respect crossing his face. He nodded. "Okay, okay. I'll go down. I guess I didn't really think you had the kid here, but I had to check. I didn't look under the beds. I didn't hear anything."

He moved past her and went back down the stairs with Angela behind him. As they walked, she slipped her phone away but left it peeking out of the top of her jeans pocket for easy access.

Jake walked past Gail and out to the dining room. Gail sighed with relief as she followed behind Angela, and they all ended up at the table. "Gail, I don't know much about this guy, but he was creeping around outside for some reason. And he's fascinated by our bedrooms. *And* he says you've been talking to Erica. And, you, Jake or whatever your name is, you need to tell me why you're here and what you want from me. And keep in mind I have things to do tonight, and it's late. For everyone, including this missing little girl."

Jake Little sized Angela up, taking into account the steel she had shown in the upstairs hallway. He nodded his head as he took her in and then eased forward, his movements smoother and more controlled than they had been on the porch or upstairs, as though the run through the second floor of the house had calmed him down a little and released some of his nervous energy. He extended his hand.

Angela took a step back, but Jake kept going, and before she could move again, he'd slipped her cell phone out of the front pocket of her jeans. Then he stepped back.

"I'm going to hold on to this so nobody makes any phone calls before we're ready to make them." He slid the phone into his back pocket and then looked at Gail. "I assume yours is in your purse there." He pointed. When Gail nodded, he went over and took the purse. He dropped it at his feet without opening it and kicked it away. "I just want to keep the police out of this for a moment, and I'm not going to say anything else right now. I think what your mother-in-law has to say is going to be much more interesting to you." Again, he looked at Gail. "Am I right? And try to hurry it up, okay? There's a child missing, a child I care about very much."

Angela had never really seen the kind of look in Gail's eyes that she saw in that moment. An added layer of toughness and contempt had appeared, and if a knife or an ax had been easily available, it would have been embedded in Jake's throat.

"What exactly do you want me to say?" she asked, her voice tight, the words coming out with an effort.

Angela's phone began to ring right then. Jake reached around and pulled it back out of his pants.

"Is that Michael?" Angela asked.

Jake pushed a button, silencing the sound. "Unknown number."

"It could still be—"

"Let's just hear this first," Jake said. "Once this is out, you can decide what you want to do next. Okay? And we're in a hurry. Quick, quick. Believe me—I get it. That's the whole reason I'm here, after all. I want to know what happened to Felicity as much as anyone."

And Angela had to admit she very much wanted to hear whatever the two of them seemed to know. Had Gail really been in contact with Erica?

Had Michael been aware of this as well?

"Gail?" she said. "Do you know something about Erica? And all of this craziness?"

Gail kept her eyes on Jake, the look in them still withering. But she said, "I do, Angela. I'm sorry to say I do."

chapter forty-four

2:05 A.M.

As she left Tiffany Flowers's neighborhood, Griffin placed a call to Twitchell. She knew he'd have his phone on, even in the middle of the night, and she needed to tell her partner what she'd just learned.

But instead of her partner answering the phone in the groggy voice of the sleep-deprived, he sounded wide-awake and alert. And he didn't say hello.

"Where are you?" he asked. "I was just about to call."

"I was just about to call you." Her excitement and lack of sleep made her words come out in a tumble. "I mean, I called you to tell you something."

"Where are you?" he asked again. "Are you home?"

"No, I'm not. I'm driving."

"Driving? At this time of night? Where? Never mind. I was about to pick you up."

"I can meet you at my place. What's going on?"

"We might have caught a break in Felicity's case. I'll see you there in a few minutes."

"Okay. I just—"

But he was gone.

It took her ten minutes to make it home. The sky had clouded over, obscuring the moon and stars. On the horizon, she saw distant flashes of lightning, a storm that might blow through Trudeau later that night. She hoped it would bring relief from the heat.

She passed few cars on the way. Solitary drivers, just like her, returning home or going out God knew where. She tried to keep what Tiffany Flowers had told her in perspective. She knew how unreliable eyewitness testimony could be, and this was being delivered ten years after the fact. But she believed Tiffany when she'd said she hadn't been watching the news, that her identification of Erica hadn't been influenced by seeing her on TV all day. It was more than anything else they had.

And wouldn't a mother have pinpoint recollection of the person who might have taken her child?

Easy, Griffin reminded herself. If Tiffany's memory was accurate, then Erica was so far guilty of nothing more than speaking to a mother pushing a baby in a stroller.

Nothing more.

"Come on," she said out loud, shaking her head. "A coincidence? Really?"

When she came in sight of her apartment building, she saw Twitchell's familiar sedan parked at the curb, the lights glowing. She saw him inside, his face illuminated by the screen of his cell phone. Glasses pushed up on top of his head, eyebrows knitted together in concentration. If Reddick was the cool mom Griffin wished she'd grown up with, Twitchell was the awkwardly nerdy dad, the one who managed to appear befuddled at the most ordinary things.

She parked. Rory and Coco would have to continue to keep each other company. They'd been fed. They'd miss her, but they'd be content. And she wasn't certain about how much they'd miss her. She might have just been trying to convince herself the cats possessed any feelings for her that extended beyond the dinner hour. She crossed the street to the sedan and opened the passenger-side door, slipping inside while Twitchell remained focused on his phone. His head didn't even move.

"What's up?" she asked.

He put the phone down and flipped his glasses into place. They made his eyes look larger, almost comic. He put the car into gear and started driving. "Remember how Phillips and Woolf were going to check on those last couple of pervs? The ones they hadn't reached yet?"

"Sure." The name "Phillips" sounded bitter to her ears. Had he blown off Tiffany Flowers ten years ago, an oversight that led them to where they were now?

"They went to the house of the one guy tonight. Todd Friedman. He refused to open the door and talk to them. And when they pressed him on it, he announced he had a gun and was going to start shooting at somebody if they didn't back off."

"Crap."

"He's barricaded in a house over on Ninth Street. Phillips and Woolf are there with a swarm of cops. They've called everyone in. Plus, there was some kind of fight at a bar near campus. We're stretched thin. They're trying to get a negotiator to drive down from Louisville. For all I know, she's on her way."

Griffin looked around. "Where are we going? Ninth Street is the other way."

"We're going to talk to Todd Friedman's former wife, Randi. She called in a while ago, said she knew something about the case as it relates to her ex-husband. They went to her house but couldn't find her, so now we're going back."

"What does she know?"

"She didn't say. But since her ex-husband's holed up, saying he won't be taken alive, we're kind of hoping it's good. If we think it's worth it, we can bring her over to his house, let her try to coax him out."

They made a series of turns, the GPS calmly naming the movements. It looked like they were heading for the northeast part of town.

"Where were you?" Twitchell asked. "Partying after a long day of work?"

He almost never asked much about Griffin's personal life. All the details he knew about her divorce from John came because she'd insisted on telling him, sharing her heartache over lunches and coffee breaks. He'd always listened patiently, offered whatever advice he could. She appreciated him for that.

"I talked to Tiffany Flowers. About her missing child."

Twitchell said nothing, but a red flush rose on his cheeks. She saw his grip tighten on the steering wheel. "Why did you do that?" he finally asked. "We said we weren't going to worry about that yet. The *boss* said it."

"I know." She waited a beat. "She ID'd Erica Frazier from a photo. She said Erica Frazier talked to her about her baby right before the kid was snatched. That's something."

Twitchell let out a long sigh. He looked out the driver's-side window of the car, away from Griffin, and made a turn as the voice instructed. "The boss talked to you tonight, didn't she? That's why she made you stay after we all left."

"Yeah." Then Griffin understood. "You knew she was going to do that?"

"Of course. I suggested it."

"You did? And you didn't say anything to me?"

"You needed to hear it," he said. They'd reached their destination, a row of apartment buildings in a middle-class neighborhood. He pulled the car over to the curb but didn't turn the engine off. "I thought it would be better coming from her. I guess I was wrong, since you didn't listen."

"What happened to partners having each other's backs?" Griffin asked.

"I do. That's why I did it."

"If you don't trust me . . ."

"I trust you. But this case, all this stuff going on, it's in your head. You're being emotional, listening to your heart too much, letting your own feelings and regrets get in the way. We can deal with the Flowers stuff later, figure out a way—"

Griffin pushed the door open and stepped outside. The night smelled like rain, and another flash of lightning lit the horizon. She started to walk away, then realized she didn't know the exact address, didn't know where they were going. Even her attempt at storming off hadn't worked.

She waited while Twitchell got out of the car and walked up beside her. He pointed at the next building. "Unit G," he said. "Are you ready?"

She refused to answer him but followed along dutifully.

chapter forty-five

2:10 A.M.

Gail pulled a chair out, its legs scraping against the wood floor, and sat down at the dining room table.

"Gail, what is he talking about?" Angela asked. She moved closer to the table, stopping at the end and eyeballing her mother-in-law, who suddenly looked her age. And flustered.

Gail's hands moved around a few moments, as though she weren't sure where to put them.

Jake Little moved past Angela and grabbed a chair across the table from Gail, sitting down as if he'd been invited to dinner. He kept his mouth shut but also seemed to be waiting expectantly for Gail to speak. His folded hands rested on top of the table, but his thumbs twiddled as he waited.

"I told you, Angela, that I was never crazy about Erica," Gail said. "I was never sure why she and Michael were getting married. I think they dated awhile in college, and then graduated and just weren't sure what to do next. So they got married. It seemed like the next step, and a lot of young couples do that. For all I know, they knew James and I didn't approve, and they married just to show us. Kids do that sometimes."

Angela made a quick inventory of the guys she'd dated in college. The steady and the casual, the embarrassing and the not so embarrassing. No, she'd never felt like marrying them was the next logical step. She'd only ever contemplated marrying one man. Michael. And she'd believed she made the right choice. She still did.

"When they split up," Gail said, "I knew Erica was devastated. She had to be. And I knew . . ." She looked at Angela. "I knew Michael . . . Well, he's more like his father than like me in that way. Michael isn't cruel—I know that—but he can be a little . . ." Again her hands waved around as she searched for the right word.

"Abrupt," Angela said.

"Yes. He'd tell her once, explain the whole thing, but then he wouldn't have the patience to talk to her again. Some people, some women, need to talk things out longer. Michael struggled with that, I know. And then he met you pretty quickly after that as well."

Jake looked at Angela, and they locked eyes for a moment. Angela saw the supposition there, his guess that she and Michael had been involved before he left Erica. Angela knew a lot of people thought that. They assumed a marriage didn't break up without an affair or something else crazy happening. She'd learned, almost ten years earlier, to ignore it and just move on. She knew. Others could think what they wanted.

"It was courtesy at first," Gail said. "I called her to check up on her. Just being friendly. How are you getting along? Is everything okay? That sort of thing. I realized the girl didn't really have anyone else to talk to, because she started confiding in me in ways I didn't think she would. After all, what did I know about the struggles of a recently divorced twentysomething? I was as far removed from her life as anything else."

"You didn't really like her, but you called her?" Angela asked.

"She was vulnerable," Gail said. "And I saw it as my duty, as a role I could play in her life. I didn't want the girl to do something rash. And I didn't want her going around saying my family just cut her off and was done with her without a second thought. I don't like to burn bridges with people."

"And this only happened when? The first few months after she and Michael split up?" Angela asked.

"It did end after a few months," Gail said. "Maybe six. The phone calls tailed off. I don't know where Erica was living at the time or what she was doing. Life went on. Michael married you. I lived my life. I figured that was the end of it with Erica."

"But I'm guessing it wasn't," Angela said.

"Do you want to sit down?" Gail asked. "We're trying to talk."

Angela didn't want to be told what to do. She didn't want anything but information. "I like standing right now."

Gail must have detected the trace of flint in Angela's voice, because she looked like she was about to say something but then thought better of it.

"Did Michael know you talked to her?" Angela asked.

It was the only question she wanted to know the answer to. She couldn't summon anything else in her mind.

"Angela, I don't want to say or do anything that would get in the way of your marriage. It's for Michael—"

"Did he know?" Angela asked.

Gail looked reluctant to speak, which told Angela all she needed to know before the words came out.

"Yes," she said, "I told him about it when I spoke to Erica during that time. And he told me, explicitly, he didn't want you to know about it."

chapter forty-six

2:22 A.M.

Erica drove Michael's car down her street, the speed increasing gradually. The neighborhood looked to be middle-class, a combination of ranch-style and two-story houses, the construction mostly brick. In the rushing dark, Michael couldn't see much else, but it appeared to date to the 1950s or 1960s, a time when they would have been filled with the first wave of families educated by the GI Bill, people looking for a place with a lawn and a little room to spread out.

Erica slowed some in front of a brick ranch with a small porch. The headlights caught the image of a tree in front that looked to be dying, as most of its leaves were gone in midsummer, but the rest of the yard looked orderly if unspectacular. Michael had expected to see more activity around the house. Reporters and gawkers. But the street was empty, the house dark and quiet. The reporters must have gone home for the evening. The police, no doubt, were pursuing other things.

Erica zoomed up the driveway and pulled around back.

"No cops," Michael said.

"They're supposed to be here," she said, distracted. "At least one car."

"Maybe they got called away to something," Michael said. "Maybe something happened with the case."

"I hope so," she said. "I'd rather they were out doing something than sitting here. Or asking me the same questions over and over again. I'm glad I don't have to deal with them."

When Erica parked, the headlights caught a small patio with two matching lawn chairs and a round table. The grass looked long and in need of mowing. Michael's eyes then fell on the swing set in the back corner of the yard, a small one with a slide at the end.

He started to say something, but Erica was out of the car before he could speak, leaving the driver's-side door open.

"Hey."

He unbuckled and opened his door. His head still throbbed but more dully, and he wondered if they even needed to stop for any kind of first aid.

He followed in Erica's wake. She went across the patio, her keys jingling in the quiet night, and soon pushed open the back door. By the time Michael reached the house, he could track Erica's progress inside by the lights flipping on in each successive room. It felt weird to be stepping into this house—*Erica's house*—but if he was going to draw the line at doing things that felt weird, he would have to erase the entire evening.

He entered a small family room. A flat-screen TV was mounted to one wall, its screen black and reflective. The furniture looked comfortable and bulky, the floor clear and uncluttered. The overhead light glowed, and Michael squinted. A small brown dog, a mutt who looked to be a cross between a collie and a beagle, came dashing out, tail wagging, tongue lolling. It came up to Michael and sniffed his shoes. He bent down, offering his hand to the dog, who first sniffed and then started licking, its nose and tongue cool against his skin. He tried to rub the dog's ears, but it dashed away as soon as he reached out.

He heard Erica rushing around in other parts of the house, the sounds of doors opening and closing, and soon enough, she reappeared in the family room by coming through the kitchen. She looked agitated, and she ran her hands through her hair as she stopped and examined the space as though she had never been there before either.

"What's going on?" Michael asked, straightening up.

"I thought . . ." Her shoulders rose and fell as she took a deep breath. She ran her hands through her hair again. The dog came back and sniffed at Erica's legs. She ignored it. "I thought maybe . . . she was here."

Michael understood. She'd darted out of the car and through the house, looking for any sign of Felicity.

Maybe she'd come home. Or been dropped off there. Even though the house was dark, the doors locked, Erica clung to that hope.

"I'm sorry," Michael said.

"Yeah. Me too." Erica wrapped her arms around herself, rubbing up and down as though she was cold. "You should sit. I'm going to go close the car."

"I'll do it," Michael said.

"I've got it. Just . . . sit and take it easy. I'm going to take the dog with me. She probably hasn't gone to the bathroom in hours." She grabbed a leash by the door and called for the dog, who was already running when she heard the leash jingle. "Come on, Trixie. I'm sorry you were here alone so long."

But Michael didn't sit while Erica and Trixie went out to the car. He wandered out of the family room, across the kitchen with its table and neat collection of cookbooks, and entered a short hallway that looked like it went to the bedrooms. Framed photographs hung on the wall, and Michael stared at them. They showed Felicity at various phases of life—infant, toddler, child. He noticed she didn't always smile, wearing a look of defiance in some of the photos, and he remembered the sadness Wayne Tolliver had talked about, the melancholy air that hung over the kid.

Michael leaned in, staring at the photos even longer. He tried to see a resemblance, something in the shape of her nose or eyes, the contours of her chin, something that he could compare to that photo of Robyn and all of them that hung by his desk. The one from the lake, the one from right before she died. He thought he saw similarities, but was he simply seeing what he wanted to see, hoping to fulfill his deep-seated wish to have a child of his own?

Erica appeared in some of the photos. In one, she held Felicity—who looked to be about three—inside an ice cream shop. In another, Felicity and Erica held hands on a beach, the tide rolling out, away from their feet. He tried for just a moment to imagine himself in any of the photos, completing the scene, but he couldn't manage to do it. He'd led a parallel life, one with Angela, and he wouldn't trade any of those memories or experiences for the ones depicted on the wall.

But he worried his absence played a part in the heavy look on Felicity's face.

Erica came into the house again, the dog running ahead of her and down the hallway. She locked the back door, and then unlocked it, her movements quick and frantic. "I don't know what to do. I want it unlocked so Felicity can get in if she comes by. But I don't feel safe if it's unlocked. That's part of the reason I didn't stay here today. It didn't feel safe in my own house."

"You said the cops were here."

"Off and on. The lead detective told me they'd keep a close eye on the house. Maybe they're up the street where we can't see them."

"Maybe they found something," Michael said. "Should you call them?"

"I will." Erica settled on locking the door and went into the kitchen. He heard the freezer open, and she came back, carrying a bag of peas. "My ice maker is on the fritz, but you can put this on your head."

Michael took it. "Thanks."

"And I can get you ibuprofen."

"I don't think I need it." He pointed at his forehead. "This is feeling better."

They stood like that for a moment, awkwardly facing each other in Erica's house, the bag of peas in Michael's hand.

Michael said, "Why don't you call them and check in? It's getting later and later."

"I'd like to show you something." She gestured down the hallway, past the pictures Michael had just examined. "I'd like you to see Felicity's room."

"I don't think—"

"You asked me what kind of kid she is, what she's like. What better way to know what a kid is like than to look in her room? Hell, the cops have already been through there today. A reporter and a camera crew went in there at one point. You're her father. And even if you don't believe that, at the very least you're helping me look for her." She rubbed her arms again. "I'd feel better if you looked, if you knew as much as possible about her before we went on."

Michael hesitated. He didn't like the idea of going deeper into the house, especially inside a bedroom. Anyone's bedroom. He couldn't imagine what he would say to Angela about doing that.

But Erica was right. He did want to know who Felicity was. What if she ended up being his daughter? What if she was found and the two of them started the long process of catching up?

What if it eased Erica's mind?

"Okay," he said, the peas still in his hand. "A quick look. And then we get going."

Erica walked past him, and he followed.

chapter forty-seven

2:27 A.M.

Griffin and Twitchell came to the door of Randi Friedman's apartment. The hallway smelled like roasted garlic with a faint whiff of either incense or pot, and despite the late hour, music played loud enough to reach them through her neighbor's door. A strumming acoustic guitar and a wailing singer's voice. Griffin tried to place it. Was it Lantern Black, Lynn Frazier's band?

Twitchell knocked, a staccato rapping against the wooden door. The two partners hadn't said anything else to each other since they'd talked on the sidewalk. Like an old married couple, they knew how to give each other space. Twitchell knocked again, and Griffin waited beside him, her hands resting on her hips.

The door swung open, and Randi Friedman, a fortyish woman with straight red hair, let out a sigh of relief when she saw Twitchell's badge held in the air between them. "Thank God," she said.

"Can we come in?" Twitchell asked.

She stepped back and let them enter the apartment, which was sparse and modern in décor. Randi wore form-fitting black jeans and a black T-shirt. Her nails were neatly manicured, her eyes lively, animated by both fear and intelligence.

"I thought you wanted to go where Todd is," she said.

"We might," Twitchell said. "But we wanted to talk to you first. I just checked in over there, and everything's under control. For now."

"I've been calling and texting Todd, but he won't answer." She threw her hands in the air and let them drop to her side. Then she lifted her thumb to her mouth and started chewing on a piece of loose skin. "This all feels like a nightmare. I wish you'd just find that girl and be done with all of this. She's been gone all day."

"That's what we want to do," Twitchell said.

Griffin walked over to Randi and placed a hand gently on her back. The woman offered no protest, allowing herself to be guided to a chair. She sat down, her body collapsing into the cushions. Without asking, Griffin went out to the kitchen and brought back a glass of water. Her second time doing that tonight. She felt a sting of anger and frustration thinking of the trip to Tiffany Flowers's residence. Did Twitchell really think that was all for nothing? Reddick too?

She remained standing while Twitchell sat on the end

of the couch closer to Randi. She decided to let him ask the questions and take the lead. She'd play nice supportive female cop, the role everyone appeared to want her in.

"You called in earlier and said you had some kind of information about your husband," Twitchell said. "Something that might be relevant to the Felicity Frazier case. Can you tell us what that is?"

She took a moment, as though choosing her words carefully. Or perhaps she was simply reluctant to say them. "Well, you know he's a registered sex offender, right?"

"We know that," Twitchell said.

She sounded apologetic. "It all stems from something he did when he was in his twenties. He never tried to hide it from me. He made a mistake and got involved with an underage girl. A teenager. He told me all about it when we first met." She looked at Griffin. "You understand. You meet a guy and he's honest about his life and his past, and you think you have some kind of prize. Right?"

"Sure."

"Okay," Twitchell said. "So you knew about his record as a sex offender. What does this have to do with Felicity Frazier?"

"Todd and I split up over a year ago. We weren't such a great match to begin with, but then I found out that the thing that got him in trouble in his twenties hadn't really gone away."

"Meaning what?" Twitchell asked, although both cops knew what it meant.

"He had pornography on his computer. Child pornography. Pictures of younger kids. I saw it one day when

I got on his laptop for something else." She shivered. The look on her face became distant as she no doubt recalled the images from the computer. "I couldn't believe what I saw. I guess I should have known. People don't get over those things. Hell, I took enough psychology classes in college. It was my minor. I guess I just thought . . . I don't know what I thought."

"So you split up over a year ago because of this. Did you tell the police about the images?" Twitchell asked.

"No, I didn't. I just wanted to be done with him." She looked at both of them, her eyes downcast. "I know I should have."

The living room window shook as a gust of wind kicked up. Griffin thought she heard a distant rumble of thunder.

"It's okay," Twitchell said. "We're not really worried about that. What is the connection to Felicity Frazier?"

"I used to work with Erica. At the credit union. I was a loan officer before I changed careers. I went back to school and became a physical therapist. Better pay, and I actually felt like I was helping people instead of just trying to take their money. But we all got to know one another a little when I worked there. Todd and me and Erica. We hung out a few times. And Felicity was there sometimes too. She was just a little kid, so she'd be off in her room while we all talked or played cards or watched a movie." Again her face grew distant. "We never had kids, Todd and I. It was fun to be around one sometimes, to kind of imagine what it would have been like. I have nieces and nephews, but they live in Alabama."

"Did something unusual happen between your ex-husband and Felicity during one of these times you spent together?" Griffin asked.

"I don't know." She looked down at her lap, where her hands rested on her thighs. She tapped her feet, nervous energy leaking out. "I know he talked to her alone once or twice. You know, he'd go to the bathroom and stop in her room or something. Just talk, as far as I know. Maybe a little odd for a grown man to talk to a kid in her room, but not so unusual."

"It might be unusual, given his past," Twitchell said.

"Right," Randi said.

"And was that it?" Twitchell asked. "He knows Felicity and Erica and has this interest in child pornography, so you think he might have done something to Felicity?"

She tapped her feet, chewed at the loose skin again. "No, that's not even the whole story. That's not it by far."

chapter forty-eight

2:30 A.M.

Angela felt a little like she'd been slapped. First, Michael had changed the passwords on his computer.

And then she learned her mother-in-law had maintained some contact with Michael's ex-wife in the wake of the divorce. Gail must have been talking to Erica at the same time Michael and Angela were starting to date and then planning to get married. Was Angela the only one in the world who didn't know about it?

Without thinking, she pulled the chair out from the end of the table and sat down. Her movements were stiff and robotic, as though she'd been programmed to make them. No one else in the room said anything, but she felt their eyes on her. She tried to keep her voice under control when she spoke.

"Okay," Angela said, "you were talking to Erica after the divorce. Did you know about the baby? Felicity? Because she must have had her back then, right?"

"I didn't know about Felicity back then," Gail said. "I didn't. I never saw Erica. We never met in person then, right after the divorce, so I didn't know what her circumstances were. But if I'd known about a child, I certainly would have done something about it."

Jake Little made a low laughing noise. "And you would have wanted them to stay together? For the sake of the child?"

"Of course not," Gail said. "I'm not *that* old-fashioned. But it would have been soon enough for me to provide financial help, to see that the child had everything it needed. I would have wanted Erica to know she wasn't alone, that someone heard her and understood her and could help her."

"Wait," Angela said. "When *did* you learn about Felicity? Tonight? Or sooner?"

"I know the answer to this one," Jake said.

Gail gave him a withering look, as if he were a servant who had spoken out of turn. Jake acted like he hadn't noticed, like the look had been intended for someone else.

"I heard from Erica again about a year ago," Gail said. "She called me out of the blue. When I heard her voice, I have to be honest, I almost fell on the floor. I just . . . hadn't thought about her much. I didn't know where she was or what she was doing. I just thought she was one of those people who'd disappeared from my life, kind of like your best friend from kindergarten or someone you knew in college but never kept up with. People just go away sometimes. They fade out of our lives."

"What did she want?" Angela asked.

"At first, just to catch up. And she offered her condolences about James. I guess she saw an obituary in the paper or online. It was a little odd, yes, but when James died, I heard from so many people I'd forgotten about. People were very kind to me. During that first conversation, I could tell there was something more going on, something else she wanted to say. To be honest, I thought she might be trying to have me put her in touch with Michael." Gail shook her head. "I wasn't going to do that." She looked at Angela, her eyes boring in on her daughter-in-law. "I wasn't. That's too complicated."

Jake Little leaned forward. "Tell her what Erica really wanted. Tell her why she called. That's the question she asked you."

Gail tried the withering look again but didn't seem able to summon quite the same force. She looked like she knew she had to answer the question. Finally.

"Something was wrong with Felicity. She needed some medical treatments for a stomach ailment."

"Pediatric pancreatitis," Jake said. "She'd had one bout, and then it came back. It was chronic, and even though Erica had a good job and health insurance, it was getting pricey to treat. The deductibles. She needed help."

"Why didn't she go to you?" Angela asked Jake.

"We'd split up again," Jake said, resigned. "We'd broken up the first time a number of years before that. I'd moved away and come back, and we got involved again, but it didn't work. And I didn't get to see Felicity as much after the second split. Only from time to time when Erica needed my help. But she didn't ask me for money. If she'd called me, I would have helped, even though I don't have a lot. I work in accounting at Hoffman Recycling, but I'd share whatever I could for that girl. I would."

"He's right," Gail said. "That's what it was, that ailment. She needed a little financial help, and her own mother had recently passed away. The family didn't have much to begin with. So she turned to me."

"And she told you that Felicity was your granddaughter?" Angela asked.

Gail nodded. "Eventually, she did. That's why I gave her some money for Felicity."

"And you believed her?" Angela asked. "Just like that."

"Think about the situation I was in, Angela. My husband had just died. I didn't have any other grandchildren. I knew you and Michael were struggling to have a baby. No one knows if Lynn can have a baby after the cancer. And even if she could, I'm not sure she'll ever marry or settle down that way. Erica told me that child was my granddaughter. So I wondered. It *is* possible. I wanted to help. Erica did say a few times that she might have to leave town with the child, pick up and move for a different job to help afford things. Maybe she took advantage of my vulnerable state, but I didn't mind. And I didn't want her to leave without my knowing the truth about Felicity. I was helping a child. There are worse things to do."

"And that was the end of it?" Angela asked. "You gave her some money for medical bills, and that was it?"

"Not exactly." She sniffled. "I told Erica that I couldn't go on doing any of it, the money, any of it, unless I knew for sure if Felicity was my grandchild. And there was only one way to know for sure."

"A paternity test," Jake said.

"Right."

"And what did you find out?" Angela asked, dreading the answer but needing to ask. "When she had the test?"

Gail shook her head. "She never agreed to one. That's when I stopped hearing from Erica."

chapter forty-nine

2:40 A.M.

Michael wasn't sure what to expect in a young girl's bedroom. He tried to remember what his sisters' rooms looked like when they were growing up. Lynn had never quite seemed like a typical kid. She had expressed an interest in music and dance as long as Michael had been aware of anything, and the only things he clearly remembered from her room were the guitars and music equipment, a pair of ballet slippers, and, at some point, posters of Bob Dylan, Lou Reed, and Kurt Cobain, her musical idols, staring down on her as she slept.

Robyn's room . . . had never changed. They lived in the house for three years after she died, and her parents had refused to touch or change a thing to do with their deceased daughter. Michael remembered that the room had been painted yellow, with matching bedclothes, but the door remained closed after her death. Michael and Lynn had talked about going in there from time to time, but neither one of them ever summoned the courage. To do so would have felt like a violation, like sneaking into a church or a museum when it was closed. He and Lynn had kept their thoughts and curiosity to themselves.

But Michael had seen his mother emerge from the room on a weekday afternoon about a year after Robyn died. He'd stayed home from school with a stomach bug and was supposed to be sleeping. But he'd felt better and wanted to sneak downstairs to watch TV in the basement. He'd stepped out of his room at the same time his mother emerged from Robyn's, her hand held to her face. He knew she'd been crying. She'd walked down the hall in the opposite direction of Michael and never saw him, but Michael stepped back into his room, feeling once again the full weight of his sister's death. He'd known then that his parents would never get over the loss of their child, that they'd carry it with them from place to place like a family heirloom, something that simply could not be disposed of. He couldn't remember what had happened to the things in Robyn's room when they moved to their new house—the house his mother still lived in—three years later. Someone had packed the things and sent them away or stored them. And the new house, of course, had had rooms for him and Lynn but not Robyn.

When he entered Felicity's room, Erica had already flipped the overhead light on and was sitting on the edge of the twin bed, her hands limp at her sides. She seemed to be staring at the floor. At nothing. Soon enough,

Trixie reappeared, sniffing the floor and the desk as though she had lost something as well. Erica didn't move her head or track the dog at all. Her posture was slack, drained of energy.

One wall was painted lavender, with a bedspread and curtains to match. A neat row of books lined the top of a small desk, and in the corner near the closet, two pairs of shoes and a pair of orange flip-flops sat bunched together. In another corner sat a ukulele, evidence of Felicity's interest in music. Everything in the room clutched at Michael's heart. By all rights, Felicity should have been sleeping in that bed at that very moment. And he should have been home with his family, miles and miles away.

"She keeps it clean," he said.

"I make her. I try to, anyway." Her voice sounded hollow.

"Are you okay?" Michael asked. "It's been a long day."

"I'm tired. But I'm hanging in. I want another cigarette, but I'm going to hold off. Plus, I'm too tired to walk outside and light up."

"What did the police do in here?" he asked.

"They went through the drawers, the closet." She lifted her hand off the mattress an inch or so, a feeble effort at pointing. "They were neat about it. They went through all the drawers and closets and everything in the house. They said they might have to come back at some point. I don't think they found anything relevant."

The dog continued to nose around. She came up to Michael and sniffed his shoes again.

"Do you think we ought to do something else?" he

asked. He still held the bag of peas and lifted it to his face, gingerly placing it against the skin. It felt good, if only because the night was so hot. "Time is passing quickly."

For a moment, Erica continued to stare straight ahead, almost as if she didn't hear. Michael was about to repeat himself when she spoke. Her voice still sounded hollow, even fainter.

"Can I ask you something? Do you think if you'd known about Felicity back then, if you'd known I was pregnant or that I'd had her, would we be together now?"

"Erica, I don't think—"

"Answer the question. Would we be together? Would we be living in a house somewhere with Felicity? And maybe another kid?"

"Is this productive?"

"Just answer. It's okay."

"If I had already met Angela, then no," Michael said. "If I hadn't . . . then I guess I don't know. I don't know what power a child would have to keep a marriage together."

"Okay. That was honest."

"Erica, I don't know why we'd want to reopen something from the past like this."

"Maybe it's not in the past for me," she said. "I see . . . *saw* Felicity every day."

"You didn't tell me about her," he said. "You didn't have to raise her without my help. You cheated me out of that time with her."

She still looked at the floor, her eyes not directed at

Michael as she spoke. "I wanted to punish you by not telling. But I also wanted to prove something. To you, I guess, even though you didn't know. To everyone really."

"Prove what?" he asked.

"That I could do it. See, there was always this thing with us. There was always the notion that you were the grown-up, you were the reliable one. You came from money and you had a career waiting for you out in the real world and nothing ever bothered you. And I was emotional and difficult and flighty. I couldn't pay my tuition bill on time or find my car keys or even remember to fill up with gas before a road trip. That was the dynamic between us, wasn't it? Always?"

Michael knew their friends had seen them that way. Opposites on the surface. Michael the grounded one, Erica something of a child. He'd frequently grown frustrated with those qualities of hers when they were together. He'd lost his patience, insisted she try harder to keep her life in order. As Michael looked back on it—on his whole life really—he'd done only two truly impulsive and crazy things in his life. The first was marrying Erica. The second was getting into the car with her earlier that night. Leaving Erica and divorcing her made complete sense. Their time together as husband and wife brought all the problems into sharper relief, and Michael came to understand he wasn't that guy, the kind who just up and married his college girlfriend because they'd been together awhile and because he thought it would make his life more interesting. If Erica didn't want to be defined by who she was in college, then Michael didn't want to be defined by that one rash decision. He stepped away from it when he could.

"Do you think things were so intense between us back then because we were so young?" Erica asked. "Do you still feel the same intensity for things? We were so honest, so open, so . . . raw, I guess." She stared straight ahead, as if seeing the past. "I remember when you told me about Robyn. How emotional you were, how real. How vulnerable."

"Let's not get into that." He saw the images that were always there. The clear summer sky, the swing set. Robyn's body bent and crumpled on the ground. The football resting in the grass twenty feet away . . .

"So you don't feel things the same way?" she asked.

"Maybe not with that intensity," he said. "But I feel things deeper now. It's different."

Erica let out a small, quiet laugh. "You mean your marriage to Angela, right?"

"That's one thing."

"Well, I knew you then, and she didn't. I'll always have that picture of who you were in college. She won't."

"It's not a contest, Erica. Time moves on."

"Can I tell you something else?" Erica asked. She yawned, not even bothering to lift her hand to her mouth to stifle it. Or maybe she lacked the energy to.

"Sure."

"I wouldn't tell anybody else this because they wouldn't understand. They'd think I'm sick in the head or a bad person for it."

"Okay," he said.

She didn't speak right away. Her body listed slightly to the right, toward the mattress. Michael took a step forward, thinking she was about to collapse onto the bed, but she held herself up.

"I used to think about moving away, about finding a better job somewhere else, starting over in a new place. But I never brought myself to do it because I always wanted you to come here, to see my life. To see the house and the yard and the dog. And Felicity. To see that I've done it. I've made it work." She slowly turned her body toward him, looking at him for the first time since they'd entered Felicity's bedroom. Her face looked pale, drained. She looked like someone fighting through a disease. "I want Felicity back. More than anything."

"But?"

She yawned again, and as she spoke, her body leaned back, heading for the mattress.

"But there's the tiniest part of me that's glad this happened so that you finally came here and saw the life I've made for myself. I've wanted that for a long time."

She fell back against the pillow, the mattress squeaking as she did, her eyes closed, asleep.

chapter fifty

2:45 A.M.

Griffin leaned toward Randi Friedman, listening more carefully than ever. She felt like a character in a sitcom hearing a juicy secret in an exaggerated fashion.

Twitchell waited patiently, his face a mask of calm benevolence. He acted like he didn't have a care in the world, even though Randi Friedman's ex-husband was holed up in a house across town surrounded by police officers. No one knew what he had in mind, whether he intended to hurt himself or anyone else.

"What else is there to the story?" Twitchell asked.

"Todd and I never had kids, like I said. We were older when we met, and we both worked. It just didn't fit our life." Her eyes opened wide in relief. "Can you imagine if we had had a kid? Sheesh." She looked at Griffin as if needing her confirmation.

"Right," Griffin said, still leaning forward.

"I knew Erica was struggling," Randi said. "Not financially, really, because her job paid pretty well. It was everything else. Being a single mom and trying to take care of a house. Dealing with child-care issues and still attempting to have a little bit of a social life for herself. You can imagine how hard all of that would be."

"Of course," Twitchell said.

"One evening, Todd and Erica went out for a drink together. They'd invited me, but I had work to do and didn't really feel like going." She looked at the two officers with intensity. "There was nothing going on like that between them. We were all friends. I didn't worry about that. They were able to go out for a quick drink because Felicity had a music lesson or something. Erica just wanted some adult conversation for an hour or so. I guess Todd was the best she could do."

"So what did they talk about?" Twitchell asked.

"Todd told me Erica vented. About all the things I just mentioned. And she expressed her concern that she wasn't going to be able to keep up with the demands of being a single mom, that she was going to end up failing. And failing Felicity. She wished she had someone to help her raise Felicity, that she thought it was so much better if two people were involved to some extent. But she didn't want to get back together with Jake, her exboyfriend. She didn't love him. She wanted it all, you know? Like all of us, right?"

"Did she ever say who Felicity's father was?" Griffin asked.

"She told me a couple of times it was her ex-husband. What was his name? Michael. She said he didn't have anything to do with her. When I suggested she go to court over it, she refused. The subject never really came up again."

"Did she ever say she wanted to get back together with Michael?" Griffin asked.

"No, she never said that to me."

"Did she ever suggest she wanted to harm him?"

"No," Randi said. "Never that. She didn't really act hung up on him." Randi snapped her fingers in the air as though something had just occurred to her. "She did post a wedding picture of them on Facebook one day. I thought that was weird."

"Did you ask her about it?" Griffin asked.

"I did. She said she had a moment of weakness, that she was feeling nostalgic for being young. I guess they married right out of college. That's all she said about it."

"Getting back to this conversation Erica had with your ex-husband," Twitchell said. "What did she say next?"

"Well, it's weird," Randi said. "Basically, she kind of offered Felicity to Todd. To us, I guess."

The room grew quiet. Twitchell shifted his weight, and the couch cushions rustled against one another. The music played in the hallway, far in the background.

"How do you mean that?" Griffin asked. "'Offered' her to you?"

"It wasn't a sexual thing," Randi said. "Not a dirty

thing. Erica couldn't have known about Todd's past. No one here did. She meant it for both of us. For us to take Felicity and keep her for a while, to give Erica a break from being a single mom." Randi shook her head as though trying to wipe the thought and the memory out of her brain. "It sounds a little crazy, I know. Todd thought it was weird. He thought she might be joking, but he said Erica was truly distraught, on the verge of tears as she talked about it."

"What did he say or do?" Griffin asked.

"He talked to her more, and she calmed down. He even said that Felicity could stay with us some night if she ever needed a babysitter. Todd's an oddball, but he can be sensitive with other people when he needs to be. And he and Erica were friends, so he listened to her." She shook her head again but with less force. "I made the same offer to Erica the next time I saw her. See, I knew her mother had died, and I guess the mom watched Felicity a lot when Erica worked or had to do other things. I think her mom's death hit her hard on several fronts. The emotional, of course, but also the practical."

"You mean she didn't have the help and support she was used to?" Griffin asked.

"Exactly. But when I talked to her about all of this, Erica said she was feeling better, that she was having a bad night when she talked to Todd. She said she'd managed to get some help from Felicity's grandmother. To help with child care and doctors' bills and things. Felicity had some health problems, something with her stomach. Or maybe her pancreas. Not long after that, I stopped working at the credit union, and I lost touch with Erica. We weren't the greatest of friends to begin with."

"Did you tell anyone about Erica's state of mind when it came up?" Griffin asked.

"You mean like child protective services or something? No, I didn't. It seemed odd . . . but not so odd that I'd report it. Like I said, she seemed to be doing better after that."

"But you called us today . . . because why?" Twitchell asked.

"I saw that Felicity disappeared. And there seemed to be some suspicion falling on Erica. No one saw Felicity in the park? No one's sure where Erica is? Right?"

She looked at both of the cops, but neither one offered an answer.

Randi went on. "I just thought of Todd. Maybe he did have something to do with it. Maybe things had gotten worse for Erica, and Todd did something about it. Maybe that's why no one saw the girl in the park. And now he's acting crazy, not coming out of the house. He seems to be up to something."

Twitchell stood up. He pointed at Randi. "Do you think he'll listen to you? Are you on good terms with him?"

"Not really. We're divorced."

"It's worth a try," he said. "Grab whatever you need. We're going over there."

chapter fifty-one

2:47 A.M.

Angela smacked her hand against the top of the table. She felt like an overly dramatic judge getting ready to make a grand pronouncement in a courtroom.

"That proves it," Angela said. "The kid isn't Michael's. If she was, Erica would submit to the paternity test. It wouldn't take long. I'm guessing you offered to pay for it?"

Gail nodded. "I would have. Sure. I even called a company that does them. It's just a cheek swab, and you mail it in. You don't have to compare the sample to the father. It's more accurate that way, but you can compare it to another relative. A parent. Or a sibling of the father."

Angela looked at Jake as though he were her jury. "See? The kid isn't his. Why else refuse the test?"

Jake spread his arms wide. "I'm on your side in this. I

don't think the kid is your husband's, but she does. Or maybe she's trying to convince herself he's the father. I suspected she'd be coming here because he has money and is connected, and we all know those things make the world go round." Jake shrugged. He looked helpless for a moment. "Maybe she thought they'd get closer again. Maybe she thought coming here and looking for Felicity would bring them back together."

"You don't really believe that, do you?" Angela asked.

"I'm not really sure what Erica has been thinking lately," he said. "Maybe she never got over your husband entirely. She talked about him sometimes when we were together. I figured first love and all that, but maybe it was more."

"That's bizarre." Angela felt a flush rising on her face, and she bit against the inside of her cheek to try to keep her temper in check. "Wait. I heard on the news that no one actually saw Felicity in the park this morning when she was supposed to have disappeared. Are you saying Erica might . . . ?"

"I'm not going that far," Jake said. But he didn't sound fully convinced.

Angela felt sick. She slumped against the back of the chair with a thud. For a moment, she ignored the two people sitting at the table with her—her mother-in-law and a complete stranger. Had Erica done something to her own child as a ploy to get Michael back? Was she married to someone who was possibly in the process of being victimized by a crazy person?

She looked at Gail. "Is that really the last you heard from her? When you asked for the paternity test?"

"That was it," Gail said. "I even called her back a couple of times to see if maybe she had changed her mind, but she never answered or returned my calls." Gail leaned forward. She reached out with her hand and placed it on top of Angela's, giving it a little squeeze. "I thought maybe she really had left town with her child. For good."

Despite the puzzlement she currently felt with respect to her mother-in-law, who had managed to keep all of this a secret from all of them, the touch felt good. Reassuring. Angela's parents lived in Florida, and she saw them infrequently. Gail was the closest thing she had to a mother on a day-to-day basis.

"But you did more than that," Jake said.

Angela looked at him and then over at Gail. Her mother-in-law seemed resigned, unable to hold anything else back.

"Okay," she said, "I did do more than talk on the phone with her and send money. Do you think I was just going to write checks?"

"So what did you do?" Angela asked. Then she understood. "You *saw* the kid?"

Gail nodded. "A couple of times. I told Erica she could have the money if I met the girl. Once we met in a park up there. I don't remember the name of it. Maybe it's the one she disappeared from—I don't know. Another time we went to lunch. This was about six months ago, and I again insisted on the test. Things grew heated, so we parted on somewhat unpleasant terms."

"And?" Angela asked. She wasn't sure she wanted to know, but she asked anyway. "What's the kid like?"

Gail nodded. "She's a sweet girl. Darling, really. A little shy, I guess, but then, I was a complete stranger she had no context for. And, yes, she bore a resemblance to my girls when they were that age. I felt that, like a piece of glass in my heart."

"You wanted a kid to make up for your dead child," Jake said. "Erica knew all about that."

Gail looked around the room, her eyes seemingly in search of something else to focus on. Emotion seemed to have gotten ahold of her for a moment, but then she turned back and looked at Angela. "I would have liked to spend more time with Felicity. And I know maybe I played into Erica's hands. Once you see the kid, it's harder to deny her something. That makes sense, doesn't it?"

"It does," Angela said.

"Understand where I was coming from. The possibility existed that this girl was my granddaughter. And Michael's daughter. If it was true, I wanted to know. But I wasn't going to drag you and Michael into something when I didn't have all the facts. That would be like rolling a hand grenade into your marriage, especially when you were struggling to have a child of your own. Angela, did you need to hear that Michael's ex-wife was saying she was raising Michael's child? What if it wasn't true, and I caused all that uproar in your lives for nothing? Should I have done that?" She squeezed Angela's hand again. "I believe you're right when you say Erica told us all we need to know when she didn't get back in touch with me. Felicity likely isn't Michael's child. Erica wanted my financial help for a while, and she got it. That was that. Maybe she took advantage of me because of James's death. Maybe she took advantage of my desire to finally have a grandchild. I get it."

"And Michael didn't know?" Angela asked.

"He didn't know. Not from me, anyway. If Erica told him anything . . . well, he would have told you if he'd heard from her."

Angela bit the inside of her cheek again. The changed passwords, the lack of access to his Facebook page. How on earth did she or anyone else know whether Michael had been in touch with Erica?

And then she looked over at Jake.

"Wait a minute," she said. "Did Erica tell Michael any of this? Do *you* know if they've been in touch?"

The corner of Jake's mouth rose a little, and he shook his head. "You think she's going to tell me? We've been on the outs for quite a while."

"So you don't know?" Angela asked.

"I don't know. I don't think she was talking to him when we first dated, back when Felicity was little. She was pissed at him for leaving, raising Felicity on her own and moving up in her job as a way to prove she was an adult. We broke up when Felicity was about four, and I moved away for a while, got involved with someone else."

"And you never got a paternity test when Felicity was little?" Angela asked. "You said you were like a father to her. You could have had the test and known for sure."

Jake was shaking his head before Angela finished speaking. He reached up, ran his hand through his thick hair. "I wasn't thinking that way. I *was* her father then.

That was it. To be honest, maybe I didn't want the bubble burst by learning differently."

"What did Erica tell you about it?"

"She was vague. But she told some friends Michael was her father. I know that."

"You got involved with a woman with a baby," Angela said. "Not many men would do that."

"I loved her. And I loved Felicity too. I wanted a family, always did. We don't get to choose the things that happen to us."

"Erica sure managed to track Michael down tonight when she needed to," Angela said. "She knew some things about him."

"It's not hard to find people," Jake said. "I found you."

Angela understood that. She'd been able to track Erica down when she wanted to. But she also wondered how much Erica knew about their lives. Had she been watching them? Following them? Was anything they'd done private?

"Who do *you* think Felicity's father is?" Angela asked Jake. "You know Erica. You must know some of the people she knows. Or you at least know stuff about her life. Who do you think it is?"

Angela should have seen the answer coming as soon as she asked the question. Before, even. As Jake opened his mouth, she knew what he was going to say.

Jake pointed to his own chest. "Hell, it's me."

"So you're really not looking for Erica so much as—"

"I want to know what happened to *my* daughter," he said. He sounded more thoughtful, a little wistful and even sad. "I know Felicity. When Erica and I were together, I spent time with the girl. Even a little after we broke up the second time. I'm the closest thing she's ever had to a dad, and I know it goes deeper than that. I *am* her dad. I know the truth." He tapped his chest. "In here."

Angela rolled all of it around in her head. The more she learned, the more questions she had. "So you and Erica met and got together right after she and Michael split up? When she was newly pregnant?"

Jake took a long time answering the question. "Not exactly," he finally said. "She and I, Erica, we started things while she was still married to your husband. Now, I'm not proud of that, but their marriage was on the downward slide. That's what Erica told me. And they did split up soon after."

Angela felt . . . what, exactly, on Michael's behalf? Anger? Betrayal?

Did it even make sense for her to feel a protective anger over something that had happened to her husband before she knew him?

Yes, she decided. It did.

Somewhere in the past Erica had betrayed Michael. And she'd shown up on their doorstep that night, furthering that betrayal in some way. Either by lying to him about being Felicity's father or by lying to him about the child even being missing at all.

She'd grown tired of sitting and doing nothing, so she pushed herself up from the table.

"What are you doing now?" Gail asked.

Jake looked up at her. "Yeah, what's going on?"

Angela hesitated, then said, "I have somewhere to go. Something to do."

Jake stood up as well. He was about three inches taller than she was and a little broader. His shoulders seemed to fill the space. "You're going to look for your husband, right?" he said. "That's the only thing that makes sense." He pointed at Gail. "She's here to watch the house in case your husband shows up again."

Angela felt boxed in. Trapped. She didn't want this man in her house anymore. She wanted him gone, and she wanted to be on the road herself the way she'd planned.

"You said you were looking for Erica," Angela said. "Well, she's not here, as you can see. So—"

"Where did they say they were going?" Jake asked.

"I'm not sure."

"Where?" He took a step forward.

Angela looked at Gail, who watched her expectantly. The air-conditioning came on with a soft whoosh, blowing cold air on the back of Angela's neck from the vent above. But the hairs there were already on end, the follicles jangling with nervous energy. "They said they were going to talk to someone who might know something about the case. Erica told Michael there was a guy, a teacher at Felicity's school, who might know something."

Jake was nodding, his gestures acquiring the frantic nature they'd had on the porch. "Yes, yes. I know who she's talking about. And where he lives."

"How do you know that?" Gail asked.

"I told you I've stayed in touch with Erica somewhat.

I see Felicity and talk to her when I can. I know who this music teacher is. She loves music. He's been teaching her for more than a year."

"Then you can tell me where he lives."

"We can go together," he said. "We *will* go together. I know the places Erica likes to go and might want to look. I know where her house is. *You* know how to track down your husband, to stay in touch with him. It's the only choice."

"I don't think—"

"Look," Jake said, leaning a little closer, his voice growing louder. "You want me to leave. I know. You don't want me in the house at all. That's fine. I'll go. But I'm not going alone. I've been getting jerked around here all day—by the cops, who wanted to come after me, and now you two. I think I'm the only one who really cares about this kid. That's my agenda. I'm not getting any younger, and I don't have any other kids." He looked around the room, appraising it. "So you're going with me, and we'll find them. Or Felicity. And then I won't ever have to come back."

Angela's mouth went dry. She'd wandered far out on the ledge and worried she wouldn't be able to come back in without falling. But she knew her primary concern, her most important goal. Find Michael and bring him home. Safe.

Angela tried to work up saliva in her mouth, then swallowed. She wondered how on earth her day had gone so sideways. "Okay, okay," she said. "Follow me. My car's in the driveway."

"Follow you?" Jake's face looked incredulous. "Didn't you hear what I just said? I'm tired of being jerked around. Erica's carelessness, the cops, all of this." He pointed to his own chest again. "I'm driving. My car. With you in it." He turned and looked at Gail. "Maybe you should go too. That way no one can call the police after I go."

"That's not necessary," Angela said. "Leave her out of it."

"I'll go with him," Gail said. "You stay here in case Michael comes back."

"No," Angela said. She felt protective toward her mother-in-law and didn't want to put her in a situation where she might be in danger. "You stay. If Michael comes back or the police or anything, you can handle it."

"But—"

"It's okay, Gail. I'll be back."

Angela spoke with confidence she really didn't feel. She wasn't certain what she was stepping into by agreeing to get into a car with Jake Little, but she had to do something. And if she could go and find Michael and keep Gail out of any harm, then she intended to do it. Jake's nervousness made Angela uneasy. It meant he wasn't sure of himself, which could make him either more dangerous or else more malleable. Or both.

She hoped the malleable side of him won out.

"It's okay," Angela said. She looked over at Jake, who stared back, his face expectant. "We're going to go together. And we'll find them. You just stay here."

"I don't—"

“It’s okay, Gail. I’ve got it.” She pointed toward the front of the house and the door. “You ready?”

Jake stepped back and let Angela walk ahead of him. But before they left the dining room, he turned and looked at Gail. “I’m leaving your phone here, and you’re not going to call the police,” he said. “Because I’ll be taking real good care of her.”

chapter fifty-two

2:57 A.M.

Michael found a blanket at the foot of Felicity's bed and unfurled it, using it to cover Erica's soundly sleeping body. He tucked the blanket around her, his mind going back to days in college when she would fall asleep in his dorm or apartment. Very little disturbed her sleep, and in the first days they dated, when he was young and lovestruck like a fool, he'd watch her sleep for a few moments at night, enjoying the peaceful look on her face, the gentle rhythms of her breathing.

A sliver of those feelings lived inside him somewhere. Maybe they always would. It didn't seem possible to feel absolutely nothing for someone he'd once been so close to, as though every positive memory and emotion had been wiped away from his brain. But he also knew nothing of great importance remained. His life, his world, resided in the house in Cottonsville, and just thinking of home told him he needed to check in there.

He left Felicity's room and walked back out to the kitchen. The dog, Trixie, seemed to have taken a liking to Michael, and she followed along, her nose pressed against his pant leg, her tongue lolling out the side of her mouth, and her tail wagging whenever he looked down. He stopped and extended his hand again, scratching the dog behind the ears.

"I have to make a phone call," he said, straightening up.

The dog's ears perked up, her face inquisitive. *Is she asking me who I'm calling?*

Then another, more pressing question entered Michael's mind. How exactly would he explain his presence in Erica's house to Angela? When he'd left the house—hours earlier now—he'd told his wife it would be a quick trip up and a quick trip back. It certainly hadn't worked out that way, and why should it have? What ever worked out exactly the way it was planned?

But he knew he needed to check in with Angela, to let her know he was safe and out of harm's way. That he hadn't stopped thinking about her even though he was off with Erica. When he'd last talked to her, standing on the side of the road with Wayne Tolliver still in the car, she'd brought up the police looking through his computer, which also meant she could have seen search histories and, yes, even photos.

But then he remembered: *No, that's not the last time I talked to her. . . .*

He'd talked to her on the road, after the car went through the fence, after Tolliver ran away. Michael's memory of the conversation was tattered and ragged, like fragments of a dream.

"Shit," he said to himself. "I must have sounded like a nut."

He patted his pockets. No phone.

He looked around the room. He saw Erica's purse on the floor, right where she'd dropped it as she came into the house. He dug around in the purse, feeling like a creep or a thief, but he found his phone.

Why didn't she give it back right away?

He pushed his suspicions aside and dialed, listening to the phone ring while Trixie moved around the kitchen, her nails clacking against the tiles and her tail still wagging.

The phone rang and rang and then went to voice mail.

Why?

He thought Angela would have been on high alert to answer his calls, even if she had fallen asleep.

He called again, and the same thing happened. Ringing and ringing and then voice mail. He couldn't leave a message. What was he supposed to say? *Hey, I'm at my ex-wife's. She's asleep in one bed, and I'm standing here with the dog. . . .*

He hung up. When he looked around, Trixie was just disappearing out of sight, trotting down the hallway toward the bedrooms. Michael worried she'd go in and jump on Erica, waking her up, so he followed behind, trying to steer the dog in another direction. But she went past Felicity's room and to the end of the hallway and made a left turn at the end, presumably into another bedroom. Michael stopped for a moment to look into Felicity's room, where Erica continued to sleep in the exact same position in which he had left her.

He went on to the end of the hallway, looking for Trixie.

When he turned into the bedroom, he saw Trixie standing on the king bed, her ears up, her snout pointed at the window.

"What is it?" Michael asked. As soon as he spoke, the dog relaxed her pose and turned around, wagging her tail again. "Are you supposed to be on the bed like that?"

As if she understood him, Trixie jumped down and ran past him, leaving the bedroom and going back up the hallway. Michael decided to let her do whatever she wanted. Maybe the amount of time she'd spent alone as well as Felicity's absence and the chaos of cops and reporters coming through the house had left her agitated. After all, he was a stranger, and he was wandering around the house while Erica slept.

He looked around the room. The bed was made, the closet door closed. It looked as neat as the rest of the house, sparsely decorated and furnished. In fact . . . He walked across the room toward the dresser.

"Holy crap," he said.

It was the furniture they'd had in their bedroom when they were married. The set had belonged to Erica's grandmother who had died shortly before their wedding. When they lived in the apartment on the east side of Trudeau, they'd used this set—dresser, bureau, bed. It still looked to be in good shape, and Michael ran his hand across the smooth top of the dresser. The feel, the look of the furniture, took him back. He remembered that first autumn, shortly after they were married, when the weather was warm and the leaves fell. For a time, he'd thought it was going to work, that they'd be together for the long haul—house, kids. Life. Michael had approached the marriage with a certain defiance. He'd wanted to prove to everyone, including his family, that he'd made the right choice, that he and Erica were embarking on a mature, lifelong journey together.

But he hadn't been able to sustain the feeling. They simply weren't a match. And soon enough, the marriage had felt like walking through sludgy, heavy water. Every day had become an effort. Michael wished none of it had ever happened.

But if Felicity was really his child, then hadn't something good come out of it all? Finally?

If she was alive . . .

From another part of the house, Michael heard Trixie barking, low, sharp sounds. He again worried that she was going to wake Erica up.

But before he turned to leave the room and go shush her, he saw a framed photo lying flat at the far end of the dresser. He recognized the frame just as he had recognized the furniture. It had been a wedding gift from his aunt, and it had sat on a shelf in the apartment in east Trudeau the entire year they were married.

He went over and picked it up. He saw himself arm in arm with Erica on their wedding day. He wore a black suit and white shirt. She wore a traditional gown. They looked happy. And young. It was the same photo she'd shared on Facebook around the time of the tenth anniversary of their divorce, the one he'd copied and kept in a folder on his desktop.

Why did she still have it out in her room after all that time? Did Felicity see it every day and ask who he was? Did Erica hide it if she brought men home and back to her room?

He picked it up. The glass was clear, dust free.

If he wondered about Erica, then he needed to wonder about himself. Why had he copied the photo from Facebook and saved it to his computer? Michael wished he could say. Curiosity first and foremost, the basic question of how his life might have been different if he'd never left Erica. Would he be happier now? No. He shook his head, standing in Erica's bedroom. No.

But would he be happy at all?

He couldn't say with certainty. And if Felicity—and maybe another child—entered the equation, then that life with Erica looked very different. The game of thinking about that alternate life simultaneously fascinated and terrified Michael.

When he'd seen the wedding photo on Facebook and saved it, he knew nothing about Felicity. But his mind still played the "What If" game from time to time by taking a peek down the road not traveled. Years removed from being with Erica, it became easy, at times, to remember their relationship as calmer and smoother than it had really been, to focus on the highs and not the lows. Like just about any married person, he could fall into the trap of focusing on the difficulties he and Angela had experienced, and that photo looked like a window into another world, one free of life's more mundane responsibilities and problems.

But he always came out of it quickly, always emerged into the clear air of his real existence, knowing he belonged with Angela.

He jumped when his phone rang. It felt like perfect timing, and he assumed it was Angela. He was surprised to see his sister's name on the caller ID screen.

"Lynn? What's up?"

"I'm checking in on you," she said.

"On me?" Michael looked at his watch. He held the phone in one hand, the wedding picture in the other. "It's three in the morning. Are you in California or something?"

"I'm not at home," she said. "And I know you aren't either."

"Oh, Lynn, it's a long story." He started to tell her, but she cut him off.

"I know all about it," she said. "Angela called me. I just now got a chance to call you back."

Michael felt his face flush. His *wife* had called his *sister* because she was worried about him? Who would be calling him next? His mother?

"Lynn, I'm fine. I don't need—"

"Just go home, Michael." Her voice sounded strained. "Let this go and head home."

"Lynn, you don't know anything about it. I don't need a lecture from you. This girl could be my child."

She sighed. "I know, Michael. I get that. But . . . you're away from your wife in the middle of the night. With your ex-wife."

"Did Angela say all of this? Did she complain about me to you?"

"No, Michael, she didn't do that." Lynn spoke with the affectionate disdain that only one sibling could have for another. "She knows it's complicated with kids for you and me. Because of Robyn. You're not thinking with your head here. I know better than anyone how sore that wound is. I know it's never healed. Remember, I'm the one who's supposed to be the oddball in the family."

Trixie made a low grumbling sound from the other room.

"God, Lynn, it's awfully late for this. We're not in high school anymore. We don't have time for one of our late-night philosophical chats. And we don't have time for the whole 'Dad doesn't respect me because I'm an artist' thing either."

"Okay, but we all know you and Angela are trying to have a baby. And struggling . . ."

"So much for privacy. My sister knows about my reproductive life."

"And I know you've talked with Erica about Robyn. You told me when you were first dating that you shared everything about Robyn with her. I remember that much, okay?" Lynn made a low murmuring sound that came through the line. "Don't make me talk about this more. You know I can't. . . . I just can't. . . . Okay? Just . . .

stop." She sounded like she was sniffling. Allergies? Or crying?

"Lynn?"

"I look at that damn picture," she said. "The one Dad took of the three of us at the lake. I know you have it up in your office. That was my birthday, July seventh. About two weeks before Robbie died."

"I know." He spoke low, consoling.

"Every year I have to put my copy of the picture away. I hide it in a closet. I can't look at it when the anniversary is coming up because I always think stupid shit like why hasn't anyone invented a time machine so we could go back. We both have money to buy anything we want, but we can't go back in time, can we? We can't undo the one thing we'd undo."

"Lynn, I'm sorry this is upsetting you."

College had been Michael's first time away from home, the first chance to really talk about his family members with someone who didn't know them, someone outside the cramped confines of Cottonsville. Erica happened to be that person he shared with back then. He took a quick glance at the photo again.

"Lynnie, this is about so much more than Robyn, okay? Don't reduce it to that. You're right, of course. We both have a blind spot for her. We were both there that day. And I know how much it hurts. It's like . . . an ice pick in my heart."

Trixie's barking became steady, incessant.

"Just go home, Michael. The problem can be solved

without you. Okay? Something will work out. The police, the reporters, all of it. Let it be their problem and not yours. For now, let it go."

Then Trixie's barking grew even louder.

Was someone at the door?

Could it even be . . . ?

Felicity? Returning . . .

"I have to go, Lynn. Not home, but something's happening here."

"Michael—"

He tossed the photo aside and ran to the front of the house.

chapter fifty-three

3:08 A.M.

They pulled up in front of Todd Friedman's house. Griffin counted five squad cars and two news vans. Even so late at night, the media had dispatched a couple of reporters to cover whatever Todd Friedman was up to. She felt cynical, angry. When she saw them, she thought the worst. They were only there in case Todd Friedman tried something really crazy. They wanted to see some kind of carnage they could play on the news, a viral clip to draw just a little more attention to their own station and reporters.

They remained in the car for a moment. Twitchell shifted his bulky body around, looking over his glasses at Randi Friedman, who remained hidden in the dark, her posture hunched and withdrawn like a small child's.

"I want to tell you what we're going to do out there,

Mrs. Friedman," he said. "We're going to find the officer in charge. That would be our colleague Detective Phillips."

Griffin felt a more acute spasm of anger when she heard his name. She caught herself feeling it and forced herself to wonder why. Did she really know Phillips had done anything wrong a decade ago when Stacey Flowers disappeared? She kind of didn't care. She just wanted to feel pissed at someone. The sound of Twitchell's voice, calm and placid, grated on her.

He went on. "When we do that, we're going to see what he needs you to do, but if we can, our hope is that you'll be able to talk to Todd and see what's going on with him. You said on the way over that your ex-husband has never been suicidal."

"No, he hasn't."

Her voice was small, emerging from the dark backseat.

"Okay, good. So maybe he's just scared and needs someone to tell him it's okay to come out of the house. Do you think you can try to do that?"

Griffin saw a faint movement in the dark. Randi nodding.

"You ready?" Twitchell asked.

He didn't wait for a response, but turned his body around and went out through the driver's-side door. Griffin pushed her door open as well, and she noted that Randi Friedman came out on her side and waited with her hands folded in front of her body, as though she expected Griffin to lead her around.

"We can head this way," Twitchell said across the car.

A light rain had started to fall, but nothing like the storm they'd been expecting. It wasn't even enough to warrant the use of an umbrella or a rain hat. The thunder rumbles and lightning flashes on the horizon seemed to have slowed as well, but the humidity grew, a thick cloak that stuck to her body.

Griffin walked behind the two of them as they approached the cluster of plainclothes officers gathered around a car. Behind them, across a small lawn, sat Todd Friedman's house, a modest brick structure with white awnings over the front porch and every window. Phillips and Woolf turned as they approached and nodded to the trio.

Twitchell handled introductions and told the other detectives that Randi was ready to talk to her ex-husband if it would help. They explained that they could summon him by telephone, but he'd told them if they stepped one foot on the lawn, he'd either shoot at them or himself.

"Do you know if he has a gun?" Phillips asked Randi.

"He had a rifle. He used to hunt. He talked about buying more, but he didn't when we lived together."

Phillips nodded, his eyes moving to the other detectives. "I'm going to reach him on the phone and tell him you're here. Okay?"

Randi nodded.

While Phillips made the call, Griffin wandered a few steps away from the cluster of detectives. The crickets chirped a rising chorus, and when the light breeze kicked up, pushing the hot air around, the trees rustled. Two uniformed cops stood with their hands on hips, keeping some gawking neighbors from getting any closer to the action. She knew those people were there for the same cynical reasons as the reporters—they wanted to see something garish and grisly. They wanted to have a story to tell at school or church or the beauty parlor. Something no one would be able to forget.

She heard Phillips's voice in the background. He spoke in low, soothing tones, like a man trying to defuse a bomb with words. She sensed someone come up next to her. And she knew who it was before she even looked.

"What?" she asked.

"I only told the boss because I was concerned about you," Twitchell said. His glasses fogged, so he pushed them up on his forehead. "I was trying to help."

"Help what? Make me look pathetic?"

"You shouldn't have gone to see Tiffany Flowers that way. Not alone. Not without clearing it with Phillips or Reddick."

"Somebody had to do something," she said.

Twitchell was silent for a moment, his lack of words filling up the space between them. Then he said, "I guess I missed the part where the two of us were sitting on our hands all day."

"I mean, *keep* doing something. Not just go home and wait."

He was quiet again. Then he said, "You know, Peg and I lost a baby before Ashley was born. Our first child."

Griffin looked over at him. He stood with his thumbs

hooked in his belt loops, his belly bulging out. She didn't say anything. She just waited.

"What I'm saying is . . . I know what it's like. You're not the only one. And maybe you need to look around. A lot of people are hurting. Not just you."

"Look—"

"And a lot of people care about this missing kid. A lot. That's why we're here." He turned to go back to the other detectives. He gave her a light, fatherly smack on the biceps. "If your head's in the game, come back. Okay?"

She heard him walk off, his shoes scuffing against the street. If his goal had been to make her feel foolish, then he'd accomplished his mission. Hell, everybody needed to be humbled sometime. Everybody needed to feel like a fool.

"Okay," she said to herself. "You're here. Help."

She walked back over, following behind Twitchell. When she arrived, she heard Phillips telling Todd Friedman that Randi was ready to come across the lawn and into the house. And no one else would go with her.

But then Randi started shaking her head. She shook it like a dog coming in out of the rain.

"Hold on," Phillips said into the phone. He covered the mouthpiece with the palm of his hand. "What is it, Mrs. Friedman? This is what we brought you here for."

She stopped shaking and said, "I don't want to go alone. I don't."

Twitchell cleared his throat. "Randi, we talked about this. A little girl's life is in danger. And we need to move fast because she's been gone all day. And it's getting late. If your ex-husband knows anything—"

Randi cut him off. "I won't go alone." Her eyes bored in on Griffin. "I won't go unless she goes in there with me."

chapter fifty-four

3:19 A.M.

Trixie stood at the back door, the one Michael and Erica had come in almost an hour earlier. The dog's tail stood straight up, and her posture looked fixed and rigid like an arrow. When Michael came into the room, the dog stopped barking but continued to stare at the door. A ceiling fan spun overhead, and on every revolution, its pull chain clicked against its light globe. Tick . . . tick . . . tick . . .

"What's the problem? Is someone out there?"

Trixie turned her head to look at Michael, her tongue running across her lips with a smacking noise. Then she resumed staring at the door but didn't bark.

The pain in Michael's head had become duller, but his heart squeezed in his chest at twice its normal rate, and he heard the blood rushing in his ears. His body felt cold, shot through with ice.

Was Felicity trying to come in the back door and return home?

He went over, the dog moving out of his way as he approached, her nails clicking against the floor. He undid the lock and pulled on the door. It stuck in the humid night air, but he managed to yank it open, almost falling backward as it came free. He expected—hoped—to see a small blond child standing there, her face expectant as she returned to her home and her mother.

But the back porch was empty.

Michael stepped out, the dog beside him. Light rain fell, almost a mist. He saw his car, the beaded moisture on the roof glistening in the glow from a light above the garage. Michael stepped farther out, looking one way and then the other. The neighborhood was quiet, the houses on either side dark. He thought he heard a car door slam out on the street but couldn't be certain.

"Hello? Hello?"

Trixie stood next to him. He caught a whiff of something sweet in the air. Honeysuckle, he guessed. He looked down to where she started wagging her tail and shifting her weight from one front paw to the other. She no longer seemed agitated, so whatever had grabbed her attention at the back door was gone. The wind? The rain?

He turned to go back in, the dog ahead of him, when something on the ground near the door caught his eye. It looked to be a piece of loose trash at first, but when Michael bent closer to examine it, he saw it was a pink handkerchief, a little crumpled and damp from being out in the rain.

He picked it up. He knew he'd hurried coming into the house, following after Erica, who was rushing inside in a panic, so he couldn't say with certainty that it had been there before.

But wouldn't he have noticed something like that?

Something bright and pink?

He examined it more closely. In one corner of the handkerchief was a stitched monogram, simple and clear in black thread. The letter "F."

Felicity?

Michael took a step toward the side of the house, hoping to look over there. But then he remembered Erica sleeping inside. She could identify it.

He dashed inside the house, the door making a soft whoosh as he closed it behind him. Trixie ran along beside him, her tail swinging as she jumped and barked at his excitement.

"Erica!"

When they passed the foyer at the front of the house, he heard something banging against the outside of the door there. The handkerchief still in his hand, he stopped in his tracks, the dog turning her attention to the unusual sound.

"Felicity?" he said, even though there was no way anyone could hear him through the door. And realizing that the girl—if it was her—wouldn't know him from the man in the moon. She might return home and find a complete stranger opening the door to greet her.

But if she was there, he couldn't let her get away.

He started to undo the lock, the bolt clacking loudly, and heard Erica behind him.

"What is it, Michael?" she asked.

He turned as he fumbled with the second lock. Erica looked sleepy, one side of her face creased from the pillow. She stood with her arms folded across her chest, her shoes off. She sniffled.

"Someone's at the door. I think it's her. I think it's Felicity. Look." He held the handkerchief up. "'F.' It's monogrammed 'F.'" He tossed it in the air between them. "She's here."

He pulled the door open.

He heard Erica say, "That's not—"

And then a body crashed into him, sending him backward and onto the floor, where he landed with such force that the breath went out of him.

chapter fifty-five

3:26 A.M.

Griffin slowed her pace as she crossed the lawn, allowing Randi to keep up with her. The woman seemed determined to walk a couple of steps behind Griffin despite being the person Todd Friedman really wanted to see inside the house. But Randi came along like a kid going into a doctor's office for a shot. Griffin resisted the urge to reach out and take her by the arm, propelling her across the lawn until she stumbled up onto the front porch.

The rain had stopped for the moment, but the grass beneath their feet remained slick and damp. The rich scent of moist earth rose from the ground like a mist. The clouds above were in motion, clearing the sky. The moon, father away and distant, peeked through briefly before being hidden again.

It had taken Phillips fifteen minutes to talk Todd Friedman into allowing Griffin into the house with Randi. She'd had to promise to leave her gun and any other weapon behind, and to keep her distance from Todd and not make any sudden moves.

"You could send me in there in a straitjacket," she'd said.

"You don't need to do this," Twitchell had said.

"Because I'm too emotional?" she'd asked. "Or because I can't separate my personal feelings from my job?"

Twitchell had almost rolled his eyes at her, but he hadn't. And he'd said nothing else until she walked away with Randi.

When they reached the porch steps and started up, the front door swung inward. For a moment, Todd Friedman appeared there, but he quickly jumped back out of sight as though he expected to be smashed by a hail of bullets. Griffin and Randi stopped halfway up the steps, awaiting further instructions from the man, reluctant to make any movements that might spook him more.

He spoke from out of sight, his voice high and frantic. "Did you bring a gun?"

"No, I didn't."

"How do I know?" he asked.

"She didn't, Todd," Randi said. "I've talked to her for a long time tonight. She's a decent cop. I can tell."

Griffin appreciated the kind words. She wasn't sure whether she deserved them. After all, she'd violated protocol by going to talk to Tiffany Flowers alone. And she'd been standoffish and pissy with her partner. Other than that, she'd been on her best behavior.

"We just want to talk to you, Mr. Friedman," Griffin said. "You can let us in, and if you change your mind, just tell us, and we'll leave."

For a moment, a silence stretched out between them all. Griffin didn't look back, but she knew her colleagues stood out at the curb watching, their eyes pressing against her back and pushing her forward. They remained silent, their collective breath held as they hoped for a peaceful resolution to the standoff.

"Okay," Todd said, his body still hidden. "But move slowly. And if I tell you to go—"

"If you tell us to go, we'll go," Griffin said. "We promise."

She nodded to Randi, and the two of them went up the steps the rest of the way and into the house. They entered a darkened living room, which smelled of cigarette smoke and stale beer. Even though she'd been standing outside in the dark, it took some time for Griffin's eyes to adjust. She waited, standing next to Randi just inside the door. She thought she heard the sound of breathing from her right, the direction from which Todd Friedman had disappeared when he opened the door and spoke to them.

She sensed the movement coming before she could react, but Todd appeared out of her peripheral vision and shoved the door. It brushed past Griffin's body, causing her to jump, and then slammed shut, blocking out the ambient noise of the street and the night.

"Just stand right there," Todd said, his voice still high but also raspy.

Griffin remained rooted in place. Beneath the cigarettes and the stale beer, she thought she could smell fear and desperation wafting off Todd Friedman. She refused to give him any reason to become more desperate and afraid.

"We just want to talk, Mr. Friedman," she said.

"Yeah . . . well . . . okay, talk."

Her eyes adjusted to the dark. Griffin made him out, about ten feet away. His hands hung limply at his sides, and she detected no weapons of any kind. At least none in his hands or clearly in view. She felt marginally better. From somewhere in the house, she heard the sound of a TV playing what sounded like a sitcom: low, tinny laughter rising and falling and then a comedic voice groaning, an odd counterpoint to their reason for being there.

"We thought you had something to say to us," Griffin said. "Or maybe there's something you wanted to tell Randi. Is there?"

He looked at his ex-wife, his eyes luminous white circles in the darkness. "She knows everything I have to say."

Randi stood with her arms crossed. "I told them, Todd. I told her. About what Erica said to you. That you could just take Felicity from her."

His eyes grew even wider. Even in the reduced light, Griffin saw the muscles in his jaw clench. He spoke through gritted teeth. "My God, Randi, why would you tell them that? With my record . . . no wonder they're here circling around me like buzzards."

"Mr. Friedman," Griffin said, "I can assure you we all only have one concern. We want to find Felicity as soon as possible, and we want her to be found safe and sound. You know Felicity. From everything I've heard, she's a great kid. No one wants to see a child suffer if we can help it. She's been gone all day and half the night."

Friedman made a choking sound in his throat. Griffin wasn't sure whether he was laughing or afraid. But he made no other response.

"Can I turn a light on?" Griffin asked. When he didn't say anything, she bent down and flipped the switch on a lamp. The yellow glow made them all squint.

Todd took a step back, his body jittery and anxious.

"Do you mind if I take a look around the house, Mr. Friedman?" Griffin asked. "I can just take a quick look in the closets and down in the basement."

"No, you can't," he said. "No."

"Okay," she said. "Did you have anything you wanted to say to Randi? Isn't that why we came in here?"

"I don't want to say it in front of you," he said. "I don't want to say anything in front of you."

"But Randi wanted me here," Griffin said.

"I do, Todd. I wasn't going to come in, except she agreed to come with me. We told you on the phone."

He didn't respond, but his eyes shifted from side to side. And his weight rocked from one foot to the other, causing the floorboards to squeak. He looked like a man planning an escape, a man ready to dart away and run.

But he had nowhere to go. He stood in the confined space of his living room with a host of cops outside of his house.

"Todd?" Griffin said. "We can talk about this all you want. We can work through it. If you tell us what you know right now, we can help Felicity and we can help you. But we need to hear all of it." She cleared her throat and decided to press him a little. "You may not want me to look around now, but I can assure you of something. We are going to look around. Those cops outside—they're going to look around eventually. And soon. So maybe we can do this the easy way?"

His head jerked up like someone had yanked it with a rope. He stared at Griffin, the fear evident in his eyes.

"Okay," he said.

"Okay what?" Griffin asked.

"I want to show you something," he said. "I really want to show Randi, but I guess both of you can come."

chapter fifty-six

3:31 A.M.

Angela could tell they were halfway to Trudeau. For a few miles, they appeared to have left most of the cornfields and vast empty spaces behind. Traffic picked up in both directions, and ahead on the horizon, like a humming glow in the dark night, she saw the lights of Simka, the small town between Cottonsville and Trudeau.

"Are we going to see this Tolliver guy?" Angela asked. "Can you tell me anything else about him? Besides the fact he's a teacher at Felicity's school."

Jake stared straight ahead. Angela couldn't be certain he'd heard her. He looked lost in thought, his mind off in some other place.

"Jake?"

"He's an odd duck," he said finally. "Tolliver." He

guided the car with one hand and gestured with the other. When a vehicle went by the other way with particularly bright lights, he squinted, moving his head slightly to the right. "He does have an unusual interest in Felicity. But I don't think it's *that* kind of unusual interest. He seems asexual to me. Like a eunuch. He's taught her for a while. I went to one of the recitals and met him."

"But he might know something?" Angela asked, her voice hopeful. "That's why we're going there, right? He might be able to tell us . . . something helpful?"

Again, Jake remained silent for an uncomfortable amount of time. Angela opted not to push. She allowed him to gather whatever thoughts he was gathering. But the longer she waited, the greater the sense of unease that had slowly been growing in the pit of her stomach. His silence, his distance, unnerved her and stood in stark contrast to the edgy franticness he had displayed at the house. Maybe he remained quiet for that very reason, knowing that it would keep her back on her heels. If he'd planned it that way, then she silently congratulated him. It worked. She felt off-balance and uncertain.

"I don't think we're going to go see Tolliver," he said, his voice as flat as the road.

"Why not?"

"Not worth it."

"Then where are we going?" she asked. "To Erica's house? You said you knew where she lived. Obviously you do."

He scratched his chin, his fingernails scraping against

the stubble and making a faint scratching noise in the car. "Not that. I bet she's not there. And if she is, we can go by later."

He cut his words off sharply, as though he were finished speaking.

Angela desperately wanted to hear more.

"Then where are we going?" she asked. "Exactly."

Angela prided herself on having a level head, on not losing her cool or focus no matter what went on around her. But the more mysterious and reticent that Jake became, the more she discovered images of Michael and, yes, even Gail, tripping through her mind. She saw her nice safe house, the orderly yard, the comfortable rooms. And the unease in the pit of her stomach started to spread, moving out along her rib cage and up into her throat, expanding like a balloon. What had she gotten herself into?

"I know someone else who might know what's been going on with Erica lately," he said after another long pause. "It's good you're with me."

"Why?"

No hesitation. "They might require a woman's touch."

"Who is it?" she asked.

"You know, you ask a lot of questions. I think this whole thing would go better if you didn't. I've got a lot of things on my mind right now. A missing kid. A missing ex. I need to think."

"I don't know exactly where my husband is," Angela said.

Jake made a dismissive noise with his mouth, something that sounded like a fart. To emphasize the point, he waved his hand in the air as well. “Wow. What a bummer for you. Your husband has been gone for . . . what? A few hours? Tough.”

The car fell into silence except for the purr of the engine. Even the radio was off. Angela listened to the hum of the tires against the road, a slight rush of wind from the driver’s-side window, which Jake had cracked about an inch.

“I’m sorry I pushed your mother-in-law about her dead kid,” he said, his voice lower. “I know it’s a sore spot.”

“Why would you even talk about that?” Angela asked. “The family is still devastated.”

“I get it. Erica told me all about it.”

“Why would she bring it up with *you*?” Angela asked.

Jake took his eyes off the road and looked over at her. He studied her as though he were making a decision. Then he looked back and said, “It’s part of her life in a way, if it’s part of your husband’s life.”

“I don’t get that. It’s an accident that happened twenty-some years ago to people you don’t really know.”

“That’s one way to look at it.” He cut his eyes at her again. He seemed to be appraising her, testing her. “Clearly Erica thinks your husband is still haunted by it. I guess he wasn’t watching his sister closely enough or something?”

Angela shivered under the gaze, although she doubted he saw it. “It’s a family tragedy.”

Jake nodded as if he understood something. “Right. You’re right.”

"And I want my phone back," she said. "I want to call Michael and find out where he is. And I want us to go there and find him."

"That's back burner," he said. "Your husband lied to you when you were together. What's going to change now? And Erica was careless with a child who may be my daughter. Who I consider my daughter. So why talk to them? Why not discover something on our own?"

"What is the deal with Erica, anyway?" Angela asked. "You were with her. Michael was. What gives?"

Jake tapped the steering wheel. Thump-thump-thump. "She was full of life. It's true. She just brought energy to everything. She can be a little exhausting at times, but when she's on, when the light is burning bright, she's beautiful."

"So it's all superficial," Angela said.

"Some of it is, yes. But not all. Look, I'm *not* trying to get Erica back. I'm trying to get Felicity back. Erica and I, we ran into a problem a little while ago, but that doesn't change the way I feel about Felicity. She matters to me."

"What's that?"

"We ran into each other again, just out of the blue, and we started talking. Catching up. This was at the grocery store, if you can believe that. Very romantic."

"Go on."

"When I saw her again, and we talked, I saw that the light she normally had was dimmed just a bit. Sure, age was part of it—some time had passed since we dated the second time—but there was more weighing on her. I could tell being a working single mom was taking a toll. How could it not?"

Angela felt a degree of empathy for her husband's ex-wife. She tried to think of raising a kid alone while holding down a job. She and Michael struggled to keep their lives on track without a child in the way. "I get it," she said.

"So I pressed my case. I said I could come back into Felicity's life, be a father figure again. Pay some support. Help carry the load. But . . ."

"But what?"

"She told me she had it, that she could do it on her own. I think it was just more of that bullshit of her wanting to prove something to the world. Or to your husband. Or maybe she just didn't want me around. Whatever it was . . . we parted on bad terms that night. And that was when someone called CPS. She managed to blame me for that. I guess because I was there and it was convenient. After that, when I pressed her for more time with Felicity or for a paternity test, she told me no. She didn't want me to know the answer to that question."

"So she doesn't know who the father is," Angela said.

"Maybe."

"Or it's neither one of you."

Jake looked over at her, his lips pressed into a tight line. Light from the passing cars danced off his eyes. But it was a mere reflection, giving a sense of opacity. She couldn't tell what he really wanted or thought.

Angela said, "If that paternity test gets taken and you

find out Felicity isn't your kid, then what happens to you? Huh?"

"I'm not stupid. I know that. But I'd rather Felicity be okay. That's more important than anything right now." He sighed. "I don't know what I'll do if she isn't okay. Or if I get near the person who did this. Just because I didn't see her every day doesn't mean that bond gets broken. I care about her. I do."

Angela shivered again.

"So no phone?" Angela asked. "And you won't tell me where we're going?"

"Not yet."

The car slowed. In the distance, they could see a stoplight, maybe two hundred feet away, the color changing from green to yellow to red as they approached. A spur went off the highway toward Simka, a path to people and civilization and town. Angela didn't plan it. She thought perhaps pure survival instinct took over somewhere in her brain or body, the unease drifting toward panic.

Her right hand slid along the inside surface of the door, fumbling for the latch.

chapter fifty-seven

3:33 A.M.

Hands clutched at Michael's face.

He tried to push them away, but it felt like there were ten of them. Stabbing, grabbing fingers working their way around his eyes and then his throat, trying to grab ahold of him. Michael pushed and wriggled, moving his body this way and then that, trying to throw the attacker off him.

The body on top of him felt lean but still strong. He managed to keep the hands away from his throat, managed to push back and keep breathing as adrenaline rushed through his body, lighting up every nerve.

But he couldn't see a face. Just a tangle of brown hair pressing against his eyes, clouding his vision.

To his left and slightly behind him, he heard Erica let out a shriek of fear. Michael managed to tilt his head ever so slightly in that direction. He saw Erica slumped against the foyer wall, her back near the baseboard, her butt on the floor, her face frightened in a way he had never seen it.

Someone loomed over Erica, another attacker, swinging his fists in a wild windmilling pattern. Erica cringed, her hands raised to ward off the erratic rain of blows.

"Michael!" she called.

Michael tried to scramble away, to move toward Erica. He reached out, his body too distant to make any difference. And he left himself open to the hands on top of him. Two quick blows landed against the side of his face, making a sharp smacking noise. They stung but inflicted little damage. He pulled his arm back, put it up in defense again.

"This is her," the other attacker, the one by Erica, said, the voice shrill and panicked. "This is for damn sure her."

As if his attacker had been waiting for that confirmation, Michael felt the pressure ease off his body. The blows stopped smashing against him as the person pushed up and away. Michael tried to seize the opportunity, making a grab for the person, but he couldn't get any real hold.

During the attack, Trixie had remained frozen in place, still in the taut, pointing position she had assumed when she first heard something outside the door. But the movement of Michael's attacker and the sound of Erica's voice crying out for help released something in the dog. She started barking, a much harsher sound than before when she had come to the door. She bared her teeth, the barks turning into a menacing snarl, and she leaped forward, snapping at the pant leg of the person looming over Erica.

The attacker turned to face Trixie, kicking a leg to brush the dog away.

Michael received his first real look at the attacker's face. He understood why the weight of the body on top of him had been so light and lean.

A woman, about his age. She wore loose clothes that made her appear larger than she probably was, and her hair was pulled back in a tight, efficient bun, allowing nothing for someone fighting against her to grab onto.

Trixie continued to growl and snap, although it seemed apparent the dog had no real intention of attacking the intruder. But she provided enough cover for Erica to slip away, so Erica scrambled across the floor closer to Michael, hoping to use him and Trixie for protection.

The woman's eyes glowed with a bright ferocity. She took a step back, inching away from Trixie but clearly contemplating the best way to continue her attack.

Michael noticed the other attacker, the one who had first come through the door after him. When he saw the face, a gasp escaped from his mouth. Not only was the other attacker also a woman, but she appeared to be older, perhaps close to sixty. And a quick examination of their faces told Michael the two women were related, mother and daughter most likely.

They edged together, standing side by side as Trixie growled. Michael and Erica remained on the floor, also side by side, their elbows touching as they came closer to each other for a sense of protection and safety.

The older woman looked every bit as angry and inflamed as her younger counterpart. Michael made a quick scan of their bodies from head to toe, looking for some kind of a weapon. He saw none, which didn't mean they weren't carrying something hidden somewhere. But he felt a slight sense of relief, a momentary hope that he could extricate both himself and Erica from the mess they found themselves in.

"Who are you?" Michael asked. "If you want money, I can reach my wallet."

But the eyes of both women, burning as they were, paid no attention to Michael. They both stared, over Trixie's gradually relaxing hackles, at Erica. Michael took a quick glance at her where she sat on the floor. Her eyes were open wide, her face showing confusion and fear on top of the crazy grief and emotion of the long day. She'd been awakened out of a sound sleep and plunged into the melee.

The younger of the two women spoke up. "We don't want money. Or anything like that."

"What do you want?" Erica asked.

"Just leave. I'm calling the police." Michael reached into his pocket and found his phone. But before he could dial, the younger woman spoke again, directing her words at Erica.

"You don't remember me, do you?" she asked.

Erica shook her head, eyes still wide. "I don't know you."

"You don't remember the day you stood over the stroller I was pushing? The day you came up to me and asked me about my baby?"

"What is she talking about, Erica?" Michael asked.

But before she could say anything, the older woman stepped forward, her eyes shooting lasers at Erica.

"You took her baby." She pointed at the younger woman, her daughter. "You're telling everyone this missing girl is yours, but you know the truth. She belongs to my daughter. You stole her ten years ago."

chapter fifty-eight

3:35 A.M.

Randi and Griffin followed Todd Friedman to a short hallway off the living room. If they'd kept walking, they would have ended up in the small kitchen. A light glowed above the sink, revealing a stack of dirty dishes and three empty beer bottles. Something smelled out there as well, something beneath the cigarettes and alcohol. Garbage. Todd Friedman clearly hadn't been tending to the household very well recently.

Then Griffin saw the object of their quest. A door on the left that Todd reached out for, taking the knob and turning.

"Where does this lead?" Griffin asked, although she suspected.

"The basement," he said, his voice matter-of-fact.

Griffin felt a new rush of adrenaline. Her palms were wet. "And what do you want to show us down there?"

"You'll see." He pulled the door open. Cool air flowed up toward them along with a musty smell that spoke of seeping walls and closed-in spaces.

"I can't go down there without letting my superiors know where I am," Griffin said. "They only authorized me to come inside here, to accompany Randi into the main level of the house."

Todd reached past the door and flipped a switch. Faint light illuminated the stairway beyond. "Well, I'm going down. And Randi's going with me. If you want to walk out, you can, I guess. But you won't see what I have down there."

"Can't you just tell me?" Griffin asked.

"Yes, Todd," Randi said, her voice quavering. "Can't you just tell her? Or me? Why do you have to make this big production out of it?"

"Because I don't want there to be any misunderstanding," he said.

"Randi," Griffin asked, "have you been in the basement before?"

She shook her head. "He moved into this house after we split up. I've been on the first floor but never in the basement. I didn't even know there was anything worth seeing down there."

"Come on," Todd said. He looked at Griffin, his face almost bemused, as though something funny had just crossed his mind. "They're going to want to know what's down there. And if you miss the chance to see it . . ."

Her mind raced with the possibilities. They unspooled in her brain like a horrible film loop. And over and over again, in the split second she stood there, she saw Felicity in that basement. Was she injured? Tied up? Dead?

If Griffin had the chance to go down there, didn't she have to take it?

She carried no weapon. No Mace, no gun, no blackjack. Todd Friedman was bigger than she was, likely much stronger. And Randi looked like little help.

She'd be on her own. Truly.

But she saw no choice.

"Why don't you let Randi leave?" Griffin asked. "I'll go down with you. And I'll tell my bosses whatever you want me to tell them. But let her go."

Todd shook his head slowly from side to side. "All of us. Or none of us. And if none of us go . . ."

He left the thought hanging.

"Okay, Todd," Randi said. "I'll go." Her voice became soothing, the kind of tone one used with a scared child or a small animal. It spoke of their familiarity with each other, to Randi's ability to read the situation and know how to speak to Todd. Griffin felt relieved to have her there, even if it wasn't entirely safe. Randi knew her ex-husband better than anyone else. "We'll go. Okay? We'll all go. Right, Officer?"

Left with no choice, either from her own sense of duty or from her desire to ensure Randi's safety, Griffin nodded. Todd answered with a nod of his own and started down the steps.

The narrow wooden staircase squeaked as Todd moved.

And the creaking grew louder as first Griffin and then Randi started behind him. Griffin gripped the handrail, felt the smooth surface against her skin. For a moment, she took a look back at Randi. She considered sending the woman away, out of the house to the safety of the police officers outside. But she just as quickly decided against it. She thought the risk of upsetting Todd was too high, and if he had something of great value to show them in the basement—something to do with Felicity or else Felicity herself—then she didn't want to do anything that might interfere with that discovery.

So they went down the stairs, Griffin's body between the former couple, a buffer that she hoped offered Randi some measure of comfort.

When they reached the bottom, Todd reached over and flipped another light switch. The fluorescents flickered on overhead, revealing a large open room, the walls and floor both concrete. Across the way sat a lonely side-by-side washer-dryer, a pile of dirty clothes on top, and on the far wall, directly across from them, stood a workbench stacked with cans of paint and assorted tools.

Griffin scanned the area once and then again, looking for something that would tell her what Todd's purpose had been in bringing them down there. But she saw nothing. It looked like an ordinary basement. Musty and dim. Functional.

"I don't see anything, Todd," she said.

"Over here." He walked to the right, moving away from the workbench.

Griffin looked behind herself once, saw Randi with

her arms wrapped around her chest against the cool, stale air. Then Griffin followed, knowing she had no choice but to see everything through.

Todd stopped in front of another door, one Griffin hadn't noticed when she'd first looked around. It sat recessed into the wall, its finish grainy and dirty. Todd reached into his pocket and brought out a ring of keys. They jangled as he flipped them around, searching for the correct one. They gleamed in the overhead light.

"What's inside there, Todd?" Griffin asked.

He ignored her. He worked at the lock, his breathing quick, and then she heard the latch click free. Todd pulled the key out and slid the key ring into his pocket.

"Is there a girl in there?" Griffin asked.

"Todd?" Randi asked. "Is there?"

He pushed the door open, flipped on the light inside the room, and moved out of their sight.

chapter fifty-nine

3:36 A.M.

The light changed to green. Angela caught the disappearing flash of red out of the corner of her eye, and as she did, the car rocked ever so slightly as Jake slid his foot off the brake toward the gas.

She knew she had to act in that moment or perhaps never at all. She'd be stuck in the car with the man until he took her . . . where?

She had no idea.

Angela had gone skydiving once in college with a group of friends. She had felt the same trepidation then when she pulled the ripcord, the same tingling, thrilling excitement and fear that the whole thing might not work.

She yanked on the door handle, pulling the silver lever back toward her with as much force as she could muster.

The lever came along perfectly, but the door remained

locked. She'd desperately hoped for the telltale clicking noise of the lock coming unlatched, the sound that offered her freedom from Jake and the car.

But nothing.

She knew what it meant. She understood right away what Jake had done.

"I've got them locked from over here," he said, his voice full of pride. "I don't want you running out into traffic. In the dark, it would be dangerous."

But they hadn't moved forward yet. A few cars streamed by in the other lane, on their left. One even honked as it went past because they were blocking the road.

Angela yanked against the door handle a couple more times, even though she understood the gesture was futile. Unless she could reach back and manually undo the lever without Jake stopping her, she couldn't get out. And she knew she couldn't manage to do that as long as he sat in her way.

But Jake reached across her body and took hold of her right hand, the one trying the latch. He grabbed it with some force and pulled, placing it roughly in her lap and then patting it. He shoved her hand between her thighs until it pressed against the material of the seat.

"Stop it," he said, his voice firm and quiet. "Just stop it."

His face hovered about a foot from hers, putting them practically nose to nose. Angela refused to be bullied, refused to show any sign of weakness just because some guy possessed greater physical strength and control of the car.

For a brief moment, she considered lashing out, striking him in the face, aiming for the eyes, just as she'd learned in a self-defense class years before. But she knew if she did that, if the two of them became embroiled in a physical altercation in the car, she'd likely lose. She held no weapons. No sharp keys, no Mace. She had only her own fists and desire, but that wouldn't be enough against a stronger man.

Jake seemed to sense that her anger and resistance had crested. He moved back, settling into his seat but still not hitting the accelerator and moving forward. Angela took a quick glance out the window, saw the traffic light cycle from green to yellow to red.

"Look," Jake said, "just cool it. We're in this together right now. When this is over, we don't have to see each other again. And maybe you'll have your husband back. And I'll have my kid."

"Your kind-of stepkid," Angela said. "If you can even call her that."

"I didn't hear the pitter-patter of little feet in your house. Why is that? Do you and hubby not want them? Or . . ."

Angela's face flushed. She hoped it wouldn't show, but it did.

"You can't have them?" he asked. "But he might have a kid with Erica? Wow. That stings, right?"

"I doubt the kid is Michael's," Angela said, her voice lower.

"He has problems? Sperm problems?" Jake smiled. "That just bolstered *my* case. Come on. Let's get going."

Angela looked over at the locked door and then back at Jake. "It doesn't seem like I have much choice, does it?"

"You want to know the same thing I want to know," he said.

"Can I have my phone?" she asked.

Jake smiled a little, but Angela couldn't tell exactly what the smile was saying.

The light changed again. Red to green.

"No," he said.

He hit the accelerator hard, jerking them both back against their seats.

They were on their way again.

chapter sixty

3:52 A.M.

It took a moment for the woman's words to cycle through Michael's brain and begin to make any kind of sense to him. He actually shook his head, like someone who had just received a strong blow.

Is she really saying what she appears to be saying?

"What are you talking about?" he asked. "You're accusing her of kidnapping her own child? *Her* child is missing."

A change came over the younger woman's face as she stood there. The anger and the defiance melted away. Before their eyes, time seemed to reverse itself, and the woman started to appear younger and more vulnerable, like a hurt and deeply troubled child, one who couldn't face what stood before her. A low, whining sound escaped from her mouth.

But her mother had lost none of her fire. She moved

closer to Erica, her right hand extended, the index finger pointed like a gun. "You're running around saying that missing girl is yours. But we know who she really belongs to. And the police think the same thing. A detective has figured it out. She's coming after you. It's true. Whether they find that missing girl alive or not, they're going to nail you for the kidnapping ten years ago."

Michael looked over at Erica. She remained on the floor, her eyes wide. She appeared to be every bit as confused and disturbed by the actions and words of the two women in front of them as he was.

"Do you know these people, Erica?" he asked.

"No, I don't," she said.

"Then I'm going to call the police and get them out of here," he said.

"Go ahead," the older woman said. "Call them. They're looking for her." Again she pointed as though she wanted to shoot lasers out of her finger and into Erica's face. "Let them drag her away in handcuffs. They came to our house tonight asking questions. They'll arrest her. I don't care what happens to me."

Michael's hands shook as he picked up his phone and dialed 911. When the dispatcher answered, he said there was an intruder in the house, two intruders, and they were acting in a threatening manner. The woman asked Michael for his address, and he admitted he didn't know it.

"Where are we?" Michael asked.

"Nine one nine Arrowcrest Lane," Erica said. "Or you can just tell them Erica Frazier's house. They'll know. Hell, they'll probably rush over here."

Michael relayed the information.

Then Erica added, "Phillips is the detective. And Woolf. Tell them. They know who I am."

Michael repeated the names into the phone, and he heard a change in the dispatcher's tone.

"We'll send someone right there, sir," she said.

Michael felt like a fool when he realized he was still sitting on the floor of the foyer with an angry woman looming over him. He slowly pushed himself to his feet, taking care not to make any sudden movement or give anyone the indication he was about to launch an attack. He kept his hands out in front of him so the women could see—he hoped—that he meant them no harm.

The mother stared at him for a moment, her eyes focusing on his pants. "Give me that." She snatched the monogrammed pink handkerchief out of Michael's pocket. "It's mine. 'F' for 'Flowers.'" Then she turned, her eyes boring in on Erica, who adjusted her position on the floor so that she sat cross-legged. She looked almost placid amid the chaos.

"Do you deny you followed her around the neighborhood, over there in east Trudeau?" the older woman said, still pointing. "That you came up to her when she pushed that baby in a stroller and acted all interested in her, like you wanted to grab her?"

Michael expected a vehement denial to come out of Erica's mouth, but instead she looked a little chastened, a little stung by the woman's words, as though they'd registered some measure of truth.

She remained silent.

"Erica?" Michael said. "Tell her it's a misunderstanding. Tell her, okay?"

Erica's mouth hung open slightly. She seemed to be formulating an answer, but what was there to formulate? Someone had accused her of kidnapping an infant. . . . The denial of the whole thing should have been easy.

Unless . . .

"Erica?" he said again, his voice sharper.

"I did sometimes talk to women with babies around that time," she said, looking at the older woman and not Michael, although the words seemed aimed at him. "It was a difficult time for me. It was after we split up and . . ."

"But you didn't take one," Michael said. "Did you?"

"Michael." She turned to look at him. "There's so much that was going on—"

"Here."

The voice of the younger of the two women—the two intruders—cut through their conversation. Every head in the foyer turned to look at her. Even Trixie, who had calmed down and stopped snarling, lifted her snout when she heard the voice.

"What is it, baby?" her mother asked.

"Look." She held her phone out, the screen turned toward Michael and Erica. As she stood there, with the phone in her hand, her face crumpled further, and tears started to flow down her cheeks, her body shaking like she was cold. "Look at this picture."

Michael looked to Erica, who remained in place on the floor. He felt he had no choice but to step over to the woman and reach for her phone. When he did, he felt his own hands shaking from the tension and adrenaline of the encounter.

He brought the phone closer to his face and examined the photo. It showed a young girl, about ten years old. About the same age as Felicity. Like the missing girl, this one also had blond hair and blue eyes, a superficial resemblance.

"This is your daughter?" Michael asked, confused.

"My cousin," the younger woman managed to get out. "Look at her. Doesn't she look like that missing girl? The one who's been in the news all day? The one she took from me. Couldn't they be related?"

"Kind of," Michael said. "In a very general way."

"No," her mother said. "Not in a general way. She looks like her. Like they're family."

Michael decided against arguing. He passed the phone over to Erica so that she could see the picture, and as he did, he understood something about the missing child and how her absence affected those left behind.

Erica stared at the photo, her brow furrowed, but didn't say anything.

"Are you saying your child was kidnapped when she was a baby, and you think Felicity is that baby?" Michael asked them.

"She admitted she had an unhealthy interest in babies back then," the mother said.

"She didn't say unhealthy," Michael said. "But, look, isn't it possible you're just seeing a resemblance to your cousin whether one exists or not? You've suffered a great loss, and when you see that missing girl, Felicity, you very much want to believe it's her." He paused for a second, gathering his thoughts. "Just like when I see her, I want very much to believe she fills a gap in my life."

Michael thought he'd made a breakthrough, a profound examination of what they were all going through.

But the older woman was having none of it. Her head wagged from side to side, and she pointed at Erica again. "Then why was she stalking women with babies? Why was she doing that? That's not made-up."

Michael turned and looked at Erica, who still held the phone. When all their eyes focused on her, she placed the phone on the floor, her face distant and a little dazed.

"Erica?" Michael said. "Tell them you weren't stalking women with babies. Tell them."

"I was. Kind of." She swallowed. "I wasn't in my right mind then. Not entirely."

"What are you talking about?" Michael asked.

"See," the older woman said.

Erica looked up at Michael, her eyes clear and focused for the first time in a few minutes. "I didn't know what to do with myself. I was losing you, and . . ."

"And?" he asked.

"And I'd just had a miscarriage. Our baby. That's why I went around doing that. That's why I took such an interest in other people's children."

chapter sixty-one

3:55 A.M.

Griffin looked at Randi, again wondering whether it made sense for Todd's ex-wife to make a break for it, to dash back across the basement, up the stairs, and out of the house. But Randi wore a determined look on her face, a combination of concern and curiosity, and Griffin could tell she wasn't going to be able to get rid of her. They were going into that little room together.

So Griffin went first, following Todd.

She wasn't sure what she expected to see as she turned the corner and walked inside. A dungeon with a small child chained to the wall? A torture chamber dripping with blood? A dead body?

She saw none of that.

Instead she found herself entering a nondescript office

with a small metal desk and wooden chair. Along one wall were shelves covered with cardboard boxes, and on the desk sat a computer. Todd Friedman walked behind the desk and bent down, rustling around in one of the drawers.

"What is this, Todd?" Griffin asked. "Why did you bring us here?"

"I wanted you to see," he said. "I wanted Randi to see most of all, but since you're here and you're a cop, you can see as well. You can see what I've been doing."

"Todd," Randi said, "what if I don't want to see this? What if I don't want to know? Let's just go upstairs and talk to the police."

"We can't." He rustled through the drawers some more and then straightened up. He held what looked like a stack of papers. "We can't until you see all of this. I don't want you to have any questions, Randi. You were good to me, and I don't want there to be any doubts about why we didn't work. You were right—it's all me."

He tossed the papers across the desk. They landed with a splat on the edge closest to Griffin and Randi. Griffin kept her eyes on Todd as he started to pace. He lifted his hands to his head, running them through his hair over and over as though he wanted to yank every strand out. Fear came off him in waves, a sweaty, musky smell that quickly overrode the damp scent of the basement.

"Todd," Griffin said, "maybe you need to just sit. Maybe Randi's right, and we need to go back upstairs and talk. You seem agitated, and I'm worried about you and the shape you're in. And we need to find Felicity."

"Just look at it," he said, still pacing. "Look at it."

Griffin took a quick glance down at the stack on the desk. She caught a glimpse of a girl, a young girl, a photo taken from a distance.

"Are these pictures of Felicity Frazier?" she asked. "Do you know where she is?"

"Just look."

"Is she hurt?" Griffin asked. "Did you hurt her? We need to know if we can reach her. If we can help her."

Todd continued to pace but stopped talking.

Randi moved forward, toward the desk, and she scooped up the stack of papers Todd had thrown down.

"They're pictures," she said.

Griffin peeled her eyes away from Todd and looked over at the photos in Randi's hands.

She'd been right about the photo on top. It showed a young girl on a playground, dressed for cold weather. But the girl in the photo had short brown hair. She wasn't Felicity Frazier. Randi started flipping through the stack while Griffin looked on, unable to turn her head away even as she feared what she might see. The photos all showed different young girls in different places. The mall, a soccer field, even a church. The girls were clothed, always going about their normal lives, but still . . . he had taken the shots from a distance as though he'd been spying on them.

"Wait," Griffin said. "Go back one."

Randi did, flipping over the last photo she'd passed.

Griffin took it out of her hand, bringing it closer to her face.

She recognized the girl in this photo. She stood outside a school building, as though waiting for a bus.

Without a doubt . . . Felicity Frazier.

Randi flipped through a few more. They came across five in a row of Felicity, including some that had clearly been taken just that summer, likely in the weeks leading up to the girl's disappearance.

Griffin stared at the photos. She felt her mouth hanging open.

She realized Todd had stopped moving. He was rustling around in the drawer again. The hairs on the back of her neck stood up, and chills shot up and down her arms.

"Did you hurt Felicity, Todd?" she asked. "Where is she? We know her mother tried to, tried to give her to you. Did you take her? Is that what happened? Did you think you were helping them? If you thought you were helping them, maybe we can work something out with the prosecutor's office."

Todd still offered no response. But he straightened up from behind the desk, holding a gun.

Randi gasped. Griffin took a step back, extending her left arm and using it to guide Randi gently behind her.

Griffin's heart accelerated. She thought she could hear it making a whooshing, huffing sound as it pumped blood to her body faster and faster. She hoped that blood didn't end up getting spilled across the walls and floor.

Todd lifted the barrel of the Glock 17, leveling it at Griffin. She didn't know whether he wanted to fill her full of holes or just get her out of the way so he could shoot his ex-wife. Either way, she'd be dead. She tried to think of who would care.

Twitchell perhaps. Her mother for sure. A few friends.

The cats.

And John, her ex-husband? What would he do when he heard the news?

"Todd, can you put that down?" she asked, struggling to get the words out with any trace of authority. "If you know where Felicity is, if you can help us find her, then it's not too late for you. You can get out of this."

"No," he said. "No. It's too late for me."

"It's not, Todd," Randi said behind her. "Todd, just put it down."

"There's a little girl's life at stake here," Griffin said. "Don't let that slip away."

He extended the gun, moving it closer to the two women. His arm looked long, the barrel menacing as it extended across the desk. Griffin felt her bladder fill, knew it would let go when she died.

I'm about to die. . . .

Todd pulled the gun back. He brought it up, placing the barrel under his chin. Before Griffin could say anything else, the sound of the shot filled the tiny room.

chapter sixty-two

5:15 A.M.

Angela thought she knew her way around Trudeau pretty well. Given the circumstances—stuck in a car with a guy who might intend to do her harm—she decided to watch the road closely, to monitor the twists and turns as they navigated what seemed like a circuitous route to the destination that remained unknown to her.

Even though the night was slipping way, and the horizon showed the first hints of the coming dawn, she lost track of her surroundings. Jake took them into an unfamiliar neighborhood, one filled with older, slightly rundown houses and several multiunit apartment buildings. Angela noticed an unusual number of beer cans strewn in the street, and more than one porch was decorated with a sagging couch or a hammock.

"Are we close to campus?" she asked.

"We are."

"Who are we seeing, then?" she asked.

"Someone who lives in the student ghetto."

He made one more turn, down a narrow alley. The moisture in the air made a hazy ring around the streetlights. The pavement was rough and cracked, jostling the car from side to side as he drove and finally parked behind a small house with a sagging back porch. A city Dumpster overflowed to their right. Before Jake turned the car off, a raccoon peeked over the top of the refuse pile, stared at them for a long moment, and then went back to eating somebody's discarded pizza.

"I don't understand why we're here," Angela said. "This is where all the students live. I thought you were worried about Felicity."

Jake ignored her. He took out his phone and started tapping at the screen, his fingers surprisingly nimble. After he sent the message, he looked to the back of the house, which showed no light except for one sad bulb burning over the back porch. He waited.

His phone pinged, and he typed a response. When he looked back to the house again, a light came on upstairs in the bedroom that faced the alley. Someone moved the curtains aside and looked down, then disappeared. Angela caught only a quick glimpse. A young face, brown hair.

"We're here to talk to a college student?" Angela asked.

"Come on," he said. "You're not going to run, are you?"

"Not yet," she said. "But I reserve the right. And you'd never catch me."

"I think you're too curious to run," he said, unlocking the doors and pushing his own side open.

He was right, Angela admitted to herself. So she opened her door and followed, stepping into the sticky night.

From somewhere up the street, they heard a drunken, triumphant whoop, likely the last war cry of the night by a fading frat boy. Instead of feeling nostalgia, Angela felt relief. She was glad to no longer live in a dumpy house, to no longer hear the late-night laughter and tears of near adults. She was glad to have a husband.

If I still have him . . .

She told herself not to think that way, not to question what she knew was true.

Before they mounted the porch and knocked, the back door came open. The same sleepy face she'd seen in the upstairs window greeted them, a pretty college student with her hair pulled back, her eyes puffy from sleep. She wore a hooded Gap sweatshirt and rubbed at her eyes like a small child.

"What are you doing here?" she asked, looking at Jake. "I don't understand."

"I need your help."

"Oh, my God," the woman said, lifting her hand to her mouth. "Do you know the police came by here earlier today and asked me for an alibi? Like I'd take a little kid or something. Can you believe that?"

"They have to talk to everybody who knew Felicity," Jake said. "Can we come in?"

The woman lowered her hand, and her face registered

surprise when she noticed Angela standing there, as though she'd materialized out of the darkness like a ghost. "Oh," she said. "You're not alone."

"No, I'm not. Can we come in? I promise it won't take long."

She nodded and then pushed the door open, holding it wide. Jake went in and Angela followed.

chapter sixty-three

They entered the kitchen, a cramped space with stacks of dirty dishes in the sink and ten empty beer bottles on the counter next to a vase of fading flowers. The woman wore no shoes, and the bottom of her shorts barely peeked out beneath the sweatshirt. She leaned back against the counter. She lifted the string from her hood to her mouth and chewed.

"What are you doing here?" she asked Jake again, speaking around the string.

"This is my friend Angela Frazier. Angela, this is Mary Beth."

"Frazier?" Mary Beth said. "Are you related to Erica?"

"No." Angela thought of leaving it at that, but how could she? "Erica was married to my husband before he was married to me. That's why we have the same last name."

Mary Beth's eyebrows furrowed. "Oh, I see," she said, although she appeared not to. "Why are you here in the middle of the night? I was asleep, and I have to work in the morning."

"You said the cops already came by here?" Jake asked.

"Yeah. They woke me up this morning. I guess that's yesterday morning now." Mary Beth sounded pouty, like her having been woken up was the worst crime committed that day. "They asked me a bunch of stuff about Erica. And Felicity. I guess they didn't find her yet if you're here asking questions."

"No, they didn't."

Mary Beth's eyes filled with tears and not because she'd been woken up again. "I can't believe someone took that kid. She's such a sweetie. Really."

"I know," Jake said. "So, what did you tell the cops? Was Erica acting weird or saying anything unusual recently?"

"Wait a minute," Angela said before Mary Beth spoke. "Who is this? Why are we talking to her?"

"Mary Beth babysat Felicity for the last . . . what? Two years?"

"Three."

"Three years. You knew me when Erica and I were together, and then I saw you a couple of times after we broke up. You were there the day I picked Felicity up for the zoo." He turned to Angela. "She's in the house all the time. She'd know if something weird was going on, right?" Jake asked.

Angela agreed even though she didn't speak. She just nodded and waited for Mary Beth to tell her tale.

"Yeah, but Erica told me not to talk to you. She said she didn't want you around Felicity or the house anymore. Maybe I should call her."

"You don't have to do that," Jake said. "She's under a lot of stress."

"Remember what happened the last time?" Mary Beth said, her eyes widening.

"A misunderstanding."

Mary Beth looked at Angela. "He came over to the house a couple of weeks ago when I was watching Felicity and said he had to see her. You know, just to hang out."

"Mary Beth—"

"So I text Erica just to see if it's okay. Next thing I know, she's pulling into the driveway and threatening to call the cops on him. She totally ran him out of the house. I didn't know."

"He has a tendency to barge in," Angela said. She turned to Jake. "Why didn't she want you around Felicity?"

"I told you at the house. She doesn't want the paternity test."

"Erica said she doesn't want Felicity confused," Mary Beth said.

"It's complicated, Angela," Jake said. "I told you she blames me for that issue with CPS."

"So was anything wrong with Erica or Felicity?" Angela asked Mary Beth, trying to cut to what was important.

"Nothing was wrong," Mary Beth said. "I mean, Erica complained about money and being a single mom. Sometimes she talked about moving away. That was it. Like I said, nothing much." She picked up the string again but didn't insert it into her mouth. She twirled it in her hand, her face lost in thought. "Hey," she said, pointing at Angela. "Is your husband's name Michael?"

Angela nodded. "Yes. Why?"

"Oh." Mary Beth put the string in her mouth. "Erica mentioned him a few times, said he might be Felicity's dad."

"Nobody really knows who Felicity's biological father is," Jake said. "Not for sure."

Mary Beth stopped talking, so Angela prompted her. "Did she say anything else about my husband?"

"She said he was rich." Mary Beth made a quick, uncertain shrug. "Oh, and she said his sister was in Lantern Black. I thought that was cool. Felicity sings all the time. Maybe it runs in the family."

Jake rolled his eyes. "Please. People get interested in music for all kinds of reasons. It's not all genetic. I love music too."

"Wait a minute. . . . Do you live down in Cottonsville?" Mary Beth asked, pointing at Angela.

"I do. Why?"

"Oh." Mary Beth looked embarrassed, like she'd said something she shouldn't have.

"What?" Angela asked, her voice sharp. She took a deep breath. "Just tell me."

"Okay." Mary Beth shrugged, trying to give off the

air that none of it mattered to her. "She went down there one day. Erica. She said she had a meeting. I figured it was a work thing. You know, she has a pretty good job at the credit union or whatever. I watched Felicity all day for her." She removed the string from her mouth again and tapped her bare foot against the floor. It made a soft splatting sound. "When she came to pick Felicity up, she looked all tired and sad. She said she'd had a long day. And then . . . just kind of out of nowhere . . . she told me it was her anniversary."

"Of her marriage?" Angela asked.

"No. Her divorce. Ten years. She got out a wedding picture and showed me. It was cute."

Angela let out a long breath. She sounded to her own ears like a hissing radiator.

"I'm sorry," Mary Beth said. "Should I not have mentioned that the picture was cute?"

"It's fine," Angela said.

"She put it up on Facebook later. I thought that seemed a little weird. But she told me I should always fight for what I want, that she had let too many things go in life without standing up for herself. I thought she was trying to empower me, you know? Like an older woman to a younger one?"

"Did you tell the cops about this?" Jake asked.

"I told them everything I knew. Yes."

"Did you mention me?" Jake asked.

"Well, yeah. I said you used to date Erica, and you came around a few times after the breakup to see Felicity. And that Erica didn't really want you around so much anymore, not since she got in trouble that time with child protective services or whatever it was. She told me you were pushing her for more time with Felicity."

"Why are you two still in touch at all?" Angela asked. "Erica told you he couldn't be in Felicity's life."

The house grew silent. Neither one of them spoke or attempted to answer Angela's question.

She grew impatient. "What?"

Jake looked away as Mary Beth said, "I felt sorry for him. That day Erica came home and threw him out, he had tears in his eyes. Real tears. I think he just wanted to be part of Felicity's life. He came by a little while after that. He said he just wanted to know how Felicity was doing. I promised I'd let him know if I could. You know, she'd been sick for a while. In the hospital. We just talked about that kind of stuff."

"Happy?" Jake asked Angela. "She kept me up-to-date on Felicity when Erica cut me off. *She* has a heart. No big deal."

"Okay, I hear you," Angela said. "Do you mind if I use your bathroom?"

Mary Beth looked at her for a moment as if she hadn't understood the question. Then she said, "Yeah, it's at the top of the stairs. My roommate, Katie, is asleep. Try not to wake her."

"Sure."

"You see?" Jake said. "I'm not a monster."

"Who said you were?" Angela asked, and headed up the stairs.

chapter sixty-four

Angela locked the bathroom door behind her. When she was done, she ran cold water in the sink and splashed some onto her face. Mary Beth's words played in her head, a fascinating loop. Erica had posted that photo on the tenth anniversary of their divorce. She'd regretted not fighting harder to hang on to Michael.

Angela knew she'd benefited from the decisions made between Michael and his ex-wife. If things hadn't gone the way they had between them, then what would her life be like?

Angela took deep breaths. And Jake Little only wanted to be part of a little girl's life, a little girl who might very well be his in every sense. Emotional. Biological. So much so, he experienced intense emotion when he thought he couldn't see her anymore.

"Okay," she said. "This is going to be okay."

But Angela didn't know where Michael was right then. All she knew for certain was that he was with Erica.

And not her.

She turned the water off and grunted in frustration. She looked around for a clean towel but didn't see one. She'd thought girls might be neater than boys, but the bathroom was a wreck. Mold in the tub, hair in the sink. The towel she picked up, white at one time, smelled like a locker room.

Someone knocked on the bathroom door.

"Jake?" she asked. "Give me a minute."

"Who's in there?" a woman's voice asked.

Angela patted her face dry and hung the towel back on the rack, promising herself she'd take a good hot shower once she returned home. She undid the lock and pulled the door open, coming face-to-face with another female college student, no doubt the aforementioned Katie.

Katie was taller than Angela, her long brown hair a tangled mess from sleep. She opened her eyes wide when she saw Angela standing there, and then her face shifted and became indignant. "Who are you?" she asked.

"Are you Katie?"

"What? Who are you? I asked first."

Angela saw all she needed to see. Like every member of her generation, Katie couldn't even go to the bathroom in the middle of the night without bringing her phone. Angela stepped back and motioned to the girl. "I'm a friend of Mary Beth's. Come in here."

Katie looked around, and, for a moment, Angela feared she'd call for her roommate. But then Katie rolled her eyes and stepped into the bathroom, allowing Angela to close the door behind her.

"Are you a professor or something?" Katie asked. "Were you at that party she went to? The one at the history professor's house?"

"Can I use your phone?" Angela asked. "I need to call my husband."

Katie shrugged, but her face remained suspicious. "I guess so." She handed it over after entering the passcode.

Angela dialed Michael's number from memory and listened to it start to ring. "Thanks." It rang and rang and then went to voice mail. "Shit," she said.

What should she do next? Call Gail and have her keep trying Michael?

"Who are you really?" Katie asked. "I swear, Mary Beth always brings somebody random home with her."

"Do you know the woman Mary Beth babysits for? Erica? I'm . . . well, not exactly friends with her, but . . . I kind of know her."

"Did they find that girl yet?" Katie asked.

"No. She's still missing."

"The cops wanted to talk to me too. I babysat for her once when MB was sick."

"What did you tell them?" Angela asked.

"Nothing. I was at work, and they said they'd come

back later. The mom, Erica, she was kind of intense. Cute kid, though. That's what's so sad. She reminds me of my boyfriend's little sister. She's twelve."

"I agree," Angela said. "It is sad."

"Can I have my phone back?" Katie asked.

"Yeah. Well, wait. Let me try my husband again."

She dialed, waiting through the rings and rings. Voice mail again.

She ended the call.

"You said you're friends with Erica?" Katie asked.

"Kind of. No."

"Oh." Katie pursed her lips, thinking. She had flawless skin and bright brown eyes despite having just rolled out of bed. Angela envied her for that. "I thought maybe you knew her friend who came by the house."

"Whose friend? Mary Beth's?"

"No. Erica's. The day before Felicity disappeared, I guess, this guy shows up here at the house, knocking on the door. Kind of hard. When I answered, he said she was looking for Mary Beth, and I said MB wasn't home. Then he asked me if I knew where Erica was. I guess he was supposed to meet Erica somewhere, but she didn't show up. This guy seemed kind of unhappy." Katie shrugged. "I said I didn't know where any of them were."

"And that's it?" Angela asked. "Who was he?"

"He didn't say his name." Katie chewed on her thumbnail for a second. "MB came home just as he was leaving. And there was a woman in the car with him." Katie opened the door and moved over to the top of the stairs. "Hey, MB, what was that guy's name? The one who came by the house the other day?"

They waited but received no response.

"Where did she go?" Katie asked, and started down the stairs with Angela following.

They found the kitchen empty and then went out the back door onto the small stoop. They stepped out just as Jake Little drove off down the alley.

"Hey," Angela said. "Shit."

But Mary Beth was there, walking back toward the house, stepping gingerly with her bare feet.

"Where did he go?" Angela asked.

"He took off," Mary Beth said. "He said he had somewhere to go." She held something out to Angela. "He gave me your phone. He said he was holding it."

"Thanks," Angela said. "I guess I'm taking Uber back to Cottonsville."

"Hey, MB," Katie said, "who was the dude who came to the house that day? The one who seemed kind of gay and was looking for Erica?"

Mary Beth's face scrunched. "That's so weird. I just told Jake about that."

"What did you tell him?" Angela asked.

The morning lightened around them as the sun rose. A chorus of birds chirped from the trees. A beautiful day except for everything else going on.

"I told him about the music teacher and the woman he was with," Mary Beth said.

"They came here looking for Erica. Or Felicity. Or both. I'm not sure."

"Who were they? What were their names?" Angela asked. Despite the warming morning, she felt a chill on her back. Her lips felt cracked and dry.

"I don't know who the woman was," Mary Beth said. "She sat in the car the whole time. But the guy is Felicity's music teacher." She looked around. At her feet. At the trees. At the sky. "Wayne. That's his name. Wayne . . . Oliver?"

"Tolliver?"

"That's it," Mary Beth said. "When I told Jake, he got into the car and took off."

chapter sixty-five

5:45 A.M.

Griffin sat in the passenger seat of the car, the door open, her legs out, feet planted on the spongy grass. The sky continued to lighten, shifting from inky black to lighter gray with smears of purple and orange beginning to appear. At some point, someone had placed a warm paper cup of coffee in her hand—she had no idea where it came from, but she sipped it gratefully, feeling soothed and comforted by the drink.

A pair of crime scene technicians entered the house accompanied by someone from the coroner's office. Curious neighbors ringed the property and the street, summoned by the flashing lights and the sirens, their voices murmuring in the night. Across the way, Randi Friedman sat in the back of an ambulance, wrapped in a blanket, while an EMT checked her blood pressure and other vital signs. Randi looked stunned, haunted, her stare distant and vacant. Griffin understood. She really did.

As much as she wished to erase the image, Griffin could still see Todd Friedman placing the gun beneath his chin, pulling the trigger. . . .

She could still see the red spray, the crumpling body. . . .

She felt ill and tried to think of anything else. Her cats. A baseball game. A trip to the zoo.

But she knew the pictures would always be there. She'd seen dead bodies before. Car accidents. Homicides. Even other suicides. But she'd never seen a head explode before her very eyes. Never felt the very life spraying out of another person.

Twitchell separated himself from a knot of cops and walked over to her. He leaned against the top of the car, his posture a forced attempt at casualness. His tie hung loose and swung in the light breeze.

"Feeling okay?" he asked.

"No."

He nodded. "Did you remember anything else? Anything he said that would help us?"

"I remember the smell of blood. And I'm pretty sure Friedman evacuated his bowels as he expired."

"But he didn't say anything else?"

"I told you everything I remember. Twice."

He nodded again, looking around. "They're bringing in a team to search. They're going to get into the crawl space, check the yard. See if it looks like anything was recently dug up. They're already examining his car."

"Where did Phillips and Woolf go? They were here, and now they're gone. Are they acting on a lead about Felicity?"

"There's something else," Twitchell said, again trying to sound casual. But he couldn't keep the curiosity and wonder out of his voice. "Get a load of this. We got a nine-one-one call from Erica Frazier's house. Some kind of disturbance."

"Really?"

"And guess who made the call. Michael Frazier."

"Is it about Felicity? Is she there?"

"No idea. They'll let us know soon." He looked around the yard again. "They're going to take those photos in, start trying to identify where they were taken and who the kids are. None of them appear to show the children in compromising positions. They look like they were taken from a distance, like he was spying on them and taking the pictures to look at later."

"You don't know if that was his plan," she said.

"No, we don't. And if a person of interest shoots himself when the police come by, we pay attention. It moves him up to being a suspect."

"And he has a history with the family," Griffin said.

"Yup."

"Look, I'm sorry about—"

Her words were cut off by the trilling of Twitchell's phone. He took it out of his pocket and checked the screen. "I have to take this."

He walked a few steps away, leaving Griffin alone with her thoughts again. She wished he'd stayed nearby.

She drained the coffee in the cup, feeling the soothing warmth spread through her torso, and looked over at Randi Friedman again. The EMT was out of sight, leaving Randi alone as well. Griffin pushed herself out of the car and started over, hoping to offer a reassuring word to the shaken woman. Or, short of that, to offer the comfort of being with someone instead of just sitting alone.

As she passed Twitchell, the phone still pressed to his ear, he snapped his fingers in her direction, an unusually harsh summons from her partner. She stopped and walked his way. She heard the last few words he spoke into the phone.

"She's here, yes. . . . I understand. . . . I'll talk to her about it."

And then he ended the call. For a moment he stood there, the phone still clutched in his hand. Griffin imagined the worst.

They've found the girl. . . . They've found her body. . . . All of it has been fruitless. . . .

"That was Woolf," he said. "Over at Erica Frazier's house."

"What happened?"

"What happened?" he said, repeating her words. "Your little emotional, ill-timed jaunt to visit the Flowers family paid off. Big-time. The two of them broke into Erica Frazier's house and attacked her. Congratulations. You really stepped in it this time. Up to your eyeballs."

chapter sixty-six

5:53 A.M.

The police made Michael and Erica wait inside the house. They retreated to the family room, Trixie at their feet, while the uniformed officers took the two women outside and placed them in the back of one of the cruisers.

The detectives asked Michael and Erica if they needed medical attention, and they both declined. Michael's back felt a little sore from crashing against the floor, but he didn't think it was anything to worry about. His heart rate finally felt close to normal, and he looked forward to sitting down someplace safe. They'd already given a preliminary statement to the officers who arrived first, telling them how the two women had burst in, accusing Erica of kidnapping. The detectives had listened with stoic calm and told them to wait while they stepped back outside.

Erica sat across the room while Michael slumped down on the couch. His mind raced. He wanted to look up at Erica but wasn't sure he could without unleashing a barrage of questions. He was intensely aware of everything he wanted to know, while at the same time trying very hard to respect the hellish and emotional twenty-four hours she'd been through.

But he couldn't hold his tongue.

"What's that you were talking about back there?" he asked. "With those women? Were you just lying to them about a miscarriage? Tell me you were lying."

"I really want that cigarette now," she said.

"Erica, what miscarriage?"

Erica looked down at her hands, which were folded in her lap. "No, I wasn't lying."

"You had a miscarriage when you were married to me? My baby?"

She nodded her head slowly, a barely perceptible movement.

"Why didn't you tell me? Either that you were pregnant or that you'd miscarried?"

"I didn't know I was pregnant until . . ." She looked up. "It was a surprise to me. I kind of suspected, but I wasn't certain. And I didn't tell you because I wanted to be sure. And we were having so many problems."

"You were on the pill."

"I didn't . . . You know I wasn't always reliable with those things."

"And you didn't tell me when it happened?" he asked.

"I didn't want you to think I was using that to hold on to you." She kept her eyes trained on his, her gaze unwavering. "I may have wanted you to stay, but I didn't want to be a charity case. I wasn't going to have a husband who saw being with me as the same as handing a dollar to a homeless guy on the street. So I didn't tell you about the miscarriage. And I didn't tell you about Felicity. Look, the doctor told me it might be tough to get pregnant again after a miscarriage. Some women struggle, so I thought it was a long shot when we kept having sex up until the end. I must have gotten pregnant about six weeks or so before you left."

"So, what these women are saying isn't true?" he asked. "You didn't . . . kidnap or whatever their baby?"

The moment stretched out with Erica saying nothing. Michael wondered if they were on the brink of a big revelation, a breakthrough or a confession of some kind. But then Erica started shaking her head. "You have the nerve to ask me that," she said. "To suggest I would do such a thing to a child."

"I don't know, Erica. You had a miscarriage and a pregnancy I didn't know about."

"That's it with you, isn't it?" she asked. "When push came to shove, you always had such low regard for me."

Michael wished he hadn't asked her about the kidnapping accusation. It had sounded insane as he said it, but he'd needed to know, to hear the denial from her own mouth. After every other revelation, he'd needed reassurance.

But he couldn't disagree with Erica's assessment. He'd never seen her in the same light he saw Angela, never seen her as a full-fledged adult. He had to admit that based on what he saw and knew—the house, the child, the job—she must have changed in some ways, and he could no longer so easily place her in a box.

"Okay, you're right." He felt chastened, but it didn't ease his anger over being deceived about the two pregnancies. *His children.*

"And you put up our wedding picture," he said. "You said things that hinted . . . you weren't over it. I saw that stuff even though we weren't Facebook friends. Hell, you made it possible for everyone to see it."

"That was the tenth anniversary of our divorce, okay? I do have my weak moments. I'm not sitting around pining for you. You know me. Something comes into my mind and I share it, so I shared the photo." She lifted her hands, indicating the room and the house they sat in. "It's a lonely life here sometimes, even with a kid around." She took a deep, shuddering breath. "And now . . . I may be on my own in a way I could never have imagined."

chapter sixty-seven

6:01 A.M.

Angela told the two students she had to make a phone call, and they seemed more than happy to go back inside. Before they left, Katie offered to give Angela a ride on her way to work. She just needed to shower and dress and drink a few mugs of coffee in order to fully wake up. Angela thanked her, amazed at how easy and simple their lives seemed, and she wished she could go into the house and spend the day with them, losing herself in their carefree routines. But she knew she couldn't.

She was very glad to have her phone back. And Jake gone. She immediately called Michael, hoping to get a response.

She did. He answered right away.

"Where are you?" she asked before saying anything else.

He paused briefly, then said, "I'm at Erica's house. We had a bit of a problem."

"A problem? What kind of problem?"

"Angela, that can be explained. . . . It just got . . ."

But Angela didn't hear the rest. She felt a tightening knot in her chest, a not-so-gentle increase of pressure against her rib cage. "What are you doing at her house?" she asked.

"It's all about finding Felicity," he said. "We needed to stop here on our way somewhere else. Erica is exhausted. She's . . . Well, you can imagine how emotionally spent she is."

"Okay," Angela said. "Fine." She didn't want to be a bitch, didn't want to try to claim her problems were worse than those of a mother with a missing child. Even if the mother of the missing child was her husband's ex and was spending time with him. "Are you *safe*? That's what I'm concerned about. I haven't been able to get ahold of you."

"I'm safe," he said, but she could tell there was more. "Someone attacked Erica. And me. Kind of."

"Attacked?"

"It's a long story. Really. But this person saw Erica on the news or heard about her from the cops and found her address online. It's not clear to me what it's all about. But she blames Erica for her own daughter disappearing. Apparently she thinks Felicity is really her kid, who disappeared right after Erica and I split up."

"I'm not even going to pretend to understand that," Angela said. She walked away from the house toward the alley, her shoes crunching over fallen leaves and twigs. A squirrel scattered at her approach, dashing up a thick tree trunk.

"Well . . . I'm learning a lot of things."

"Join the club."

"She . . . Erica . . . Look, she just told me she had a miscarriage before we split up. My baby. That's why these people—the mother and the grandmother—think Erica took their baby. Erica had miscarried and was distraught. Can you believe I didn't know that?"

"Are you really asking me that?" she said. "You didn't know about Felicity either."

"You're right. I know."

"Michael, there's . . ." She stopped herself. Did she want to be that person, the one who told her husband everything she knew about his ex-wife? Did she want to fight dirty? "I'm not home, Michael. I went out looking for you. Or for Felicity. I needed to do something. I'm in Trudeau now, near the university."

Michael said nothing. She imagined she could hear the gears grinding in his head as she held the phone to her ear. "I can't believe you did that. What if something happened to you? And you called Lynn and got her on me too?"

"You get to have an adventure, and I don't? And I've learned some things." She decided to play her cards. She just wasn't sure which order to play them in. It seemed too cruel to let him know that Erica might have been cheating on him at the end of their marriage. After all, how did she know she could believe Jake when he said it? He wanted Felicity to be his child, so wouldn't it make sense for him to claim to be involved with Erica back then? But the news about Michael's mother, she had that right from the source. Gail. "Did you know your mother was giving Erica money in the past year?"

"Excuse me?" he said. "I don't understand."

Angela explained about Felicity's health scare and Erica's request for money from Gail. "Your mom went along and gave her money. She even went and saw her from time to time. And do you know what made Erica cut off the relationship? Do you know when she stopped taking your mom's calls or having anything to do with her?"

"I have no idea. I didn't know they were talking to each other."

"Your mom told me she never told you about it. I guess she didn't want to get you worked up over nothing. She didn't want to disrupt our lives."

"She did not tell me," Michael said again, trying to emphasize the point.

"Erica stopped talking to your mom when your mom asked for a paternity test," Angela said. "Your mom wanted to know, needed to know, that Felicity was really her grandchild before she got too attached or involved. And that's when Erica cut her off."

A few exasperated, sputtering noises came through the phone. Angela took a deep breath, trying her best to keep her cool.

"I've never heard any of that," he said.

"I believe you," Angela said. And she did. "But if Erica is right there, why don't you go ask her about this? Why don't you find out what game she's really playing?"

"Angela, I will. It's all chaotic here—"

"Wait. What's the name of the guy you went to see? The teacher or whatever?"

"Wayne Tolliver. Why?"

"He was here, Michael. He came to this house. I'm at Felicity's babysitter's house. Never mind why. But he came here just two days ago, and he acted upset, like he was unhappy with Erica. Did he tell you anything? Does that make sense to you?"

"I don't know. He acted strange. He said Felicity had missed some music lessons, so maybe he was worried about that. He also ran away from us a couple of times."

"Ask Erica about all of this. Your mother. Everything. I'm going to call the detective and tell her this stuff about Wayne Tolliver."

chapter sixty-eight

6:17 A.M.

The cops remained outside. When Michael was off the phone, he looked out the front window, moving the blinds apart with two of his fingers. He saw the two women who had come through the door intent on attacking them sitting in the back of a police car. The detectives were standing outside, arms crossed, engaged in a discussion.

The blinds snapped back into place.

Erica was at the kitchen table, the dog at her feet. She sipped from a mug of coffee, the color still drained from her face. She looked like she'd aged five years since the previous evening when she appeared on his doorstep. But he told himself not to fixate on that, not to feel any more empathy for her until he understood what was really going on.

Trixie's tail thumped against the floor as Michael approached. The dog had decided she liked him, had tried her best to protect both of them when they were attacked.

"Erica?"

She looked up from the mug, her eyes bloodshot, the steam rising past her face. She didn't say anything but waited for him to speak.

"That was Angela," he said. "Have you been talking to my mother? Have you been getting money from my mother?"

Erica barely blinked. She showed little reaction to his question. No surprise, no fear or trepidation.

"It's been a while," she said. "Six months or so since we last talked."

"Why? How?"

Erica looked at the tabletop before speaking. While she did, Trixie looked up at her, sensing her owner was having a difficult time. "Felicity had a medical condition. A serious one. And I needed money. Years ago, your mother said I could always turn to her if I needed help. My mother had died a year earlier, and she didn't have much money anyway." She looked up. "I looked into other things. A second mortgage. Selling the house. Cashing out my 401k. But none of those would have been as fast. I thought of your mom. I knew she had money, and I knew she might help."

"And she gave you money?"

"She did."

"Is that it?" Michael asked. "Just money?"

Again Erica was slow to answer. Finally she said, "I saw her a few times after that. She wanted to meet Felicity."

Michael knew he was standing on the kitchen floor. He looked down and saw the linoleum beneath his feet. But for a moment it felt as though a hole had opened below him, leaving his body suspended in the air, ready to plummet from a great height. It took a number of heartbeats for his equilibrium to return, and when it did, he still didn't feel able to speak.

But he did.

"My mother met Felicity? She saw . . . you and Felicity?"

Erica nodded. The dog looked from Erica to Michael and back again.

"Why didn't she tell me?" he asked. "Did you tell her you thought Felicity was my child?"

"I did."

"And is that when she wanted the paternity test?"

Erica's head snapped up quickly. She almost smiled. "Well, I guess Angela knows a little bit of everything, doesn't she?"

"Why didn't you agree to the test?" Michael asked. "Why turn tail and run right there?"

"Michael . . . It's just . . ." She stopped. The steam still rose from her mug, swirling near her chin.

Michael remained quiet.

Erica looked like she was considering waiting him out, playing a game of chicken until Michael either said something else or grew bored. But he knew he wouldn't give in. And so did she.

"I didn't know, for certain, that the baby was yours," she said.

Michael felt the floor opening beneath him again. "You're talking about Felicity and not the miscarriage, right?" he asked, his voice calmer than he'd imagined it would have been.

Erica nodded. "I know the miscarriage was yours. Look, Michael, I know Felicity is your child as well. I feel it in my heart. I've felt it all along."

Michael was backing away, his hand up, asking for silence. He didn't want to hear any more. He didn't want to know. But after taking a few steps away, he returned, walking closer to the table than he had been before.

"Who?" he asked. "Why?"

"You can guess why," she said. "Our marriage was falling apart. You were so checked out. I knew everything was going to end. I wanted someone to care about me, to pay attention to me."

"So it's my fault you cheated?"

"I didn't say that," she said. "Look, Jake was kind to me. He listened to me, and I really needed someone to listen to me. He was really good for me back then."

The disappointment sank inside Michael like a lead weight, settling in his guts, almost pulling him to the floor. "So you have no idea if Felicity is my child. She may not be. Probably isn't."

"I don't know for sure," she said. "She very well could be yours."

"Could be," Michael said. "What a phrase."

Erica looked to be on the verge of tears. She placed

her head in her hands. Michael warned himself not to be taken in by the gesture, not to feel sympathy where it wasn't warranted. "I needed help tonight," she said. "I turned to you because I knew you would help. We can do the paternity test. We can. When . . . if . . ."

"When," Michael said. "And you took advantage of my mother. She was vulnerable, grieving. You knew about Robyn."

He wanted to leave it at that. But he couldn't. He needed to ask one more thing.

"Did anyone else in my family know about this with Felicity?"

Michael looked around the house. He felt crowded and suffocated. He saw sun behind the blinds, wished to feel fresh air on his face. He wanted to walk away from Erica, head to the front door. But before he did, her voice stopped him.

"Your sister saw Felicity too," she said.

"Lynn? She came here and saw Felicity?"

"Yes," Erica said. "Your mom told her, and she got in touch with me. We were friends, Michael. Remember? I think it meant a lot to her for the same reasons . . . you know, because of Robyn, because of everything that happened with her. And you and Lynn . . ."

"Don't," Michael said. "You did a nice job of hooking us all in, didn't you?" Michael turned back around and went outside.

chapter sixty-nine

6:35 A.M.

Griffin returned home, greeted by the two cats. She'd been cast away from the crime scene at Todd Friedman's house after answering and re-answering the questions she knew were coming. When the questions were finished, Reddick called her on her cell.

"You have to step aside," the chief said. "We can't have you around the case right now. Go home. Take a couple of days off. We'll figure out where to go with this."

Griffin wanted to ask what was going to happen to her. Would she be fired? Suspended? Demoted?

But she'd feared finding out the truth. And she'd feared her boss's disapproval even more. She'd felt tears pushing against the backs of her eyes as she listened to Reddick's voice. Even though the boss had remained cool and professional, never yelling, never screaming, Griffin had felt the disappointment oozing through the phone. She'd slinked away from the Friedman house without even saying good-bye to Twitchell.

The cats weaved through and between her lower legs. She bent down and gave each of them equal time, scratching their ears and rubbing their backs. She felt the thrumming of their purrs and appreciated the fact that someone—something—still liked her. The cats wandered away, and she kicked her shoes off. She slumped onto the couch, and when she did, the images of just a few hours earlier flooded back into her head. Todd Friedman with the gun. Pointed at her. Then jammed under his own chin.

Then the shot. The spray of blood glistening on the wall, a single white chip of bone she'd seen on the edge of the desk. She shivered, felt nausea surging through her like a roiling tide.

She reached for the remote and turned the TV on. Yes, she was curious about the night's events and wanted to know if anything new was being said about the case. She also wanted to chase those images away, drive them out with the distractions of the television. The weather report, a cooking demonstration. Anything.

The local news had stationed a reporter at Todd Friedman's house. She came in during the broadcast, the reporter on Todd's lawn, face suitably serious. Griffin turned the volume up and leaned forward while Rory jumped past her and then settled on the couch.

"Sources are telling us that the police consider Todd Friedman a suspect in the disappearance of Felicity Frazier. As we speak, equipment and personnel are arriving to aid in the search of the property. While officials aren't formally commenting on what they hope to find here, we can certainly assume that they are embarking on a potentially grim task."

"Can you see where they're searching?" the anchor asked.

"I've already seen an officer in a coverall go into the crawl space under the house. I've also seen officers walking the perimeter of the property, out in the back where there are some woods. Some of the officers have even gone into the woods—"

Griffin's phone rang, making her jump. She checked the screen. An unknown local number. She sighed. Could it be a reporter? Should she let it go to voice mail and hole up?

The cop instinct in her couldn't resist. What if there was news? What if someone needed her? Even if it was just another ass chewing, she couldn't ignore the call.

"Hello?"

"Is this Detective Griffin?"

"It is." The voice sounded tentative. Almost friendly. Not adversarial or professional like a reporter or someone from work. And was it familiar somehow? "Who is this?"

"It's Angela Frazier. You were at my house earlier. Well, last night I guess."

Griffin muted the TV. "I remember. How are you?"

"I'm fine. A little confused. A little on edge like everyone else."

"Of course."

"I know you've had a long night. I've heard about all this crazy stuff going on. But you said to call if I needed anything."

Griffin sat up straighter. Rory looked at her, shaking her head. "Right. What do you need?"

"This may sound crazy," Angela said. "But I'm here in Trudeau. It's a long story."

"Okay."

"Do you remember my husband left our house with Erica Frazier to go talk to some guy? Some teacher of Felicity's?"

"I remember. Yes."

"I don't know why this seems so strange to me, but that guy, Wayne Tolliver, showed up at Felicity's babysitter's house the day before she disappeared. He seemed upset about something, like he was mad at Erica. Look, does that seem odd to you? Like it does to me?"

"It does. Sure."

"Well, maybe someone should look into it. I'm here in Trudeau if you want to talk about it more. . . ."

Griffin easily calculated all the reasons to stay away. But there was one compelling reason to go—to find Felicity. To restore her standing with her peers and superiors.

And to protect Angela Frazier, who might be getting in over her head.

She bounced off the couch, startling the cat.

"Tell me where you are."

chapter seventy

Griffin drove them toward Waync Tolliver's house, while Angela rode shotgun. As they went, the sun rising higher, the day's heat already felt through the windshield of the unmarked car, Griffin asked questions, trying to find out what was going on.

Angela answered, filling her in on her travels through the night with Jake Little and ending with the young women in the house, the college students, revealing that Wayne Tolliver had shown up looking for Erica just two days earlier.

"Did he say anything threatening?" Griffin asked, her brain going faster than the car. "Did he say what he wanted her for?"

"No. He just seemed pissed off."

"And there was a woman in the car while he came to the door?" Griffin asked.

"Apparently. But they didn't see her."

Griffin didn't know what to think. It could have been anything. She knew Felicity had missed her voice lessons. She knew Phillips and Woolf had already talked to Wayne Tolliver, checked him for priors, confirmed his alibi, and turned him loose.

But could they have missed something? Couldn't anybody when they were rushing the way they all were, fighting the clock while Felicity remained missing?

"Is this guy dangerous?" Angela asked.

"Nothing on his record," Griffin said. "That's no guarantee he won't do something crazy."

"Shouldn't you call for backup or something?" Angela asked. "Isn't that what cops do?"

"I'm kind of freelancing right now," Griffin said. "And my colleagues are busy at another potential crime scene."

To her great relief, Angela dropped it. Griffin just wanted to explore the lead. If she opened up another trail, she'd follow with her coworkers' help. If Tolliver was another dead end, another roadblock on the way to finding Felicity, she'd walk away quietly and let the whole thing go.

She stopped in front of Tolliver's small house. The street remained quiet in the morning light. A sprinkler chattered on a neighbor's lawn, its misty spray of water catching the light and glistening like diamonds. Two doors down from Tolliver, an elderly man with a stooped back placed an American flag on his porch, his face full of pride.

"Stay in the car," Griffin said. "Just wait for me."

"Okay. But can I ask you something first?"

"Sure."

"Michael said he was attacked by some woman who thinks Erica stole her baby," Angela said. "Where did that crazy idea come from?"

Griffin felt her face flush. "Yeah, that's kind of a long story. He's okay. I know that. Just wait here."

Griffin started across the lawn. She wondered once again what she was doing there, whether her presence on another rogue mission might mean the end of her career. But just as she felt a certain empathy for Erica Frazier, left behind and rejected by her husband, she also felt the same thing for Angela Frazier. The woman had no idea what her husband was up to and what the end result of the night's activities was going to be. Would she come away from the evening holding the unexpected title of stepmother? Now that she had seen that old wedding picture on her husband's computer, would her marriage even survive?

As Griffin approached the door, she slowed. It appeared to be ajar about a foot. She looked to one side of the yard and then the other, seeing nothing and no one. She reached down and drew her weapon, the textured grip of the Glock 22 bringing her a measure of reassurance.

She reached the door, the sun warming the back of her neck, and called out.

"Mr. Tolliver? Trudeau Police Department. Mr. Tolliver?"

She listened at the door and heard nothing. She used

her foot to nudge the door open all the way. For the second time that night, she stepped across a threshold, unsure of what she'd find on the other side. She hoped for a better result than with Todd Friedman and took comfort in actually being armed.

"Mr. Tolliver?"

A sound came from the kitchen. A moan? A grunt?

"Mr. Tolliver? Trudeau Police."

"Here . . ."

Griffin moved through the living room and headed for the kitchen. When she reached the entrance, she saw the table canted to one side and an overturned chair. Then she saw a man on the floor, his hand held to his jaw, his right eye puffy and half-closed.

"Wayne Tolliver?" Griffin asked.

"I am," the man said from the floor. "Can you help me up?"

Griffin kept the gun out and maintained her distance from the man. "Are you alone in the house?"

"I am. My attacker left."

"Are you armed?"

"Would I look like this if I was?"

Griffin bent over and patted the man, checking his pockets. Then she holstered her gun and helped him to his feet, guiding him into a kitchen chair, which scuffed against the floor as he sat.

"Thank you," he said. "This has been a hell of a night."

"Who did this to you?" Griffin asked.

"I don't know," Tolliver said. "He must have wanted my TV—"

Griffin leaned closer. "Who did this to you? And I'll give you a hint—I already know."

Tolliver considered her, his head turned so he could see her out of his good eye.

"Don't make me say that despicable man's name."

"You have to. Who did this to you?"

"Can I get some ice?"

"Maybe in a minute. Give me the name."

Tolliver looked resigned. He shifted his weight on the chair, his movements making the vinyl surface squeak. "Jake Little."

Griffin walked to the freezer. On her way, she grabbed a plastic bag from the counter and filled it with ice. She brought it back and handed it to Tolliver, who gently placed it against his forehead.

"Why did he do this to you?" she asked.

"I think I need a lawyer."

"That's your right," Griffin said. "But if you help us find this girl, I'll do what I can to make everyone forget that you didn't tell us everything you knew yesterday morning. That's impeding an investigation, so you might want to do what you can to get out from under that charge. And if you really care about helping Felicity, as I think you do . . ."

"Okay," he said. "I do care about her. And not in the way her mother suggests. All I've ever done is try to help the girl. That's it."

"Help her how? And what does it have to do with Jake Little?"

"I'm not sure, to be honest."

Griffin raised a warning finger. “Time is short.”

“Okay, okay. Look, a year and a half ago, I got to know Lynn Frazier. She was playing some music around town, some solo shows and things, in different clubs. And I used to go listen, so we got to know each other. Apparently she found out from Erica that I was Felicity’s music teacher.”

“Okay. We knew Erica was talking to members of Michael Frazier’s family.”

“Right. About a year ago, Erica and Lynn came into contact again. Don’t ask me how. I got the feeling they hadn’t spoken for a while. Maybe not since Michael and Erica split up. I think it was Michael’s mother who got them back in touch. That’s what Erica said. Anyway, I saw Lynn about six months ago at a show, and she mentioned it to me. Very casually. We were drinking some beers, maybe too many, and she said she thought there was a good chance Felicity was Michael’s daughter. Her niece. I don’t know if that’s true or not, but she seemed unhappy that the kid might be growing up without knowing a big part of her family. I saw her again about a month ago, and she seemed pretty concerned about the kid because she knew about the child protective services call. Again, I don’t know how. Maybe from Mr. Little.”

“Lynn and Jake Little were talking about Felicity? Are you sure?”

“They knew each other.”

“How?”

“Look, I’m telling you what I know.” He removed the bag and wiped moisture off his face with his other hand.

Then he placed it back on his eye. "When Felicity missed those voice lessons, three days in a row, I got worried. I called Lynn and asked if she knew what was going on since she said she knew the kid and might have been related. For all I knew, she was involved in the kid's life. That might have been a mistake."

"Why?"

"I didn't know Lynn was so vulnerable, so concerned about Felicity. She immediately went into overdrive, trying to get ahold of Erica and not being able to get a straight answer from her. To be honest, maybe Erica was avoiding Lynn because Lynn was so worked up. I don't know."

"Is that why you went to the babysitter's house?" Griffin asked.

"Yes."

"With Lynn Frazier in the car?"

"Yes. Erica had promised to meet Lynn that day. I think Lynn just wanted to be part of Felicity's life. She wanted to get to know her better. But Erica stood her up. So we drove around looking, including at the babysitter's house. We didn't find them, so eventually I told Lynn I had things to do. That was the end of it for me, until yesterday morning when I heard Felicity was gone. The police came and questioned me. I told them what I knew about Felicity missing her voice lessons three days in a row and hearing nothing from Erica. I also told them my alibi. I was teaching a class at the community center. Rock-solid. Thirty-five senior citizens saw me. That convinced them."

"Did you tell the police about Lynn's concerns?" Griffin asked.

"Are you talking about Michael's sister?"

The voice from the kitchen doorway made Griffin and Tolliver look over. They saw Angela Frazier standing there, her lips parted, her eyes expectant.

"You should wait outside," Griffin said.

"You were gone for so long," Angela said. "What if something had happened to you? And now I come in here, and you're talking about my sister-in-law. Right? What does she have to do with this?"

"I'm not sure," Griffin said. She turned her attention back to Tolliver. "Well? Did you mention Lynn to the police?"

"I didn't. Given her fame, I wanted to keep her name out of it. And she told me she was heading out of town that night, the one before Felicity disappeared, so I didn't think it mattered. She certainly didn't *seem* like she was going to hurt Felicity. But I did freak out a little when her brother showed up at my door. What if Lynn had hurt the child? Or taken her? I'd gotten her all stirred up by calling. I just wanted to stay out of it. I didn't want trouble, so I ran when I could. But, really, the focus should be on Erica." He winced, as though he'd been hit with a stab of pain. "At least I thought that this morning."

"What's different?"

He used his free hand to point to his face. "Jake Little came by and did this to me. He wanted to know where Lynn Frazier was. He thought I was lying to him. He thought I knew where she was because we'd gone to

Mary Beth's house together the day before Felicity disappeared. I told him the truth. I haven't seen Lynn since that day, and she's supposed to be out of town. Working."

"She *is* out of town," Angela said. "She's doing a session or something."

Tolliver spun around, turning his body so he could see Angela in the doorway. "Right. See? She's away."

"What does Jake Little think?" Griffin asked.

Tolliver turned to the detective. "He's on his way back to Cottonsville. He said he was there earlier looking for her, and he's going to try again."

"Call your sister-in-law," Griffin said. "See where she is."

Griffin took out her phone and called for assistance. She needed someone to keep an eye on Wayne Tolliver while she headed for Cottonsville.

chapter seventy-one

6:59 A.M.

On the porch in front of Wayne Tolliver's house, the two women stood with their phones to their ears. Angela watched the detective, who seemed to be processing the conversation they'd just had as she made her phone call. Angela tried to process it herself.

Erica had stood Lynn up, and so Lynn spent time trying to find Erica the day before Felicity disappeared. And then Jake Little had showed up at Tolliver's house, trying to find Lynn. And had been so upset, he beat Tolliver. And now appeared to be off looking for Lynn, even though she was supposed to be out of town.

"Do you think Lynn's in danger?" Angela asked. "You don't think she knows anything about Felicity, do you?"

"I'd certainly like to talk to her, even if she is out of

town," Griffin said, a thoughtful look on her face. "Did you reach her yet?"

"Voice mail." Angela held her phone out. "I already left one message, but I tried to sound normal. Should I warn her?"

"Just tell her she needs to call you back. Or me."

"Lynn's never been in any trouble."

"I'd like to be able to ask her about it myself," Griffin said.

Angela called again. While she listened to the ringing on the other end—a ringing that went on and on too long—her mind raced. It went to voice mail again, and Angela left a message, her voice as calm as could be, asking Lynn to call her when she had the chance.

When she finished, she looked at Griffin. "Nothing again. Voice mail."

"So I heard."

"I can call Michael. Or my mother-in-law. Maybe they've heard from her."

Griffin nodded. "Do that. Since your husband's out and about, try your mother-in-law first."

chapter seventy-two

7:03 A.M.

Griffin listened to the ringing. She stepped away from Angela Frazier, who was leaving a voice mail message for her mother-in-law. Griffin moved away, but not because she didn't think the woman already knew what was going on. She did. Clearly. But if Griffin's call didn't go as well as she hoped, if she ended up receiving a tongue-lashing—or worse—she wanted it to be between her and her colleagues rather than something witnessed by a civilian.

"Yo."

Twitchell sounded rushed. Harried.

"It's me."

"Oh," he said. Voices came through the line in the background. A low rumbling like a truck. "Hey."

"Where are you?" she asked. "I have to tell you something."

"I'm in paradise," Twitchell said. "I'm at the Friedman house. We're all over it. This guy's basement is a Pandora's box of porn. I may not eat for a week."

"I'm sorry. Did you find anything there yet?"

"We found a kid's shoe at the edge of the woods. It doesn't match what Felicity was wearing when she disappeared, but it's the right size. We don't know if she's the only kid he had an interest in. Word's out. We're getting calls from every jurisdiction within five hundred miles that has a cold missing kid case. Davenport County was never so popular."

"I bet. Look, I—"

"Are you at home? I can call you later. But I'm knee-deep in this shit right now. Reddick's here riding herd on everybody. State Bureau of Investigation is on the way. Maybe the feds."

"I can—" She stopped herself. She didn't want to beg, didn't want to open herself up to more scolding. But she couldn't remain quiet. "Look, I can help."

"Easy, tiger," Twitchell said. "I already asked Reddick. She's going to call you later. But right now you're too hot. The press caught wind that someone attacked Erica Frazier. Soon enough, they're going to know a cop goaded them into doing it."

"I didn't goad anyone."

"Look, I bet they let you come back later today. Just let everyone cool off. Okay? We'll talk later—"

"Wait," Griffin said. Her throat felt tight. Here she went, out on the ledge again. "I've got a line on Jake Little."

"Really? The prodigal ex-boyfriend and quasi stepfather?"

"Yes. Him. The very one."

"Where is he?"

"He's heading back to Cottonsville. He's looking for Lynn Frazier, who we think is out of town." She told him about Wayne Tolliver helping Lynn search for Erica the day before Felicity disappeared. And then Jake Little's appearance at Wayne's house and the subsequent beating.

"How do you know all this?" he asked. Then he groaned. "Oh, shit. You're there, aren't you? Tolliver's house? Get out of there. That jackass will make a stink or sue the department so fast, it will be like getting hit by a hurricane. Are you kidding me?"

"But we've got to find Little. After he smacked Tolliver around, he headed for Cottonsville."

"Okay. I'll call it in. But you get out of there."

"Everybody needs to get down to Cottonsville. That's the center now."

"*That's* the center?" Twitchell asked, his voice getting higher. "We've got a house full of porn here and woods full of spaces to hide a tiny body. What else do you want? Why the hell would you fixate solely on this Jake Little stuff when we have all this here? You saw the guy blow his brains out as we were closing in."

"Shit, can't you just . . . not be so rigid? Can you try not to be such a . . . company man?"

A silence dropped over the call like a curtain. Griffin looked back to where Angela Frazier was talking on the phone, her words too low to be heard. She did hear breathing through the other end of the line, Twitchell's huffing as he tried to rein in his anger. She'd stepped in it, pushed too hard. She almost squinted her eyes shut as if bracing for a blow.

"I'm going to pretend you didn't say that," Twitchell finally said. "I'm going to let it go by. A mulligan because I know you're upset with yourself for cocking this up. Now, I'm going to get off the phone and go back to work. And while we look for a kid's cold corpse out here in the woods, I'll also tell Reddick what you learned, and she'll peel somebody off to go check on it. But I suggest you go home and take a nap. I think you're losing it. I really do."

The call ended. Griffin stared at the dead phone for several seconds. Then she looked over at Angela Frazier, who was talking to someone.

"Is that your husband?" Griffin asked.

She nodded.

Griffin wiggled her fingers in the air, asking for the phone. She handed it over.

"Mr. Frazier? This is Detective Griffin from the Davenport County sheriff's office. Where are you right now?"

The man's voice sounded far away. Faint like he was tired. "I'm at Erica's house. There was a disturbance here. But more police just came and got Erica. They're taking her to a potential crime scene to identify some of the items they found. They want to know if they belong to Felicity. A shoe . . . and some other clothes. Detective Phillips, was it?"

"Do you know where your sister is?" she asked.

"No, I don't. Angela said she was out of town. And I think this is kind of crazy. Angela was saying—"

A Trudeau police cruiser came down the street and stopped in front of Tolliver's house. The help she had called for, allowing them to go.

"Stay put. We're coming to get you."

chapter seventy-three

7:12 A.M.

Michael rode in the backseat while the detective drove. Angela sat up front on the passenger side, not saying much and letting the soft, cool air-conditioning brush against her face.

"Thank you for picking me up, although I don't fully understand all this talk about my sister," Michael said. "And who is this other guy? Erica's ex-boyfriend?"

"Can you call her? Your sister?" the detective asked.

"I just talked to her during the night," he said, "and she seemed fine."

"Was she home?" the detective asked.

"She said she wasn't."

"Did she say she was out of town?"

"No, she didn't."

"Try her."

But when he wasn't able to reach her, the detective suggested he try his mother. So Michael did, reaching her right away.

"Mom?"

"Oh, Michael. I'm so glad to hear from you. I see Angela tried to call me too, but I was just getting out of the car. Are you okay?"

"I'm fine, Mom. I'm fine. I was never . . . I wasn't really in danger."

"But you were with Erica," she said. "Was that . . . okay?"

Michael heard a teakettle whistling in the background. "Shouldn't I ask you the same thing?" he said. "I'm finding out all kinds of stuff about you."

"Michael, I was just trying to help Erica when she was in need. And I didn't tell you because you have a life of your own, separate from Erica. If there was nothing to tell besides a little money changing hands, then why bother you? I help a lot of charities. How is this different?"

"Because this one was my ex-wife," he said. "I can't believe this, Mom."

Angela turned her head to the left, looking over her shoulder into the backseat. Then she turned forward again.

"And she's claiming that kid is my daughter," he said.

"She cut me off over the paternity test," his mother said. "I doubt the child is yours. And, honestly, why weren't you more careful back then? None of this would be going on—"

"Enough, Mom. Enough. Don't try to turn it around

on me." Michael fought the urge to end the call. But something prevented him from treating his mother so harshly. Even if she deserved it sometimes. He knew he had a reason to call, a real reason. "Have you heard anything from Lynn?"

"No, I haven't. Angela told me to try to reach her, but she was very cryptic. The whole night has been rather cryptic, to be honest. But I did what I was told. I just went by Lynn's house, but she wasn't home. The place was locked up pretty tight. Blinds down, and the flowers on the porch looked unwatered." His mom lowered her voice. "She's supposed to be out of town, isn't she, Michael? You know she doesn't always tell me when she travels."

"Did you go to the lake house?" he asked.

"No, I didn't. I called out there, on the landline, and it just rang and rang. Michael, I don't know where she is. Can you tell me what's going on? I'm getting worried. I called Lynn's cell phone, and she didn't answer that. You'd think with all of us calling her, she'd answer. Wouldn't you?"

"I'm sorry, Mom. Don't worry. I talked to her a little while ago."

"Well, I am worrying, Michael. You've been off all night. Now something is going on with Lynn. You're my children."

"We just need to find Lynn because she might know the whereabouts of Erica's ex-boyfriend. His name is—"

"Jake Little. Yes. I know who he is."

"Yeah, Angela told me." Michael pressed his lips together until they hurt. He let it go for the moment.

There were larger things at stake. "The police think he knows something about what happened to Felicity. And he's looking for Lynn for some reason."

"Oh, God, Michael."

"Mom, just We'll go by the lake house."

"Who will? You and Erica? Michael—"

"No, Mom. I'm in the car with Angela." He paused. "And a detective. We're going to go to the lake house to see if we can find Lynn."

"None of this makes sense to me." His mother remained silent for a moment. "Michael, this is crazy. I thought this man on TV, the one who shot himself, did this. They think he might have hurt Felicity. Maybe even other children."

"I know. I don't understand it all either."

His mom made a noise, a worried rattling sound between a sigh and a moan. "Please tell me what happens, will you?"

"I will."

"And Michael . . . I'm sorry for all of this. I feel that . . . I wish I'd never taken a single call from Erica. I think it opened some old wounds, for all of us. Going back to Robyn and everything . . ."

"I'll let you know what happens, Mom."

After he ended the call, he leaned forward. "My sister isn't at her house, and she isn't answering her cell."

"Is that unusual?" Griffin asked. "Does she usually answer?"

"She does," Angela said.

"Unless she's recording. Then she might be away from it."

"What about her house?" Griffin asked.

"My mom just went there. No answer. But our family owns a lake house. It's just a few miles outside of town. We should check there, since you seem so worried. Lynn spends more time at the lake than the rest of us."

"Just tell me where to go," Griffin said.

chapter seventy-four

The Fraziers had bought the house on Cravens Lake when Michael was five years old. He remembered the first days going there with his family, when Lynn was a toddler and Robyn hadn't even been born. It had seemed to Michael that the sun always shone at Cravens Lake, that his parents always seemed patient and relaxed, that everyone around them—neighbors and friends—laughed all the time when they were near the water.

Cravens Lake sat seven miles outside of Cottonsville. The houses that ringed the water were mostly small cottages. Recently, people had started moving in from out of town, buying up one or two of the cottages, tearing them down, and building waterfront minimansions. Michael had always respected his parents' refusal to do that. His father had said he'd sell the place, or let it sit there empty and unused, before he sold to someone who just wanted to tear it down and build something gaudy. Michael also wondered if his father hadn't been able to let go of something from the past, a reminder of the times before Robyn died. . . .

But the family rarely went anymore. Every spring and summer, Michael and Angela made a vow to spend more time there, but they'd never made it more than once in a season. His parents almost never went, even though they still owned the property and paid for the place to be maintained. It seemed to Michael as though they'd forgotten they enjoyed going there or that the place had ever meant anything to them. His mother certainly hadn't been there since his dad died.

Only Lynn went regularly. Michael knew she spent days at the lake, using the quiet, solitary space to work on songs, to rehearse, or to just be away and alone. She tried from time to time to invite the rest of the family out there, to gather everyone together like they had done when they were kids, but it had never happened. Like Michael, she grumbled about their parents' lack of interest in the place. She'd even approached Michael once, several years earlier, and asked if he minded if she took over the property when their parents were gone.

Michael had told her he didn't care.

They approached the cottage on the familiar narrow road. Trees, their leaves rich and green in the summer morning, reached over the car from both sides. Between the houses they passed, Michael saw the dark water shimmering in the sun.

"There's a road up there," Michael said. "Turn right, and the house is the second on the right."

The detective made the turn and found the house without saying anything else. She pulled into the small driveway, the gravel pinging against the underside of the car. Disappointment crept over Michael. No other cars in the driveway, no sign of Lynn. The house remained closed up and shuttered. Michael couldn't be sure anyone from his family had been there all spring. Maybe the woman who cleaned or the guy who took care of the lawn had come by. None of the neighbors were out either, but on the water, a boat cruised by, leaving a foamy wake.

They sat in the car with the engine still running, the air-conditioning rushing over them.

"See anything unusual?" Griffin asked.

"No," Michael said. "It looks empty."

"Well, let's go look. Just to make sure."

Michael reached for the door handle, but Angela's voice stopped him.

"Detective," she said, "can I talk to Michael for a second?"

Griffin nodded. "Sure. I'll try the doorbell, see if anyone's in there."

She left, and the two of them were closed back inside the car. Angela turned around in the front seat, adjusting her body so she could face Michael. She looked tired, yes. Her hair slightly greasy, her eyes red, the lines just starting to form at the corners of her mouth more pronounced. But she also looked beautiful. Michael thought that every time he saw her face.

"Michael, I don't care what happened out there," she said. "You did what you had to do."

"Nothing happened," he said. "I mean, nothing you would have to be worried about."

"I get it that you and Erica were together, so there's an intimacy between you that may never go away. It's not a big deal. And if you have a child together—"

"I'm not sure we do," he said. "She told me Felicity may not be mine."

"Oh. Okay."

"You don't sound surprised."

"It doesn't matter," Angela said. "I mean, you're going to care about this kid whether she's yours or not. Your mother did. I can't be mad about someone who doesn't want to turn his back on a child." She waited a moment before adding, "I get it. I do."

"Thanks. Really." He wasn't sure what had prompted the words, but he welcomed them. After a long, crazy night with possibly more craziness ahead, he'd needed to hear them. And then he wanted to do more, so he reached out and took her hand in his, squeezing it. "You'll always come first."

"I know."

Michael thought they were finished, but Angela made no move to leave the car. She kept her eyes on Michael with clearly something else on her mind.

"Are you ready for this?" she asked.

"For what?"

Angela nodded toward the house. "For what we might find in there."

"The detective said there was another potential crime scene," Michael said. "At some other guy's house."

"True," she said. "They're checking everywhere, I guess. But we can't really know. . . ."

Michael looked past her at the house, saw Detective Griffin pressing her head against a window, trying to see in. "Looks like nothing so far."

"Let's just hope Lynn's safe. And Felicity."

Michael squeezed Angela's hand. She smiled back at him.

"You're right," he said. "Absolutely."

chapter seventy-five

8:03 A.M.

Griffin watched the two of them, Michael and Angela Frazier, exit the car and walk toward her at the front of the house. She'd given them a moment alone, and she could only imagine what they'd had to say to each other. At times like that, when she contemplated the complications and awkward moments in a marriage, she felt lucky to be single, to have only Rory and Coco for company.

"Do you have a key?" she asked.

"I know where it's hidden." Michael went to a flower bed, one filled with purple, pink, and white perennials, and upended a small ceramic frog. Something rattled inside, making a pinging noise, and then a key fell out. "Security is pretty light out here."

"I'm guessing your sister knows about that," Griffin said.

"Sure. The whole family does. We've never carried our own keys to the lake cottage. It's been a while, but we wouldn't forget that."

Griffin stepped aside while he inserted the key and, after some maneuvering, unlocked the door. He looked back at her.

"I'll let you go in first," he said.

"I need to." She went past him, stepping into the small foyer. "Hello?"

The walls were paneled, the carpet thick and out-of-date. Ahead, she saw the living room, the furniture rustic and past its prime. But everything appeared neat and orderly and well maintained. It looked like a lake home should look—comfortable and inviting.

Griffin went into the living room with the two of them behind her. She called out again but received no response.

"Lynn?" Michael called.

They waited. By that point, Griffin didn't expect to hear anything. The place felt empty and unused. She doubted anyone was there.

Michael and Angela fanned out, going down the hallway where Griffin presumed the bedrooms were. Griffin walked through the living room and then the small dining room, seeing nothing. She went out to the kitchen and lifted the lid off the garbage can. Empty. She pulled open the refrigerator door. A jar of pickles, one bottle of an obscure IPA, and a box of baking soda.

Griffin tried not to feel disappointment, tried not to see the whole trip to Cottonsville and then the lake house as a failure. But how could she not? She'd risked a lot coming out there after the disaster she'd stirred up with the Flowers family. If she came away with nothing again . . .

"Find anything?" Angela asked, walking into the kitchen.

"No. Looks pretty empty."

"Nothing in the bedrooms either."

Griffin looked around the kitchen, examining the walls, the cupboards, and the counters, hoping to see something. Anything. She pointed to a row of hooks next to the refrigerator. "The keys. There's an empty hook."

A set of small hooks mounted on a strip of wood hung next to the refrigerator. Each hook contained a set of keys . . . except for the last one on the right. It was empty.

"Are they always full except when someone is using a set of keys?" Griffin asked.

"I thought so. Michael?"

"What are the keys for?" Griffin asked as they waited for Michael to come to the kitchen.

"The shed out back. The garage. And the car."

"A car?"

"Yeah."

Michael came into the room. "What's up?"

"Isn't there always a set of keys on that last hook?" Angela asked. "They keep a car in the garage here. An old station wagon. It's just for guests to use or whatever. Right, Michael?"

"Yeah," he said. "Maybe my mom did something with them. She might have taken the car somewhere. Hell, she might have sold it. She was talking about it."

"Let's go check the garage, okay?" Griffin said. "Just to be sure."

They left the kitchen, heading back toward the front of the house. Michael pointed the way, indicating the door that led from the house to the garage. It was in the hallway where the bedrooms were.

He hesitated, looking back at Griffin. She read the look on his face. He didn't want to open it, so she stepped forward. She twisted the small lock and pulled on the knob.

The garage smelled like a combination of motor oil and gas fumes. The car sat there, its grille and headlights looking at Griffin like a giant face. She felt the disappointment again, creeping through the center of her body.

Then Michael stepped up beside her. "Shit," he said. "Oh, shit."

"What?"

Then she saw it.

The car wasn't a wagon. It was an SUV.

And the front bumper and fender were smashed as though it had been in an accident.

chapter seventy-six

8:19 A.M.

Angela watched as Michael went past her and the detective. He walked to the edge of the car, reaching out with his hand to touch the damage to the bumper.

"Don't," Griffin said.

Michael didn't. But he also didn't move away from the vehicle. He stared at it as if transfixed.

"That's not the car that's supposed to be here," Angela said, anticipating the detective's question. "That's Lynn's car. Her Lexus."

Michael remained frozen in place, the look on his face distant.

The detective moved to the passenger side. She reached into her pocket and brought out a small flashlight. She shone it through the window, moving the beam around the interior of the vehicle.

Angela moved forward, stopping alongside Michael. She reached out and placed her hand gently on his arm. "Do you want to come inside and let the detective work?"

"Where is she, Angela?" he asked. "Lynn's hurt. She's in trouble."

"We don't know that for sure. Maybe this accident happened a while ago."

"And no one knew? Why hide the car here? What if someone took . . . I don't know."

"What?"

"What if this Jake Little hurt both of them?" he asked. "What if he did something to Felicity and hurt Lynn?"

"It looks like she had an accident, Michael. The only question is why she put her car here and took your parents'. It means . . ."

"Someone else could have done it."

"I guess. But . . . well, we don't know anything, do we?"

Angela looked over at the detective, hoping for reassurance or support. She would have settled for and been happy with a good old-fashioned shrug.

But the detective stood stock-still, the beam of the flashlight fixed on one particular place inside the car. Something Angela and Michael couldn't see.

"What is it?" Angela asked. One horrifying thought popped into her head. *A body. A dead person.*

A dead child.

She started shaking her head to wipe the image away, but it stayed.

"What is it?" she asked again.

"Blood," the detective said. "There's a bloodstain on the seat in the back. A pretty big one. And it looks relatively fresh."

Her words released Michael from his spot. He moved forward, following the beam of the flashlight with his eyes. Angela came up behind him and saw what the detective had seen: a bloodstain the size of a dinner plate on the backseat of the car.

Angela turned to say something to the detective, but the beam disappeared.

Griffin had her phone out, calling for more help.

"I'm calling Trudeau," she said. "I'm letting my colleagues know about this."

chapter seventy-seven

8:22 A.M.

Michael continued to stare into the backseat of the car, even after the detective removed the flashlight beam and the garage fell back into its murky midmorning gloom. He remembered not to touch the car. But he stared and stared, wishing that the bloodstain on the backseat of Lynn's car would resolve itself into something benevolent.

Spaghetti sauce . . . chocolate syrup . . . Hi-C . . .

But nothing else fit. It looked like blood. Coupled with the damage to the front of the car, the conclusion was obvious.

From what seemed miles away, he heard the detective making phone calls. First requesting some kind of assistance from the local police, and then a longer call in which she appeared to be arguing with her superiors.

Only snippets made it through the halo of fog that enveloped Michael's head.

"I know I'm not. . . . I really found something. . . . As soon as you can . . . Yes, of course I told them. . . . No, I'm not leaving the scene. . . ."

Then Angela leaned in close, practically whispering in his ear.

"Michael? Why don't we go into the house?"

"She's hurt. Lynn's hurt. That man, that Jake Little . . . You said he beat up Tolliver. He's violent."

"We don't know anything for sure. Let the police look into it."

"Why would there be blood in the backseat if Lynn was okay?"

"I can't answer that," Angela said. "Why don't we go inside?"

"Where else might she be?" Griffin asked. "Where does she go? Where does she have friends?"

Michael looked at Angela. "Nashville is one place. She has friends all over the country. New York. California. She's traveled everywhere. She said she wasn't home."

"Anyone else?" Griffin asked. "Boyfriends? Girlfriends? Other relatives?"

Michael started to list a few names, old friends of Lynn's he'd met on a few occasions.

"Where would she go if she were in any kind of trouble?" Griffin asked. "If she needed to feel safe? Or secure?"

But before he said anything, they heard the sound of a car arriving, the tires crunching over the gravel right outside the garage.

"It's Lynn," Michael said. "She came back."

Griffin held her index finger in the air, asking for quiet or calm or both. She left the garage, going back through the house. "Stay in here," she said.

Michael started to follow the detective, but Angela placed her hand on his forearm, stopping him. She looked into his eyes, their gazes locking in the garage.

"They'll find her," Angela said. "Okay? Both of them."

"My mom . . . I keep thinking of her. I don't want her to have to experience another loss. Of any kind."

"Let's not go there yet. We can't."

"You talked to Lynn on the phone last night too. Did she sound normal?"

"Mostly. She said she was tired. That was all."

"So you don't know where she was?" Michael asked.

"The police will figure that out with the phone records. They'll do everything they can."

Michael tried to corral his racing thoughts. He moved past Angela, taking a few steps back into the house. The sunlight came through the windows, brightening the space enough to make him squint. Angela followed along behind.

"Who would she turn to if she got into a jam?" Angela asked. "If she needed help?"

Michael shrugged. "Us. Mom. Her family . . ."

"Would she go to your mom's house?" Angela asked.

"I don't know. . . ."

Angela reached out. She took Michael in an embrace, pulling him close so he felt her warmth, felt the comfort of her body against his. He closed his eyes for a moment, his mind stumbling back to images of Lynn as a child, seeing her young and vulnerable and innocent. The sun-bleached days in the yard. The late nights talking in her room.

The day at the swing set.

"I don't want anything bad to happen to her," he said, feeling the brush of Angela's hair against his face.

"I know," she said, her voice a comforting whisper.

Michael pulled back. "Wait. Where's Detective Griffin? Why isn't she back?"

"She's outside."

"Let's go see," he said. "It could be her."

They walked to the front of the house, hand in hand. But when Michael pushed the door open, he saw Detective Griffin in the yard, standing over a squirming man. Despite his erratic movements, she managed to work a pair of handcuffs loose from her belt and slap them onto the man's wrists. The way his face was mashed into the grass looked painful.

"What the hell?" Michael said.

"That's him," Angela said. "That's Jake Little. Erica's ex-boyfriend."

"Let me up. Let me up." Jake's words were strained, his face red.

Detective Griffin stood over him, her index finger raised. "Mr. Little, I'm handcuffing you for your own safety and the safety of others. I'm going to check your pockets now."

"Stop," he said. "I didn't do anything."

The detective patted his pockets, then slipped her fingers in. She tossed aside keys, some tissues, a crumpled piece of paper, and a wallet.

Griffin took the man by one of his arms and rolled him over so his face came out of the grass. He squinted as the sun fell across his eyes.

The detective raised her index finger again. "Now, Mr. Little, do you know the whereabouts of Felicity Frazier or Lynn Frazier?"

"No."

"Mr. Little, a child's life is in jeopardy. We saw the wrecked car, the blood. What were you coming back here for? Where are they? You need to cooperate."

Anger surged through Michael, a force that propelled him toward the man. "Where are they?" he shouted. "Where?"

He felt Angela take hold of his arm, try to pull him back.

"Mr. Frazier. Please."

But the man on the ground craned his head around, looking at Michael as best he could from his position. "You're him. We finally meet."

"Where are they?" Michael asked.

"Where's your sister?" Jake Little asked. "That's who I'm looking for."

"We know that," Griffin said. "Where are they?"

"I don't know." He spat the words with such force, Michael thought they might knock the detective down. "I don't know where they are. I've been looking all night. I came here to find her. Lynn. I know her family owns this house. Erica told me once about their lake property."

A slow-moving unease crept through Michael's body. He'd staked everything on this man knowing where Lynn was, where Felicity was. He spoke with such conviction. . . .

"Have you had any contact with Lynn Frazier?" Griffin asked. "Any at all?"

"Not since before Felicity disappeared."

"How do you even know her?" Michael asked, his voice shaky.

"I met her at Erica's house. Once. She was there, visiting Felicity, I guess. And Erica and I had just split up for the second time, so things were shaky with us. I went by to see Felicity, and this woman was there. She was introduced as your sister. I didn't stick around and interfere with the visit."

"Was my mother there?" Michael asked.

"No. Just Lynn."

"And you talked to her?" Griffin asked.

"Very briefly," he said. "That time."

"So then you talked again?" Michael asked.

"When Erica cut me off about a month ago, after the CPS call, I wanted to get back in touch with Felicity. I didn't want to be cut out of her life. I didn't know who else to turn to, so I tracked down your sister. It wasn't hard to do, considering how well-known she is. I just e-mailed her through her Web site. I told her we had a mutual interest, and she wrote back."

"What mutual interest?" Michael asked.

The man stared at Michael, his eyes bright with anger and fear. "Why? Can't you guess?"

"Tell us," the detective said.

The man kept his eyes on Michael, his glare as hot as the sun.

"You want to know?" he asked. "Are you sure? Fine. Because she's the one who was supposed to approach Felicity yesterday. That's what we decided. Wherever your crazy sister is, she has the kid."

chapter seventy-eight

Michael took a couple of steps back.

He felt as though he'd been shoved, that a giant hand had landed against his chest and pushed.

"You're full of it," he said. "That's bullshit."

Detective Griffin bent at the waist, moving her head so close to the man on the ground that she spoke directly into his ear. But she didn't whisper. Her voice cut through the still air like a revving engine.

"What are you saying?" she asked. "*Why* did you both want to take Felicity?"

"I didn't want to *take* her," he said. "I just needed something from her. And so did Lynn."

"What did you need from a nine-year-old?" Griffin asked.

Before the man answered, Angela spoke up beside Michael.

"The paternity test," she said.

Both the detective and Michael turned their heads toward Angela.

She was nodding, a look of certainty on her face.

"You wanted a paternity test," Angela said. "To prove who her father is. You just needed spit or something, a cheek swab."

The man on the ground almost smiled as he looked up at Angela. "Very good," he said. "I didn't want to hurt Felicity. I wanted to prove I was her father." He turned his head toward Michael again. "And your sister wanted to prove *you* were her father. But Erica kept ducking us. She'd agree, and then she'd change her mind. She was giving us the runaround."

"So get a court order," Griffin said. "Get a lawyer."

"We were going to. But *his* name is on the birth certificate, and that makes it tough for anyone else to make the claim. The courts don't just easily let any random person off the street come in and ask for a paternity test. You have to have a compelling reason. You have to build a case, and that takes time and money."

"So?" Griffin said. "Take the time."

"Erica threatened to leave town, to take Felicity away and never come back. And to not tell us where she'd gone. When we heard from the music teacher that Felicity had stopped showing up for her lessons and Erica blew Lynn off, we panicked. We thought she might have left. But

Tolliver kind of knew Erica's routine. He knew where she walked the dog in the morning, so he told Lynn."

"He'd called Lynn because he was worried about Felicity," Griffin said.

"Yes. I don't think he knew he was causing any trouble for Erica. He just thought Lynn wanted to check on her. He thought Lynn would be a good influence on Felicity's life, with the love of music and all."

"That's why Tolliver didn't tell us that little detail about sharing Erica's routine," Griffin said. "He didn't want to be blamed. Or charged with anything. I guess that gave him even more reason to run away a couple of times. He thought he might be in too deep."

"No shit," Jake said.

"So Lynn went to the park to get the sample?" Griffin asked.

"Erica told me if I came around Felicity or her, she'd call the police. Like I said, she blamed me for the child protective services call, even though it wasn't my fault. I didn't think she'd really call the cops, but why risk it? So we thought Lynn would have a better chance. She'd met Felicity a few times, and Felicity liked Lynn. She thought she was her cool aunt, the rock star. What kid wouldn't think that?"

"So she kidnapped her?" Griffin asked.

"No. I don't know what she did. She wasn't supposed to do anything crazy. She was just supposed to get the swab and leave if she could get Felicity alone. If she couldn't in the park, she might try another way. Maybe go over when the babysitter was there. So when she got the sample, she could compare it to herself or to me to see who the winner was. I don't know what the hell went wrong yesterday. If I knew where Felicity and Lynn were, I wouldn't be looking for them all over town. I wouldn't be eating dirt right now."

Michael closed his eyes for a moment. He felt Angela's hand on his arm, offering support. The sunlight turned the insides of his eyelids red.

"I know about your dead sister," Jake said. "The one who fell off the swing. I know *all* about it and how it fucked you and Lynn up. Erica told me everything when we were dating."

"Shut up," Michael said, but his voice was faint.

"I told Lynn about the CPS call. I was trying to let her know how urgent things were. Maybe that got her worked up even more. Maybe I said too much, but I wanted to know once and for all whether I was the father."

"Stop talking," Michael said.

Lynn took Felicity. . . .

Lynn had Felicity. . . .

But the wrecked car, the blood, the unanswered calls . . .

Where was she?

He opened his eyes again. Griffin was on the phone calling for more backup, reporting what she'd learned, the man again squirming on the ground.

The sun caught something in the grass, the light reflecting off silver.

Michael stared at the keys, then looked up to the end

of the driveway where Jake Little's Impala sat, the sun shining off the glass and chrome.

Michael pulled free of Angela's grip. Without breaking stride, he snatched the keys from the grass and started for the car.

"Mr. Frazier, wait—"

"Michael—"

"If you know something—"

He ignored them. He unlocked the car and jumped in, driving off, the tires throwing up a spray of gravel.

chapter seventy-nine

Michael drove Jake Little's car back toward town, back toward Cottonsville.

Back toward the house they grew up in.

The house where Robyn died.

While he drove, the sun bright in his tired eyes, the air-conditioning blowing against his face, he tried to comprehend the enormity of what he was experiencing.

Was Lynn hurt or in danger? Injured with Felicity?

No no no no no no no no.

He hoped she was just sitting there, at the house, writing a song or playing music.

Maybe she'd had a fender bender and needed the car from the lake for the short term.

Maybe Jake Little had lied.

Michael hoped for all of this as he drove.

But the blood. The unreturned calls. Jake Little's story.

And if Lynn didn't know where Felicity was, who did?

He entered the neighborhood, navigating through the familiar streets, the houses looking a little smaller than he remembered, a little older, but still nice. Still a place a family would want to raise children.

Michael worried about Lynn, the anxiety and fear churning in his blood like a roaring sea. He made two right turns, passing kids playing in their yards, an older man washing a shining red car. He felt the ache of nostalgia in his chest, the familiar sights and sounds bringing it all back as though time hadn't moved.

He saw their former house at the end of the street. A few cars lined both sides, but not the station wagon. The sun glared off windshields and mailboxes. Michael tried to remember the last time he'd been down there. He'd driven by a few years earlier, alone. Coming home from a meeting, he'd found himself nearby and taken the slight detour. He wasn't sure what he'd expected to see. He'd cruised by the house that day, going slow. The lights had been on, the blinds closed. A family had lived there then, because he had seen kids' bikes and a basketball in the yard. Michael had found the experience unfulfilling. In a way, it bothered him that someone else lived there, that a family went about its life, never knowing about his sister's death.

But what did he expect? An entire house turned into a memorial? A giant reminder of his sister?

Maybe, he thought. *Maybe.*

When the house came up for sale a few months earlier, he'd resisted the urge—the strong urge—to go through it, to visit during an open house or make an appointment to see it.

He'd even talked about buying it and then knocking it to the ground. But Angela had talked him out of it, helped him let that thought go.

But maybe Lynn had looked at it. Angela suspected she had.

Maybe she'd done more than just *see* the house.

Michael parked in front. Before he pushed the door open, his phone rang. He checked the screen and saw Angela's name. He knew what she was calling to say. She would tell him to turn around and leave, to let the police handle as much as they could. She wouldn't think he needed to be at that house, reliving everything that had haunted him for more than twenty years.

The images from that day. What they had both seen.

How he'd turned his back and let it happen . . .

He felt awful ignoring Angela's call. He never wanted to do that.

But he did. He silenced the ringer and climbed out of the car.

He stepped onto the sidewalk and looked up at the façade of the house. The blinds were all down, the driveway empty, the garage closed. The grass and bushes were untrimmed, and some leaves overflowed the edges of the gutters. The state of casual neglect made Michael reconsider. Maybe Lynn hadn't bought the house. Maybe no one had. But he saw no For Sale sign. If someone else owned the place or was living there, they weren't tending to the property as Michael or anyone in his family would have.

He walked across the lawn, his shoes making soft sounds as they moved through the grass. When he reached the door, he leaned close to peek through the window. The glass was tinted, but he made out the foyer and the living room beyond. He saw no furniture, no sign that anyone lived there or had been there recently. He stepped back.

As far as he could tell, it was the same door as when he was a kid. Weathered and a little more beaten, but the same door. He couldn't say how many times he'd come and gone through it, alone or with his family. In the fifteen years he lived in the house, it must have been thousands.

He reached out to the left and rang the bell. He rang it two more times before giving up, not surprised that no one responded. He stepped down off the porch and walked around the side of the house and moved toward the back. As he walked, a choking sense of dread and anticipation filled his chest, a pressure as though the heat in the air had come alive like a squeezing fist.

He knew the swing set was gone, taken down and removed by a handyman shortly after Robyn's death. He remembered coming home and seeing it gone. His parents never commented on it, and when they moved, they never bought another one. But it didn't matter whether it remained there or not. When Michael turned the corner, he saw the spot where the swing set once stood.

He froze in place. He wasn't sure what he'd expected to see. It was simply a regular suburban backyard, one of millions in the country. Grass and some small trees, a rectangular patio that sat empty under the bright sun. He could have been anywhere, in any everyday yard.

But he knew what had happened there. He'd been shaped by it.

And so had Lynn.

He turned his head to the right, looking at the house.

He refused to walk away.

chapter eighty

Michael tried the back door and found it locked. He studied the glass, which was divided into twelve smaller panes. He tugged the knob harder, but it still didn't budge.

No surprise.

Michael scanned the area. His heart sank because he saw nothing he could use. Then his eye settled just off the patio where a fist-size rock sat in the grass. Michael bent over and picked it up, felt the sun's warmth against his palm. He brought it back over to the door and studied the glass pane nearest the knob.

Michael looked to the left and then to the right. He couldn't see the neighbors' houses, couldn't see any people in their yards. With the heat of the day rising and the air conditioners going, Michael doubted anyone would hear the glass breaking. But he also knew if he broke the glass, he was crossing a line.

What if Lynn *wasn't* inside? What if all of it was for nothing?

Michael refused to turn back. He'd risk an unpleasant interaction with the police or a pissed-off homeowner. He brought the rock back and then forward, smacking it against the glass.

Nothing.

He swung back again, farther, and hit the glass again.

It gave way, his hand going through as well. Michael felt the small shards cutting into the skin, tiny stings. He slowly withdrew from the jagged opening, taking care not to cut himself any more. He shifted the rock from his palm to his fingertips and used it to clear the rest of the glass out of the pane. When he was finished, he tossed the rock back into the grass.

He checked his hand. A few cuts bled, and Michael gently picked some small shards out of his skin. But the damage didn't look too great, nothing that would require stitches, nothing that would stop him from going ahead.

He stepped forward and reached through the broken-out pane. He hoped the house wasn't so secure that they had a double-sided dead bolt, one that required a key to open the door from the inside as well as the outside. It hadn't been like that when they were kids, but that didn't mean a later owner hadn't changed it.

Michael fumbled around and felt relief when his fingers took hold of a small knob. He easily turned it and heard the lock click open, so he straightened up again and tried the knob. The door swung wide.

Michael felt a cool rush from the air-conditioning. He stepped inside, his shoes sinking into the soft carpet. He paused for a moment after closing the door behind him, taking care not to tread on the broken glass. He listened and heard nothing.

He'd stepped into the family room, which was also empty of furniture or pictures or art. Something else struck Michael as he stood there—the smell. He couldn't say what it was—some combination of years of human habitation—and he must have been experiencing an olfactory hallucination, but he would have sworn it was the same smell he remembered from his childhood. And it took him back. To the days and nights spent around the kitchen table, to the many evenings watching TV in the family room.

To the deadly somber day of Robyn's funeral when the house had filled up with friends and relatives, almost all of them in dark clothes. And Michael had sat in a corner, trying not to cry, ignoring his cousins and their insistence that he come outside and play baseball. Even Lynn had come by and tried to draw him out, but he refused.

Michael shook his head, releasing himself from the memories. He started forward, heading toward the front of the house, to the stairs to the second floor. When he reached the bottom of the steps, something caught his eye. He looked down, trying to make it out. Then he saw it was a bandage, a piece of gauze marked by a quarter-size bloodstain.

He left it on the floor and looked up to the top of the stairs. He reached for his phone and was drawing it out of his pants pocket in preparation to call the police when he heard the floor squeak above him, the sound of someone moving around.

Michael tensed. He took an involuntary step back. What if someone up there had done harm to Lynn and Felicity? And he'd put himself in danger's way by breaking into the house?

He pressed the nine on his phone, ready to summon the police.

But someone emerged from the bedroom at the top of the stairs to the right. The bedroom Robyn had slept in when they were little. Michael saw a blond head, a child's body.

A cry caught in his throat. He tried to process what he was seeing. The girl looked so much like Robyn, except . . .

She was there. Alive. And wearing a bandage on her forehead. Michael recognized her from the photos.

"Felicity?" he said.

The girl nodded, looking shy. Then she waved her hand at him, summoning him up the stairs.

chapter eighty-one

8:39 A.M.

Griffin helped Jake Little to his feet and led him over to her car. She opened the back door on the driver's side, guiding him in and reminding him not to hit his head. She also told him to sit quietly and behave, and he did, looking peaceful and resigned. Whatever fever had been driving him up to that point appeared to have broken. He seemed to have accepted that his part in the drama was over.

Griffin came back across the lawn in the direction of Angela Frazier, who stood on the grass with her phone to her ear. Griffin knew she was calling her husband, and she could tell Angela wasn't getting an answer. She looked like she wanted to throw the phone across the yard.

"Where did he go?" Griffin asked. "He seemed to have an idea."

"Lynn keeps a studio downtown," Angela said. "A music studio. It's a small space, but she plays there with friends. Or by herself."

"Okay," Griffin said. "But it's a little obvious. She knows we'd look there."

"You're acting like you think she's a criminal," Angela said. "I think this is all a gross overreaction. It's just a wrecked car. Lynn might be hurt. We still have to find Felicity. When Michael gets back, he'll—"

Griffin cut her off. "Where else might she go? Anything you can think of, no matter how ridiculous."

"I'm thinking," Angela said.

"Mrs. Frazier, the police are on their way here. My colleagues from Trudeau are on their way as well. We need to have answers for them if we can." She realized she'd been speaking loudly. "Is there anywhere else she might have gone? You're right. There's a missing girl involved here, one who might be your husband's child."

Griffin noted that Angela Frazier showed no negative reaction to the statement. Either she'd accepted the possibility herself, or she was damn good at hiding her discomfort.

"Anything you can tell us would be very helpful," Griffin said. "No matter how far-fetched."

Then it looked like a thought had jumped into Angela Frazier's mind. She opened her eyes wider. "The other house."

"Which house? Your mother-in-law's house?"

"No, not that. *Their* old house."

Griffin started nodding her head. She remembered

talking about it with Angela the previous evening when they'd discussed her husband's family. "The house where their sister died. Is that what you're talking about?"

"I bet that's it," Angela said. "I bet that's where Michael went."

Griffin took out her phone and called the local police. She identified herself and gave them the address to check for Michael. And then she called Twitchell, letting him know.

chapter eighty-two

8:55 A.M.

As Michael reached the top of the stairs, he slowed his pace. His limbs felt stiff, his joints frozen.

He understood that going into that room was going to take him past some line, some unseen point at which everything would be different. Forever. A fleeting thought crossed his mind, one that told him to turn around and go, to pretend he'd learned and seen nothing in the house. But just as quickly that thought went away.

He'd seen her.

An entire community waited, desperately hoping to locate the girl. He couldn't walk away. He never could have, not since the moment Erica rang his doorbell.

Michael sucked in a deep lungful of air and turned the corner into the room.

The blinds were half-closed, the light coming through diffuse. A handful of sun rays slashed across the floor, but the bed remained in shadow.

Felicity stood there on the far side of the room, her head turned toward the door, toward Michael. She made the waving gesture again.

Michael saw someone on the bed. On the bedside table, next to a digital clock, sat some crumpled tissues and a half-empty glass of water. Michael came closer, recognized the figure lying on top of the covers. Her leg was propped on a pillow, an ice pack resting precariously on her knee.

"Lynn?" Michael said. "What the hell is going on?"

"Oh, Michael," she said. "Thank God you're here. I thought maybe you were the police breaking in. I was ready to hide, but my knee is killing me."

"What are you doing, Lynn?" Michael raised his voice. "Everyone is looking for Felicity. Do you know how much of a mess you've stirred up? The police, the media. Everyone."

"I know, I know, Michael." She grimaced, adjusted her position on the bed. She reached down and moved the ice pack into a more stable position. "Michael, I get it."

"You were in an accident," Michael said. "Right? With Felicity in the car? And you left your car at the lake and came here to hide out?"

She cleared her throat and reached for the glass of water. "My knee is killing me. It swelled during the night. I can feel it. Yes, I banged it in the accident. I took the station wagon. It's in the garage. We hit a tree in my car. I was rushing, coming to Cottonsville a back way heading for the lake house, and went off the road. I just wanted to hide out there, spend some time with Felicity. We were lucky. . . .”

Michael walked across the room. He bent down in front of Felicity and looked at the bandage on her head. “Are you okay, Felicity?”

“I hit my head,” she said. “When the car crashed into the tree.”

“Did you cut yourself bad?” Michael asked. “Do you think you need stitches?”

“She doesn’t,” Lynn said. “I took care of it.”

“How do you feel?” Michael asked Felicity.

“I’m okay,” she said. “I’m hungry. I want to go home.”

“I know,” Michael said. “We’re going to take you home.” He reached out and squeezed the girl’s shoulder in what he hoped was a reassuring, comforting gesture. Then he turned back to his sister. “Why did you take her?” Michael asked. “You still haven’t told me what you were thinking.”

“You weren’t doing anything about her.”

“*Doing* anything? I didn’t know she existed. I think you’re groggy.”

“Stop talking about her like she’s not in the room.”

Lynn looked over at Felicity. She made a gesture, asking the girl to come closer, but Felicity remained rooted in place. The girl looked up at Michael.

“Is my mom here?” she asked.

“Not yet, but soon. I suspect the police and a lot of

people will be here any minute. It's okay, honey. You're safe." Michael leaned past her and turned on the bedside lamp. The walls were painted dark blue, nothing at all like when they'd been children. And why wouldn't that be the case? So much time had passed. More than twenty years.

"Michael, all I wanted to do was get the paternity test. I just wanted to find Felicity in the park—hopefully she'd be alone—and take the swab. And then leave. That's all I was supposed to do. That's it." She winced, but the look quickly passed. "When I got there, I talked myself out of it. I told myself the whole thing was wrong and foolish. I was ready to go home. But then . . . I saw her. Felicity. Alone in the car. It seemed like it was meant to be, you know? It was there for me to do. And it wouldn't hurt anyone."

"You can't just do those things without her mom's permission," he said. "You can't just go up to a kid and take a saliva sample."

"Erica wouldn't let us," Lynn said. "She kept jerking us around. And Mom wanted to know. It was killing her."

"Mom knew about this idiotic plan?"

"No, she didn't. But I was doing it for her. And for you and me. Michael, she might be the only grandchild Mom ever has."

"We don't know that."

"Why haven't you and Angela had a baby?" she asked. "With my cancer, I may never. You understand that, don't you?"

"I wouldn't have solved the problem this way," he said.

Lynn turned her head away from the lamp and toward the window. "I didn't mean any harm, Michael. But when I was there, with her . . ." She turned her head back to Felicity. "Michael, she looked so sad. And lonely, left there in the car in the park. It felt like fate, like she needed me. And I knew child protective services had been called recently for the same reason. Because Erica left her alone. I knew that. Jake told me."

"It's still not your place to intervene. What did you think was going to happen?"

"And I saw her blond hair. And her eyes . . . Michael . . ."

Then Michael saw it. He got it. All the gears clicked into place in his mind.

"You thought she looked like Robyn," he said.

Lynn nodded, her eyes full of tears. "She was Robyn all over again. You don't know what happened the day Robbie died. You don't know what I did. Michael, I couldn't let Felicity go. I just couldn't."

chapter eighty-three

Before Michael could ask a question, he heard a car door close outside. Then another.

He stepped over to the window, the one that looked out onto the street. Felicity came up beside him, bouncing from one foot to the other as Michael peeked through the blinds. He saw a Cottonsville police cruiser and two uniformed officers, their badges glistening in the sun. Then another car pulled up behind them. Detective Griffin emerged, her face determined, her stride brisk.

And then Angela got out of the car as well. . . .

"Felicity? Do you want to do me a favor? Will you go downstairs and wait for the police officers to come inside?"

"Are they with my mom?" she asked.

"I don't think so. But she might be here soon. Can you go downstairs and do that? I'm going to talk to my sister a little longer, and then we'll be down too. Tell them that if they ask. Tell them we're okay in here, and no one's seriously hurt. Okay?"

The girl didn't say anything else but simply walked out of the room, her hand to her bandage. He heard her soft footsteps on the stairs, and he hoped for more time with Lynn before the weight of everything that had happened fell on them.

When she was gone, Lynn lifted her head, removing her hands from in front of her face. "I thought I'd killed her, Michael."

"Who?"

"Felicity. When we had the accident and hit the tree, I thought she was dead. I thought I had done it again. I saw the blood." She buried her head in her hands. "I'm sorry, Michael. It all went sideways so fast."

Michael came over and sat on the edge of the bed. He reached out and patted his sister on the arm. "Lynn, what do you mean you thought you'd done it *again*? Why are you saying that?"

Her words came out in a tumble, like boulders sliding down a hill. "I didn't tell Mom and Dad. I didn't tell the minister or the therapist they sent us to. You made my burden yours, for all these years."

"It's not *your* burden," Michael said. "I was supposed to be watching you both. I was older. I should have been there instead of wandering away, lost in my head. Daydreaming. I hate that I did that, that I let my attention waver."

Lynn remained silent. She stared at Michael and then turned away, her eyes trailing over the walls and up to the ceiling.

"What's the matter, Lynn?" he asked. "Why are you not saying anything?"

"It's not your fault, Michael. Robyn . . . It's not your fault. You didn't kill her."

"I know that. She fell. It was an accident. But I could have, *should have*, prevented it. I should have been there to try."

She still kept her head turned away.

"Lynn? Talk to me."

She said something under her breath. Michael didn't understand, so he leaned closer.

"What are you saying, Lynn?"

"It's not your fault, Michael." She turned to face him. "It's me, Michael. It's me. I killed Robyn. I killed her that day."

chapter eighty-four

9:04 A.M.

Griffin watched the two uniformed cops approach the house. She stayed back by the car with Angela Frazier, letting the local authorities do their job unless they needed her help. She'd stepped on enough toes, rocked enough boats. She told herself to avoid more trouble.

But you were right, she reminded herself. *You were right.*

And when the Cottonsville cops and crime scene technicians had shown up at the lake cottage to process the car and secure Jake Little, she was more than happy to leave, heading for the house where she hoped they'd find Felicity.

And she hoped the girl would be alive. . . .

When the cops stepped up onto the porch, their

movements cautious, their hands placed near their weapons, the door suddenly swung open.

For a moment, everyone froze. The thought dashed across Griffin's brain that the cops were going to draw their guns, spring into action, or fire at whoever emerged.

But they remained rooted in place. And when they saw the tiny figure emerging from the front door, their postures relaxed ever so slightly.

"It's her," Griffin said.

"It is," Angela said next to her.

Griffin hadn't realized she'd said the words out loud.

She moved forward, asking everyone for calm, her hands out. "Hold it, hold it. Easy, guys. Easy."

But they *were* taking it easy. One of the cops bent down and offered the girl his hand. And then Felicity came farther onto the porch, blinking against the bright sun. Griffin reached the bottom of the steps, and the cop, a burly guy with fingers like sausages, eased the girl along, placing her tiny hand into Griffin's.

"It's okay, honey," Griffin said. It felt weird to have the child's hand in hers. The touch, the feel of Felicity's soft skin against hers, summoned a raft of emotions, but foremost among them was relief. The kid was alive. She wore a bandage on her head and her clothes looked a little dirty, but she was alive. And with Griffin. "Why don't you come over here with me to the car?"

"Is my mom here?" the girl asked.

"She's on her way."

They came up to Angela Frazier, who stood with a smile on her face, greeting the child. Her stepchild, perhaps. "We've got some water bottles and crackers in the car. Are you hungry or thirsty?"

Felicity nodded, so Griffin led her over to the car. As Angela opened the door and rummaged around for the snacks, another vehicle came down the street and stopped behind Griffin's. She recognized it and the driver right away.

Twitchell stepped out on the driver's side, and the passenger-side door swung open at the same time. Erica Frazier jumped out, her face a mask of worry and anxiety. It took just a moment for her to see her daughter standing at Griffin's side.

"Mom!"

"Oh, baby!"

Felicity tore out of Griffin's grip and ran to her mother, jumping into her arms like they'd been separated for fifty years instead of one night. But Griffin remembered being that age, knew that one night of fear and terror away from her parents would have felt like fifty. She closed her eyes, pressed against the lids with her thumb and index finger.

Someone came up beside her. She assumed it was Angela Frazier offering support.

But a familiar male voice said, "I always knew you were a softie."

She opened her eyes and saw Twitchell, his pale bald head shining in the sun. He reached out, offering her a tissue.

"Thanks."

"No, thank *you.*" He reached out again and gave her

upper arm a soft squeeze. "You did good, kid. You did really, really good. I'm glad you called me to bring her down. It's nice to see a happy ending for a change."

They all, including Angela Frazier, stood and watched Erica clutch her daughter to her chest, apparently intending to never let go.

chapter eighty-five

9:14 A.M.

What are you talking about, Lynn? Robyn fell. She was up too high. She lost her balance. That's what you said back then. That's what you told Mom and Dad and the police. There's nothing more to it than that."

Lynn shook her head, looking away again.

Michael had seen Robyn on top of the swing set before, arms out like a gymnast on a balance beam. She would be silhouetted by the sun, looking almost like an angel or some otherworldly being, high above them, bright as the day, possessed of an incredible ability to walk and balance in the air.

"What did she say to you that day?" Michael asked. "I heard you both yelling. I know you were fighting, but I don't know what it was about."

Lynn sniffled. She reached to the side of the bed and picked up a tissue. She rubbed her nose vigorously and then locked eyes with Michael. She seemed to be looking through him and down the tunnel of years back to the day she could also see so clearly.

"She always taunted me because she could do things physically I couldn't," Lynn said. "The gymnastics, the climbing. Even though she was younger, she was stronger and braver than I was."

"Than either of us," Michael said. "But she always had Dad egging her on in a way he never did for us."

"True." Lynn's cheeks flushed, the tips of her ears turned red. She adjusted her body a little, causing the ice cubes in the pack to jostle against one another. "I hated her for that, Michael."

"For her bravery?"

"For Dad's favoritism," she said. "For being his 'Robbie-girl.' I was never his 'Lynnie-girl.' He never cheered me on that way."

"He was proud of you. Until the day he died, he was proud of you."

"Maybe. He never understood the music, the lifestyle. It baffled him." She swallowed hard, sniffled again. She looked small, shrunken into the bed like a child. "Maybe I never outgrew being nine and feeling like he loved Robyn more."

"She said something to you that day?" Michael asked. "Something that caused a fight?"

Lynn nodded. "The usual. She told me I was slow, that I couldn't do the things she could do. She said it as she climbed up on top of the swing set. It used to scare me so much when she did that. I used to feel sick, watching her climb so high."

"Me too."

"And I know she was just being a brat, just trying to get my goat. I should have ignored her. You always did."

"I was older."

"And a boy," Lynn said, her voice a little envious.

"And that was it?" Michael asked. "That's all she said? Why are you saying you killed her?"

Lynn shook her head slowly from side to side. Her whole body trembled, as if the ice in the pack covered her body. "She told me Dad liked her more than me *because* she could climb that way, because she could do those things better than I could." She reached for the blanket, pulled it up over her body. "Your football was there in the yard, sitting in the grass. I picked it up. Hell, I didn't even know I could throw a football worth a damn."

"What did you do?"

"I threw it at her. It hit her on the shoulder and knocked her off-balance. She teetered there for a moment. I didn't think she'd fall. She *never* fell. She was like a cat, Michael—you know that. She could do anything on a ledge or a branch. She was always okay."

"But she . . ."

"She screamed, Michael. When she saw she couldn't hold on, she screamed." Lynn lifted her hands to her ears. "I can still hear it. Over and over, I hear it. Do you hear it too?"

"It was an accident, Lynn. You threw a ball at your sister. You didn't mean . . ."

He left the thought unfinished. It hung in the air between them.

He heard voices downstairs, heavy shoes moving through the house.

"What are you saying, Lynn?"

"I *meant* to hit her. I *tried* to hit her. I wanted to knock her off the swing set. In that moment, I wanted her gone, Michael. I *wanted* to hurt her."

Michael stood up from the bed, the springs squeaking as he rose, and took a step back. "That's not possible. She fell. It was an accident."

"And the way she landed, on her neck and shoulder . . . and head. I knew, Michael. I knew it was bad. Then Mom was there and you, and I thought Mom saw from the house. I thought she saw me throw the ball at her, but she never said anything. She must not have been looking. I lived in terror that I'd be caught, but no one ever knew."

Michael heard footsteps on the stairs, somebody coming closer.

"I was going to tell you," Lynn said. "After the funeral that day, I was going to tell you. At the house, *this* house, when everyone came over, I wanted to take you aside and tell you. But you were so sad. I couldn't do it. And the more time that passed . . ."

The room didn't spin, but it felt like it should have. A swirling, chaotic twirl, a maelstrom that would pull Michael down.

But the spinning was in his head. In his heart.

Everything moved and shook inside him, a quake that couldn't be stopped.

"You let me feel responsible all these years," he said. "You let me carry the burden alone. My God, Lynn, do you know how much that's weighed on me?"

"I do. That's why I wanted to get Felicity, to prove she was part of our family. I wanted to help fill the gap that everyone felt. Including you—"

And then the police were coming through the bedroom door, coming to take Lynn away.

epilogue

SIX WEEKS LATER

Michael and Angela walked through the parking lot, the midday sun radiating off the blacktop. When they reached the car, Michael opened the door for his wife, making an elaborate display of taking her hand and guiding her into her seat.

Angela rolled her eyes and shook her head at him. He was acting like a clown.

When he came around to the driver's side and started the car, they sat for a moment while the air-conditioning ran and the low voice of a newscaster came out of the radio. Michael turned it off, then faced his wife.

He smiled.

"What is it?" Angela asked.

"I just can't believe it," he said. "It worked. We're having a baby."

"I knew it would." She leaned closer, kissed him fully on the mouth. "It's been working that way for millions of years. We've been trying pretty hard, remember?"

"I remember."

"I knew it would work out."

Michael watched her closely. Was it possible she was glowing already? Had a month or so of pregnancy already caused her to radiate?

But she also looked thoughtful. Distracted.

"We can go by and tell your mom," she said, her voice hopeful. "It might be a good thing. It might help her to have some good news."

Michael nodded. "Yeah. I think you're right."

"This is a painful time for her, Michael. Lynn's going to spend some time behind bars. Even if they get it down to a Class D felony, to . . . What did they call it?"

"Unlawful imprisonment," he said.

"That sounds worse. I'm not making excuses for her. She cooked up that plan with Jake Little, and he's getting punished too. They both made it happen."

"Yeah," Michael said. "And everyone knows. Everywhere."

"Anyway, your mom's going through hell. And she's dealt with a lot. All the stuff with Robyn came back up. And she learned things she couldn't have imagined about the day Robyn died. We all learned it, I guess."

"I know. I'll call her." He paused. "She'll be happy to hear. And, yeah, we're all still dealing with what Lynn admitted about Robyn." He watched the heat waves radiate off the parking lot. "I'm still processing it—that's for sure."

Angela leaned over and rubbed his upper arm. "I've been thinking, Michael. And this is totally up to you. But if she's a girl, I don't mind if we name her Robyn. Even if it turns out to be a boy, we can name him Robin. If that makes everything better, we can do it."

"I don't . . ." He reached out and squeezed her hand. "That's a really great gesture, but I don't think we need to. There's only one Robyn. And I'd like to keep it that way."

"If you're sure."

"I'm pretty sure," he said.

"Okay."

"You hungry?" he asked.

"Yes."

"Me too." But he didn't drive away. He let the car run, still facing Angela.

"What?" she asked.

"What are we going to do about Felicity?" he asked.

"Hmm. Yeah. What do you want to do?"

"I can call Erica," Michael said. "We can see Felicity this weekend and tell her in person."

Angela smiled. "That sounds good. She's going to be excited too."

"I think she will be. It's an adjustment for her, having us in her life. And she doesn't know yet how complicated siblings are."

His comment felt weighted. It hovered in the space for a long moment.

"We've gone from no kids to two in six weeks," Angela said. "After a couple of years of not being able to have any. We're on a roll."

Michael let out a deep breath. "Let's hope the excitement's over for the summer. In fact, I may not answer the door ever again."

"I don't know. It worked out, didn't it? You have Felicity now."

"*We* have Felicity in our lives now."

Angela squeezed his hand back.

He put the car into gear, and they drove away.

acknowledgments

Thanks to Kara Thurmond for her Web site design . . . and redesign.

Thanks to Ann-Marie Nieves and everyone at Get Red PR.

Thanks again to everyone at Berkley/Penguin.

Thanks to Jane Steele for her copyediting.

Thanks again to Jin Yu for her marketing wisdom.

Thanks again to my amazing publicist Loren Jaggers.

Thanks again to my wonderful editor, the brilliant Danielle Perez.

Thanks again to my stupendous agent, the unstoppable Laney Katz Becker.

Thanks again to my family and friends.

And thanks to Molly McCaffrey for everything else.

READERS GUIDE

SOMEBODY'S DAUGHTER

david bell

READERS GUIDE

questions for discussion

1. Michael has had no contact with his ex-wife, Erica, since they divorced a decade earlier. Are you surprised they haven't been in touch? Do you think it is unusual for people to have a "starter marriage" like this one?

2. Erica chose not to tell Michael about Felicity because she wanted to prove she could raise a child on her own and be mature and responsible. Do you understand her reasoning? Or do you think she should have told Michael, since he was likely the child's father?

3. Angela, suspicious of Erica when she shows up out of the blue, tries to talk Michael out of going with Erica. Would you have objected to Michael's going with his ex-wife if you were Angela? Do you understand why Michael wants to go with Erica to look for Felicity? How much do you think this might be related, even

subconsciously, to Michael's feelings about his deceased sister?

4. Angela learns that Gail has been in contact with Erica. She has even met with her and met Felicity. Do you understand why Gail wanted to see Erica in person and learn more about Felicity? Do you blame her for cutting Erica off? Was she right not to tell Michael or Angela?

5. Detective Griffin becomes emotionally involved in Felicity's case, going as far as to overstep her bounds as a police officer. Do you understand why she cares so much? Do you blame her for anything she does?

6. Angela and Jake Little join forces to try to track down Michael and Erica. Do you understand why they form this unlikely partnership? Do they share the feelings of being somewhat jealous of and concerned about Michael and Erica's relationship?

7. Michael and Angela are struggling to have a child of their own. Do you think that makes Michael's desire to find Felicity more powerful? What would it be like for Angela to have to adapt to Michael's having had a child with another woman?

8. We learn early in the book that Michael's sister died in an accident. How do you see Robyn's death affecting Michael's family more than two decades later?

9. Lynn's initial goal is to learn who Felicity's father really is. Do you understand why Lynn has an intense desire to prove Felicity's paternity?

10. Erica admits that at times she feels overwhelmed by the pressures of being a single mother. Is it understandable that sometimes she wanted to leave her responsibilities to Felicity behind? Do you think all single parents feel this way at some point?

11. We learn that Robyn's death wasn't exactly the accident the family thinks it was. How much do you blame Lynn for what happened that day on the swing? Do you blame Michael for not keeping a better eye on his sisters? Do you blame Michael's parents—especially his father—for favoring Robyn and making the other children jealous?

12. With all that they've learned, what challenges do Michael and Angela face at the end of the book?

Read on for an excerpt from David Bell's
latest novel of suspense,

KILL ALL YOUR DARLINGS

Available now

chapter one

Connor

PRESENT

Grendel doesn't bark when my key hits the lock.

That's when I know something is wrong.

Grendel, an eleven-year-old beagle mix, still barks at the mailman, the neighbors, squirrels, cats—any strangers at all, despite his age and flagging energy. And I can count on him barking with joy when I come in the back door every evening. If not for him, I'd always be greeted by stone-cold silence.

And that's what I hear tonight.

I toss my keys onto the kitchen counter and slip my coat off.

"Grendel?"

Everything looks normal. Grendel's food bowl is nearly empty, which means he's eaten while I was out at the library. I usually manage to keep the kitchen clean, mainly because I don't cook. The appliances are here, and everything appears to be in order.

But something *feels* wrong.

Without Grendel's barking, the house seems unsettled.

Off.

A chill flash-freezes up my spine. I feel like an intruder in my own home, like I've walked in on something.

I move toward the front of the house, stepping carefully. The ancient floorboards squeak, each one sounding like a gunshot.

Grendel typically spends his time on the couch when I'm gone. When he hears something outside, he likes to lift his head and look out the picture window. He lets out a series of barks that make him sound much more vicious than he really is, and once that's out of his system, he flops back down as though he's just run twenty miles.

By now I should hear his collar jingle, his nails on the hardwood.

He's an old dog, I tell myself. *Old dogs don't live forever.*

"Grendel?"

When I reach the entrance to the living room, I freeze in place.

Everything is where it's supposed to be. The lamp I always leave on is on. The furniture is arranged the way it's been arranged for years. Nothing is disturbed. Nothing is broken.

And Grendel sits on the floor, his tail flopping back and forth when he sees me.

Everything is where it's supposed to be except that someone is sitting in the recliner, legs crossed, hand gently scratching Grendel between the ears.

"Hello," she says.

My mind is slower than my body. My body reacts instantly. My muscles tense. My hands clench. My knees bend into a defensive crouch, and adrenaline shoots through me like rocket fuel.

But my mind is still trying to make sense of this scene before me. A young woman with long hair dyed an unnatural shade of red sits in my recliner petting my dog. And she greets me like she's supposed to be there, like I've asked her to wait for me to come home this evening. She wears a red coat, black jeans, and heavy boots, and her face is mostly obscured by large owllike glasses.

"Who the hell are you? You need to get out of here—"

The woman lifts her hand from Grendel's head and holds it up, cutting off my words. Grendel bounds over, sniffs my shoes. He would have barked when she first came in, because he always barks the first time he meets someone. Then he gets used to them. He looks happy to see me.

"You know who I am, Connor," she says, "and once you remember who I am, I think you're going to know why I'm here."

"I don't know who you are," I say. "But I am going to call the police if you don't get out. If you didn't take anything and didn't hurt my dog, you can just leave, and I won't press charges."

She ignores my threat. With a slow theatricality, she

lifts the glasses off her face and folds them, placing them carefully in her lap. She blinks a couple of times but remains quiet.

"If you want food, you can take it. Or money. I'll give it to you. But you have to go."

"Connor."

And then I finally see it. Her face is suddenly familiar. The eyes are bright blue. The shape of her face. Thinner. Much thinner. But recognizable.

She must realize that I'm starting to really see her because she smiles knowingly, like a chess master who has just outfoxed a lesser opponent.

"No," I say. "No. You're not supposed to . . . I mean, you're supposed to be . . ."

She lifts her eyebrows. "You mean, I'm supposed to be dead? Is that it? I'm supposed to be dead."

"Not dead," I say, my voice lower. "Not exactly dead."

But she's nodding. "Oh, yes. I'm supposed to be dead. I'm supposed to be written off. Forgotten. Erased. Tossed in a ditch or a river or a forest, my bones scattered to the winds and slowly returning to the earth. Dust to dust and all that. Isn't that where I'm supposed to be?"

"Yes," I say. "That's what we all thought. I'm glad that's not true, but I'm . . . This is all very disconcerting. You're here. . . ."

She leans forward and reaches behind her. She brings out a familiar-looking object and holds it up between us. She looks like she's on television, presenting something to the viewing audience.

"Isn't this what we need to talk about, Connor?"

It's my book. The book that was published today by a major New York publisher. The one I was at the library reading from and signing. The one that represents a dream come truc for me.

I don't answer her question.

I come all the way into the room and sit on the couch across from Madeline O'Brien. I sit across from my former student, the young woman who disappeared almost two years ago, just months before she was supposed to graduate.

chapter two

Madeline, are you okay?" I ask. "Are you hurt? Do you need me to call someone? My God, does your mother know you're okay? Do the police?"

She turns the book around and studies the front. She runs her hand over the cover in a small circle, her skin against the paper making a rustling noise. "We can discuss all that in a minute. I want to talk about this book first."

"How can we talk about anything except why and how you're here? People have been looking for you. They're worried about you. This is all a shock."

"All in good time."

Grendel has come back into the room, and he yawns

and stretches out by my feet. He's already bored by the rare appearance of a visitor in the house.

"My Best Friend's Murder," she says. "That's a great title. Did you think of it yourself, or did the publisher come up with it?"

"It's my title."

"I remember you saying in class once that most writers don't get to use the titles they want. The publisher always rejects them or changes them, so good on you getting this one in."

"Do the police know you're . . . here? Alive."

"I've been following this," she says, tapping the book. "Just because I was gone doesn't mean I didn't know what everyone in Gatewood was doing. If you can get to a computer, you can visit social media. I could keep track of my friends and family. What's left of them. You. Other professors. You sure posted about this a lot on social media. Almost every day for the last six months. You must *really* want this book to sell. You used to tell us not to spend our time online, that social media is ruining us. I guess that all changes when you have a book coming out and you want to pimp it."

"That's part of a writer's job," I say. Like any teacher—I hate having my own words used against me.

"I guess so. Social media can be used for a lot of things. Promoting books. Searching for missing people."

When she speaks and gestures, I see the Madeline I once knew. One of my best undergraduate students. Bright. Talented. Elusive. She talked a lot in class and wrote raw, vivid stories without giving the impression she'd revealed too much of herself. Her stories were always about troubled families with absent fathers, and the mothers were always calling the police on her lousy new boyfriend. It was hard for me not to assume they were autobiographical. In our conversations outside of class, she hinted at a difficult home life but never provided any details.

She looks like she's lost about twenty pounds, and I wonder what she's been doing for the past two years. Has she been in danger? Sleeping on the streets?

She also does one of the things I remember most about her, a nervous tic she occasionally resorted to in class. She did it only on rare occasions, usually when one of her stories was being discussed. Madeline reaches up and rubs her index finger across her right eyebrow and then pinches her thumb and index finger together, plucking a single tiny hair out of her skin.

"I bought a copy of the book this morning," she says, lowering her hand from her forehead as though she's just done the most normal thing in the world. "At Target. That's pretty sweet to get your book there. I started reading it in the parking lot, and I've been reading it all day. Except when I went to the library to hear you speak."

I thought so. She was standing in the back of the room, obscured by the people I knew and many who I didn't. I remember seeing the slim young woman with the bright red hair.

It turns out I *did* know the woman. She was Madeline.

"You left before the book signing," I say.

"I don't like crowds. And there were a lot of familiar faces there. I needed to be careful."

"How did you get in here?"

"The basement. You should get a dead bolt down there."

"It's Gatewood. Most people don't even lock their doors."

"That's a mistake," she says. "You never know who will come in."

It's strange. When Madeline disappeared at the age of twenty-two, I was anguished. Scared. Confused. Devastated that someone so young could fall victim to a seemingly random and horrible crime. Her disappearance—and apparent death—during her senior year of college brought back a lot of feelings I'd been working to move past, feelings that lingered from the losses I'd unexpectedly suffered when my wife and son died. For weeks after Madeline disappeared, I wandered around in a haze. And so did my colleagues on campus and my students. We were all shocked.

But I don't feel relief with Madeline sitting in my living room. Her reemergence is so abrupt, so disconcerting that I scramble to think of ways to get her out of the house. If she doesn't want my help, if she won't let me call the police, then I'm not sure I want her here at all.

I don't want her there because I know what she really wants.

"I told you I started reading this book earlier today," she says. "And I haven't stopped. I haven't stopped even though I know every single thing that's going to happen."

chapter three

Madeline

SPRING, TWO YEARS EARLIER

Dubliners billed itself as an authentic Irish pub. Madeline had never been to Ireland, had never been anywhere, really, but she felt certain the bar wasn't close to authentic. Posters on the wall showed foamy crashing waves and lush green fields. Or else ads for Guinness. The bartender sometimes spoke with an accent, although he once told her he grew up two hours away in Lexington, Kentucky. And that was about it for authenticity.

But the students didn't care about authenticity. The beer was cheap, and the pub was close enough to campus to walk.

Sometimes, when business was slow, the bartender didn't bother to card. It didn't matter to Madeline, who was twenty-two, or to her classmates in advanced fiction writing since everyone was a senior and old enough to drink legally. But it sure made Dubliners appealing to a lot of students, even though the place smelled like stale beer and fried food. And your shoes stuck to the floor pretty much everywhere you walked. *Step-stick. Step-stick.*

Dr. Nye—or "Connor" as he let them call him on those occasions when they all went out drinking—said anyone who was over twenty-one and wanted to go out for a beer should gather at Dubliners after their senior fiction-writing seminar. His treat. No student was going to pass up that chance. When professors offered to drink with students—*and to pay*—students showed up. Madeline had learned—from hard experience—there were professors she didn't mind being around when they were drinking and professors she knew she needed to avoid when they were drinking.

Madeline ordered a pint of Harp and stood at the end of the bar, tapping her foot to the Lynyrd Skynyrd song a guy in a red flannel shirt had played on the jukebox. She had been hoping to speak with Dr. Nye after class anyway. No, not just *hoped* to speak with him. She *needed* to speak with him. She *needed* his advice. That was why she had come to Dubliners more than anything else. Not for the free beer—although she certainly didn't mind that. But for his wisdom and knowledge.

Connor met her eye once but was surrounded by the three or four neediest students in the class. They were the ones who laughed loudest at his jokes, spent the most time in his office hours, wrote stories not because they wanted to write them but because they thought Connor would like them. Madeline felt certain he was smart enough to see through it. She gave him credit for being able to cut through the bullshit.

But she hung back, waiting. She wanted to talk to Dr. Nye, wanted to talk to him about her thesis.

She wanted to talk to him about so much more. But the thesis she'd turned in the day before was at the front of her mind. Almost the second she'd handed it over to him and walked out of his office, she regretted it.

She wished she hadn't written about things that were so real and raw, even though that was exactly what Nye always told them to do.

But Madeline feared she'd been just a little too real and raw. . . .

And it was going to bite her in the ass. Hard. And she was doing what she always did, what she'd been taught to do since she was a child—look for the exit. Find the fastest way out. Don't wait for trouble to pin you down.

No, she told herself. *Try to stay for a change. Try not to run. . . .*

Someone slipped up next to her, a guy she'd taken a few classes with over the years, Isaac Frank. Isaac wrote science fiction stories riddled with grammatical errors. Madeline wanted to pull her hair out when she read them. But he was a nice enough guy, someone she liked to talk to before class. Isaac was trying to convince his parents to pay for him to travel abroad over the summer before he went to graduate school. Not study abroad. *Travel* abroad. Travel. As in . . . just for fun. But Isaac had told her just the other day his parents were willing to pay for only three weeks of travel instead of the four he wanted. Madeline listened, pretending she could in any way relate to Isaac's first-world problems.

She hoped summer plans weren't on Isaac's mind in Dubliners. He leaned in close to Madeline at the bar, sipping from a Guinness, and she decided if he started complaining about not going to Prague she was going to dump a beer on his head. She just couldn't listen.

"Hey, Madeline," he said.

"What's up, Isaac?" she asked.

Madeline didn't listen to Isaac's response. She stared down the length of the bar where Connor stood with the sycophants. One of them, a sorority girl named Hannah, was going on and on about something, and Madeline watched Connor listening and occasionally smiling. But the smile looked forced. His mouth moved. His teeth showed. But his eyes remained flat.

"Should we go rescue Dr. Nye?" Madeline asked. "Hannah won't shut up. She literally hasn't taken a breath in five minutes."

"He's on, like, his fourth drink."

"He's a writer. What do you expect?"

"We've only been here an hour or so," Isaac said.

She started tapping her index fingernail against her glass. *Ping. Ping. Ping.*

"Nervous much?" Isaac asked.

"What?"

"You seem kind of stressed. Or something."

"I'm fine, Isaac." She realized she'd snapped at him. And he looked like a hurt puppy. Isaac was clearly one of those guys who couldn't handle a woman speaking harshly to him. "I'm sorry. No. I mean, I just turned my thesis in yesterday. It's a novel."

"Oh. Sweet. One step closer to graduation."

"Yeah. Maybe. It's pretty . . . Well, I put some stuff in there I don't know about. I want to ask Nye about it."

"Is it sex stuff? Nye doesn't care about that."

"Not sex," Madeline said. "Just . . . Well, I think I want it back before he reads it. I might change it. Maybe write something different. Something less . . . real, I guess. I'm afraid Nye will think the wrong things about me. And other professors might get the wrong impression of me."

"Really? He's pretty chill."

"Professors tend to stick together," she said. "They're like cops. You know? The blue wall?"

"They do that in the Mafia too. They call it omorta."

"You mean *omertà*. That's the code of silence. I read a book about it once."

Isaac glanced at Nye. "Well, he looks pretty sad," Isaac said.

"Wouldn't you if Hannah was babbling in your face?"

The music seemed to get louder. The TV showed the university's basketball team running up and down the court, shooting and passing. It looked kind of pointless to Madeline, all the back and forth, back and forth. But it was Kentucky, and everyone in the damn state talked about basketball all year round. Even Isaac watched it, his face deadly serious, like he was viewing a documentary about World War II or some other major historical event. Had she heard someone say it was an important tournament? Something called the NIT? Was that a big deal?

"It's not that," Isaac said, eyes on the TV. "He's sad because his wife and kid died. Tragically."

Madeline wanted to sigh, but she held it in. She'd been corrected by professors before because she sighed when her classmates said something particularly stupid. The rumor had been going around as long as she'd been an English major that Dr. Nye's wife and teenage son had died a few years earlier. Sometimes the story said they'd died in a car accident. Sometimes people said they'd been murdered. Once Madeline heard they'd both died when a neighbor's dog went mad and attacked them in the backyard. When Nye had come home from work that day, so the story went, he found the dog standing over their mauled bodies, licking his bloody chops.

"That's all bullshit, Isaac," she said. "He looks sad because he wants to spend more time writing novels, and he can't because he has to teach. He's into the tortured-artist thing. It's kind of appealing to be all sad and broody."

Isaac's lips spread across his face as he turned away from the TV. He looked like a condescending schoolteacher. "It's not a rumor." He sipped his beer and leaned his elbows on the bar. Isaac was a tall guy. Not overweight but kind of . . . doughy. He looked like he hadn't been outside in two months. More like Dr. Hoffman, although obviously Hoffman was a lot older. And just thinking of Hoffman made her shiver and remember what she had to talk to Connor about.

And Isaac wasn't like Dr. Nye. Or Dr. White. Guys who managed to stay fit even in middle age. Stay fit and look good.

"I Googled it one night and found an article," Isaac said. "I guess Nye's wife is—was—some kind of researcher. Like management consulting or something. She had to go to some conference up in Maine, and she took their son, who was, like, fifteen years old, with her. And while they were there . . . Well, it's really kind of a freaky story."